THE QUEEN
HAS A COLD

Praise for *The Holiday Detour*

"*The Holiday Detour* had me with its opening scene and it didn't let go until its very end. Jane Kolven knows the importance of a hook and uses it most effectively…This book showcases her ability to use dialog effectively and masterfully. She can create tension and drive the plot forward in the most amusing and engrossing ways…I would encourage anyone who loves fun, quirky romances to read *The Holiday Detour*. It's a highly entertaining and completely satisfying read."
—*Lesbian Book Blog*

"Kolven has a keen eye for what makes a narrative work and, just as importantly, she handles everything with a light touch. There were several points while reading this book that I actually smiled or laughed out loud."—*Medium.com*

"This is a bit of a madcap connection story…It's a little mish-mash of *Planes, Trains and Automobiles* meets a rom-com and it's sweet and silly by turns. Dana runs hot and cold, which makes her less appealing than Charlie, but they do figure out that they are a match. I liked that they did 'get' one another, and their futures have enough flexibility to accommodate a new/first relationship."—*V's Reads*

By the Author

The Holiday Detour

The Queen Has a Cold

THE QUEEN HAS A COLD

by

Jane Kolven

2021

THE QUEEN HAS A COLD

ISBN 13: 978-1-63555-878-4

This Trade Paperback Original Is Published By
Bold Strokes Books, Inc.
P.O. Box 249
Valley Falls, NY 12185

First Edition: April 2021

CREDITS
Editor: Cindy Cresap
Production Design: Stacia Seaman
Cover Design by Tammy Seidick

Acknowledgments

This book was possible because of the generosity of intersex activists who share their experiences and campaign against medical intervention for intersex kids. I'm especially appreciative of Hans Lindahl for serving as a consultant on this manuscript in its first stages. I'm grateful to Pidgeon Pagonis, Cary Costello, and Georgiann Davis for everything I've learned from conversations with them and from their public work. Thanks to Hanlon McGregor and Jordan Rosenberg for serving as sensitivity readers between drafts, and my editor, Cindy Cresap, for always remaining diligent and thoughtful in her work.

For TJ, my unwavering friend and cheerleader,
and for intersex kids everywhere

PROLOGUE

Her Majesty Queen Clotilde, fifty-seventh monarch of Montamant, widow of the late King Georges, twice named "Most Fashionable European Royal" by *Femme Dynamique* magazine, globetrotter and diplomat, recipient of seven honorary degrees, did something that Sunday morning no one could remember her doing before.

The queen sneezed.

In Her Majesty's rooms, her trusted confidant and capable assistant, Madame Pouvoir, immediately produced a tissue, and to her professional credit, her eyes only widened for a second. It was enough for Marie-Claire, the chambermaid who had been laying out Her Majesty's outfit, to see and give a similarly surprised gasp. But discretion reigned in the palace. Marie-Claire caught herself and turned her attention back to her wardrobe selection: a pair of green suede L.K. Bennett pointed-toe pumps and a yellow wool shift from Akris.

Madame Pouvoir resumed her recitation of the day's activities. "After lunch, you have an appearance at the annual meeting of the cheesemakers' association, which will include a tasting of this year's releases, and we have some remarks for you to—"

"Haaaa-choooo!"

It was not a petite sneeze. It was not the delicate sound of someone with money and power and staff to do things like sneeze for her. It was full-bodied, followed by the sound of an elephant trumpeting as Her Majesty blew her nose.

This time Madame Pouvoir made no attempt to hide her concern. "All right, Your Majesty," she declared, snapping her leather portfolio closed, "you're going back to bed."

"I am not!" Queen Clotilde pulled her silk robe tighter across her chest. "There is a lot to do today, and it is not your job to decide what I can and cannot do."

"Your Majesty—"

"Waaaa-shooo!" This time the queen's sneeze sprayed all over her robe, and she scrambled for the bedside tissue box to mop up the mess.

Madame Pouvoir dutifully helped and tossed the used tissues in the garbage without fuss. She reached into the pocket of her gray wool blazer and produced a small bottle of hand sanitizer, which she squirted onto the queen's hands and then her own.

"Your Majesty, respectfully, I think you should return to bed. The octocentennial is on Saturday. You need to be well rested for it."

"Thank you, Madame. I had completely forgotten the founding of the monarchy over which I rule."

They stared at each other, two iron-willed, intelligent women in their fifties, neither capable of backing down.

Unaware of the growing tension, Marie-Claire approached the bed and gave a miniscule curtsy. "Your Majesty, your clothes are ready. Do you want to carry a bag today?"

Madame Pouvoir shot her a killer glare. "The queen will not be needing those clothes today."

"Yes, I will."

"No, you won't."

"Pouvoir, do I have to remind you which one of us wears the crown?"

"You're sick."

"Sick!" Her Majesty laughed, but it turned into a cough. "I am not sick. I am never sick. In the twenty years since my coronation, I have never...once...been sick." A final cough punctuated her sentence, mocking its intention. She sighed. "Actually, I do feel a little hot. I might sit down for a moment." She sank to the bed and nestled into the mountain of pillows. She shut her eyes. "Will you wake me in twenty minutes?"

"Of course, Your Majesty." Madame Pouvoir gestured to Marie-Claire, and they crept out of the bedroom and pulled the heavy double doors shut behind them.

"I thought you said she had breakfast with the bishop," Marie-Claire said.

Pouvoir shook her head. "She's not having breakfast today. Or cheese. Let's hope she's better by this weekend, or else we might have to call you-know-who."

Marie-Claire gasped. "Madame, no!"

"If Her Majesty remains ill, there will be no alternative!"

"In that case, we must make sure Her Majesty gets better!"

Madame Pouvoir gave one solemn nod of her head. "I will have the kitchen send up some tea and soup. And let's have the bishop say some prayers."

CHAPTER ONE

Remy found a parking space not too far from the entrance to the building and sauntered to the electronic card reader that granted access to the back stairwell and elevator bank. They held their card up to the reader, but the red indicator light didn't change to green. They waved the card, but nothing happened. They removed it, tried again, and still nothing. Remy was locked out.

They sighed and trekked through the alley that led to the street entrance. The main lobby door was also secured, so Remy knocked on the glass and held their ID up for the security guard inside. The guard buzzed them in.

"Name and purpose of visit?" The guard sounded bored as he clicked a pen open to take down Remy's information.

"I'm supposed to move in today, but my card isn't working."

The guard made a *gimme-gimme* hand gesture, and Remy passed their card over the desk. The guard inspected the front and back suspiciously, leaving Remy to wonder if there was a lucrative market for fake university IDs. Satisfied with whatever he saw, the guard rose from his chair and went to a machine on the back counter of his workstation.

"Did you pay your tuition bill?" he asked as he swiped the card in the machine.

"Of course!"

"Did you leave a check or pay online? If you paid by check, they might not have gotten it processed yet. It can take up to three days, and it won't post to your account until it's processed. If it's not posted to your account, your account will still show it's past due, and your card will be deactivated."

"I paid my entire semester tuition weeks ago," Remy informed him. The bill had come to Pierre's house because Remy didn't want their mother to see it. Pierre had waited two days before remembering to give it to them, which had enraged Remy. They didn't want anything to get in the way of this plan. They'd paid the bill in full that night, just to be safe.

The guard didn't seem impressed by Remy's financial solvency. "You put this next to a cell phone? It gets demagnetized that way."

"No. I only got it an hour ago."

Whatever the guard had intended to learn from the machine failed. He returned to his chair and sat down, causing it to let out a whoosh of air under his weight. "Let's look you up in the system."

"Thank you."

Remy watched impatiently as the guard used two index fingers to type their information. One of the things Pierre had reminded them when they'd set off on this adventure to graduate school was to be patient and kind, especially to those with less education and privilege. Although it was funny advice from someone as snobby as him, Remy tried to heed it. But sometimes it was hard.

"Looks like you're in Room 312."

The guard could have asked them that. Remy was carrying the confirmation letter with their apartment assignment. "I know."

"I'm not sure what the problem is. Should be working."

Remy fought the impulse to bang a fist on the counter. "But it's not."

The guard placed his palms on the desk and used them to hoist himself up. He unclipped a tangle of keys from his belt. "You parked out front?"

"In the rear parking lot."

Wordlessly, the guard started to walk toward the back door. It took Remy a moment to realize they were supposed to follow, but as they nearly caught up, the guard turned around and went back to the desk. Uncertain if they were needed, Remy turned and followed. The guard leaned over the counter and produced a small standing sign that read "Back Soon." He placed the sign on the countertop, then pushed past Remy wordlessly. Remy again trailed him to the back door.

The guard inserted a metal key in the back door and opened it. He tapped a door opener in place with the toe of his scuffed black shoe. "Bring your stuff in, and then I'll unlock your room. Can't leave this unlocked for too long."

"Bring my stuff in?" Remy looked at the sparse gray cement and cinderblock hallway. "How do I do that?"

"There's a cart over there."

Remy bit their lip. "I'm supposed to take my luggage out of the car and bring it in myself?"

"That's usually how they do it." The guard turned and shuffled in the direction of the front desk.

Remy put their hands on their hips. It wasn't that they had brought too many bags. Only five. They'd assumed they would go shopping or order things online to fill the small apartment. They would round out their wardrobe once they'd seen what the other students were wearing and had a better idea of how to blend in. It wasn't even that much of a shock that they were expected to transport their own belongings. Not that they'd thought about the logistics in advance, but if they had, they probably could have guessed the school didn't have porters. No, it wasn't the shock that frustrated them so much as how hard it was to do everything in the United States. Harder, more time consuming, and much sweatier.

"You chose this," they reminded themselves as they opened the trunk of the car they'd bought two days earlier. They'd anticipated that trying to hire a car service for every errand and outing would be a pain. At home Remy had been taught how to drive at age eighteen but never actually allowed to do it. Owning a car now meant freedom.

They were still sulking over the five suitcases they'd crammed into the trunk when a rusted maroon hatchback came sputtering into the parking lot and took the only remaining space in the back row. Out of the car climbed a lanky young woman with long blond hair, a tanned complexion, and deep red lipstick. She was too attractive to be driving such a shoddy automobile. She paid no attention to Remy on her way to the door, but she gave a small "hmm" of surprise when she saw it was already open. She went inside, and a moment later emerged with a cart with a small flatbed, which she pushed to her car.

Taking their cue from her, Remy went inside to find another cart. There weren't any.

"Hey!" they called across the parking lot. "That's the only cart!"

The young woman hoisted a giant blue plastic tub out of the back of the car and plopped it onto the cart, which she expertly kept steady with a foot. "Yeah, there's only one. Sorry, guess you'll have to wait a minute."

"I was using that!"

She made a face. "It was sitting in the hall."

"Yes, but I was in the process of taking my bags out."

By this time, the woman had added another tub to the cart. She shrugged and reached for a beat-up checkered suitcase, which she loaded, along with a table lamp. She slammed the hatchback shut and slowly wheeled her load past Remy.

"You're going to abandon me?"

"How is your stuff my responsibility?" she asked.

"Can we at least share? We're both going inside, yes?"

She pursed her red lips together, displeased, though Remy wasn't fazed. They stared back. After a tense moment, she maneuvered the cart in a giant donut and pushed it toward Remy's car. She wasn't able to stop it in time, and the edge of one of her cheap tubs collided with the rear bumper, nicking the silver paint. "Oops." She didn't sound very sorry.

Since the car was brand new, Remy was vexed, but a few American dollars getting the paint fixed wasn't presently as much of a concern as getting their belongings inside and concluding the exchange with the attractive but unpleasant fellow graduate student.

They took the first Louis Vuitton suitcase out of the trunk and placed it on the rear of the cart, where there was still a little room. Their five bags weren't going to fit unless she moved some of her belongings or they put a suitcase on top of her tubs, but they didn't want to push the issue. They reached for another suitcase, but it was heavier than it looked, and it banged against the bottom lip of the cart, sending the lamp tumbling to the pavement. Its glass base shattered.

"Hey! I just bought that at Target!"

"It was an accident," Remy said with a shrug. "What's 'at target'?"

She scowled as she picked up the remains of the lamp. "What do you mean, 'what's at Target?' I just said this lamp was."

"I know, but…" It wasn't worth trying to get clarification. "I'll buy you a replacement when we're done here."

"You will?" She turned her face toward Remy. Her eyes were outlined in black, which made their greenish-brown color glow. Her mascara was long and dramatic, and the overall effect with her ruby lips was the image of a model going out on the town. Although her impeccable makeup clashed with her cheaply made jeans and plain pink T-shirt, Remy envied her freedom to wear so much of it in public.

They wondered how she had learned to apply it so well. Had she spent time watching video tutorials online from the secrecy of her bedroom? Or had she learned from a mother or older sister out in the open?

"I like your eye makeup."

The woman blinked a few times, her lashes opening and closing like dark butterflies. "Thanks. You still owe me a lamp."

"Yes, of course. Can we bring my bags inside first? The guard was mean about my card not working."

"Why doesn't your card work?" She moved between the cart and the trunk and reached for one of Remy's remaining suitcases. When she hauled it out, her thin arms showed tight muscle underneath her tanned skin. "Did your loan check not come in yet? I think they can give you an emergency loan to cover the tuition bill to keep your card active until the money comes in. It's kind of weird, since it's money from the school to pay the school, but it'll tide you over."

Remy wasn't entirely sure what she was talking about, but judging from the rust on her car and the uneven stitching on her clothing, they could tell she wasn't a person of means. She probably knew lots of tricks to stay financially afloat.

"Thank you for the advice."

Remy offered to pull the cart, since it was so heavy with their suitcases. The young woman went ahead to summon the elevator. Once they were settled inside, they both reached for the "three" button, and their fingers touched.

Remy pulled theirs back in haste but dared a side peek at her. She was still wearing a huffy expression, obviously annoyed at sharing the cart and having her lamp broken, but there was a pink tint to her cheeks that hadn't been present in the parking lot. Maybe it was from the physical exertion, but the possibility that she was blushing over their accidental touching pleased Remy. They bit the inside of their cheek to suppress a smile.

The elevator climbed slowly. When it finally dinged open on the third floor, she led Remy to the left of the elevator, down a wide hallway with deep blue industrial carpet, and stopped in front of apartment 313.

"It's 312 actually," Remy said, gesturing to the door immediately across the hall.

"No, it's 313." She swiped her card, and the door opened.

"Oh." Remy was uncertain of whether this was a good or bad development. "I guess we're neighbors."

❖

Sam had barely opened the lid on the first plastic container when her phone beeped with an incoming FaceTime call. She darted to the beige laminate kitchen counter where she'd left it and stabbed at the screen.

"Hi, Mom! Hi, Dad!"

"Hey, kiddo!" her father greeted her. "How's it going so far?"

"Just starting to unpack, but I'm already questioning this decision. Is this a terrible idea? I should have picked a school closer to home."

"You needed to go somewhere with a good program," her mother said. "They offered you a teaching assistantship."

"I know." Sam was aware the package she'd been offered by Boylston University far exceeded what she'd been offered by the two other institutions that had accepted her. The cost of living in the Boston area made that extra money necessary, but five full years of guaranteed funding to complete her PhD, a much smaller teaching load, and the promise of research support over the summer to conduct field work had contributed to the overall desirability of Boylston over other universities. Plus, the library had a special archive of nineteenth century gossip newspapers Sam anticipated using as research for her dissertation. "I just miss you guys."

Her father put an arm around her mother, and they smiled. Sam loved watching their easy intimacy. It was going to be hard living some place where comforting touches and hugs weren't available on demand.

"We miss you, too," her father said. "And we love you."

"Have you met anyone?" Mom asked. "Made any friends yet?"

"I've only been here two hours."

"It took me five seconds after I met you to decide I liked you."

Sam couldn't help smiling. "Come on, Mom, that's different."

"You were purple and screaming, but I could already tell you'd be a good person with a kind heart."

Sam shook her head. Loving a child after giving birth to them was hardly the same thing as making friends as an adult. "I guess I have talked to one person. Some annoying rich person who broke a lamp I had bought this afternoon. I splurged on this beautiful glass lamp at Target that was five bucks more than the plain ones. I just wanted one pretty thing to make this feel like home, you know? But this person knocked it over in the parking lot while we were unloading our cars, and it shattered. They acted like it didn't even matter." She glanced at the door. "Actually, they were a jerk, but they did say they'd take me to Target to buy a replacement." She wondered what time they were supposed to go or if she was supposed to knock on their door when she was ready.

"See?" her mother said. "You're making friends already."

"Hardly. Some rich person with a shitty attitude."

"Language," Dad scolded her. It didn't matter that she was twenty-five.

"I hope everyone's not like that here," Sam continued, giving voice to a fear that had been itching at the back of her mind for months. "What if they're all East Coast snobs, and I'm..." Midwest trash, her brain finished. Not good enough. Not smart enough. One of the many people who starts a PhD and never actually finishes. A failure.

But for the sake of her parents and all the sacrifices they had made to help her get to this point in life, she couldn't say those things aloud. Instead, she said, "I'm worried everyone here will be stuck up."

"You will win them over with your charm and your brains." Her mother's pronouncement left no room for debate. It was reassuring to have someone in her corner, so Sam let herself accept the words as truth. She would win over the jerk across the hall with her charm. And maybe teach them some manners along the way.

CHAPTER TWO

*H*ow's it going? Ready to come home yet?
The text alerts on Remy's phone beeped with derision. No, they were most certainly not ready to return home. Things were going fine. Sort of.

It was too much to explain in a text, so Remy tapped the icon for a video call and waited patiently. Within two rings, Pierre's haughty face appeared. His brown hair was sticking out in every direction, and his cheek was creased from sleep, but where some men's good looks came from grooming, nothing so pedestrian could ever stop Pierre from looking every bit his noble self.

"That badly, hmm?" He smirked.

"No, it is not going badly," Remy said. "New York was amazing."

"I know, so amazing you had time to call me to tell me what you were doing every two hours. How is Boston?"

"I've only just arrived."

"And your little school?"

Remy was getting annoyed. They had done plenty of sightseeing and clubbing in New York, as well as serious things they hadn't shared with Pierre. Keeping in touch with him didn't mean they were sitting in a hotel room lonely for his company. And Boylston was hardly a "little" school. It had a world-class reputation. Pierre might have attended Paris IV before its merger and renaming as Sorbonne, but he hadn't attended graduate school and had little room to scorn Remy's choice. Universities in the United States weren't all terrible. Boylston meant anonymity. No one in Boston knew who Remy was. That hadn't been true when they were an undergraduate with some of the lesser Grimaldis or when they went on a grand tour at eighteen and ended up being spotted at dinner with Prince Carl Philip in Stockholm. Now, where no one even knew the name of Remy's country, Remy was looking forward to being incognito and consequently free.

"I'm living in one of the wealthiest and most powerful nations in the world," Remy reminded him. "How are things in your little city-state?"

"*My* little city-state?" he scoffed. "I would think it's more yours than mine—unless you're planning to never come home?"

The thought had occurred to Remy. "We'll see how it goes tonight."

"What's tonight?"

"I have a date." Remy said it with pride, though a loose plan to take someone to buy a lamp was hardly a date. They hoped they could turn it into one, assuming she was open-minded about the gender of the person she dated, because she, whatever her name was, had been hot.

Remy also knew the idea of them on a date would annoy Pierre. There was nothing between them other than a lifetime of growing up together in a tight-knit society, especially since Pierre saw Remy as too masculine to be interesting. In return, Remy thought he was fun to party with but too superficial for anything other than friendship. They were friends, nothing more, but Pierre didn't like it when anyone else came before their friendship.

On cue, he gave a sigh of disappointment. "You're always interested in women. Now you're chasing *American* women, even worse."

Remy wasn't the promiscuous one. Pierre had spent the summer dating around Barcelona and Cyprus. "Only one American woman."

"You have a crush!"

"Maybe. It's not sure yet."

"When will it be sure?"

"After I buy her a lamp."

"That's a very unusual gift for a lover."

"I broke hers when we were moving in," Remy said. "She lives across the hall. I'm taking her to buy a lamp, and after that I'll probably never see her again except occasionally in the elevator."

"But you'd like to see her?"

"I don't know how to handle the, er, secret."

"Which one?"

There were two, both of which were fairly big and complicated. But Remy was referring to the one that a sweet American who bought fast fashion on clearance would probably never be able to tolerate, even if she benefited from a new lamp because of it.

"I think," Pierre said, "that this is why your mother wanted you to stay in Europe. You could have come with me to Italy. I already know who you are."

"How would that be any fun?" Remy propped their chin on their fist with a wink. "I wanted to be incognito. I still do. I know it'll become public eventually, and when it does, it'll spoil everything."

"Don't decide it's a failure before you even try. If you really like her, give it a chance. Whoever she is, she would be a fool to reject you."

Remy smiled. "Thank you."

"Oh, before I forget, I meant to tell you. Your mother missed a reception yesterday. No one is saying why, but there's a rumor that she's having some cosmetic surgery done before Friday."

Their mother was vain enough for cosmetic procedures and had undertaken several, despite publicly denying it, but it was strange for her to miss an official function. She didn't like to disappoint people, and she hated it when rumors began circulating. They shrugged. They'd moved away from home. What their mother did or didn't do was someone else's problem.

"All right, my friend, I'm going to buy a lamp."

Pierre rolled his eyes. "Don't have too much fun." He was back to his petulant self. "I wouldn't want you to get any ideas about staying in America."

❖

At 6:15 p.m., there was a brisk knock on the metal fireproof door to Sam's apartment. In anticipation, she had already freshened her makeup and put her purse together. She'd unpacked a few reusable shopping bags, which she tucked neatly into a pocket of the purse. She was hungry and had intended to buy groceries after unpacking, but that would have to wait. The sooner they went to Target and replaced the lamp, the sooner she could be home, either to run to the grocery store if she still felt up to it—or, more likely, to get some takeout from the Thai place down the street. Takeout wasn't a habit she could afford to develop, but since it was the first night in her new apartment in a new city, starting her PhD, she felt she deserved a special treat.

As soon as her transaction with the jerk across the hall was concluded.

She opened the door to find the jerk standing there with a smug grin. "We never introduced ourselves," they said. "I'm Remy."

"Sam," she said, extending her hand for a shake. "I use she/her/hers."

Remy looked at her hand in confusion. "Use she/her/hers to do what?"

Sam waited a moment to see if they were joking. "Okay, so just—" She used her left hand to make Remy extend their right and forced them into a handshake. "I use she/her/hers as my personal pronouns. Which do you use?"

"Oh! I would like to be called 'they.'"

"Great! Then that's what I'll do." She looked down to where they were still holding on to each other's hands. "Don't you usually shake hands with people when you meet them?"

"Of course." Remy yanked their hand away. "Shall we go?"

They turned and headed toward the elevator, leaving Sam to check that her door was fully shut and locked. So much for courtesy, she thought as she trailed behind them. It was in Remy's blood to be a jerk. And weird.

Neither said anything until they reached the parking lot, at which point Sam stopped in front of Remy's sporty silver car and watched while they sauntered over to hers. They looked at each other.

"Did you want me to drive?" she asked. "I just figured..." She had figured that Remy's car was nicer and Remy had said they would take her to Target, which implied they would do the driving. Did Remy actually want to ride in her shitmobile? She shrugged inwardly and joined them at her car. She unzipped her purse and began fishing around for the car keys. She could feel her student ID, her wallet, lip balm, lipstick, and her phone, but no keys. Then she remembered she'd left them on the kitchen counter because she had presumed Remy would be driving. "I'll have to go back upstairs to get my car keys."

Remy frowned. "I have mine," they grumbled.

The interior of Remy's car smelled factory fresh, and the seats were made of buttery black leather. Sam doubted she'd ever been in a car so nice. "Did you just buy this?"

"Yes, for school."

"How much did this cost?" she couldn't help asking aloud. "Never mind, don't answer. That's a rude question."

"Where do you want to go?" Remy asked, pulling up a map on a display screen in the spot where Sam's car had a broken radio. "Is there a lamp store nearby?"

"Well, I got that one at Target, and they had a few more on the shelves, so I was hoping we could go back there."

"'At Target' is a store?"

"Yes." Sam peered across the darkened cabin. Remy wore a pair of glasses with thick clear plastic frames and had a mop of dark hair that was artfully tousled forward with shaved stripes underneath the arm of the glasses on the side facing Sam. She hadn't paid much attention to their appearance earlier in the parking lot, but now she could see that they were also in jeans and a loose-fitting T-shirt, with an aquamarine scarf tucked around their neck despite the early September date and their bare arms. They dressed in the casual style of someone with enough wealth that they didn't need to impress, but it was more than that. They looked…

"Are you from a different country?"

"Yes."

That would explain their clothing, the slight accent she heard, and their lack of knowledge of Target, which in Sam's world was one of the most important aspects of American culture.

"Which one?"

"You haven't heard of it."

Sam smarted. "I know Americans are typically terrible at geography, but I am a graduate student with a bachelor's degree in anthropology. I think I know my way around a world map."

"Mon-tam-aunt."

"Excuse me?"

"The name of my country," Remy explained. "Montamant. It means 'loving mountain.' Have you heard of it?"

Sam had not.

Remy gave a satisfied little chuckle as they threw the car into reverse and sped out of the parking lot. They turned the wrong way onto a one-way street and roared to the nearest intersection, barely pausing at the stop sign before joining a sea of traffic up a main thoroughfare. Several cars honked. Sam clutched her seat belt and cursed under her breath.

"What about you?" Remy asked once they were in the flow of traffic. "Do you prefer to date men or women?"

"Excuse me! That is a very personal question!"

"You asked me what pronouns people use to talk about me."

"I asked what pronouns *you want* people to use to talk about you. It's to make sure you refer to someone in a way that is respectful of their identity."

Remy was silent for a moment before saying, "I wish more people thought that."

It was clearly a delicate subject, probably one best left alone for now. Sam tapped the screen on the console. "You never entered an address. Where are we headed?"

"I thought we could eat dinner first, if that is okay with you." Remy glanced over at her. "Have you eaten yet? I know you Americans like to have dinner early."

"Actually, no, I didn't eat yet, and I am a little hungry." She wondered where Remy planned to go and if she would be able to afford it. She didn't want to blow her monthly spending money on the first night.

As if reading her mind, Remy added, "I invited you. I will pay."

Sam opened her mouth to protest. She didn't like being beholden to people. Was this just because they felt badly about breaking her lamp? "Why?"

Remy smirked. "It depends."

"On what?"

"On how you answer the question."

It took Sam a few seconds to realize which question Remy was referring to, and then she felt a rush of exhilaration mixed with fear. Remy might have been sensitive about their gender, but their attitude about everything else was typical of someone raised with a silver spoon in their mouth. Sam didn't want to like them. She didn't want to tell them what she found attractive in a partner because Remy would no doubt take it the wrong way and assume she was someone whose affections could be bought with a nice meal.

More than that, she didn't want to have the slightest entanglement, antagonistic or not, romantic or not, with someone right now or for the next five years. Her mind needed to be focused on passing her graduate courses and after that passing her qualifying exams, getting her research done, and writing her dissertation. She couldn't afford to let something—or someone—get in the way of her dreams.

"I have a boyfriend," she lied.

❖

Once Sam said she was involved with someone else, the evening felt a little sour and much less interesting to Remy. They contemplated veering from the plan to go to dinner and instead buying a lamp and being done with it. Or, better yet, they could order one online and have it shipped to her. But Remy, who had bristled at much of their upbringing, had nonetheless internalized the idea of being gracious.

Boyfriend or not, they had promised to buy Sam dinner, so that's what they would do. If he had been in the car, Pierre probably would have told them to keep trying. In high school and college, "boyfriends are just obstacles, not barriers" had been one of his favorite expressions, and Remy had watched him use his charm, wit, and wealth to break up couples and win over the women he desired. While Remy had to applaud him for going after what he wanted with so much gusto, they also doubted they could ever be so ruthless with people's emotions.

If Sam had a boyfriend, Remy would respect that.

They drove in silence for a few minutes before Remy realized they didn't know much about Boston and only had a vague idea where to go, based on scouring maps online before moving. They'd looked up plenty to do and see and had made a mental note of a couple of restaurants to try. One was a new effort by a chef who'd led a Michelin-starred restaurant in New York before moving to Boston. The menu and photos looked excellent, and it was one of the places Remy thought they could get to by memory from the online map.

In some parts of Europe, Remy wouldn't have needed a reservation if they gave the host their last name, but they doubted their family name carried any clout in the United States. That was the point of moving here, wasn't it? Sam didn't seem like the type of person to be impressed by Michelin stars and immediate seating. She would probably feel uncomfortable, and neither of them was suitably dressed.

What would make someone like Sam comfortable, Remy wondered?

At a red light, Remy pulled their phone out to look up a recommendation and access a map without Sam seeing it on the screen between them. She was being remarkably quiet, neither asking questions nor protesting their aimless journey, and Remy wondered if she found their company tolerable after all.

Boston's best lobster rolls for cheap, the website declared. That was perfect. Remy had never had a lobster roll and wasn't even sure what it was. But they enjoyed lobster, and if it was the regional specialty, it would be fun to try. Plus, "for cheap" meant it would probably be somewhere Sam would like.

"Okay, I found a place," they announced. "This is going to be great."

Ten minutes later, they pulled onto a busy street. There were cars parked on one side next to the curb, but parking wasn't something Remy had practiced. Doing it in a brand-new car with Sam in the passenger seat was too intimidating. They passed the cheap storefront restaurant, but down the block was a fancier place that had a valet out front. Remy eased as close to the curb as they could manage and put the car in park.

The valet opened Sam's door as she unbuckled her seat belt. Her eyes sparkled. "Wow! This looks really nice!"

Remy frowned as they got out and handed the keys to the valet. "Er, yes, it does. I was actually thinking we'd go over there, though." They pointed down the street, where the forest green awning gave way to scaffolding over a glass storefront with faded pictures of food in the window.

They could see Sam's disappointment.

"We don't have to—I thought you might prefer—I've never tried lobster rolls, and I thought it might be fun."

"Would you be embarrassed to be seen with me in a nice restaurant?" Sam asked crisply.

"Absolutely not!"

"Do you only spend money on people you think are worthy? Or is it because I said I'm dating someone, and therefore I don't deserve a nice dinner?"

"It has nothing to do with that," Remy argued.

"So what then? This is your way of testing someone to see if they're only interested in you for your wealth?"

"No, please stop making these assumptions." Remy realized what Sam had said and paused. They looked at her. She was huffy, clearly displeased with the choice of a cheaper restaurant, but it was more than wanting a night out at Remy's expense. They could see more complicated feelings lurking behind her expression. "Are you interested in me? Do I need to test your motives?"

"I have a boyfriend."

There was something about the way she said it that made Remy skeptical. Probably her insistence. When Pierre seduced women who were already in relationships, their protests were usually half-hearted.

They'd mumble the words they knew they were supposed to say but didn't want to. Sam was defiant.

"Do you really?" They stared at her until her icy glare cracked.

Her cheeks glowed in the warmth of the streetlight. "No."

"Do you even date men?"

Sam rolled her eyes but was smiling as she admitted, "No."

The smile told Remy everything, and they reciprocated. They held out a hand. "Please allow me to buy you a lobster roll, and if you want, tomorrow I will take you somewhere with more gourmet food."

Remy counted in their head: *un*, *deux*, and it wasn't until *trois* that Sam put an end to the flutter of nerves in Remy's stomach when she put her hand in theirs.

CHAPTER THREE

Lobster rolls were gross, Sam learned. She had never been a fan of mayonnaise, despite most Midwestern potluck dishes being smothered in it. She preferred ranch, which was a gift from the gods compared to the empty tang of mayonnaise. But the restaurant also served fresh French fries that were crispy on the outside and fluffy on the inside, and Sam happily dredged hers through a puddle of ketchup she'd squirted onto the red and white wax paper her sandwich had been wrapped in.

Remy ate with delicate manners, never getting so much as a speck of food on the corner of their mouth, while Sam must have gone through four napkins in ten minutes. Not that she cared too much. She wasn't trying to impress Remy, but she did find them to be tolerable enough company.

"Okay," she said through a mouthful of fries, "tell me about this place you're from. Mountain Amount?"

"Close." Remy pursed their lips through a sip of soda. "It's called Mon-tam-ahnt."

Sam couldn't hear the difference. She was a visual learner anyway. "Spell it."

"M-O-N-T-A-M-A-N-T." Remy pronounced the letter "a" as "ahh."

Sam tried to picture the word in her head. She'd taken two years of French in high school, but the pronunciation and vocabulary were distant memories. "Mont-amand?" she tried.

"Very close!" Remy sounded praising. "I'm not surprised you've never heard of it. It's only fourteen square kilometers."

"That hardly helps me. How big is that in miles?"

"It's about…" Remy laughed. "I have no idea." They reached for their phone and converted the measurement online. "Nine miles."

Sam gaped. "My family drives farther than that to the grocery store!"

"We are seven times bigger than Monaco." It was obviously a point of pride.

Sam tried to imagine her mom taking the car to a different country to pick up chicken and potatoes. Maybe the difference was that the country was densely populated, so the small size didn't matter. Sam had grown up in Indiana, where the houses were spaced with expansive green lawns between them. "How many people?"

"There were 2,163 as of May 1."

"How do you know that off the top of your head?"

Remy shrugged. "I know a lot about my country."

"How old is this place? Why haven't I ever heard of it? Where is it, anyway?"

"Eight hundred years old. We are celebrating the octocentennial this week. You have probably never heard about it because your American media doesn't care about anything that's not American. It's between France and Switzerland, about an hour and a half from Genève, er, Geneva, south of Lac d'Émosson, in the Chablais Alps."

Sam could hazily picture the border between France and Switzerland and knew the Alps were an important mountain range between the two countries, but she had never heard of lack-de-motion or the sha-blay Alps and couldn't pinpoint Geneva. Still, the idea of a tiny country nestled in the mountaintops sounded quaint and romantic. She felt a little foolish that she'd never heard of the place, especially given her research interest in Europe, and vowed to look it up later.

"What are you doing in the US?" she asked. "You're going to Boylston, obviously, but why?"

"The same as you. I'm going to get a master's degree."

"I'm getting my PhD." She had already put in her two years at the master's level, and though she wasn't trying to be snide, it was a point of pride that she had worked hard enough to be accepted into a PhD program. "I research gender in affluent historical societies."

"What does that mean?"

"I'm not entirely sure yet," Sam admitted. "I have two years of coursework before I'll begin my dissertation. Our library has a special archive of gossip newsletters from the nineteenth century that I thought might be cool to look at."

She didn't want to prattle on and on, but she really liked talking about her ideas and hoped Remy would ask a follow-up question. Or three.

"Where did you get that idea?"

"It's kind of a riff on my master's thesis. I was trying to learn more about gender roles in the Middle Ages. I found out about this Danish prince who used to cross-dress, even at public events, and seems to have been more accepted for his transgressive gender expression than we typically expect from that time period."

"Hrodohaid," Remy said with a nod. "The name can be for a boy or girl. It is as if his parents knew what kind of person he would be when he was born."

Sam put down the fry she was holding. It had taken her four months of research to find Hrodohaid to use as the centerpiece of her master's thesis. She had made countless calls and emails to libraries around Europe when she was in the research stage, and almost no one had ever heard of the eighth century royal. There only existed a few documents about him. Her own parents, who had held her hand through every step of her master's degree, would probably be hard-pressed to name the figure Sam had spent so much time studying and writing about.

"How did you know?"

Remy looked uncomfortable. "I...have my own fascination."

"You're lying. What did you do, google me before you came over to my apartment? Try to find a few things to talk about, so it wouldn't be so awkward?" She frowned. "Is that how you try to get people interested in you? You seduce them by talking about things they like?"

She regretted saying the word "seduce," but now that it had been said, it hovered in the air between them, an uncomfortable reminder that Remy had flirted with her and that she had admitted she was single.

"No, truthfully, Hrodohaid was an idol for me when I was a child."

Sam knew she had the looks of a cis woman with the privilege of never having to think about gender expression as a marker of power. But she'd been told she didn't "look lesbian enough" during countless pride celebrations, and more than one woman had turned her down because they assumed she was straight and just experimenting. Even her master's thesis advisor, while ultimately supportive of her research, had questioned Sam's choice to investigate someone who cross-dressed. While Sam knew there were things about being trans or nonbinary she would never understand, she also felt it was her academic duty to call greater attention to the historical examples of gender and sexual expression that defied what society presumed had always been the norm.

"You know you're safe with me, right? I think European colonial cultures have done a lot of damage to all of us by forcing us into rigid male and female roles, and I would never be anything less than supportive of someone's expression of identity."

"That's very kind." Remy wadded up their napkin and tossed it down onto the counter. "Shall we get your lamp?"

❖

"At Target," Remy learned, was a very large store called Target with cheap prices and a range of products from groceries to the lamp in question to beach balls. A competitor to the giant American Walmart. Remy knew superstores existed and had read plenty about taxes, trade, and labor policy. Although Montamant was too small to have that kind of retail store, Remy had set foot in Monoprix in France and Tesco in the United Kingdom but never the American Target. The goods sold there didn't appear much different from what could be found at other superstores around the world, but facing a fairly empty apartment made the towels and picture frames more appealing.

Remy found an aisle full of American-style coffee makers and a few presses. Then they spotted a one-touch machine that looked like the Nespresso they'd used for survival as a university student. The coffee it made never tasted the same as espresso from a cafe, but it was fast and convenient for someone with a lot of homework to do.

"Look at this. This is a good price, I think."

"I have no idea how much those things cost," Sam said. "I've never had one."

"You cannot survive without it as a student. Wouldn't it be nice to push a button and, voilà, you have coffee in the morning?"

"It would, but it uses plastic cups that you throw away after each use. I hear it's pretty terrible for the environment."

Remy pointed to a shelf below and reached for a reusable filter. "You can put your coffee in this. It's a little less convenient if you have to fill it yourself each day, but the machine is still faster. Unless you prefer espresso?"

"Me? What do I have to do with it?"

"I will buy this for you." Remy took a large box off the shelf and held it out for her. "It's a gift."

Sam folded her arms across her chest. "You're supposed to be buying me a twenty-dollar lamp, not a two-hundred-dollar coffee machine."

"Is there someone to take this to the cashier?"

Sam took the box and set it on the ground. Then she muttered, "I'll be back in a second," and walked away.

Remy hovered in the coffee aisle in search of an espresso machine that would make her happier. There were a few options, but they didn't like the brands. Giving Sam a gift that broke in a week was hardly an act of generosity. They could order a better one online and have it sent to Sam as a surprise. Not only would she get better quality, but she also couldn't say no. They put the box back on the shelf.

A few minutes later, Sam returned with a bright red shopping cart. One of the wheels squeaked and spun backwards, and every few steps Sam had to kick it back in place. She looked annoyed when she finally turned to Remy and asked, "Where's the box? Put it in here."

"Oh, I'm not getting that one anymore. Let's go get your lamp."

They could hear her grumble over the chirping of the shopping cart wheel.

In the aisle with the lamps, Sam selected the same glass one Remy had broken earlier, looking pleased there was another available. It was cute, with three perfect glass spheres stacked as a base, but for a bedside lamp, Remy preferred something a little less decorative in case they tossed and turned in their sleep or fumbled too hard to find their glasses in the morning. They chose one with a simple metal neck and added it to the cart.

"What else do you need?" Sam asked.

"Everything and nothing. What do *you* need?"

"I have zero money, and we just picked out the one thing you promised to buy me, so I'm done. Also, I should get home and finish unpacking because I have a meeting tomorrow with the professor I'm serving as a TA for."

"There is nothing in this giant store that you want or need?"

"Not really. I don't like taking charity from strangers, and I don't like having someone try to buy my affection."

Her words stung. Mostly because Remy had never attempted to buy anyone's affection, especially not with housewares. They had never been interested in someone who didn't have their own means. Maybe that was Sam's appeal. Although she didn't hold back from saying what was on her mind, she lacked that haughty sanctimony so many of Remy's friends had. They doubted she was naive enough or superficial enough to be bought with pretty trinkets.

"I'm not trying to buy your affection. I want you to have a nice apartment. Why is that bad?"

"Because that's not your responsibility."

"But I have more than you. Why shouldn't I share it?"

"It's more complicated than that."

"It doesn't have to be."

"It always is," she sighed. "You say you're giving me a gift today, and tomorrow you'll expect something in return. Or we'll fall into some pattern where you're the superior one, and I'm supposed to bow down to you just because you have a fatter wallet—"

Remy couldn't help laughing a little because, in fact, if they had been in Montamant, then Sam's insistence on shaking hands would have actually been offensive. She would have been expected to bow to them. But she didn't know that, and they didn't necessarily want her to know it.

"Why are you laughing at me?" she snapped.

"I'm not laughing *at* you."

"See? This is what I mean. You rich people are all the same. I'm here to get a degree and nothing else. I don't have time for socializing." She put her hands on the cart. "Can we go now?"

At the checkout, Remy paid for their two lamps with a new Visa their mother didn't know they had applied for. Once Remy had turned twenty-five, a portion of their inheritance had fallen under their control, and the benefit was being able to do things like pay tuition, buy a new car, and splurge on a lamp for a pretty young woman who seemed sympathetic to Remy's gender but intolerant of their wealth.

By the time they wheeled the broken shopping cart to Remy's car, it was dark outside. The garish LED lights in the parking lot brought out the golden highlights in Sam's hair. The angrier she was, the more attractive Remy thought she looked. Her cheeks grew pink, and her lips pouted, and Remy wanted to kiss her until she smiled again.

Instead, they put the two lamps in the trunk of the car and got inside.

"Hey, you have to put the cart away!" Sam wheeled it across the parking lot to a metal corral and shoved it into a row of other connected carts. As she climbed into the passenger side, she added for good measure, "I don't know what they do in Mount-ammo, but here you're supposed to put things away when you're done with them. We don't have servants."

Remy gripped the black leather of the steering wheel. "I have been nothing but nice to you, and it's upsetting that you—"

"Nothing but nice? You broke my lamp, kidnapped me, took me to some shitty dinner because you don't think I have good enough table manners for a real restaurant, or maybe you were pissed because I said I was seeing someone, then when I said I was single, you changed your tune completely and tried to buy me off with a K-cup machine. I don't know who you think you are, stomping around like king of the universe—"

Remy couldn't help snickering again, though they really did not want Sam to know their secret. It was funny how right she was about their different places in life, even if she thought it was pretense on Remy's part.

"What is so funny?" she snapped as Remy's phone rang. The call routed through the screen on the dash. The phone number had the international country code for Montamant. "Please take me home. I am tired of your games."

Remy tapped a red icon on the screen to reject the call and pushed the car's ignition button. The quiet engine turned to life, and Remy put the car in reverse.

❖

When they got back to the graduate housing building, Sam had cooled off enough to remember her manners. She thanked Remy for the lamp as they parted ways to their respective apartments. She wouldn't allow herself to peek back at Remy as they opened their door and went inside, though she wanted to. Remy had been unusually quiet on the drive back. Although she had meant to put them in their place, to force them to recognize that an economic divide between them did not mean Remy could treat her however they wanted, she also hadn't meant to deflate them. She wondered if their feelings were truly hurt or if they just didn't know how to respond.

It didn't matter. Their relationship was purely transactional. Remy broke the lamp; Remy replaced the lamp. There was no need for further interaction.

She brought her laptop to the laminated wood coffee table and sat on the floor. She checked her new school email and saw that she already had a message from one of her professors notifying students in their graduate seminar that they should read an entire book before their first class session next Monday.

Sam hadn't purchased any textbooks yet, in hopes that she could find free versions online or read them at the library to save money. She hadn't expected a reading assignment before the semester even began. Between that and preparing for her first teaching duties, there was a lot to get done this week, and her apartment wasn't even unpacked. Remy had kept her out far later than she had wanted, without asking her if she minded, and it felt good to blame them for how rotten the evening had turned out.

She wanted to wipe the smug grin off their face. Smash a sloppy lobster roll into it.

She opened a new browser tab and typed "Mount Almond" into the search. She couldn't remember how Remy had spelled it. After guessing a few different spellings, the search engine thankfully understood what she was asking and redirected her to the official government page for the tiny city-state of Montamant. The site was in French, but Sam's browser offered to translate it for her.

"This is not how you should be spending your time," she said aloud.

She clicked on the tab for "History" and began to read. It was a much more elaborate version of what Remy had told her at dinner: Montamant had been established eight hundred years earlier and impressively ruled by the same family ever since. The Vallorcins.

It was strange that nothing had come up about the royal family of Montamant when Sam was doing her master's research, and she felt a little embarrassed to think her skills as a scholar might be lacking. She had read everything she could on the Grimaldis in Monaco, the Windsors of the United Kingdom, the Glücksburgs of Denmark, the Orange-Nassaus of the Netherlands, the Liechtensteins, the Belgians, the Bernadottes of Sweden—which had led to a major crush on Crown Princess Victoria—and even the shared governance of tiny Andorra. But nothing about Montamant had ever come up in an online search or any historical document Sam had accessed.

Who were the Vallorcins? Why hadn't Sam ever heard of them? She clicked the tab for "Royal Family" to find out more.

There was a headshot of a stunningly beautiful woman who looked in her mid-forties. She had immaculate makeup tracing her wide brown eyes, which were creased with enough lines to make her appear stately but far fewer than should have been there if she was truly the age the website gave, fifty-two. She had a tan Sam guessed was either from a spray bottle or a vacation in the Mediterranean, glossy pink lips over ivory white teeth, and perfectly highlighted brown hair that was coiffed into an elaborate style around a diamond tiara. *Her Majesty Queen Clotilde*, the image was captioned. Sam imagined she was the kind of rich woman who ate her servants alive for breakfast.

A short bio explained that Queen Clotilde had inherited the throne at age thirty-two as the only child of her father. She had ruled alone since the death of her husband, Georges, in 2010. The site also listed her charitable work and passion projects, which included preservation of Montamantien culture and history.

Unlike the queen's entry, which was lengthy and slick, probably put together by a public relations team, the entry for the heir apparent was bare bones. There was no photo or bio, only a few words: "Her Royal Highness Princess Remy."

Sam gasped. She forced herself to read it again. *Princess Remy.* Sam clicked over to a fresh tab and asked the search engine how to turn off the translation feature. She followed the instructions to reset her browser settings, returned to the Montamant page, and refreshed the screen.

In French, the entry said *la Princesse Remy.*

It couldn't be a coincidence.

Even without a photo, Sam knew it was the same person. So many of the strange things that had happened that evening made sense: how Remy didn't think to pick up their trash or put their own shopping cart away, how they had expected someone to magically appear to carry their luggage and shopping, the obscene wealth, the secrecy. Sam had made jokes about bowing down before them without knowing that Remy was, in fact, royalty.

She sat with this reality for a moment. She'd never met royalty before. She'd barely spent time with anyone outside the lower middle class. What was Remy doing in graduate housing when they could have rented a real apartment? Or bought a condo? Even a whole house? Why did Remy want to get a graduate degree, anyway? Was it something they were doing to pass the time?

She looked at the page again. The contrast between the amount of pride with which Queen Clotilde was introduced and the paltry line naming Remy as her heir was alarming. And the listing of them as a princess. Did that mean Remy had been assigned female at birth? When had Remy stopped identifying as female—or had they never identified that way?

That's what Remy had meant when they said Hrodohaid was an inspirational figure to them. Born of royal blood but unable to wear the crown because he never accepted his place as a future king, instead seeking a husband of his own. Hrodohaid had been able to forfeit the crown to a younger brother, whose marriage and subsequent children had secured the family line, and Hrodohaid had vanished into the depths of history.

Hrodohaid hadn't lived in the social media era.

On a lark, Sam opened the Instagram app on her phone and searched for "Remy Vallorcin," but there was no user by that exact name. Sam next tried "Remy Montamant," and there was one entry. Listed as a person who lived in Switzerland. The account was set to private, but the profile picture was an image of a person with their back to the camera, facing a sunrise or sunset that blotted out most recognizable features. But Sam knew it was her Remy, trying to be part of the world but not knowing quite how.

She sent a follow request, along with a message: *I know who you are, Your Royal Highness, and your secrets—both of them—are safe with me.*

CHAPTER FOUR

Although Remy wanted to find a liquor store or a bar, they didn't want to have to deal with the security guard letting them back in. With nothing to drink or eat in the apartment, Remy hunted online to see if there was an alcohol delivery service. There was, and it promised to arrive within an hour. They ordered a bottle of champagne to celebrate their first night at graduate school before hunting for food delivery options.

Ninety minutes later, Remy was stretched out on the micro-sofa with one leg slung over the wooden arm. The champagne bottle was nearly empty, the pizza was half eaten, and there was nothing good to watch on television. But it didn't matter. It was a perfect night, the kind Remy could never have had at home and the kind they'd been chasing with this plan to move to the US.

Despite sending Remy away from Montamant so often during their childhood, Clotilde, Madame Pouvoir, and the others had been disappointed by and disapproving of Remy's choice to attend graduate school in the United States.

"You will come home vulgar," Clotilde had predicted the night Remy finally summoned the courage to tell her their application had been accepted. She had been drinking a very expensive brandy, and in her anger, she gesticulated wildly enough that it sloshed onto the carpet. "You'll sleep with vulgar men and learn terrible habits."

Remy hadn't argued back. It wasn't American vulgarity—or, to put a more positive spin on it, the casual nature of American culture— that they were looking forward to, so much as freedom away from a predetermined fate. In the United States, as in Montamant, one's birth had a significant bearing on the course of one's life, but the great

American myth was that people could make their own destinies. For someone whose future had been determined since the moment they were conceived, that myth was appealing.

On television, a reality series about brides buying their wedding dresses was airing, and Remy got so lost in the mindless program that they ignored a few text messages. They heard the chime, but in their sparkly champagne stupor they couldn't be bothered to figure out where the phone was.

Then the phone rang with the special ringtone Remy had programmed for the palace's central number. They hadn't given their American number to anyone at home except Pierre, but they'd programmed the palace number in case of emergency. Apparently, they were right to do so. Pierre must have betrayed them by sharing the number, and now Her Majesty was probably calling to criticize Remy's decision to attend Boylston under the guise of a motherly check-in. That was exactly why they didn't want her to have the number in the first place. Remy let the call go to voice mail and pledged to yell at Pierre later.

A moment later, the phone rang again. On the second ring, it disconnected and immediately rang again. Then again. And again.

"Damn!" Remy swore in French. They got to their feet and went in the direction of the noise. The phone was lying on the kitchen counter next to the car keys, and it skittered across the counter as it rang once more.

There were a few notifications from various apps, several voice mails, and a preview of the most recent text, which said in French: *Swan. Respond immediately—Pouvoir.*

"Swan" was a code Remy had dreaded receiving their entire life. It was the Montamantien security code name for Queen Clotilde, and Madame Pouvoir would not use it unless the unthinkable had happened. Fully alert now, ready for a phone call that would change their entire life, Remy stared at the screen. Their heart quickened, and tears pricked unexpectedly at their eyes.

The phone rang again.

They drew in a shaky breath and answered. "So, Madame, it has happened? My mother is dead?"

"My apologies, Your Highness." Madame Pouvoir didn't sound like someone in the midst of a monarchical crisis. "Your mother is very much alive. We did not mean to alarm you."

"You sent the swan code. And called nine times."

"Five." Pouvoir had never tolerated hyperbole. "It is regarding Her Majesty. She is alive, but she has fallen ill."

"Ill?" Remy couldn't picture Clotilde in anything less than perfect health. "What do you mean?"

"Your Highness, we do not wish to alarm you, but under the circumstances, we thought it best that you knew."

"Knew what?" Remy imagined the possibilities. Cancer? Plane crash? Rare exotic disease picked up on a vacation to the tropics? "What's wrong with my mother?"

"The queen has a cold."

Remy squeezed their eyes shut. They contemplated asking Pouvoir to repeat herself, but they were certain they had heard correctly. Remy tried to picture Clotilde coughing and sneezing, the perfect nose she'd gotten when Remy was in primary school red and swollen. It was gross and unusual, as Clotilde's steely disposition usually crushed any viruses that might try to take hold of her the same way she crushed the wealthy businessmen who tried to woo her. But Remy didn't understand why this necessitated a code-name phone call and why Madame Pouvoir, the unflappable manager of all things Vallorcin, was concerned over something so trivial.

"You are joking."

"I am not."

Madame Pouvoir always referred to Remy as Your Royal Highness, in keeping with her job and Montamantien custom, but she had also been the one to wipe Remy's dirty face after meals and kiss them good night before bed. Until recently, their relationship had been characterized by Madame respectfully but firmly disciplining an unruly child.

Remy was an adult now. Although Madame might have dedicated her life to the palace and the Vallorcins, she was not one of them. Remy was the heir. If a bona fide call about the swan ever came, Remy was the one who would have to give up Boylston, the dream of a graduate degree, and life in the United States. It was Remy's job to make certain Madame Pouvoir understood that, until such a day arrived, Remy's time was precious. The minutiae of Queen Clotilde's life weren't Remy's problems anymore.

"Thank you for that update, Madame, but in the future, refrain from using the swan code unless it is truly an emergency." Remy clarified, so as not to leave any confusion, "In the event of Her Majesty's death."

"Your Royal Highness, I don't think you quite understand. We may need you to—"

"Thank you, Madame, give my regards to everyone at the palace." Remy terminated the call.

The queen's cold seemed coincidentally timed to the start of Remy's semester. When Remy was four and still living at the palace, their father had approved their request to study ballet at a nearby dance school. For the annual recital, the ballet mistress had cast Remy in a pas de deux with another girl, since there were more girls than boys in the class. Four-year-old Remy hadn't thought it was unusual and had liked getting to hold Isabelle's hand while she twirled. But a few days before the recital, Clotilde had taken Remy to see a little girl who was sick in bed with pink dots all over her face. After that, Madame Pouvoir had put Remy on bed rest, insistent that, although no symptoms had appeared, Remy was going to develop chicken pox. They had missed the recital and, eventually, spent a week miserable with the itchy disease. After they recovered, they were never permitted to take dance lessons again.

Remy looked at their phone screen, seeing the missed calls, texts, and alerts from various apps. If Clotilde wanted to use technology to exert her control from afar, Remy could win that game. They turned off their phone and went to bed.

When Remy didn't respond to Sam's follow request or message, she decided to let it be. Maybe Remy didn't like having their secrets exposed, even with her promise not to tell anyone else. Or maybe Remy didn't want to be friends on social media. Maybe Remy didn't even want to be real-life friends.

Sam showered and got dressed for the day, taking longer than usual to select an outfit that fit the muggy weather, expressed her personality, and also read as professional for her meeting with Dr. Grant in the afternoon. She picked a red skirt with white buttons down the front and paired it with a short-sleeved white blouse with a Peter Pan collar. Yellow ballet flats she'd gotten on clearance for five dollars completed the look. Comfy, professional, but not boring.

She next tended to her makeup. During professional development workshops in the first part of her graduate school career, senior faculty had cautioned them against overdoing it on makeup because of implicit biases male faculty, and unfortunately some female faculty, still had against women in academia. Fancy hairdos and too much lipstick or eyeshadow could give the impression that a young woman was more focused on her appearance than her research. Sam hated that idea, especially for women working in gender and sexuality studies, which ought to be a department where transgressing gender presentation boundaries and breaking down stereotypes based on appearance were encouraged.

She used the flat iron to put loose curls in her hair and colored her lips with her signature red Revlon lipstick. She was proud of how she looked for her first official day at Boylston.

And she changed her mind about Remy. Did they really think they could write her off with some lobster rolls and a Target lamp? Or that they could avoid talking to someone who lived directly across the hall? Maybe it was a matter of protocol. If she knew Remy was royalty, was she now expected to curtsy and defer to Remy's every wish?

She was not going to do that.

She gathered her school bag and ID card and strode across the hall. She rapped eagerly on Remy's door. She looked and felt good, and she was going to demand that Remy take photos of her and be her friend, whether they wanted to or not.

Remy opened the door, bleary-eyed, brown hair pointing in different directions. They were wearing a thick robe over their pajamas. "What are you doing here?"

"Your Highness," Sam declared, fanning her skirt and bending her knees in an elaborate curtsy.

Remy swore in French and yanked her by the elbow out of the hall and into their apartment.

"Why didn't you answer my message last night?" Sam demanded.

"What message? How did you find out?"

"Research. I'm a professional researcher, remember?" Sam set her bag on Remy's kitchen counter. Actually, Remy's name and identity hadn't been that easy to find, but it annoyed her that Remy would assume she was incurious or incapable of looking them up.

"I didn't want you to know." Remy's slippers made a swishing sound as they shuffled across the laminate flooring to the sofa, where they collapsed. "The whole reason I came here was because no one knew."

"Then you should delete your Instagram."

"It doesn't even show my face."

"You're also listed on the government website." As a princess, but Sam wasn't going to say it. Remy no doubt knew, and it was probably painful, maybe what had even led Remy to travel so far from home.

They looked up at her in alarm. "You saw the government page?"

"Yes." She plopped onto the sofa next to them, pushing their bathrobe aside to make room. "I read the whole history of the country. Ask me anything. Go on, quiz me."

"You saw the line of succession?"

Sam knew what Remy was asking. "I'm not going to tell anyone. As far as I'm concerned, it's a mistake. You already told me your pronouns."

They were quiet for a long moment, during which Sam tried to communicate all her support on this important issue. She could see the fear and hope shining back in Remy's dark eyes.

"Thank you, Sam."

"It's what friends do. If you want to be my friend? It's hard to tell since you didn't approve my follow request."

"I thought you decided I was a rich person who wanted to use my credit card to get you in bed," Remy reminded her.

Sam shrugged. "Well, yeah, but you're also the only person I know in Boston, so technically that makes you my best friend here." She stood and smoothed her skirt. "Besides, I'm wearing my favorite skirt, and I need someone to take a picture before my curls fall out, so I can send it to my mom. She has a picture of me on my first day of school every year since kindergarten."

Remy laughed. "You look amazing today." Sam gave them her phone, and they organized an impromptu photo shoot in front of a bare wall. "But, please," they said, "don't remind me about mothers."

"Why?" Sam heard the phone camera snap and laughed in embarrassment. "Wait, I wasn't ready!" Remy hit the button again. "Stop! I'm not posing yet!"

Remy took three more photos and then studied the phone screen intensely. After a moment, they waved it toward her. "You don't need to pose. Look."

"No, it probably looks terrible!" There was a difference between feeling confident and being camera-ready, and Sam didn't really want to see photos of herself with one squinty eye. But she gasped as she looked at the screen. Remy had caught her mid-smile. She looked happy and natural. "You made me look beautiful."

"You *are* beautiful."

Remy turned away before Sam could see what they meant by it. Embarrassed, she pocketed her phone. She'd text the photo to her mom later. Remy had probably said it in the way they'd tell anyone they were beautiful because everyone had their own beauty. It probably hadn't meant anything more than that.

"What are you doing today?" Remy asked. "I need to buy textbooks, so I want to go to campus."

"You're actually *buying* your books?"

"I plan to succeed in graduate school."

"That's not what I meant. Textbooks cost a ton of money. No one buys them, or at least, not from the campus bookstore."

"How do students get their books?" Remy's question was good-natured, but there was a hint of a smile on their face. Sam realized they were enjoying her horror at their wasteful spending.

"Order them online, but then of course, you have to accept the environmental damage of shipping, not to mention putting real humans and local stores out of business. Or you could buy used copies at the bookstore, but that's still kind of expensive, and they're usually in pretty terrible condition. Depending on the book and the class, you can rent them."

"Rent?" They said it like a dirty word.

"Yes. You read it and send it back at the end of the semester. I'm sure they sanitize each page before shipping it out again."

"You're mocking me."

"Yes, I am. I also need to go to campus to meet with a professor, so…want to get some breakfast first?"

"Give me a minute to get dressed."

"You never said why mothers were annoying to you!" Sam called as Remy went into the bedroom.

They shouted a few words back, but Sam couldn't understand through the closed door. She moved closer to it and aimed her voice toward the crack. "What?"

"My mother, the queen!" Remy yelled. "She is interfering in my life here!"

"How?" Sam's voice echoed off the cinderblock walls of the mostly empty apartment.

Remy threw the door open in exasperation. "Please don't watch," they pleaded.

Sam raised her palms to show she had no bad intentions and took several steps backward. "I'll be on the couch."

She could hear a dresser drawer being opened, and then Remy continued, "She had the palace staff call me with the emergency code phrase, which they are only to use if she dies."

"Holy shit! Is she okay?"

"Yes, yes," Remy said. "It was a ploy to interrupt my time here."

Sam thumbed through the photos on her phone and picked the best one. She sent it to her mom. She always knew when her own parents were sick and vice versa. She couldn't imagine having a parent so diabolical they would fake death to disrupt her life.

"What did you say?"

"I told them not to contact me unless it's a real emergency."

They emerged from the bedroom in another loose T-shirt. They wore the same jeans from the night before, this time with a lemon-colored canvas belt. It matched Sam's shoes, and she wondered if they had selected it on purpose.

"I think they wanted to remind me they have the power to prevent me from attending graduate school here if they want, and I needed to remind them that I'm an adult."

"But if something were to happen to Queen Clotilde..." Remy would have to quit school and return home, and they would accede to the throne, wouldn't they?

Remy put on a pair of black Buddy Holly glasses. Yesterday's clear frames had made it easier to see their eyes, but this pair framed their face, made them look more polished and distinguished.

"You look good! Maybe we should take your first day of school photo."

"No."

"Oh, come on, you took mine!" Sam took her phone out and pulled up the camera app. "Let me take one."

"Absolutely not. I'm serious." Their tone of voice was harsh, spoiling the mood between them. Remy must have recognized that because they cleared their throat and said more genially, "I don't like photos to be taken of me because I don't know where they might be posted and who might see me dressed like this. You asked what would happen if Clotilde died? I would have to go home, I would have a coronation, and the rest is complicated."

It sounded like an invitation to talk more. "Why is it complicated?"

"Sam, think about every monarchy. How does the line of succession work?"

Sam shuffled through the European monarchies she could name

off the top of her head. "Some operate by primogeniture, and some by absolute primogeniture, though laws about girls ascending tend to be newer."

"What are the children of the monarch called?"

She could see what Remy was getting at. It was the same problem she'd recognized in her research of Hrodohaid. "The boys are called princes, then kings, and the girls are called princesses, then queens. And, of course, there's no system for referring to someone who's not a boy or a girl." She dared to glance at Remy, whose chin was lifted ever so slightly. "Is that why you're away from your family?"

"The advisors call me Princess, and Clotilde wants me to marry a man who can become king. She thinks the monarchy will have a better chance of survival with a man sitting on the throne beside me."

"How progressive of her," Sam couldn't help saying. "Does that mean you've always identified as nonbinary?" Remy squinted, and Sam wasn't sure if they understood or if there were different words used in French. "Nonbinary, like neither male nor female, something outside the choice of only two genders? Since you use 'they' pronouns. How do you express it in French?"

"It is more complicated in French," Remy said, "because your English 'they' must be specified as masculine plural or feminine plural. To answer your question, there were some complications to my anatomy when I was born."

Anatomy didn't equate to gender, but it sounded as if Remy was trying to explain why they had been declared a princess at birth and why that label was wrong for them.

"Are you intersex? Is it okay if I ask that?"

Remy pursed their lips, but after a moment they nodded. "I don't know how much Clotilde understands about the condition, since she didn't tell me when I was a child. I've never talked about this with anyone close to me, not even my best friend."

Sam recognized what it meant that Remy was willing to talk to her. "I know it's private. I'm here to listen, but I don't want to force you to share."

"Since you know about Hrodohaid, I think it is okay to talk to you."

"We can talk about as much or as little as you'd like."

"I was born with male and female characteristics. I do not know much about what happened when I was born, but I was always raised as a girl. After my father's death, I learned that the medications they had been giving me for a few years were hormones."

Sam wondered which hormones exactly and what their intended outcome was. Probably something to regulate Remy's estrogen cycle, if they were forcing Remy to be raised as a girl, but she didn't really know how hormone treatments worked for intersex people.

"I stopped taking the medication this summer," Remy continued. "Before I came here, I went to a doctor in New York, and he told me the medical condition. One minute." Remy went to an unpacked bag and rooted around inside. They produced a small leather notebook and flipped through the pages. "Partial androgen insensitivity."

"I don't know much about that," Sam admitted. She would look it up later, though.

"It is caused by a gene on the X chromosome," Remy read. They put the notebook down. "The doctor gave me new medications, better ones. He said they will help me stay healthy like this, not change me into a woman. He said based on my development, it is unusual that I did not have many surgeries when I was younger. Apparently, that is common. He thought Clotilde had been a very good mother for not allowing it." Remy looked at Sam. "Of course, I did not explain that surgery would have alerted the press, given who my family is, and they were probably trying to avoid gossip by leaving me this way. It was not because she was a good mother at all."

Sam wondered when Remy had first recognized that "female" and "girl" were the wrong labels and how Remy had told the queen. It sounded as if living as nonbinary was something they'd only been able to do fairly recently.

The "Royal Family" section of the website had only listed Queen Clotilde and Remy. Depending on whether the queen had siblings or an extended family, the future of the House of Vallorcin could rest in Remy's hands. Queen Clotilde must have worried deeply about Remy performing as a woman, marrying a man, and producing heirs. Assuming Remy could.

"If your mother is the sovereign, and your father is dead, then Montamant must allow women to rule on their own."

"I don't want to be queen."

"What do you want to be?" Sam asked. "I mean, you want to be you, obviously, but how do you want the kingdom to call you?"

Remy smiled and, to Sam's surprise, took her hand in theirs. Their palm was silky soft and cool, and when they squeezed Sam's hand, she felt a shiver run through her body. "You're the only person in my life who has ever asked me what I want. What pronouns I prefer, how I want to be called. Apart from the medical clinic in New York and Boylston, I've never been asked by anyone close to me."

Sam felt something swell inside, urging her to close the distance between them and kiss Remy, and she wondered where that urge had come from. She shook it away.

"Well," she said amiably, taking her hand back, "what do you want?"

"I want to be Remy." They went to the kitchen and stuffed a wallet in their back pocket. "When I was a child, I was told every day that I would be the leader of Montamant one day, but we're a tiny country, and we're realistic that we may not have a future. When the EU was formed, we strongly considered going with Switzerland and not joining. Since the mountain passes connect us more easily with France most of the year, we went with France instead and joined. It's easier to keep a closed border on the Swiss side. But there was a referendum to abolish the monarchy and sell our state-owned land and property to France. If France had accepted, we wouldn't have been a country anymore, just another French province, and my family would have become ordinary citizens."

In her research the night before, Sam hadn't seen any information on a referendum like that. "What happened?"

Remy handed her school bag to her and led the way out of the apartment. As they walked to the elevator, Remy explained, "This was a long time ago, before France was the global leader it is today and long before we adopted the euro. It would have meant changing currency, laws, nearly our entire way of life. There were some members of Parliament who supported the idea because they presumed they'd be able to remain in power in our territory without my family's intervention if we became part of France, but by constitutional law, a decision so big had to be voted upon by the people. They voted no."

As the elevator doors closed, shielding them from the ears of anyone else, Sam turned to Remy. "If the people of Montamant wanted to stay independent, maybe that means they love the monarchy. Maybe they love the country more than they love the gender binary."

"That vote was a long time ago. Times change, and people change."

"But you don't know *how* they change."

"Neither do you," Remy pointed out. "Do you think it is worth taking a risk to find out?"

Sam was irritated to think that no one knew how the public might respond to Remy's physical appearance and identity. It bothered her that no one had asked Remy about their desires for the future. Remy looked approximately her age, so this wasn't a new issue. Why had the government officials and queen's staff swept the matter under the rug instead of dealing with it in a way that was respectful to Remy?

The elevators dinged open, and Remy turned in the direction of the parking lot. Sam pointed toward the front door. "There's a diner right down the block, and then we can catch the T to campus."

"We can drive."

"Oh, come on, it's a beautiful day, and parking on campus is a hassle, and we're in Boston. Don't you want to ride the T? It's the oldest subway in the US."

Ignoring Remy's frown, Sam considered it a victory when they walked out the front lobby together. She linked her elbow through Remy's, daring a quick side glance to see if they seemed perturbed. It was only a few steps to the diner up the street, and Remy held tight the whole way.

CHAPTER FIVE

Although she had complained about the cheap dinner they'd eaten the night before, Sam's choice for a breakfast spot wasn't exactly a step up. The restaurant was bustling, with people huddled over chipped tables and sitting on ripped vinyl chairs. Plastic potted plants lined the hostess booth, where they were given two laminated menus containing misspellings even a non-native English speaker like Remy could spot. Sam ordered an "omlette" with ham and bell peppers, but Remy suspected that any attempted imitation of classic French cuisine would be terrible and opted instead for an American breakfast platter, which came with eggs, bacon, toast, and a pancake.

"I won't need to eat lunch," they joked.

The food was not delicious, but it was plenty enough and hot, and Remy scarfed it down between gulps of watery coffee.

"What textbooks do you need?" Sam asked. "How many classes are you taking?"

"They recommended taking two courses per semester, but each has a list of fifteen or more books. I don't know them off the top of my head."

"The books? The bookstore will have a list posted next to your course. Then under each book, they'll mark whether it's required or recommended. Actually," Sam said as she pulled her phone out, "they might have that listed on their website. What courses are you in?"

"I don't know the names of my courses."

"You don't know the names of the courses you signed up for?"

Remy bristled. "I registered last spring after receiving my acceptance letter, and I selected the first two required courses. The names were all similar: Ethics in Public Policy, Economics and Public Policy, Global Public Policy, Public Policy Analysis."

"Let me guess—you're studying public policy?" They shared a laugh, and their eyes caught for a long second. Sam's eyebrows were lifted slightly, and Remy knew she was leaving an opening for them to explain why they'd chosen to study public policy. Or maybe why they'd chosen to come to graduate school at all. Now that she knew they were royalty, the idea of explaining felt like a relief. They could finally voice what they'd only ever been able to express in their application essay.

"I wanted distance from my family, but I wanted to be certain I was getting an education that would prepare me for the future. When I was younger, I wasn't the best student. I didn't always pay attention or do my homework. Now that I'm older and more mature, I realize my education was inadequate. Montamant might be an inconsequential nation, but we have laws and taxes and public assistance programs. Too often the sovereign is a figure only, not a real leader. I want to be capable of leading."

"That's very noble of you."

Remy could see they were winning her over from her first impression of them as a bratty millionaire, and they liked that. But they were in an awkward position now. Sam knew their secret, so it was no longer possible for them to remain casual acquaintances. And they knew so little about her in return, other than that she had pretty hair and was kind to them.

"What about you? Tell me about your life."

Sam shrugged. "I'm still questioning whether I should be so far away from my family. I know that compared to how far away you are, that sounds silly, but my parents and sister and I are really close. After college, my older sister, Becca, moved back home, and here I am, halfway across the country. I guess it was kind of like what you said. I felt like I had more to learn. The world is such a big place, and there's so much I don't know about." She tapped the rim of Remy's coffee cup with her fork. "Like the fact that there's a country called Montamant led by a family called the Vallorcins. How do people shut themselves off from learning when the world is so big, and there's always more to discover? I've never really understood that."

Remy didn't share Sam's passion for education, but they could understand wanting to see more of the world than her small corner of it. They felt the same way. They knew how it felt to be torn between family obligations and personal discovery. Maybe, they dared to hope, Sam could understand them in return. She could never fully internalize how it felt to be labeled a freak of nature or to be rejected by her own mother, but maybe she could understand feeling different from her family and wanting to carve her own path. Remy had friends, but they were people with whom they could dine and go to clubs. Pierre had been their constant companion since they were toddlers. He knew almost everything about them, but he accepted them out of familiarity more than he understood them. Remy wanted to be understood. And appreciated.

They sat quietly for a few moments. At first, it didn't feel uncomfortable, but once the coffee mugs were drained and their plates had been cleared, Remy wasn't sure where to look. They could feel a mounting pressure to do or say something to break the silence. But they feared saying something embarrassing.

Finally, they dared to glance at Sam, who was pointedly looking into her empty coffee cup. Her hair was fluffy and summery, not the icy blond of Scandinavian women but a warm honey that made Remy think of California and sunshine. Her lipstick had a cakey, cheap texture, but the effect of its crimson color was to plump her lips and draw the eye toward them. Remy wondered how those lips would feel against their own. Was Sam the type who took the lead, or did she wait to be kissed? Would she like it if Remy slid their hand around the back of her neck, between her tanned skin and her hair? Did she tilt her head to one side?

"If you're finished staring at me," she said without lifting her eyes from her mug, "we pay at the front, so we can leave at any time."

"Good." They slithered out of the vinyl booth. "I wasn't staring."

"Yes, you were."

"No, I wasn't."

At the cashier stand, Remy reached into their back pocket for their wallet, but Sam moved in front of them and thrust a blue card out.

"It's my treat, and you were staring."

"You don't have to do that," Remy said. "You should save your money."

The cashier looked between them before deciding to take Sam's card.

"It's my treat," Sam repeated. "You bought dinner last night, and I'm returning the favor. I need you to know that I'm not just friends with you because of your money." She flicked her hair over her shoulder, accepted the card back, and put it in her wallet. "But you *were* staring."

"I was not staring!" They found their way outside, and in the dense noise of the morning traffic, they added, "How would you know, unless you were staring back?"

Sam's red lips curved into a smile. She put her hand around Remy's arm, and Remy promptly crooked their elbow and held her hand tight with their free one. Walking side by side with arms linked, they took up too much space on the sidewalk, and they couldn't walk very quickly, but Remy basked in the closeness.

"You were staring," she repeated one last time, "but I didn't mind."

❖

Sam arrived at Dr. Grant's office a few minutes early, which she thought sent the message she was prepared and enthusiastic for the semester. It didn't matter because Dr. Grant's office door was shut, and she didn't respond to Sam's knocking. Sam hesitated outside the door for a moment, but if Dr. Grant arrived, she didn't want to pounce on her, so she decided to go to the bathroom and check her makeup. A minute later, she went back to the office and knocked again. Still no answer.

She looked up and down the hall, hoping that one of the other professors in the department was around to ask if they knew where Dr. Grant was or whether it would be appropriate to call or email her to see if she wanted to reschedule the meeting. But all the office doors were closed.

She rooted through her bag for her phone. She and Remy had exchanged numbers on their way to campus, so she composed a text: *Professor not here. What do I do?*

After a moment, Remy responded: *Break in and steal copies of the exams.*

Sam shook her head. It wasn't worth explaining that graduate school didn't work that way. She typed out a cheeky response, second-guessed herself, deleted it, and was in the process of writing a new message when Dr. Grant's door flung open and a woman with lavender-colored hair poked her head out. With her body-contouring black dress and hot pink heels, she looked only slightly older than Sam, though Sam knew from reading Dr. Grant's professional biography that she must have been in her late forties.

"Samantha?"

"Uh, yes, uh, Dr. Grant?" Sam threw her phone back in her bag. "Hello."

"I've been waiting for you."

Dr. Grant didn't say anything else, just turned and went back into her office. Sam was too nervous to explain the knocking and the stalling by going to the bathroom. There was a single chair stationed beside the desk, which was clearly intended for her. It was wooden and barely wide enough to support Sam's slender frame. On the desk were several stacks of thick books, two tidy file folders, and a syllabus that had already been highlighted.

For the next half hour, Dr. Grant explained her process for teaching Introduction to Women's, Gender, and Sexuality Studies, which involved a lecture every Monday and smaller group sessions on Wednesdays that Sam would lead. The carefully highlighted syllabus indicated when each assignment was due, and Dr. Grant, clearly used to working with novice graduate students, laid out a precise grading rubric Sam was to follow. Although Sam had witnessed graduate teaching assistants at work earlier in her academic career, the prospect of now being the one to come up with discussion questions and determine student grades felt daunting but exhilarating. Dr. Grant's demeanor was intimidating, though, and Sam wasn't sure their working styles would mesh well—which was unfortunate, since she had hoped Dr. Grant would agree to be her dissertation director and advisor.

By the time the professor had explained the process for the final exam in December, Sam's head was spinning with information and instructions, but she knew to just keep nodding and smiling and accepting the photocopies being handed to her. Then Dr. Grant tapped her palms lightly on the desk and sighed.

"Well, now we can talk about the real stuff."

"The real stuff?"

The professor leaned back in her chair. "I was on the graduate admissions committee this year, and I remember your application. Researching gender nonconformity among the social elite in Europe, right?"

Sam nodded, trying to mask her delight that her application had made an impression. "Historical societies," she added, in case Dr. Grant didn't remember every detail. "The project was inspired by this research I did on monarchies—"

"I came across an interview in which Prince William commented on what it would be like to have an LGBTQ child, and I thought of you." At this, Dr. Grant slid another set of photocopied pages to Sam.

"Wow, thank you," Sam said as she began flipping through the pages. "I really appreciate..." She trailed off as she noticed writing in the margin. Dr. Grant had responded to the article and given Sam her marked-up copy. But instead of notes that might serve as reference in Sam's research, the comments ranged from *WTF?!* to the more intellectually cutting *Contradicts Foucault, History of Sexuality, Part IV, see page 78.*

Dr. Grant hated the article and possibly Prince William himself. From Sam's quick skimming, it seemed like a puff piece in which a twenty-first century royal presented himself as the opposite of a giant homophobe. Nothing too controversial. Why would someone spend so much effort analyzing it?

"It's not much," Dr. Grant said, despite the copious notes that had clearly taken time, "but maybe it'll set you on a better path. Historical examples of transgressive social elites are just not viable as a dissertation. Your advisor will, of course, help you craft your project once you're finished with coursework and ready to present your research proposal, but I don't want you to spend two years spinning your wheels over something that could never come to fruition."

"Why couldn't...why couldn't it come to fruition?"

The professor looked at her for a long, uncomfortable moment. In that time, Sam could see that the cool hair color and carefully winged eyeliner masked a stern-faced middle-aged woman. Her piercing gaze made Sam feel small and stupid. She shifted uncomfortably in the wooden chair, squeezing her inner thighs to keep her knees together in her skirt.

At long last, Dr. Grant explained, "Your project is historical. This isn't a history department. We don't train graduate students in historiographic methods. And even if you were trained, you wouldn't find evidence of something that would have been systematically covered up, ignored, or otherwise forgotten."

Sam wasn't sure if this was one of those times when it was best to speak up in her own defense or just listen. "Queen Christina of Sweden," she began, but the professor interrupted.

"Queen Christina, sure, but there are already plenty of books about her, and royalty used to have relatively more freedom when it came to appearance. Not today, of course, with tabloids and the publicity machines, but you didn't specify royalty. You said social elite." Dr. Grant sighed as if the conversation had grown wearisome. "It's as if you're ignoring the most basic principle of gender studies, that all gender is contextual. You want to apply a topic of fascination for you today to a society that didn't have the same vocabulary or concept. It's ahistorical. At best, it won't work. At worst, it's as if your very premise indicates a failure to grasp the most fundamental concepts of the discipline."

Sam choked on any further questions. Dr. Grant hated her idea and didn't think she belonged. Sam wondered if Dr. Grant had voted against her admission to the program.

When she was finally sure no tears would fall, she looked up. Dr. Grant was typing on her laptop with her back to Sam. Their meeting had concluded.

Sam gathered her papers and got to her feet. "Thank you for your time," she mumbled as she hurried to the safety of the hallway.

❖

The student union was a labyrinth of corridors and offices, and the sparse signs didn't indicate the location of the one office Remy was trying to find. After circling the main floor twice, Remy went into the campus bank to ask for help. The employees pounced on them, and fifteen minutes later, Remy emerged, the newest account holder at the Boylston University Student Credit Union, with a free pen and directions to the ID card office.

When Remy finally got to the right room, a student worker with red curly hair hanging down his forehead greeted them politely. "New or replacement? Ten dollars for a replacement."

"I don't need a card," Remy explained. "I got a card yesterday at check-in, but it doesn't work. I couldn't use it to get into my housing."

"Did you pay your tuition bill? If you paid with a check, they might not have processed it yet, and your card might be—"

"Yes, yes, yes." The young man looked up, startled. "I'm sorry. I have been told this already. I paid the tuition. That's not what the situation is."

The worker gestured for the card, which Remy handed over. The worker looked at it intensely for a moment, then ran it through a machine as the security guard had done the night before. He typed on the computer, frowning and stroking the trace of red stubble on his chin.

"Is there a problem?"

"There's missing information from your personal profile." He angled his computer screen toward Remy, but it didn't move very far.

Remy leaned over the counter to get a better look, but they could only make out a blur of yellow and white text on screen. "What information is missing?"

"We have your name and home address, but there's no phone number."

"Oh!"

Remy felt a wave of relief. That was simple enough to correct. They hadn't had an American cell phone when the school had originally asked them to fill out their information, and they hadn't wanted to give an international number they didn't expect to use in Boston. They recited their new ten-digit American number to the student worker, who typed it slowly into the system with two forefingers. When they finished, they stared back at Remy without saying a word.

"Will my card work now?"

"No, there's more missing."

"What else?"

"Your emergency contact."

Her Majesty Queen Clotilde, Royal Palace of Montamant, Remy wanted to say, just to see the student's reaction. Instead, they gave Pierre's name and number.

"And now my card will work?"

"Your, um…" The student cleared his throat and turned the computer screen back toward himself. With dread, Remy could feel what was coming. "It doesn't have a gender."

For a moment, Remy thought the student was referring to them as an "it," but then they realized the student meant their personal record in the student database.

"My ID card won't work until I specify a gender?"

"I guess." The color of his face was starting to match the color of his hair. "Should I put, um, F, or, um, M?"

Remy's fist clenched below the counter, out of sight. "Are there any other options?"

"It's, um, it's a dropdown menu."

"And when you go down," Remy said, gesturing a mouse scroll with his forefinger, "there are only two choices?"

To his credit, the student moved the mouse to find out. "Just the two."

"Is it possible to write something else in?"

"I don't think so. Hang on, let me try saving it and maybe the other information we added is enough." Tap, tap, tap. He shook his head. "Sorry, it's not letting me save it until all the information is entered." He seemed equally embarrassed by the situation. "Um, which one should I put?"

Remy could feel a wave of anger rising inside, and at least getting angry meant they wouldn't cry in front of a student employee who probably didn't understand why having to pick between M or F could reduce someone to tears.

"May I have my card back?"

When the student extended their hand, Remy ripped the card away and stormed out of the office. They looked for a bathroom, but in the main corridor, there were only the male and female restrooms. The all-gender individual bathroom was somewhere in the building. Remy knew this because they had looked it up prior to coming to Boylston, but in this moment they didn't have time to find it.

Between the men's and the women's restroom, the women's seemed like a better choice for a meltdown. Remy ran inside, found a stall, locked the door, and slumped against it. The tears fell immediately.

Although it had a good reputation, Boylston wasn't Harvard or Yale or Cambridge. Remy had chosen to attend a less prestigious school because Boylston promised to erase some of the troubles Remy was running away from. Their admission materials had stressed their inclusivity: the all-gender washrooms, housing by student preference rather than public gender expression, and the option for students to change their name on all official campus documents. The name option was a real litmus test, even if it was an option Remy didn't need to exercise. Although Clotilde had spent Remy's life forcing them to live as a girl, King Georges had understood at Remy's birth that a name used for girls and boys might be best for the baby, given Remy's exceptional situation. Remy had never wanted to change their name, but if they had, their father's death would have reinforced their affinity for it. Knowing Georges had chosen it, Remy felt that keeping it was one way to feel close to their father.

Clotilde had once told them she hated the name Remy.

They unrolled the toilet paper into a long strand, which they used to blow their nose. Boylston was supposed to have been their escape. Since no one knew Remy here, Remy had looked forward to making a new identity, not only away from being royalty but also by exploring what it would mean to live without having to choose M or F. No one had ever said that Remy wouldn't even be able to open the door to their graduate apartment without making that choice.

It didn't seem fair. It seemed more than unjust. It seemed negligent on the part of the university to make promises to students it couldn't keep. It seemed cruel to act so welcoming and then make Remy feel like such a freak.

They felt their tears subsiding as they got angry again. They slammed a fist into the rickety stall door, causing the whole row of stalls to shake.

Their phone chimed with a text alert, and they took it out of their pocket, hoping it would be someone to offer words of comfort. But Remy wasn't sure who that person might be. Their phone showed three missed phone calls from Madame Pouvoir and a text from Sam.

Done with professor. Didn't go well. Hates my ideas. :(Meet you at the bookstore?

Remy wanted to tell Sam they'd also had a bad day, but writing it out sounded exhausting. Sam didn't want Remy to think she was using them for money, and she didn't want to be subject to Remy's financial charity. Remy felt the same way about their identity. They didn't want their friendship to be founded on Sam's pity. The more she knew about how hard Remy's life could sometimes be, the less she'd see them as a real person. They would be reduced to nothing more than a charity case, and being supportive of Remy would only help Sam to feel good about herself.

Remy figured not telling her what had happened to them was the best option. If she'd had a bad afternoon, Remy could charm her and offer sympathy. They would listen carefully and tell her that the meeting probably went better than she realized.

At the same time, Remy wasn't sure her ideas were that great. What did Sam really know about anything? She had read some books from the United States in the twenty-first century about people and places distant to her. She wanted to study people who defied gender norms, but Sam, with her wavy hair and perfect lipstick, hadn't lived through the experiences she studied. The experiences Remy had had. Sam didn't know what it was like to have photographers chasing her to get a picture, to have her own mother send her to Switzerland for the summer, so no one could see how she looked in a bathing suit, or to have her traditional sixteenth birthday celebration, at which she would be officially named heir apparent, canceled because her father had died and the palace was in a period of mourning. Sam's parents still called and texted her, and maybe they didn't have any money, but they loved her. Sam had no idea how hard the world could really be.

OK, they texted, and they washed their face in the tiny bathroom sink before heading to the bookstore.

CHAPTER SIX

Although she had held out for two days, canceling functions that were less important and suffering through the ones that couldn't be canceled, by Monday night Queen Clotilde had lost her voice, and her nose was a giant red blob. After a few hours of constantly extending a hand for a cough drop or tissue, she abandoned her Louboutin shoes and Elie Tahari dress for a puffy sweatshirt she borrowed from Remy's closet, the bottom of Georges's old flannel pajamas, and a pair of fuzzy slippers. She stuffed tissues and cough drops into the pockets of the sweatshirt as her cough evolved from delicate throat-clearing to phlegm-filled fits that lasted several minutes and left her and the chambermaids gagging.

"Oh dear," Madame Pouvoir declared. "She's gotten worse."

"Yes, Madame," Marie-Claire agreed from behind the surgical mask she was wearing. "This is her third box of tissues today." With a hand protected by a latex glove, she reached for a pile of used tissues next to the bed and placed them in the wastebasket. She pulled a can of sanitizing spray from the bottom cabinet of the nightstand and waved it around the room.

Madame looked at Marie-Claire, dressed for biological warfare, and Her Majesty, who could have won awards for reenacting the Black Death. It was clear the queen was suffering from more than a routine cold. She pulled out her phone and dialed 4, the shortcut for Dr. Lemal.

He answered after half a ring. "Yes?"

"The queen is ill." Madame stabbed at her phone screen to disconnect the call, knowing her message was sufficient to make the doctor come as quickly as he could.

Queen Clotilde croaked, "I'm fine," and then winced as the words scratched their way out of her throat. She stuffed another lozenge in her mouth and dropped the crinkly wrapper into the trash can at her bedside.

Within ten minutes, a valet showed the doctor into the queen's suite. With a silent nod to Madame Pouvoir, he set to work taking the queen's vital signs, making disappointed noises after each test. He asked her to stick her tongue out and prodded in her nose and ears. Then he rummaged through his bag and produced a syringe and vial.

"Vitamin C," he explained. "I will give Her Majesty this and an oral pain medication, perhaps some electrolytes, but unfortunately, there is not much more we can do."

"I'm nearly better," the queen whispered. "It's almost over."

"Doctor, is this true?" Pouvoir demanded.

"How long has she had these symptoms?"

"Since yesterday morning."

"I would say it is hardly close to running its course in that case," Dr. Lemal said. "I would expect at least a week, maybe two, for the worst of the symptoms. After that, there will still be a lingering cough, and she probably won't feel better for a solid month. Her Majesty is also dehydrated. It is important to drink plenty of water and remain in bed."

The queen shook her head and raised herself to a seated position. "Tonight is the—"

"Her Majesty must remain in bed," the doctor reiterated. "The immune system operates best when adrenal hormones have time to rest, so sleep is imperative when the immune system is fighting off disease. The longer you remain active, the longer you will remain sick."

Queen Clotilde pleaded silently with Pouvoir. She knew the queen wanted to be at the octocentennial, from the opening breakfast on Tuesday to the closing royal ball on Friday night. Every event of the celebration had been designed to have Her Majesty presiding over it, and many of the expected attendees had never before visited the palace or met the queen. To cancel on them would raise suspicion, generate rumors, and give the impression that the queen felt she was too good for her own people. Rescheduling was impossible. It was written into the Montamantien constitution that the proclamation of sovereignty had to be read by a member of the royal family on the anniversary of the country's founding every one hundred years, or the royal family would lose its claim to the throne. With King Georges dead, God rest his soul, that only left them with one option.

"We must summon Her Royal Highness."

"No!" Queen Clotilde and Marie-Claire cried in unison.

"Madame, you mustn't!"

"Absolutely not," the queen croaked. "I forbid you."

It was Madame Pouvoir's job to hold the kingdom together. If that meant displeasing Her Majesty in the immediate for the long-term benefit, so be it. It was better to find herself among Her Majesty's enemies than to tell Her Majesty she could no longer legally be called by that title because Montamant was no longer led by the House of Vallorcin. The crown princess was their only hope.

Pouvoir made lip service to obedience and excused herself from the queen's chambers. She waited until she had walked across the central wing of the palace to her office, shut and locked the door, and reached for the phone to call Remy.

Determined not to tell Sam the humiliating story of what had happened at the ID card office, Remy adopted a casual pose, leaning on a display case filled with Boylston-branded jewelry. Sam came slumping into the bookstore with her head down.

"You look happy."

"It was awful!"

She proceeded to rehash bits and pieces out of order, interrupting herself to tell Remy other rude things Dr. Grant had done and said as they pushed through the crowd to the section of the store where the textbooks were stocked. Remy interrupted once to ask for help figuring out where they were supposed to be looking. Sam insisted they find their course schedule online, again chiding them for not knowing what they were going to be studying.

"It does not matter," Remy started to explain, but Sam interrupted to say that, yes, it did matter, not only to Remy's future but also to their intellectual journey.

"Sam, please." Remy put their hands on their hips and looked at the ground for a moment, trying to figure out how to express their thoughts in English. "Certainly, each course matters. I respect the faculty who devised the curriculum. Please don't lecture me about my future. There are enough people at home to do that, and I wouldn't have come here if I believed the courses I am taking were unimportant."

"I'm sorry." She tilted her head alluringly to one side. "You're right."

"I meant that it doesn't matter which courses I am taking this fall and which come later. I'll have to buy all the books and take all the courses eventually."

"You can't buy all the books today." Sam held out a hand for Remy's phone. She touched the screen with her two index fingers and flung them apart to magnify the course schedule Remy had accessed. "Okay, over here."

She found the shelf containing the books for Remy's classes and began putting them in Remy's outstretched arms. When they realized she was choosing all dog-eared used copies, they protested and reminded her that the cost wasn't an issue. Sam huffed at this but exchanged the used copies for new ones.

"That's the last one you need," she said. "Should we head to the front?"

"What about yours?"

"I'll get them later."

"Why wouldn't you get them now?"

Remy knew she wanted to huff a little more and protest that the campus bookstore was too expensive, or maybe that she was too embarrassed to make the purchase in front of them or that she didn't have enough money in her account. It wasn't worth reminding her that Remy could afford to buy the books for her. They could tell by the heat in her eyes that she knew Remy wanted to offer.

"I can't take advantage of you whenever I need something I can't afford," she finally said.

"I'm considering it an investment." Remy was thinking of it in terms of an investment toward gaining Sam's affections, but they explained it somewhat differently to her. "If I spend a little money on books for you now, you'll be able to do your research, and you'll figure out all the answers to the problems people like me face."

"Not even close, since Dr. Grant doesn't think my ideas are remotely viable."

"What does she know?"

"Enough to write three books on gender."

Remy waved this away. This momentary setback on Sam's academic journey was hardly as serious as Remy being a nonentity in the eyes of the university because they didn't have an easily codified gender.

"Books are a swindle to force students to spend money on things they could find on the internet for free."

Sam gasped. "That is alarmingly anti-intellectual of you!"

"No, it's anti-capitalist."

"Says the one offering to buy all my books for me?" She put her hands on her hips, which she could do, since she had made Remy carry the entire load.

"I can be anti-capitalist and spend money," Remy argued. "I spend on other people, like you, to correct an unequal system that has given me more than my fair share."

"I don't want to be bought off so you can prove how progressive and socialist you are."

They resisted the urge to roll their eyes. "I am not a socialist, and I am not trying to 'buy you off.' If buying a book for you can make things a little easier for you, why wouldn't you let me do it?"

"I don't need anyone to make things easier for me. Graduate school is supposed to be hard. I came here for that challenge."

While Remy appreciated that she didn't want to be handed her successes, there was a difference between being challenged academically and being challenged economically. Economic challenges weren't something people could overcome with mere determination. Remy had seen that firsthand at home, where the average worker toiled their whole life to pay their bills and keep their family fed without a chance of ever gaining a fraction of the wealth Clotilde and Remy were born into. If Sam couldn't afford her textbooks, she'd be forced to take on debt or additional work to pay for them, which would mean less time for her academic study—and, more importantly, less time to spend with Remy. She was foolish not to take the help when it was offered.

"There's nothing shameful about accepting a gift from a friend," Remy told her. "Where's the section for your department?"

Sam selected three or four books, which she reluctantly added to the pile Remy was carrying. For all the anxieties she had about allowing Remy to pay for her books, she didn't seem to think twice about asking them to carry them. Remy didn't mind, but as they waited in the long checkout line, they couldn't resist the urge to tease.

"You know, people don't usually make me carry their things for them. I don't even have to carry my own things. I have staff for that."

Sam's red lips fell apart, and immediately, Remy knew they'd made a mistake. She started to reach for her books.

"No, no, I am teasing." Remy smiled at her. "I don't mind."

"Are you sure?"

"Yes, really. I'm sorry. I was teasing."

"It's hard to tell," Sam said. "You've got that dry French wit. I can't always tell when you're joking. Plus, you know, I don't know what the rules are for being around…" She glanced around, but the other students in line looked bored, and most were staring at their phones if they had a free hand. "Royalty," she finished in a whisper.

Remy cringed. Even saying it softly was too risky in their eyes. "There aren't any rules. You aren't one of my subjects. You're a friend."

"When did we become friends exactly? Because less than twenty-four hours ago, you hated me."

"I did not hate you."

"Yes, you did. When I stole that cart from you."

It was Remy's turn to gape in surprise. "So you admit it! You knew I was going to use the cart, and you took it anyway!"

"You seemed like one of those rich jerks," she admitted with glee. "I wasn't going to let you do whatever you wanted and get away with it."

"I'm hardly one of those rich jerks," Remy said.

"You're exactly one of those rich jerks. But you're also pretty sweet."

Remy wondered what had caused her change of heart, since they had never been "pretty sweet" with Sam. In the day they'd known each other, Sam had mostly spent her time telling Remy all the things they did and said wrong. She'd searched online to find out about them. While she'd been nice enough about what she'd found—*Your secrets are safe with me*—they hadn't been her secrets to learn in the first place. There was a reason Remy didn't introduce themselves as royalty or intersex. Maybe it didn't matter to Sam, but Remy had traveled across the world to protect their identity. Whether she knew it or not, Sam was probably only drawn to Remy because they were an enigma, an object of fascination for their indecipherability. As attracted to Sam as Remy was, they didn't want her pity, and they definitely didn't want to be her experiment.

Sam had insisted she wasn't using Remy, and she wasn't, not for money. She had made that clear by resisting every offer, and Remy could gauge her sincerity on that front. But that wasn't the only way Remy could be used. They had learned in their previous experiences dating that some people were only interested in them for the claim of having dated royalty. Intimacy, emotional and physical, was difficult for Remy, who had been betrayed by others' intentions and who had to safeguard the secrets of their body. To let someone in—to let Sam in—would require a lot more trust, even if she already knew who they were.

All the frustration Remy felt about their ID card not working, about Madame Pouvoir constantly phoning to interrupt their time in Boston, about twenty-five years of being hassled and mistreated and misunderstood bubbled up, and Sam, who was looking at Remy with a mix of curiosity and concern, was the most convenient target.

They stepped up to the cashier, another student worker who looked overwhelmed by the crowd, and Remy spilled the books onto the counter. "Is this all together?"

"Separate." Remy pushed Sam's books to one side and pulled out a credit card. "This is for these."

It felt good to show Sam they were still in control, that Sam couldn't do and say whatever she wanted and expect Remy to continue catering to her whims. Remy was the one with royal blood in their veins.

They dared to glance at her from the corner of their eye to see if she was going to yell at them and make a scene. Instead, she was looking down, and her lower lip looked wobbly. She wasn't in fight mode. She was ready to cry. Remy felt a pang of remorse, but it was too late to undo what they had said and done. They paid for their books and took the bag. They waited near the entrance to the bookstore, where they could still hear Sam say, "No, thank you, not today," and leave her books behind.

They saw her wipe a tear from her cheek, crying as Remy had cried after their visit to the ID card office. Maybe now she would understand how injustice felt. As she hurried past, ignoring them, Remy felt another icy stab of regret in their stomach. They had gone too far. They thought about following her, to apologize and wait for her to tell them how wrong their actions had been.

They couldn't do it.

They walked to the transportation office and asked for help summoning a cab to take them home.

❖

"Hello, Peaches!" Mom greeted her. "How was your meeting with the professor?"

"Oh, Mom!" The tears begin to fall. It was a bittersweet kindness that no matter how far from home she went, no matter how much she convinced herself she wanted to pursue the wrong dreams and friendship with the wrong people, her mother was always there to welcome her back with nothing but love. From the warmth of her mother's embrace, she felt like a horrible child.

She couldn't tell her mom that her only so-called "friend" in Boston had tricked her into picking out textbooks only to humiliate her at the checkout. She hadn't even wanted to take Remy's money, and they'd insisted. How could they have been so cruel? And then there was Dr. Grant. How could Sam explain to her parents that this project she had come all the way to the East Coast to pursue wasn't going to work? That something she'd talked about, even researched and written about as a master's student, a project she believed in—that someone who knew better and had more years of experience had told her how stupid it was?

"I'm fine." She sniffed. "Just a hard day."

"Do you want to talk about it?"

"I don't want you to be disappointed in me."

"Now, how could that be? If you're not ready to share details, that's okay, but I'm still here. You can ask us about what we've been doing." It was a gentle chide, a reminder to Sam that she wasn't the only one with a life worth sharing and that she couldn't let herself get so absorbed in Boston that she neglected her family.

They talked for a few minutes about Sam's brother-in-law, who had started a new job as a mechanic in the service department of a Honda dealer, and about how Sam's dad had volunteered to serve as an assistant coach for a junior high football team. It was nice to hear about the normal things her family was doing in light of her whirlwind time in Boston meeting royalty and finding out she was never going to get a PhD.

When they were caught up on family gossip, Sam felt ready to share. Between the meeting with Dr. Grant and the bookstore with Remy, Dr. Grant was the bigger blow of the day. If she hadn't already felt low from that meeting, she probably wouldn't have cried over Remy being an asshole. Although they'd opened up a little more this morning, and breakfast had been nice, in truth Sam had expected the asshole to rear its ugly head again. And right now she wasn't sure she wanted anything more to do with them. She could justify their aloofness and their abrasiveness as partly cultural, partly royal, and partly a defense mechanism for someone who had been mistreated by the world. But there was no justifying the deliberate cruelty they'd shown at the checkout counter.

"Dr. Grant doesn't think my research project is viable." She was ready to launch into a larger explanation when she blurted, "Also the asshole across the hall was an extra asshole today, and I guess I should have known better, but I really thought my first impression was wrong and we could be friends."

"You were hanging out with her again?"

"Them, Mom, and yeah, we had plans to do some stuff on campus together. I guess I thought we could be friends if I was understanding enough, but I was right yesterday. They're a jerk."

"I thought this was about your meeting with Dr. Grant?"

"Well, it was, but then Remy had to go and screw everything up when I was already upset about the meeting with Dr. Grant." She sniffed and ran a crooked finger under her eyes, wondering if her mascara was streaking. "Dr. Grant was—"

"Where is Remy now?"

"I don't know. We came back to the graduate apartment building separately. I took the bus. They probably hired a limousine or something."

Her mother made a face Sam couldn't interpret. "Do you think they'll apologize to you?"

"We're hardly friends, Mom. We've only known each other for one day. I don't want to talk about them."

Her mother continued as if she hadn't heard. "I think it's nice you're making friends, and I hope you straighten it out. I got the text with your first day of school picture."

Sam felt bedraggled now after being out in the daytime heat and crying and smearing her makeup, and she'd already forgotten how hard she had worked to look and feel good this morning. The day had been full of promise. She had wanted to impress Remy and Dr. Grant. Now they both hated her, her curls had fallen out, and all she wanted was to put on her pajamas and give up on today.

"Technically, the first day of school is next week. This week is orientation and meetings. I'll take another picture the first day I have class."

"Well, I thought you looked nice today. Did your neighbor take the picture?"

Sam wiped her eye. "Come on, Mom. Can I please tell you about my meeting with the professor? I don't want to talk about Remy."

Sam saw a smirk on her mom's face despite the lousy lighting of their video call. It peeved her. Why was her mother so insistent they talk about Remy? Their Royal Highness wasn't worth the time or energy. Sam didn't want to patch up their friendship. She didn't even want to live across the hall anymore. The school year would be great if she never saw Remy again.

CHAPTER SEVEN

Y our Royal Highness, I beseech you." They weren't words Madame Pouvoir was accustomed to saying. She was beseeched by incompetent staff members and desperate journalists. She never did the beseeching. But these were desperate times. "Your mother is very ill, and we are concerned that she cannot attend the upcoming octocentennial events."

"I do not see how this is my problem," Remy responded. "Frankly, I'm resentful you continue to call me at this number, which you shouldn't have in the first place."

"We have all your contact information. We would never let you loose in the world without knowing where you are and how to get in contact with you."

"I have a few angry words for Pierre for giving this number to you."

Pouvoir shook her head. The princess sounded like the same petulant child she had always been, more concerned with her own trivial day-to-day affairs than any issue of real substance. "Monsieur Lefaux was persuaded to share your phone number in his duty to the state. Even if he hadn't, we could have easily obtained it on our own. With all due respect, I do not think you grasp the urgency of what I am saying. Tomorrow is the opening breakfast, at which the proclamation of sovereignty must be read. Her Majesty cannot stand for long periods, and her vision is blurry. Her voice is nearly gone. Do you recall the significance of the proclamation of sovereignty? And how important it is for Her Majesty to read it?"

Pouvoir knew the proclamation had been part of the princess's education because she and King Georges had personally designed the royal and historical curriculum, and Madame Pouvoir had been responsible for hiring the constitutional lawyer who had come to the palace each week for an hour to tutor Remy after school.

When Remy didn't answer, Pouvoir resigned herself to the idea that the education she had so carefully devised had been a failure. She began to explain, "The constitution of Montamant declares that every—"

"Every one hundred years the proclamation of sovereignty must be read before the entire Parliament and ten percent of the population, or the presiding royal family forfeits its claim to the throne. In that case, the prime minister will be immediately authorized to assume full leadership of the nation, thus ending the reign of the House of Vallorcin and beholding the nation to an untested provisional government until Parliament can determine an appropriate governing structure."

Her Royal Highness did remember. "Then you can understand my grave concern that your mother is physically unable to read the proclamation. The law allows another member of the royal family as a substitute for the reigning monarch."

"And I'm the only remaining Vallorcin."

"May God rest King Georges's soul."

Madame Pouvoir said nothing else, waiting for the princess to decide how she wanted to proceed. If she believed in Montamant, cherished her rightful place as its future sovereign, and held tight to the values of duty and tradition, she would do the right thing. But since the king's death, she had run wild, insisting she was not a girl and now fleeing to America to escape family and responsibility. Pouvoir wasn't sure she knew the princess very well anymore. She couldn't be certain what she might decide.

When she didn't respond after a moment, Pouvoir added, "Please."

"I haven't made a public appearance since the funeral."

Not since an article had been written in the Montamantien newspaper. At the funeral, Remy had been a teenager in the throes of puberty. Her Royal Highness's body had not been developing in ways that might be expected of a young woman, and one prying reporter had managed to get someone at the palace to divulge that Queen Clotilde and King Georges weren't entirely sure Remy was a girl. Even with the newspaper's admittedly small circulation, the scandalous story about how Remy liked to wear boys' clothing and didn't menstruate had been a violation of privacy and potentially damning to the Vallorcins.

Sending Remy away to school had been the best option to protect Montamant—and Remy.

"*Mon chou*," she whispered, hoping the child who had wanted to be cradled after scraping a knee was still somewhere inside. "She has made a lot of mistakes, but she is still your mother. She—we—need you."

She held her breath.

"I'm not going to let Montamant fall apart," Remy said. "Tell me the plans."

Pouvoir's eyes fell shut in relief. "Thank you, Your Highness."

With only two hours until the charter flight was due to depart, Remy didn't have much time. They waved at the bartender and asked for the check. They dropped a few American bills on the damp surface of the bar and stumbled outside. Squinting into the bright afternoon sun, they immediately regretted the glass of Macallan. Feeling tipsy in a dimly lit bar was more fun than feeling tipsy on a public sidewalk in the late afternoon heat.

They had to hurry back to the graduate dorm, but there weren't any cabs to be found. Remy paused at a bus stop to ask the tiny old woman who was waiting there how they could get home, but her only suggestions were walking or taking the bus with her. She told Remy the fare and reminded them they had to have exact change. Remy had left their last remaining dollar bills on the bar and wasn't sure which stop was closest to their building anyway. Walking seemed like a simpler solution, but also another reminder of how sweaty life in the United States seemed to be.

By the time they got back to the graduate apartments, their glasses were slipping off their nose from the perspiration. Their hair felt sticky and wet, and they wondered if they had time to take a shower before heading to the airport. Returning to the comforts of royal life had its appeals.

They approached the security guard, went through the same dispiriting ritual about their ID card not working as the night before, and finally were let into their apartment. They found a mostly empty suitcase and tossed in a pair of pants. In truth, they probably didn't need any of their clothes. They would have to wear whatever the palace decided, which would probably be a dress unless Clotilde was so ill she was willing to accept that Remy wasn't the daughter she'd always expected them to be.

Although a charter flight wouldn't leave until its passenger was ready, the scheduled departure was 6:30 p.m. With the flight duration and time zone change, as well as the drive from Geneva to Montamant, Remy was due to arrive at the palace only a few minutes before the breakfast ceremony and reading of the proclamation. There was no time to waste.

Once Remy had their bag ready, they turned off the lights around the apartment and opened the door to the hall. They stopped for a moment, looking at Sam's door. Was it worth telling her they were leaving for a few days? Would she even care? After the way they'd abandoned her at the bookstore, she probably never wanted to speak to them again.

Remy's phone rang with Madame Pouvoir's custom ringtone. "Yes, Madame?"

"Your Royal Highness, I wanted to check on your progress at getting to the airport and give you another update on your mother."

"I've barely had time to get home and pack. I'm leaving for the airport momentarily. What's going on with Her Majesty?"

"She has now lost hearing in her right ear and developed an ear infection although Dr. Lemal says the hearing will come back once the infection has run its course. As a result of the fluid in the inner ear, she has developed vertigo and cannot stand or sit for long periods without losing her balance."

Remy pictured Clotilde tripping over her stilettos and landing facedown in the embroidered carpets that covered the palace floors. They wanted to laugh, but there wasn't time, and although Remy didn't care if Clotilde was suffering, they cared about Montamant plunging into anarchy because of it. Maybe more than they had first realized.

"I'll deal with that when I arrive." Remy yanked up their suitcase handle and rolled it into the hallway. "Thank you for the update."

"Have you had a chance to eat?"

Did a glass of Scotch count as eating?

Pouvoir didn't bother waiting for Remy's answer. "I will have dinner ready for you on the plane."

"Thank you, Madame, that would be appreciated."

"We'll see you soon, Your Royal Highness. Travel safely."

"I will, Madame. I'll see you in the morning."

The door to Remy's apartment slammed shut automatically, and Remy realized they couldn't get back in if they were missing anything. Too bad, they thought. If they didn't have something, they would have to make do without it.

As Remy turned toward the elevator, Sam's door creaked open a few inches. She peeked out, then ducked back inside and shut the door.

"Sam?"

She didn't open the door again.

Remy didn't have time for games, but they couldn't resist knocking on the door. "Sam?"

The door cracked open again, and Remy could see one eye peering out. "Sorry," she said. "I wondered what all the noise out here was."

"It's me. I'm leaving for Montamant."

"You're what?" She pulled the door fully open and held it with a foot so it wouldn't close on her. She was wearing a tank top and didn't have on a bra, and Remy tried hard not to look at the delicate points of her nipples poking against the thin cotton. "Why are you leaving?"

"There is a problem with Her Majesty, and the palace is worried enough to send for me."

"Oh, Remy, I'm so sorry!"

Remy squinted at her. "Why are you being nice?"

"I'm not being nice."

Remy noticed her makeup was mostly gone, except for a few black smudges around her eyes, and they wondered if she'd been crying. Once again, they felt awful about what had happened that afternoon, but they didn't know how to convey that to her.

"You're staring again," she pointed out, her voice glum.

"Sorry." Remy reached for the suitcase handle. "I didn't mean to make so much noise out here. I'd better leave."

"Just like that? You're just going to leave without saying anything else?"

"Uh, good-bye?"

"Why did you do that to me at the bookstore?"

Sam wasn't the type to mince words, which Remy appreciated. Frankness was a part of Montamantien culture, and tiptoeing around the truth was one reason why Remy's childhood had been so miserable. Any another day, they would be grateful Sam was willing to share her frustration so plainly. But Remy's mind was already halfway across the Atlantic, and they were anxious to get to the airport.

"I don't know."

"Well, have a safe flight," she said crisply. "I'm sorry to hear about Her Majesty. Truly." She turned to go back into her apartment.

Remy couldn't stand the idea of leaving for a week on bad terms. They grabbed her door before it latched shut. "I'm sorry. I'll buy your books when I get back next week, if it can wait that long."

"It can't. I can't go without doing the reading for class for an entire week. And I'm tired of your games. So you can go back to Mountamount and just...fuck off." She lifted Remy's fingers off the side of the door and pulled it closed. It latched, locking Remy out.

They felt awful. Sam was an adult who could figure out how to get her own books. She hadn't even wanted Remy to buy them. But as soon as they had offered, they had taken responsibility. To go back on that now, to leave her without those books for a week, made Remy the kind of person they didn't want to be. Unreliable. Untrustworthy. Not the qualities of a good future sovereign.

They pulled their wallet out of their back pocket. It was a risk, but Sam hadn't done anything to indicate she was untrustworthy. They slid their new credit card under the door.

"Sam," they called, "if I don't leave for the airport soon, I'm not going to make it home in time. I'm sorry for what I did. There was no excuse. You can use my credit card to buy your books."

"It's not about the money," she called back. "It's about the way you hurt my feelings."

Remy closed their eyes. "It was my student ID card. They told me it doesn't work because I didn't specify male or female on my student profile. I was angry and embarrassed about that, and I took it out on you. I shouldn't have done that. I'm sorry. Can I call you when I return?"

Remy waited a moment, but Sam didn't reply. They once again turned to walk to the elevator. They only made it a few steps before Sam stepped out into the hallway, her foot holding the door open again. She had Remy's Visa in her hand.

"What did you say about your student ID?"

"The student at the ID card office said my profile is invalid because gender is a required field, but my profile does not have an M or F label."

"Boylston has a third gender option." Sam tapped the Visa against the palm of one hand. "I mean, there should be more than three. It's not as if everyone who's not male or female has the same gender, but... All students, undergraduate and graduate, are allowed to choose their gender on student documents, and we have an 'other' option. That shouldn't prevent your ID card from working."

Remy shrugged. It had made them feel like garbage at the time, but "other" didn't sound that much better. "That's what the student worker told me. Anyway, I have to leave."

"How are you getting to the airport? Do you need a ride?"

"I'm driving myself. I'll leave my car there." Sam arched an eyebrow, but before she could mention the high price of parking, Remy reminded her, "This is one time the cost does not matter, Sam."

She turned back to her door, reached inside, and flipped the lock backward, so her door couldn't close shut and lock her out. She followed them to the elevator. "Why didn't you tell me about your ID? I could have helped you. You just have to go to the graduate school office for the override. It's a total pain, and it's not right that you have to take extra steps other people don't, but that's how you do it. It shouldn't prevent you from being able to access your housing, especially when you've already paid for it."

When the elevator arrived, Sam stepped onto it, and Remy wondered if she planned to follow them all the way to the car in her pajamas and slippers.

"That happened before we met at the bookstore?" she continued. "Is that why you were in such a shitty mood?"

"I don't want to talk about it."

"Why didn't you tell me that instead of taking it out on me?"

"I said I didn't want to talk about it now, and I definitely didn't this afternoon. Do you know how humiliating it was?"

"No," she answered to their surprise. "Of course I don't. There's no part of me that can ever fully understand your lived experience, no matter how much I empathize."

No one had ever quite put it that way before. Usually people either didn't care, or they tutted and frowned and said they could imagine how difficult things were—if Remy dared to express that they were different in the first place, which wasn't often. Never had they trusted someone with their secret and had that person admit candidly they didn't understand. Somehow it sounded more supportive than the tuts and frowns.

"I may not understand what it's like to walk in your shoes, in your body," Sam continued, "but I know something about humiliation. I was told today that my research is stupid, and there's no way I can pull it off. And I had to sit there and nod and agree. I felt humiliated, too, but that was professional. It was worse when my own friend humiliated me."

They made their way from the lobby to the parking garage. "You're right that my behavior was unacceptable. I apologize. Sincerely. I'm not good at handling anger and sadness since my father died. It's something I need to continue trying to improve, and I regret if I damaged our friendship."

"Thank you." Sam sighed. "That was one of the best apologies I've ever heard."

"Then I am forgiven?"

"For now," she teased them with a coquettish purse of her lips. She handed Remy their Visa card, and Remy took a moment to open their wallet and slide the card in. "I'm sorry about your father. That's another thing I know I can't fully understand. Now your mom…and I'm going on and on about myself. How selfish of me."

She was good at apologies, too. She was the kind of person who actually stopped to consider other people's perspectives. It was gracious and charming.

"I understand how disappointed you must have been after your meeting with the professor," Remy said. "I know how important school is to you."

She came back to life then, the effusive person they'd met the day before. "So disappointing! I'm sitting there listening to her tell me there's no way I can ever know anything about gender norm defiance among the social elite, and I can't tell her the most obvious piece of evidence I have."

"You mean me?"

"Well, yeah! I couldn't very well say, 'Hey, Dr. Grant, guess what? You're completely wrong because the nonbinary person across the hall happens to be royalty.'"

They had reached Remy's car, and Remy put their suitcase in the trunk. There were so many things they still wanted to say to her. They wanted to thank her for not revealing anything to Dr. Grant. They wanted to tell her in more detail how awful they felt about what had happened at the bookstore, how much they regretted their actions, and ask if the smudges of mascara were because they had made her cry. They wanted to tell her that being the cause of her tears broke their heart, too.

She was standing on the asphalt in a pair of gray slippers. She wore a pair of tiny shorts that matched the tank top. Even though her legs had been bare underneath her skirt all day, she looked more naked now, vulnerable without her makeup and styled hair. Remy wanted to thank her for being brave enough and forgiving enough to follow them down to the parking lot to patch up their fledgling friendship.

"I guess I should go."

Sam stepped forward and hugged them, and it felt as good as Remy had hoped. She smelled like lemons and the sweat of the day, comforting and arousing at once.

"I'll miss you," she murmured against their ear. "Will I see you again?"

Remy had assumed they'd perform their duties and be back in time for classes to start. Was there a chance the affairs of state would force them to stay in Montamant? They didn't like that thought. School was too important. Life in Boston, with all the freedom it offered, was too important.

And they didn't want to leave Sam.

In the space of two days, she had become important to them. There were so many awful things waiting for them at home: Clotilde's cold judgment, figuring out how to dress and what to be called in front of Parliament, the looks and gossip that would circulate when Remy made their first official appearance in ten years. Remy didn't want to face any of it, especially not alone.

"Come with me."

"What?"

They hadn't known they were going to propose it until the words were out, but now it seemed like a remarkable idea. "You should come with me to Montamant."

"What?"

"I don't know, Sam. I know I have to go, and I don't want to leave you behind." They took a risk to reach for her hand. She didn't pull away. They saw the trepidation and a little excitement in her eyes. "I felt awful when that happened at the bookstore, awful for myself and awful for what I had done to you. I convinced myself you're only interested in me because you pity me or because you want to say you know some mixed-up person."

"You're not a mixed-up person."

"Aren't you a little bit curious to see royal life?"

"Remy, I wouldn't know what the rules are for someone like me to be there and how to act, and this is terrible timing with your mom so sick, and we start school in a week…"

"Sam?"

"Yeah?"

"Come with me. I'll make sure you are back before classes start. Just come with me."

Remy caught her eyes again and felt their heartbeat quicken. With Sam in Montamant, they'd have someone to lean on, someone who understood them in ways no one in the palace did. They could keep talking, keep working on their relationship and getting to know each other.

"You can do research. I will make sure you have access to our historical archives, and you can watch a contemporary monarchy firsthand."

"I don't have a toothbrush or any clothes." She looked down at her body and, for the first time, seemed to realize what she was wearing. She dropped Remy's hand and folded her arms over her chest in modesty.

"We can get you clothes. Anything you need."

"Leave the country?"

She would be leaving her home country. That meant she'd need a passport. Remy had a diplomatic passport that enabled them to move in and out of foreign countries with relative ease—not that the US customs official in New York had understood why they merited the passport, having never heard of Montamant or the House of Vallorcin. But Sam wasn't a diplomat or even a Montamantien national. She'd need a passport when they landed in Geneva, and they would need to submit her information to the American aviation regulatory body with their flight plan before takeoff.

"Do you have a passport?"

"Yeah," Sam said with a knowing smile. "I applied for one last spring. It was really expensive and took a long time to come. I just got it in the mail last week. I brought it with me to Boston because part of my funding package was summer research money, and I was really, really hoping to figure out how to get to Europe this summer—"

"Are you telling the truth?"

Sam grinned. "I'm not lying, I know it sounds like I am, but I was hoping to go there this summer. I've never been before, I just wanted to—"

"Do research," they said in unison.

"Sam." Remy's voice was softer now, indulgent. "We don't have time to waste."

"Oh, right, the plane! You can't miss the plane!" She turned back to the building and ran for the door, calling over her shoulder, "I'll be back down in two minutes!"

Of course, the back door to the building had shut, and she didn't have her ID to swipe in. She had to run through the alley to the front of the building, where she would have to beg the security guard to let her in the same way Remy had to.

Remy got in the car and started it and moved it closer to the back door. They sent a hasty message to Madame Pouvoir to notify her that Sam was coming and to make a few special requests in consideration of Sam's generosity.

Sam was true to her word and emerged within a few short minutes, waving her passport as she jumped in the car. She had a bag and was carrying a pair of sneakers.

"Did you bring a bra?" Remy asked.

"Oh my God!" Sam put a hand over her face in mortification. "For your information, yes, it was sitting on the chair in the living room, where I'd taken it off a few minutes before you were banging around the hallway. Which you were probably doing on purpose, so I'd pop out and see what was going on."

"I was not." Actually, Remy thought, they may have done that subconsciously. They had been looking for a way to make amends with Sam and had been too cowardly all afternoon.

"You were, too. And who talks about someone having a bra?"

Remy gave their lips a little lick of delight as they pictured her pulling it off. "I'm only asking because I figured you'd be embarrassed not to have one to wear all week."

She glared for a second, then relented. "Couldn't you just whip out a credit card and buy me a new one?"

"Oh, no," Remy said with mock seriousness. "Unfortunately, we have very strict laws about the royal accounts. The law clearly states that any palace guest who does not arrive without her own undergarments must suffer without them for the remainder of her visit."

Sam shook her head with a smile. "You're ridiculous. I grabbed my phone, but then I realized I can't use it on the plane, and it won't work in Europe, so I guess that was dumb."

"You can use mine if you need to call your parents."

"How did you know I wanted to call my parents?"

Remy shot a glance at her as they pulled out into the Boston traffic. "Because I've been paying attention."

Even though Remy had their eyes on the road, they were also paying attention when Sam bit her lip and turned her head to the window to cover her widening smile.

"I can't believe I'm doing this!"

"I can't believe it either," Remy said. "But I'm really glad."

CHAPTER EIGHT

Sam had never flown on a private plane. She'd never even seen one. Her family preferred the flexibility and economy of driving and didn't often have occasion to travel the kind of distances that necessitated flying anyway. She knew enough about airports to expect to remove her shoes and stand in line for a long time for the security check. This experience was different, though. When they arrived at Logan, Remy avoided the main terminals and drove into a parking lot immediately behind a small building. As soon as they were out of the car, Remy grabbed Sam's hand and ran with her inside. Within a minute, they were being led across the open tarmac to a small jet. Sam climbed a flight of stairs onto the plane, imagining herself as a celebrity. She resisted the urge to turn around and wave to an imaginary crowd.

Inside, the plane didn't look like any plane Sam had ever seen. Two giant leather seats framed a shiny wooden table on one side of the cabin. On the other was a leather couch with a long table in front of it. The lighting was bright but inviting, not garish fluorescents, and the floors had a rich maroon carpet instead of the vinyl and industrial carpet of ordinary jets.

Before she could figure out where she was supposed to go, a woman in a crisp white blouse and navy blue tie appeared. She introduced herself as Sophie and offered to take their bags.

Remy passed her their suitcase and Sam's duffel, and Sophie took them into another room, which was separated from the main cabin by a wall and door instead of those dorky curtains that separated first-class from everyone else on regular airplanes.

Sam looked to Remy for guidance.

"Sit anywhere you want," they said.

Without assigned seats, Sam had to make a choice: sit in a chair by herself, forcing Remy to also sit alone, or sit on the couch and hope Remy would join her. Since it was a six-hour, overnight flight, they'd probably want to take turns sleeping on the couch later. She sat in one of the armchairs, and Remy joined her at the other. Sophie reappeared and asked them what they wanted to drink.

"Did they order us dinner and breakfast?" Remy was clearly accustomed to flying this way. Sophie nodded. "What did she get me?"

"Who?" Sam asked.

"Madame Pouvoir."

"We have a full tapas meal catered by Toro," Sophie reported. "When they phoned to say there was an extra passenger, we contacted the restaurant to make sure the order was changed for two. So, please, no worries. Would you both like a glass of wine before we take off?"

It wasn't long before they were in the air, and soon they were being served dinner on a white linen tablecloth. Whoever had picked it out had done a terrific job. They shared an assortment of smaller nibbles like dates, Marcona almonds, and olives, then moved to ham, spicy potatoes, and grilled corn. Sam's belly was already full and her head light from the red wine Sophie kept refilling when Sophie announced it was time for the main dishes. She set down a platter of octopus and another of duck drumsticks.

The food had thus far been unusual but extraordinarily delicious. Octopus and duck, though, Sam wasn't sure about. She looked at the platter and then looked at Remy.

"You must try. Please." They took a duck drumstick and ate it with their hands to her surprise.

"Duck, maybe, but I can't eat octopus."

"Why not? Have you ever had it before?"

"No."

"Then how do you know you won't like it?"

"I've never had sex with a man before, but I already know I won't like it."

It had to have been the wine. Too much wine, plus it was getting late, and it had been an emotional roller coaster of a day. There was no other reason why she would have said something so direct, so personal, and so…awkward in front of Remy.

She felt her cheeks growing hotter than the wine had been making them, and she couldn't look up. In desperation, she reached for a piece of duck and took a bite to give her an excuse to stop talking. She had expected it to be like chicken. It certainly looked like chicken. Instead, it had a fatty texture and gamey flavor she found unpleasant. She reached for her linen napkin and spit it out.

Then she realized what she had done. It wasn't as if she could hide the napkin. There were only two passengers on the plane. Once Sophie cleared the plates, she would take Sam's napkin and realize there was a lump of food inside it. Then she would know Sam wasn't sophisticated enough to keep her food down. She was mortified. And horrified on Sophie's behalf that she would have to touch a napkin full of half-chewed duck.

Her head fell in embarrassment, and she covered her eyes with her hand. She slouched in her chair, trying to get as low to the table as possible. If she could just make herself smaller, maybe the moment would pass.

Then something began roiling inside her, and before she could control herself, she let out a giant, noisy burp. It brought the awful taste of the duck back to her mouth, making her nauseous enough to gag, and her hand flew to her mouth to contain the food that threatened to come up.

Pffffffttt.

Sam looked up in time to get a face full of wine as Remy did an actual spit take with laughter.

"Hey!" she yelled, causing another unpleasant duck burp to escape her mouth.

Remy laughed so hard they choked. Then it turned into a coughing and laughing fit, and with one giant cough, Remy jerked forward against the table and spilled the remains of the wine glass all over the octopus, which made them laugh harder. Sam scrambled to mop it up with her duck-filled napkin, and then remembered she had sticky wine drops on her face and pressed the cloth against her cheek. The napkin was wet with wine and octopus, and she threw it in disgust. It landed against Remy's chest, spilling open some of the contents against Remy's shirt. Reflexively, Remy jerked back and knocked the table, spilling more wine and causing the napkin with chewed food to fall open on the floor.

They both exploded into another round of laughter. Remy couldn't talk and their face was bright red. Sam was laughing so hard she thought she might pee her pants.

Eventually, they settled enough to summon Sophie for help. It took her a few minutes to get the table cleaned up, and she gave them wet wipes to use on themselves while she did. By then, they had both calmed down. They left the messy table area and settled next to each other on the couch. Sophie poured them two fresh glasses of wine. It was warm and fruity, and Sam could feel it pulsing through her veins. Her cheeks were hot with its effects, her head light, and she leaned into Remy's body warmth, momentarily forgetting they didn't have that kind of relationship and Remy was royalty.

"At least now you don't have to try the octopus." Remy slid an arm out from behind her and wrapped it around her shoulders, pulling her in close. She knew it meant something that Remy was letting her feel the contours of their body. Their embrace was comforting. And comfortable, like they had always fit together.

"Have you really never had sex with a man?" Remy asked.

"Can you pretend I didn't say that? I'm so embarrassed."

"You don't need to be." Remy's hand started to play with her hair. "Tell me."

"No," Sam said. "Have you?"

"Yes." She was surprised to hear that and wanted to ask follow-up questions, but Remy asked her, "Do you always date women?"

"Yes. You?"

"Yes. Usually." Remy paused before asking, "Could you date someone like me?"

"Yes."

"Even though I'm not a woman?"

"Yes."

It wasn't that she only dated women but that she didn't date cis hetero men. Anyone else was fair game in the name of queerness. The fact that Remy was intersex and nonbinary wasn't the issue. It was more that their economic and social differences should have made them unappealing to Sam. She didn't fully understand why she was drawn to Remy, but she was aware enough to see that her behavior could only be the result of attraction.

"Sam, I have to tell you something." Their hand stopped touching her hair, and Sam sat up to look at them. Their brown eyes were avoiding her behind their glasses. She wondered what further important thing Remy could be withholding. The last two secrets had been pretty significant, and they hadn't even volunteered the information. She'd had to get it herself.

"What?"

"I have a friend, Pierre, and I think he will be at the festivities."

Remy swallowed. "No, not 'think.' I know he will. I don't want you to be surprised."

"Wait a second, I'm confused. How will I know who is at the festivities?"

"What do you mean?"

"What do *you* mean?" she repeated. It sounded as if Remy meant she would be at the octocentennial, but Sam wasn't a citizen, and she only had the clothes on her back. She hadn't jumped in Remy's car and gotten on this airplane in the hopes of attending official palace events. She thought she was going there to support Remy through the death of their mother, one of the worst moments of their life. She didn't even expect Remy to be at the events more than was required of them.

"At the octocentennial, I want you to be prepared to meet Pierre. Sometimes he's not the nicest person, but he—"

"So, wait, you're saying I'm supposed to come? To the events?"

"Of course! Why wouldn't you?"

"Because I'm not from Montamant, and I'm wearing a tank top."

"Oh, that!" Remy leaned forward and called for Sophie.

She stuck her head out, and Remy said, "The package?" She nodded and vanished again.

A moment later, she brought out a giant silver gift box and presented it to Sam. Sam looked at Remy, who nodded encouragingly. She lifted the lid to the box. Inside were a pair of pink silk pajamas with tissue paper between the layers of fabric. She lifted the pajamas out and was surprised to see there was more in the box. She pulled out a toiletries kit with a toothbrush, toothpaste, floss, and face wash. No makeup, but she thankfully always kept the essentials of her own makeup collection in a small zipper bag in her purse. There were also colorfully striped socks, bikini underwear in a tasteful shade of nude with lace trim, and a fresh, clean T-shirt made from buttery soft jersey.

"Really?" she gasped.

"While you were getting your passport, I had to let Madame Pouvoir know we were adding a passenger, so she could give your details to the aviation company. I asked if she could have some things sent for you. I thought it would be helpful if you had some clean clothes for the morning."

How had Madame Pouvoir been able to get dinner and the equivalent of a weekend getaway bag in the time it had taken Remy to drive them to the airport? Had Sophie gone to the store herself before the flight, or were there special delivery services for things like this?

Was this how the wealthy traveled? Anything they wanted, they could immediately get?

And Remy had wielded that power to make sure she was taken care of.

"I really appreciate this, Remy. This was really thoughtful of you." Sam put the lid back on the box to keep her treasures safe and clutched the pajamas to her chest. "I'm feeling that wine. Do you mind if I put these on and try to get some sleep?"

"Of course. Sophie, would you help with the beds?"

After Sam changed her clothes, she settled into one of the leather armchairs, which was now reclined almost flat. There was a crisp sheet on it and a pillow and blanket waiting for her, and she chuckled internally at her earlier belief they'd have to take turns sleeping on the sofa. Between the long day, the red wine, Dr. Grant's hazing, and now the giant shift in her relationship with Remy, Sam was more than ready for sleep. She was grateful she didn't have to lie down with her bare skin sticking to the sofa leather.

As Remy settled in the other chair, Sam felt the absence of their body heat against hers. She wondered if what she had been feeling was all because of the alcohol and if it would vanish in the light of day. She was starting to suspect it wouldn't.

Sophie dimmed the lights in the cabin. They decided to put on a movie. The media library contained a huge selection of contemporaries and classics, and they opted for the first black-and-white film on the list, *Some Like It Hot*. It turned out to be a movie with Marilyn Monroe that depicted two men masquerading as women to hide from the mafia.

"I didn't know this was what this movie was about," Sam said. "Do you find it offensive?"

"Honestly," Remy said with a yawn, "I'm enjoying it. You see how hard it is for them? Now imagine how exhausted they would be if they actually felt they were women."

"Wait, are you saying you feel like a woman?"

"Not really." Remy snuggled deeper into their blanket. "When you look at me, do you see a woman?"

Their conversation was waking her up, partly because she wanted to hear Remy talk more about these things and partly because she wanted to make sure that in her stupor she didn't say something careless.

When she didn't answer, Remy pressed. "Do you see a man?"

Sam knew the answer to each question should be no. Remy identified as nonbinary, and it was her obligation to respect that identity. Now that she was starting to learn about intersex, she knew she needed to do more research, learn more, and grow in her understanding. She expected her knowledge and attitudes to change a lot through her PhD as they had during her master's. But one thing she had come to understand in the last few years was that personal values were sometimes different from historical precedent or even mainstream social attitudes. Supporting a nonbinary person's existence was important. Telling Remy she understood them as nonbinary, as Remy wanted, as they understood their own identity, that was the most important thing. Especially since they were flying across the Atlantic Ocean to a place where no one else gave them that kind of support.

"I guess I just see you as…you," she answered finally.

"What does that mean, 'you as you'?"

As much as she was squirming in the hot seat, Sam appreciated that Remy wasn't going to let her off easy. She took a moment to gather her thoughts and put them into words.

"When I look at you, I see someone who tells the world they don't care about anyone else's expectations for them. You wear your hair how you want, you dress how you want, and you're basically telling the world to fuck itself if it doesn't like who you are. It's kind of hot."

Sam knew it was a bold admission, but she didn't let herself look away from Remy. She waited to see whether they would blow her off or reciprocate their interest. Remy held her gaze for a long moment as their own cheeks grew a little pink. Sam's heart was pounding in her chest, and it was hard to get her breath. Finally, Remy nodded with a slow, smug smile.

Sam cleared her throat. "So when we get to Montamant, how are you going to handle it?"

Remy took off their glasses and laid them gently on the table between their beds. For a moment they had that confused, bug-eyed look of a nerd whose glasses had been stolen by the class bully. They rubbed the bridge of their nose, stimulating life where the frames had left indentations, and when they opened their eyes again, Sam saw a face that was soft, eyes that were deep and kind, someone she could tell all her secrets to. Sam wished they were still on the couch, close to each other. She wanted to reach for Remy in the darkness and press into their warmth. To wake up tangled together, smelling of each other, and know that their night on the plane had united them.

Maybe it was crazy, and she certainly didn't understand where these thoughts had come from, but she felt the ache in her body.

Remy gave her a sad smile. "Clotilde will be upset about my appearance, since with this hairstyle I cannot—how do you say it in English when you look a certain way, and people think something about you?"

Remy's hair was kind of punk and cool, but Sam didn't think it necessarily said "male" or "female." It was just hair, but she thought she understood their point.

"Do you mean 'passing'?" She thought that might be what Remy was referring to, though in her gender and sexuality classes, Sam had learned that the better way to phrase it was that people assumed things about someone, rather than that person stealthily trying to pass as something they weren't. "You mean that with your hairstyle, you won't pass as female? People won't look at you and immediately think female?"

"Something like that. I am certain Pouvoir and Her Majesty will complain about it."

"Do you realize," Sam said, "that you always call her 'Clotilde' or 'Her Majesty'? I've never heard you call her 'Mom.'"

"We aren't like you and your mother."

Obviously. But could they become that way, if they tried? Did they even want to have a closer relationship before it was too late? It didn't seem as if Remy did.

"Were you always this way? You and the queen?"

"No." Remy gave a forlorn sigh, one that was out of character, but Sam was certain that's what she'd heard. "My appearance was always a problem, but we were closer before my father died. I think if he were alive, he would understand. Clotilde never will. And once he died, everything that had connected us vanished. She was happy to send me away for school and vacations, anything to keep me away from the press, the palace, and her."

"I'm sorry about your dad."

Picturing life without her own father was impossible, but if King Georges had been the glue that held the family together, no wonder the Vallorcins had become so distant from each other. With the queen nearing death, Sam couldn't imagine how much pain Remy was in.

Perhaps, if Queen Clotilde could retire and establish Remy as sovereign this week, the two could mend their rifts. Not that anything would ever make up for losing a parent, but it might give Remy some peace of mind if they reconciled before she died. And Sam would get to say she not only visited a palace but saw a coronation. How incredible would that be?

"Can the queen turn the crown over to you, or can you only inherit after death? How do the laws of inheritance work in Montamant?"

"Only after death."

"That's a shame." Remy looked at her quizzically. "I don't mean that you should stage a rebellion or anything. I mean that it would probably be nice for her to see you ascend to the throne, to know the country is in good hands. It would be a privilege for a parent to get to see their child step into that role. I guess if you can't become monarch until her death, she won't get to, though."

"Mm," Remy said noncommittally. "Of course, that's years away."

"Years?" Sam sat up in her bed. "I thought you had to rush to Montamant because she was dying."

"She's not dying. The queen has a cold."

CHAPTER NINE

While they were sleeping, Sophie had lowered the window shades, and Remy awoke in the dimness of the small safety lights on the floor. After a minute, their eyes adjusted. Sam was still asleep, her hair thrown across her face and her mouth hanging wide open. They were due to land in an hour, and Remy wanted to eat breakfast.

"Sam, are you awake?" She made some incoherent mumbling noises, and a clumsy hand tried to push her hair off her face. "Sam? What did you say? I couldn't hear you."

She blinked to life. "What time is it?"

"In Boston or Montamant?"

"Were you trying to wake me up?"

"No," Remy fibbed, "I thought maybe you were already awake."

"I am now." She sat up and flipped her hair over her shoulder. "Did we finish the movie?"

"You fell asleep before it ended."

"What happened?"

"The rich man said he didn't care if Jack Lemmon was really a man."

Sam grinned. "Really? That's kind of daring for back then."

"You like that?"

"Well, yeah, you know, everyone gets their happy ending."

"You like the idea of someone not caring what gender someone really is?"

"Yes, of course. Did you wake me up to talk about the movie? Or my attitudes toward gender?"

"I woke you up because I'm hungry."

"So you admit you woke me up on purpose." Sam fumbled around with the chair to try to get it to sit up, but when she couldn't figure out how, she slithered out of it to her feet. "I guess I should get dressed, then." She gave them a pointed look. "I wouldn't want Queen Clotilde to see me in my pajamas while she's on her deathbed."

"I'm sorry," Remy said. "It was a misunderstanding."

"You exaggerated on purpose."

They were repeating the same arguments from the night before. "I did not. You assumed. If she doesn't recover from her cold in time for breakfast, and the proclamation doesn't get read by a Vallorcin, the future of the monarchy is at stake."

"So you've said." She padded across the cabin toward the bathroom. "Hold that thought while I try to get ready. I wish I had a flat iron."

If they made it to the palace in time, she might be able to shower and do her hair. Or one of the palace chambermaids could style it for her. That depended on how quickly they cleared customs in Geneva and whether there was a lot of morning traffic. Once they got outside Geneva, the drive should be simple enough. Later in the fall, some roads would close due to falling boulders and snow blocking the mountain passes, but this early in September, the roads were usually clear.

While Sam was in the bathroom, Sophie set up the big table for breakfast. "Coffee, Your Highness?" she asked.

She hadn't referred to them by their title until this moment. It was a startling reminder that Remy was about to lose their individuality, to become only "Your Highness." To go from feeling like themselves, like they had started to in Boston, to feeling wrong.

People born as commoners probably thought being royal was glamorous and full of perks. How little they understood about the sacrifices royals were often asked to make for the greater good of their nations. At least elected officials had term limits and were allowed to retire. For royalty, the job was never over.

They should have watched *Roman Holiday*.

By the time Sam emerged from the bathroom, looking gorgeous and impossibly fresh despite having only minimal grooming supplies, Remy had made a mental list of the things she'd need to know before they reached the palace. They settled on the couch with espresso, orange juice, croissants, and fresh fruit while Remy tried to prepare her.

"Madame Pouvoir is in charge of the household, and even though you'll be there as my guest, you should do anything she tells you to do. She will prevent any trouble."

"What kind of trouble do you anticipate me getting into?"

"None, but there are aspects of palace culture you don't know. Madame gives everyone advice about where to stand, when to sit, whose hand to shake, those things. She's an encyclopedia of royal protocol. In fact, I think Clotilde added 'protocol officer' to her official job description."

"You sound fond of her," Sam observed.

Remy plopped a piece of melon in their mouth. "I am. She raised me. She's a terrifying person, but she's efficient at her job, and in her best moments she was a tender nanny."

"Remy, she misgendered you your entire life. She forced you into an identity that wasn't yours. That's abuse."

Remy definitely harbored some longstanding resentment toward Clotilde—and the world—and occasionally it angered them that Pouvoir hadn't been more willing to speak up on their behalf. But abuse? That was crossing a line. Sam hadn't been there and didn't know enough about their family to say such a thing.

"Let me be clear. I appreciate the way you make me feel as though I'm not a monster, but that doesn't give you the right to talk about my family however you want. It is me who decides who I want in my life and how I want them there. Madame Pouvoir may be authoritarian, but she also read me stories before I went to sleep. She did the best she could to make sure I had a good childhood while trying to help my parents protect the monarchy. Please, not an unkind word."

"Sorry." Sam's voice was soft and low. "I promise I'll listen to her."

Remy was on a roll and wasn't ready to hear her quite yet. "Should I remind you that twenty-five years ago the world was different?"

"Hey," she snapped, "do you need to tell the person getting a PhD in gender studies that social attitudes toward gender change over time? No, you do not."

"Sorry," they echoed. They hadn't expected to feel so protective of Madame Pouvoir, but they didn't want Sam to have bad feelings about her before they even met.

"So am I. I wish you'd had a better childhood, and I'm angry on your behalf. But you're right. It's not my place. You're the only one who can decide whose fault it is and who you choose to forgive."

Sam was sincere in her apology, they could tell, and they didn't want her to feel badly. They knew she was only concerned about them.

What she didn't understand was that Madame Pouvoir, in her own way, was also. Everything she had done, even the things that now seemed wrong, had been out of concern for Remy and desire to protect them. Although Remy's childhood hadn't been easy, they didn't fault Pouvoir for it.

They put a hand on Sam's cheek to show her there was no real argument. She leaned into their touch, putting her own hand atop Remy's. They gazed into each other's eyes, and for one perfect moment, Remy imagined what life would be like with her. How simple it would be, despite all the political, economic, and social complexities that stood between them. To kiss Sam's soft lips, to hold her hand, to feel her body against theirs like last night but know they didn't have to wake up and separate as they went about their daily lives. To go through life together.

Remy was becoming infatuated with her.

They squeezed their eyes closed. The reality was that in a few hours, they would stand in front of a huge gathering of people to secure the Vallorcin line. No matter what happened now on the plane, no matter how they organized their lives back in Boston, for the next few days, Sam couldn't be anything other than a friend. It wasn't done. Remy had to marry royalty—or at least nobility. Prior to plans for marriage, it was inappropriate to make public appearances with a casual lover.

"What else before we arrive?" Sam's lips parted slightly, an invitation for Remy.

"There's a lot I want to do before we arrive." Remy's voice was breathy, the heat rising in their body.

They both leaned forward, and Remy closed their eyes as their lips gently pressed to Sam's.

❖

It took Sam a moment to get over the shock of feeling Remy's lips on hers, their mouths opening and their tongues slowly dancing around each other. She slid a hand around the back of Remy's neck and pulled them in closer. Remy tasted like espresso and kissed with soft intensity. It went on and on, growing deeper until she heard herself give a little moan of desire. Remy put a hand between them and squeezed her breast. Sam wanted more. She needed more. And she could tell Remy felt the same way.

She untucked her shirt and guided Remy's hand up and underneath her bra. Their thumb found her nipple and circled it, and Sam's head fell backward in release. Remy took the opportunity to nibble delicately at the skin of her neck. They kissed downward to the neckline of her new shirt, but Sam didn't want it stretched out before she had to meet the queen, and she wanted them closer. She leaned back against the arm of the couch and pulled Remy down.

Remy wasted no time in slotting their legs around each other. They braced their weight on their elbows and gently caressed the hair at Sam's temples as they looked into her eyes. Sam felt naked, exposed, and treasured. Remy gave their lips a tiny lick and bent down to kiss her again.

This time the kiss was slow and meaningful but just as hot as the frenzied rush from a moment before. Sam reached for Remy's ass and squeezed it. She wrapped a leg around them, daring them to press harder against her.

Remy ended the kiss then but gave one final, delicate press of their lips to hers. "I want you so badly," they whispered. Their breath was hot on Sam's face. "I've wanted you since the first time I saw you."

It was the declaration she had been waiting for. Confirmation she hadn't imagined all the tension between them. Sam searched her own heart, wanting to protect herself and Remy at the same time. For many, the question would probably be whether she was only attracted to Remy's wealth and royal bloodline, but for Sam those were inconvenient obstacles. When she looked at Remy, she saw someone she could have long, deep conversations with. Someone whose upbringing and worldview were different enough to make for interesting discussion but whose core values were in harmony with her own. She wanted to see and touch their body. To show them it was beautiful, however it was made. And she wanted to be responsible for making them come undone, to see, finally, behind the shields.

"I want you, too." Her words came out in a breath, and she clutched tighter to Remy.

"You can have me," they said, but their voice was tinged with sadness. "Whenever you want, you can have me."

Sam leaned back enough to get a good look at them, and she understood the sadness. She gave her own sad smile back. "But I can't. Because right now Montamant has you."

Remy sat up and adjusted their clothing. They ran a hand through their hair and took a sip of the espresso that was probably cold by now.

Sam swung her feet to the floor and adjusted her bra and shirt. She fluffed her hair and wiped a trace of saliva from the corner of her mouth. It was hard not to feel disappointed, and these little actions gave her a moment to put herself back in control.

A minute or so after their makeout session ended, Sophie entered the main cabin. Sam envied how perfect her hair and makeup were after the all-night flight and wondered what tricks she knew. And she admired Sophie's careful timing. She had probably heard everything and waited until they were done to make her entrance.

"Your Royal Highness, we're nearing descent into Geneva, so if you wouldn't mind fastening your seat belts?"

"Of course, thank you," Remy replied.

"She said 'Your Royal Highness,'" Sam whispered as Sophie retreated.

"She started doing that once we entered European airspace. I think Madame Pouvoir instructed her to use my given name last night as a gesture toward my independence."

"She didn't curtsy."

"She didn't need to. She had already spoken with me once. You only have to do it the first time you meet and the last time before leaving."

Sam was beginning to realize that studying royalty and encountering it face-to-face were two different things, and she was underprepared for the latter. "What other rules do I need to know? If I mess up, what will Her Majesty do? She sounds like the type who doesn't let things go unchecked."

"Ordinarily, she would correct you, but Pouvoir says she's barely conscious at this point." Remy found a seat belt nestled between the cushions. "Then you are still coming?"

"Where else would I go?" Sam wondered. "And why would I waste an opportunity like this?"

What she wanted to say—but was too self-conscious to admit aloud—was that she was willing to come even if it meant watching Remy from the shadows. Being there as Remy's weird foreign guest was still better than not being there at all. She would take the scraps Remy could give her while she figured out how much more she dared to hope for.

She kind of hated herself for it.

Remy reached across the space between them and put their hand on her leg. Sam regretted that she was no longer wearing the shorts from the night before and that Remy's hand wasn't on her bare skin.

"Thank you, Sam. If you can be patient with me this week, I promise to do right by you." They squeezed her leg suggestively.

She took Remy's hand and curled their fingers together. "I promise to do right by you, too."

When they landed, they climbed down the short flight of stairs off the plane and into a waiting vehicle that led them across the tarmac to the terminal. The driver explained they would need to clear customs. The driver came inside, managing their bags for them, and Sam was surprised to see there were no lines of people waiting to have their passports stamped.

"If you come to Europe again," Remy said, "don't expect this in the commercial terminal."

In French, they introduced her to the customs officer. Remy's passport merited only a quick glance, and Sam wondered if it was because Remy was a diplomat or because they were from a nation within the European Union. Hers got more scrutiny, but she was excited that she was about to get her first passport stamp ever. After a moment of scanning the pages and comparing the photograph to Sam in the flesh, the officer slid the passport to her without doing anything to it. She looked at Remy in confusion, and they must have sensed her disappointment.

They said something to the officer, who smiled benevolently and took Sam's passport back. They stamped one of the back pages and, in English, wished her a good visit.

"Will I get another stamp when we reach Montamant?"

"First, we drive across the Swiss-French border, but we're in a diplomatic vehicle, and we have already entered the EU, and Montamant doesn't have its own border control, so no."

"Oh, well." She smiled at the fresh stamp and then closed the passport and slid it into her bag. She wasn't that disappointed, since a day ago she hadn't even expected to use her new passport. "It's still exciting. Three countries in one visit."

"Three countries in two hours," Remy corrected her.

On the other side of the customs desk, a young man in a suit was holding up an iPad, the screen of which said "Vallorcin." Sam glanced around the airport. She knew Montamant was a small nation with nonexistent global power, but she had imagined a little more fanfare for the heir to the throne.

"Doesn't anyone care that you're royalty?"

"They will. But not here."

Sam wondered if Remy meant it was a matter of security to remain low-key at an airport, perhaps to avoid terrorism or kidnapping or some other political gesture? Or maybe they meant that no one in Geneva, Switzerland, in a private airport full of the world's wealthiest people, thought Remy was special.

Sam thought they were special. She thought the whole experience was special, like something she'd only seen in movies. They were led to a shiny black SUV with two flags affixed on each side of the hood. The flags had a pale blue background with one perfect white triangle in the middle and a red heart in the center. She remembered seeing that flag on the Montamant website. "The loving mountain," Remy had explained, though "mountain of love" was maybe a better translation. The flag was an adorable depiction of that.

The man in the navy suit held her hand as she climbed into the vehicle. She slid over to the far side, and Remy climbed in after her. A driver in an actual uniform and cap was waiting behind the wheel. He greeted Remy in French, and then Remy introduced him to Sam in English. They said his name was "Jeel," and after a few seconds of confusion Sam understood that Remy meant Gilles, which she'd always thought was pronounced "Jy-els." If she was going to survive this week, she needed more than a brush-up on the French language.

In the meantime, Remy was being courteous by continuing to speak in English, so she could follow the conversation. "Pouvoir didn't come with you?"

"No, Your Royal Highness." Gilles's accent was nowhere near as clear as Remy's, and he spoke haltingly. "She thought it was more prudent to manage the situation with the prime minister from the palace. She sends her apologies to Mademoiselle Ide."

Sam wondered who Mademoiselle Ide was. Remy just looked at her.

"Me?" Sam realized. "Madame Pouvoir sends apologies to me?"

"You know her?" Gilles asked with a glance in the rearview mirror.

"I've never heard of her until yesterday. She sounds scary."

He smiled. "She is."

"Stop, Gilles, you're going to scare Mademoiselle Hyde away." Remy turned to Sam. "Gilles is Pouvoir's nephew. He's teasing."

"She gave me this job," Gilles explained. "She can be very precise, but she is not mean."

"And what about the queen?" Sam couldn't help asking.

He shook his head but didn't take his eyes off the road. "My apologies, Mademoiselle, but I will not and cannot say a bad word about Her Majesty."

"It's all right, Gilles," Remy told him. "You can speak freely with us." Again to Sam, they explained, "There's an old law that criminalizes speech against the crown. I doubt anyone is ever prosecuted for it anymore, but Clotilde likes to keep it as a law, as you can imagine. Gilles, Sam is going to meet Her Majesty for the first time. What was your experience when you first met her? Do you remember, or were you too young?"

It was obvious Gilles didn't want to say, even with Remy's blessing. "She is beautiful and just."

Remy snorted with laughter. "If you say so."

"She is at the moment very sick," Gilles reported. "My aunt told me she is not feeling good, and she is not able to talk or go out. I understand that is why they have asked you to come home. Though I have been instructed not to discuss the malady with anyone else."

"That's what I heard, and that's why I'm here." Remy rooted in their pockets and produced their phone for Sam. "Do you want to call your parents? It's…nearly midnight in Indiana, I think. Is that too late?"

"No, my mom always waits to hear from me before going to bed. Can you show me how to do it?"

Sam didn't really want to talk to her mother in the car with Remy and the family driver, since she expected her mother to ask a lot of tough questions about her spontaneous decision to fly to Europe. She'd probably grill Sam over her choice to do it with Remy specifically. But if she didn't check in, her parents would be worried.

To her surprise, Remy unbuckled their seat belt and climbed into the front seat. They narrowly missed kicking Gilles in the face, and one of their shoes fell off. Sam passed it to the front.

"To give you privacy," they explained. "I will put up the…" They gestured up and down with their hand and gave her a gentle wink, a promise that they understood. Then they pushed a button that raised a piece of dark glass between the front and back.

Sam pushed the green button on the phone to connect the call. The phone rang a few times, and she tried to figure out exactly how to explain where she was and why.

CHAPTER TEN

No, no, no, I cannot do it!" Marie-Claire protested. "My job is to tend to Her Majesty's clothing! I won't!"

Pouvoir closed her eyes to Marie-Claire's histrionics. Bringing Queen Clotilde her breakfast tray was nothing to fear. She turned to Marie-Pascale, who worked in the kitchen and would have less reason to protest. "Please get Her Majesty's tray while I explain to her."

Marie-Pascale, who had assumed her only job was to bring the tray up from the kitchen and leave it outside the queen's suite, exchanged a terrified look with Marie-Claire. Pouvoir gave them both her best authoritative stare. After a moment, Marie-Pascale's eyes lowered and she reached for the silver tray.

"After you, Madame," she murmured, following Pouvoir into the bedroom.

"*Bonjour*, Your Majesty!" Pouvoir announced. She wasn't going to be afraid of the queen's reaction to the news even if all the other palace staff were. She pulled the heavy drapes apart, flooding the room with sunlight, and assumed a position standing at the foot of the bed.

Queen Clotilde slowly opened her eyes, blinking in the bright sunshine, and raised herself to a seated position. Pouvoir waited patiently while she blew her nose several times. The nose-blowing led to a coughing spell, which lasted a solid minute and only concluded when the queen produced a ball of phlegm from deep in her chest and spat it into a tissue. Pouvoir willed her face to remain neutral, though she was gagging inside.

When Her Majesty had settled, Marie-Pascale set the tray on the bed, and Pouvoir began to speak. "Your Majesty, I hope you can recognize that you are not in a state to attend the breakfast ceremony this morning."

Queen Clotilde drank a small glass of orange juice, cringing when she swallowed. "Burns," she croaked, touching her fingertips to her swollen glands.

"The vitamin C is good for you, even if the acid makes your throat a little tender. Now, because you are not well enough—"

"Proclamation," the queen whispered.

"Indeed, that is what I have come here to tell you. Because you are not well enough to read the proclamation as required by law, we have ensured that another Vallorcin will be available to take your place."

The queen blinked a few times. Then she shoved the breakfast tray out of her way and got to her feet. Scratchy throat forgotten, she launched into a diatribe at Pouvoir, who summoned her resolve to stand erect, listening but not reacting.

"What were you thinking?" the queen concluded. She collapsed back into bed in a coughing fit.

"Your Majesty has employed me to ensure the successful running of the palace and the protection of the royal family. By having Princess Remy read the proclamation in your stead, I have done just that."

"You've gone too far this time, Pouvoir." The queen's hands flew to her forehead, rubbing her brow. A headache no doubt exacerbated by the unnecessary shouting at Pouvoir for performing her duties so admirably. Queen Clotilde snuggled back against the pillows. "If Remy's here, then I can sleep?"

"Of course, Your Majesty. We will leave your breakfast on the table if you awake hungry." She nodded to Marie-Pascale, who gathered the tray and brought it across the room.

"Bring her to me when she gets here," the queen croaked hoarsely.

"Naturally."

Pouvoir nodded once more to Marie-Pascale to signal it was time to leave the room. She pulled the heavy drapes closed again, and they crept out, shutting the tall bedroom doors behind them.

"She yelled at you!" Marie-Pascale gasped once they were safely in the corridor. "She said that she hated you and that you were fired."

Indeed, the queen had said that and worse, but more importantly, by falling back asleep, she had demonstrated that she lacked the capacity to perform her duties. Pouvoir had not gone too far; she had done exactly what needed doing.

As for reconciling mother and child, that was another matter, and she had another hour to figure out how to solve it.

❖

"Honey, I can barely hear you." Mom's voice crackled, and the screen keep freezing and pixelating. "Think...reception..."

"Sorry, I think we're going into the mountains."

"Mountains?"

There was no point in beating around the bush. "I'm in Europe. With Remy. They had a family emergency, and they asked me to come here with them. As a friend," she added.

Her mother's response was garbled. Sam decided to assume she had said something positive.

"We'll be back before school starts," she continued. "I don't know how often I can call you, but I wanted you to know where I was, so you wouldn't worry."

They drove through a patch with crystal clear reception in time for Sam to hear her mother say, "I thought you didn't want anything to do with Remy?"

"Yeah, but..."

"You'd better not be doing something stupid in the name of love. I thought getting your degree was your singular goal right now."

The conversation was so unfair. Her parents had said all summer that Sam should try to make friends in Boston, and yesterday—right before she'd boarded the plane, in fact—her mother had pushed her to reconcile with Remy. Now that she was doing what they suggested, Mom was scolding her choices?

The screen froze again, and Sam was too annoyed with her mother's reaction and the technology to try to continue their conversation.

"I'm here for research, I swear," she insisted. "I'll be home Monday. I love you!"

She ended the call. Her mother's reaction had surprised her. She had expected concern about things like safety, but she also presumed Mom would think it was cool Sam was getting to have this once-in-a-lifetime experience. She certainly didn't know how to tell her mother she and Remy had made out on the airplane, and there was no way she could tell her mother that she probably was doing something very stupid in the name of love.

❖

"If I may say so, you seem remarkably calm, Your Royal Highness."

Remy felt anything but calm, and having Gilles speak to them in such a formal way was only adding to the stress of the morning. They'd known each other for twenty years, after all.

"Do you remember when we were little, that time we went swimming in Nice?"

"I do."

"Do you remember the big fight about my outfit?"

"You didn't want to wear a top."

"Clotilde hated that."

Remy had only been seven or eight years old when they had gone on holiday along the Côte d'Azur for a few weeks. Madame Pouvoir had brought Gilles, and the Lefauxes were there with Pierre. It was before Pierre's mother divorced his father and moved to Spain, and several years before King Georges died. The three children had played together, and the differences between the other two and Remy hadn't seemed strange, only natural points of curiosity. When Remy had seen that Gilles and Pierre got to swim in trunks and didn't have to wear two pieces, they had wanted to do the same. Georges had given permission, but even at such a young age, Remy had understood they had said something to upset their mother. She had made them feel as though they had disappointed her with their behavior, but as a child Remy hadn't understood why.

It was also one of the last times Remy could remember being allowed to socialize so freely with a commoner. The children had played, eaten, and even napped together. At that tender age, Remy was often told they were going to be the next leader of Montamant, but they didn't really understand how that made them different from Gilles. It had been a simpler, happier time, and Remy remembered it now with fondness, but in some ways, these terrifying and complicated days were better because at least now Remy knew who they were.

"It's strange to see you like this," Gilles admitted. "Can I say that? I guess I was expecting someone more…feminine."

"With long hair and large breasts, you mean." Remy adjusted their scarf protectively. They hated it when their silhouette could be seen under their shirt. "I'm scared other people will feel that way, too. I don't know how they'll react."

"You're still our heir. I think that will matter more to most people."

Remy bit their lip and felt something welling up inside them. Relief? Gratitude? They couldn't label it. They only wished more people had said things like Gilles before they'd had to run off to the United States in shame.

"Thank you, my friend."

Their drive continued in amiable quiet, interrupted only by their stop at the French border. Remy tapped on the glass and lowered the divide between the seats. Sam had finished her phone call, and she sent her passport to the front seat for Gilles to hand over to the border agent. They were soon moving forward again, heading out of the villages of Switzerland and onto the highway through France. They climbed steadily higher as they passed through small towns of the Haute-Savoie.

Sam pointed out the buildings she found interesting, which was nearly all of them, and cooed over the breathtaking views of peaks and valleys. Some day in the future, when they would have time to stop and visit everything, maybe Remy could bring her back. They'd show her the old churches and cottages, eat wine and cheese, walk along the icy rivers hand in hand.

Today, Gilles rushed past, their car chugging higher into the mountains and toward their destination, everyone desperate for them to arrive on time.

❖

At 8:30 a.m. precisely, their sleek car turned onto a road flanked by two stone gates. They climbed one last steep hill, angled around a curve, and arrived face-to-face with an iron gate and several security guards whose jackets were embroidered with the flag of Montamant. Gilles rolled the window down, allowing the guards to peer inside.

"Your Highness," they greeted Remy.

Apparently, the visual confirmation of Remy's identity was sufficient to allow the car entry. Sam had expected pat downs or retinal scans or something, but so far, every aspect of this trip had been characterized by underwhelming security procedures. She supposed that said a lot about the peace and safety of life in Montamant.

The guards stepped back from the car, and the gate slid open.

Gilles rolled his window up and moved the car slowly forward. They drove underneath a stone building, through a narrow archway that Sam wasn't sure was any wider than their giant SUV, and finally they parked in the middle of a cobblestone plaza. Remy was let out of the car first, in accordance with royal protocol. When Gilles opened Sam's door and helped her out, she gasped at what she saw.

They were inside a square courtyard, around which stood the walls to the palace. Directly in front of them, the building was made from tan-colored stone, pockmarked with age, and the doors and windows were small and gloomy. Based on the design and amount of erosion, Sam thought it must have been built in the Middle Ages. To the right was another stone wall, this one perfectly rectangular, with red bricks, ornate white stone trim, and floor to ceiling windows. It had to have been constructed centuries later as an addition, maybe when the monarchy outgrew the first, cramped section of the palace. On the opposite side of the courtyard, to the left of the medieval section, was a white plaster section with dark brown Tudor-style beams crisscrossing the facade. The windows in that section were stained glass, though Sam couldn't make out what they depicted. Behind their car, the Tudor and revival wings met through a series of ramparts, along which two guards kept watch down the mountain. With four wings, the palace was gigantic. An architectural feat throughout the centuries, packed with history. Remy didn't live in a house, not even a mansion. They lived in a museum.

A row of staff in outfits ranging from business suits to maid uniforms to chef's jackets were lined up side by side. The oldest woman was wearing a black blazer and pencil skirt and carrying a thick leather binder. Next to her was a red carpet that stretched from the courtyard to a tiny stone doorway in the medieval portion. In unison, the row of staff bowed to Remy, the men folding at the waist and the women dipping into curtsies. Sam knew Remy was royalty, but seeing a dozen people bow with such formality in the middle of a palace courtyard, she suddenly understood exactly who the person she had kissed on the plane was.

The older woman took three confident steps toward them. Remy extended a hand, which she shook heartily. She had a tight smile on her face, but her eyes betrayed her severity. There was a twinkle of genuine affection in them. This, Sam could tell, was the famous Madame Pouvoir.

"Your Royal Highness, your hair!" she said. "Your clothing!"

"Madame, please."

"The staff didn't even blink at their outfit," Sam interjected.

Remy and Madame Pouvoir both turned to look at her, making Sam feel very small. Her first breach of protocol had been made. Clearly, she wasn't supposed to speak unless spoken to.

"You must be Mademoiselle Hyde." Madame Pouvoir extended her hand to Sam, gave it one cursory shake, and withdrew. "You may call me Madame Pouvoir. Marie-Francine will take you to the room we have assigned you. You will no doubt want to freshen up." She looked Sam up and down. "We have laid out some appropriate clothing for you as well."

Madame Pouvoir turned her attention back to Remy, and they exchanged some words in French. Sam tried to pretend she wasn't eavesdropping, but for all she knew they had forgotten she didn't speak French and were waiting for her to chime in. Then Madame Pouvoir put her arm around Remy's shoulder and led them down the red carpet. They approached the medieval stone doorway, ducked to avoid hitting their heads, and disappeared into the darkness of the palace. Sam didn't know where she was supposed to go or what she was supposed to be doing. Following them? Awaiting further instructions? This didn't seem like the kind of place where guests were encouraged to explore on their own.

"Mademoiselle Ide?"

A woman who didn't look much older than Sam came forward. She was wearing a simple black shift with a white apron over it and black ballet flats.

It was nice to see the important traditions, like having servants and making them wear ridiculous uniforms, were being honored, Sam thought cynically.

"I am Marie-Francine. If you will please come with me, I will take you to your suite."

They walked away from the medieval side of the palace to the more beautiful side.

"Excuse me," she asked, "do you know how old this wing is?"

Marie-Francine opened a giant door that must have been ten feet tall. "This part of the palace is from the Renaissance." She gestured for Sam to step through.

Inside, the ceiling looked about twenty feet high. The space was cavernous, and the sound of the door closing echoed across it. The walls were covered in pale blue silk and lined with oil portraits of ancestors and picturesque scenes of people picnicking with their Saint Bernards. The furniture looked several hundred years old—Baroque or Louis XIV, Sam thought, though she wouldn't have been able to tell if it was authentic or re-created. Old but elegant. Fashionable and ornate with brightly colored silks and elegantly carved wood. The ceiling was carved plaster and trimmed in gold leaf. It was all so impressive Sam couldn't believe it was real.

"Right this way, Mademoiselle."

Marie-Francine led Sam up a wide staircase to the second floor, which was lined with an expansive overlook to the lobby below. They went through a set of double doors and into a bedroom that looked like a suite at the most expensive hotel Sam could imagine. There were heavy curtains that fell to the floor, plush carpets over the wooden floors, and a four-poster bed with at least ten pillows. In the middle of the room was a dress form with a simple red cotton shift draped over it. On the floor, a pair of nude stilettos with a sharply pointed toe had been arranged. Without asking, Sam knew the outfit was what she was supposed to wear to breakfast. It wasn't exactly her style, but she could tell even from a distance that they were probably the most expensive clothes and shoes she'd ever seen in her life.

Maybe there were some perks to being a royal guest.

CHAPTER ELEVEN

The palace staff were concerned about Remy having a chance to shower and dress before the opening breakfast ceremony. Remy wondered if they thought the shower was needed to wash off the remnants of the United States. Their old bedroom had thankfully been redecorated from when Remy was a child, when the walls were pink and the sheets had depicted lollipops and fairies. Since Remy had left for university, the walls had been painted in a sophisticated textured cream finish, and the furniture changed to dark wood. It didn't feel familiar like home, but Remy appreciated how adult and neutral the room was. One of the new maids, whose name Remy hadn't yet gotten a chance to learn, hustled them toward the bathroom. A standing shower with glass doors, something Remy had never had as a child or teenager, had been installed, and it looked welcoming after the long journey.

After Remy had been in the shower for only a few minutes, someone knocked on the bathroom door and reminded them time was running out to get ready for the breakfast ceremony. One of the chambermaids blew Remy's hair dry while another helped Remy select a pair of trousers, socks, and shoes. Then she held up two options for a shirt, both in Montamant's signature sky blue. One had seams at the bust, tailored to a woman's build, and one was cut straight, a men's shirt. She offered them as equal possibilities, her face neutral about what each shirt would signify. Remy appreciated that, but neither would look good on them.

They wished they could just wear a T-shirt.

They opted for the men's shirt and said no to the fitted jacket the maid next offered. This was Remy's first public appearance in ten years, so they knew their transgression of the expected, feminine manner of dress would be a lot for the people of Montamant to swallow. But dressing in clothes that clung to their body would only encourage speculation about how that body looked. Going without a jacket would make them seem more casual, more approachable. They said no to a jacket and tie and instead found a green-patterned belt in the bag they had brought from Boston.

Before putting on the clothes they had selected, Remy shooed the maids out of the room. It was atypical for the royal family to dress themselves, but they were uncomfortable with the idea of letting strangers see their body. They also knew they could throw on clothes faster than a maid with careful precision would.

They wanted to give their eyes a swipe of mascara and put on some pink lip gloss to finish the look, but they didn't want to give Clotilde and Pouvoir more ammunition for calling them a girl. They put on a coat of clear lip balm instead and opened the door to their suite to signal they were ready.

The whole process of getting dressed and allowing the maids to make final micro-adjustments to their clothing took only three minutes, but since time had been short to begin with, there was no way Remy could visit Clotilde before the ceremony. Instead, Madame Pouvoir greeted them in the hallway. As they headed down the grand staircase together, she prompted them in the lines for the proclamation of sovereignty.

"I've got it," Remy assured her. It had only taken two run-throughs before the words came flooding back from all the after-school lessons at which they'd been required to recite them. "What about Sam? Can someone show her to the room? Which room are we in, anyway?"

"The South Wing ballroom," Pouvoir reported, and they took a sharp left turn down the hallway that would take them to the wing of the palace constructed nearly five hundred years earlier. It was Remy's favorite section with its wood inlay floors and glistening stained glass windows. "Mademoiselle Hyde will be escorted down. Please do not worry."

"Do you think the people will be disappointed to see me and not Her Majesty?"

"Montamantiens love all members of their royal family."

It was such a silly line, the kind Pouvoir was very good at spewing to get around having to say anything controversial. It was telling that she had taken that approach. If she believed the people wouldn't care how Remy looked, she would have said so directly. She must have been equally nervous.

"What can you tell me about this new prime minister?"

"He's young and inexperienced, but he thinks he knows everything. He shows no respect for your mother, and frankly, I worry that he is not a royalist. That's part of the reason why we called you."

The last prime minister had been Clotilde's age and had gone to school with her. This new one, Jacques Âne, sounded like trouble. "Have you briefed him on Clotilde's illness or my arrival?"

Pouvoir grimaced. "We notified him of her illness yesterday, but we had hoped she would feel well enough to read the proclamation. He doesn't know you are the substitute." She checked her watch. "You have two minutes to get there."

"They can surely wait a minute for me to arrive."

"The proclamation has to be read on the anniversary precisely. We've allotted five minutes for introductions, which means you now have less than two minutes to get there or else you'll have missed the window."

"And this trip here will have been for nothing." Remy gave her a wave and took off in a jog down the corridor. They could hear her tutting after them. Running wasn't seemly for royalty, but Remy hadn't flown overnight to risk being one minute late and watching an upstart young prime minister try to dissolve the monarchy on a technicality.

In the South Wing ballroom, circular tables covered with blue and white tablecloths were populated with Montamant's ministers, the social elite, and the fortunate citizens who had won the lottery to attend the ceremony. A breakfast buffet made of five tables lined one side of the room. As soon as Remy concluded the reading of the proclamation, everyone would be welcome to eat and enjoy conversation.

Although there had not been a proclamation reading in several generations, Remy remembered watching formal state events as a child. The wealthy and historically powerful families of Montamant would clamor for time to speak to Clotilde about business affairs, eager to bend the monarchy's ear on matters affecting their bottom line. The regular citizens who had never been to the palace before and probably never would again would clamor equally for the queen's attention, but to take photos to prove their visit.

After the introduction by the bishop, Remy stepped up to the podium. There was a little murmuring in the room as the crowd realized

Queen Clotilde was not in attendance. At the head table, the prime minister, Jacques Âne, couldn't manage to hide his displeasure.

It was now or never. Remy was going to have to speak. If the crowd had expected a woman who looked more like Sam or Clotilde, there was nothing that could be done now. Remy had to pretend they weren't aware of any judgment.

They made direct eye contact with the prime minister as they said into the microphone, "Hello, everyone, and my apologies for the absence of Queen Clotilde. I have come in Her Majesty's place to officially begin the celebration of eight hundred glorious years of our tremendous nation."

The room applauded generously. Even Monsieur Âne felt compelled to join in.

On the podium was a printed copy of the proclamation. As with so many Montamantien traditions, it was important that Remy not mistake a single word, lest Âne use that as justification for declaring the proclamation had not been fully read according to the law. Better to ensure the proclamation was read word for word, perfectly, in case Âne was the type to look for trouble. Besides, the proclamation was only read once every hundred years. Clotilde would never get an opportunity to do it. No one alive now would ever get a chance to hear it again. This was Remy's first chance to be in the spotlight, and it was a giant one. They wanted to do it right.

The room fell quiet as everyone waited for Remy to begin the recitation. There were a few stray coughs and a few rustles as people shifted in their chairs, but all eyes were on Remy.

The door at the back of the ballroom creaked open, and three hundred people craned their heads to see who had dared to arrive late.

A figure in red stepped into the room and stopped in her tracks. She was wearing a simple but perfectly tailored dress, and her hair was a fluffy halo of blond curls. From their distance at the front of the room, Remy saw the signature red lipstick, a perfect match to the dress, that told them it was Sam. She stood still, unsure where to go and what to do with so many eyes upon her.

"Please, have a seat," Remy called in French, knowing she couldn't understand but wanting to ease the moment for her nonetheless. To have invited her to sit in English would have only called attention to what an outsider she was in a nation where French was the official language. They used the formal "you" because using the informal would let on that the tardy person was their acquaintance. They nodded to one of the stewards, who approached Sam and led her to an empty seat at one of the tables for the lottery winners.

Remy cleared their throat. The time for hesitation was over. If they didn't recite the proclamation now, they might miss the window. They glanced at the paper, then flipped it over. They closed their eyes and trusted their memory.

"On this day and every one hundred years following this day, we come together to declare the sovereignty of Montamant, our beloved home and nation, free from outside influence, true to our most basic principles: to love ourselves, each other, and our country. We declare today and forever that we will be led by the House of Vallorcin, noble and just in their guidance, leading us with honor for our traditions and vision toward the future. Today, we celebrate: vive le Montamant!"

"Vive le Montamant!" the crowd echoed. The room exploded with applause.

As Remy gazed out at the ballroom, at so many people who had come to witness this moment, they couldn't help but smile. No one had stopped them from taking Clotilde's place. No one had jumped up to interrupt because they didn't look like the princess the country imagined them to be. They basked in the applause for a moment. They had done it. The first, important step in protecting the monarchy was accomplished.

Without a translator, Sam relied on the reaction of the crowd to gauge how well Remy had done at reading the proclamation. When they erupted in cheers and applause and some women even dabbed their eyes with their napkins, she knew Remy had done well. She felt ashamed at how wrong her first impressions of Remy had been. Now she was sitting in a royal palace somewhere in the middle of Europe, and she didn't understand how in a few short days her life had taken such an upside down turn.

She did know: it was because of them.

They came down from the dais and began shaking hands with the attendees, starting with a horde of men in identical suits, most of whom looked over fifty. Sam guessed they were the members of Parliament, and with bitterness, she observed there wasn't a single woman among them. Soon the people at her table were joining a line along the edge of the ballroom, next to the carefully molded wood paneling. By the time Sam stood to join in, the line had wrapped around three walls of the room.

Not wanting to break custom but unsure of her place, Sam leaned toward the very short woman in front of her. Her silvery hair was curled into a complicated up-do, her knit dress stretched tight across the slight bulge of her stomach, and her shoes were covered in scuff marks. For someone from a different country, she didn't look that different from the people Sam knew and saw every day in the United States. She definitely wasn't a member of the aristocracy, who were sitting in the front and dressed in nicer clothing. Sam assumed it would be okay to approach her.

"Excuse me, what are we standing in line for?"

The woman turned around, her wrinkled mouth turning down at the sight of Sam. She said something in French and turned back to the front.

Sam hadn't expected that. But of course. These people spoke French as their primary language. It was rude to just start speaking to them in English. She searched her brain.

"*Parlez-vous*...English?"

The woman turned around again. "Of course I speak English. What eez your question, Mademoiselle?"

If the woman spoke English, why hadn't she just answered the question in the first place? Sam repeated it again.

"In line to meet wis zee princess." The woman's English was heavy with her accent, and "friendly" wasn't the adjective Sam would have used to describe her first encounter with a Montamantien. "And then, after that, we *mange* zee breakfast."

"The princess," Sam clarified, though it sounded wrong to her ear, "shakes everyone's hand? Or do we bow?"

"You are not from here." The woman hadn't asked it as a question, just a statement of observation. Did she want Sam to apologize for being foreign?

"I'm just visiting."

"There are people who live here who wait zer entire lives to see zee palace."

Sam cringed. It wasn't exactly a dream come true for her to be a guest at the royal palace, since she hadn't even known it existed until a few days earlier. She could imagine how it might seem to someone who spent their life hoping to get a chance to meet their royal family in person.

"Doesn't the palace ever offer tours?"

"They are *finis* after zee death of King Georges."

"Well," Sam said with as much tact as she could manage, "it is an honor to be here. I am very lucky, and I'm glad you were lucky enough to get the chance, too."

After that, her new "friend" turned forward, the conversation over. The line had barely inched forward, though the members of Parliament were now returning to their tables with plates full of food. That rankled Sam.

When she was in junior high, she had gone to a big family dinner at the home of her friend Katie's grandmother. She, Katie, and the other kids had had a wonderful time playing adventure games in the backyard, and somewhere around dusk, they were told dinner was ready. Sam had been starving at that point, having worked up an appetite running up and down the acreage all afternoon. But Katie's grandmother had told her to wait. She had summoned the teenage boys and shut the back door behind them. It had taken several more minutes for Sam and Katie to be told they could get in line for food.

Later, Sam had asked Katie why. To her embarrassment, Katie had told her mother and grandmother, who had called Sam into the kitchen for an explanation. The adult and teenage men in the family ate first, she explained, to honor the family's past in which they toiled in the fields all day. Next came the children, who were growing and needed nourishment. Finally, the adult women got to eat whatever was left. As a twelve-year-old, Sam counted as an adult woman and had to go last.

The family's commitment to tradition meant it hadn't mattered that the men hadn't lifted a finger all day and had instead drunk beer and watched football. Sam had hated watching Katie's male cousins saunter by with their plates full of dessert while she was still eating her barbecue sandwich. She had been more embarrassed than she could express that Katie had told her mom Sam's question, and she had been angry at the answer she'd received. She had skipped dessert that night, opting to sit by herself under the stars to contemplate why the adult women were considered third-class compared to everyone else in the family.

The opulence of this breakfast at the palace couldn't mask that it was similarly organized around archaic understandings of who was important and who was considered less than. The ministers, she decided, should have sat in the back and waited for their constituents to eat to show that they served the people.

Across the room, the one person who, by Montamantien law and ancient belief, did actually come before everyone else, was working harder than anyone else in the room. Remy accepted bows from each guest and returned some with handshakes. They were smiling and nodding with the kind of attention and charisma that made people feel listened to. Neither Remy nor the guests seemed to mind that the line was so long; all that mattered was the thirty seconds in which they shared a brief conversation. This Remy was hardly the antisocial person Sam had met in Boston. Watching them now, Sam could see they were born for this role.

She couldn't help smiling. She felt something inside, a feeling hard to put a name to. Maybe pride.

"Mademoiselle Ide?" One of the staff members in a sky blue blazer approached her. Like the other staff Sam had encountered, he said Sam's last name without the "h." "If you will please come with me?" He gestured for Sam to step out of the line.

"I haven't had a chance to say hello to Remy yet."

"If you please, Mademoiselle."

"What about breakfast?"

"We will ensure you have plenty to eat." The man gestured with a white glove toward a side door, through which Sam was escorted. They emerged into a wide corridor with ornate red carpets and gold chandeliers. The walls were lined with portraits of previous sovereigns, their names indicated on small brass plates underneath.

"Wasn't I supposed to be in line?" she asked, as they made their way down the corridor. It was hard not to admire the space and the paintings, and the emptiness of the corridor gave Sam the sense she was seeing something the rest of the public could not. But she hadn't been able to see or speak to Remy since their arrival, and she wanted to congratulate them on the awesome job they had done with their speech. "Was the line just for citizens?"

The man didn't answer, but after a moment, he stopped in front of what looked like a wood-paneled wall. A black seam running from floor to ceiling gave away that there was a hidden door, which the man pushed open for Sam to step through. He didn't follow.

She entered a room full of glass cabinets with china on display. It wasn't a very big space, but with six-foot-tall cabinets lining every inch of the walls, there must have been thousands of plates, cups, and gravy boats in dozens of patterns. She wondered how often someone stomped too hard or a vacuum cleaner butted against a cabinet, and something broke. Then she wondered if the china was even replaceable. Probably not.

"There you are!" Madame Pouvoir rushed into the room from the far end, shaking her head as if Sam were a long-lost puppy. "We'll need to hurry before the doctor returns, but we've been waiting for you."

"I'm sorry, what? I thought I was already waiting for Remy, and then the man—"

"Not the princess," Pouvoir cut her off. "Her Majesty."

❖

It took over two hours for Remy to meet everyone who had attended the opening breakfast, and by the end of it, their hand hurt from all the shaking, their feet hurt from standing in one place for so long, and they were starving, having watched everyone else eat from the copious buffets while they continued to greet guests. But it was worth it.

If the members of Parliament and the civilian attendees had expected their princess to look more feminine, they had enough tact to hide their surprise at Remy's appearance. Instead, they had politely referred to Remy as "Your Royal Highness," bowed, said a kind thing or two about Clotilde or asked Remy to take some facet of their life into consideration, and been on their way. Remy wished the staff standing with them had been paying closer attention and had taken notes. They weren't sure they'd be able to remember everything that was said. Mostly people were concerned about rising housing costs and stagnant wages, which were perpetually a problem in a landlocked country with little room for new development. Without expanding its territory into France or Switzerland, Montamant could only build up. Unlike Monaco, which had successfully capitalized on its miniscule size with high-rises, Montamant didn't sit at sea level. There was a limit to how high buildings could be constructed for stability, and with so many of them designated as historical, there weren't a lot of options for tearing down the ones that didn't use space efficiently.

Remy made a mental note to hunt down that urban planner they'd met on holiday in Greece the year before. Maybe that guy, whatever his name was, would have some ideas.

As the crowd began to thin, Remy realized they hadn't seen Sam since her stunning entrance before the reading of the proclamation. The clothes, they presumed, must have been bought or borrowed especially for her, though how Madame Pouvoir knew Sam's measurements was anyone's guess. Who had dressed her, whether she liked what she'd been forced to wear, and where she was now, Remy didn't know. They were annoyed to have coerced Sam into coming if they weren't going to have any control over what happened to her. What if Sam had left in anger when she realized Remy was too busy to talk to her? What if she had fled in horror at seeing three hundred people bow at Remy's feet?

At long last, Remy found Monsieur Lapin, Madame Pouvoir's right-hand man, and made an imperceptible but regal nod that brought Lapin immediately to their side.

"Mademoiselle Hyde was here at the beginning of the ceremony, but I didn't see her in the reception line. Do you know where she went?"

"Her Majesty's suite," Lapin reported, cringing as he produced the words.

Likely, Remy thought, he was waiting for Remy to explode at this news, a reaction that would have been entirely justified. There was no reason for Sam to meet Clotilde if she was a sniveling, dazed mess, and the idea of having the two of them meet while Remy was otherwise occupied was inconsiderate. How could Remy mediate? It would be so intimidating to Sam. It was insensitive. It was…diabolical.

And only one person in the palace had a mind cunning enough and power absolute enough to pull it off.

"Her Majesty must be feeling better."

CHAPTER TWELVE

Sam took three tentative steps into the darkened room, willing her ankles not to wobble in the sky-high heels she was wearing. Her palms were sweating, and she pressed them to the side of her dress to wipe them off. She had no idea what to do or say, yet here she was.

She was meeting the queen of Montamant.

Queen Clotilde was reclining on an ivory sofa underneath a white and gold wool blanket. Her nose was pink, the tip of it swollen, but otherwise she looked every bit the stunning beauty Sam had seen online. Her dark hair hung in loose waves around her shoulders. She wore a modest amount of makeup that made her skin shine without detracting from her natural beauty, and the nude lip gloss accentuated lips that were a little too plump for a woman of her age. Collagen injections, Sam presumed, but unlike the women who did it on reality television, the queen didn't look grotesque. She looked gorgeous.

The realization that she found Queen Clotilde attractive only compounded her nerves. But there was no real risk or harm. It wasn't as if she was going to make a move on her. Certainly not with the age and class difference between them, the queen's illness, Sam's growing feelings toward Remy, and—most importantly—not with knowing how the queen had treated Remy as a child. Queen Clotilde's physical beauty paled in comparison to Sam's growing appreciation for Remy's soul.

An appreciation that the queen was probably about to squash.

When she was within earshot, Sam said, "Your Majesty," and offered a curtsy. Those yoga classes she had taken over the summer paid off when she managed to both bend and rise again without quivering.

Queen Clotilde said nothing. Sam could feel the scrutiny as the queen's eyes raked over her hair, face, chest, and hips. She felt like a piece of meat, the way she had felt at straight bars on Friday nights in college before she and her friends had found the gay- and lesbian-friendly places to go. She willed herself to stand up straight and keep her chin slightly lifted. She didn't want Queen Clotilde to see her timidity.

At long last, the queen gestured to the matching ivory sofa facing her own, but sitting proved to be another challenge. Sam had to lower herself carefully, knees together so as not to let the hem of her dress ride up too far, and once seated on the plush cushions, she wanted to fall backward and relax into them after the long flight and drive. Instead, she kept her feet squarely on the ground and held her spine rigid several inches from the back of the sofa. Good posture was a sign of wealth and class, wasn't it?

Sam readied herself to hear that she was American trash who needed to keep away from Remy. That the queen hated Remy's appearance and didn't want Sam to support their nonbinary identity. If they'd had a chance to prepare for this meeting on the plane, Sam would have asked Remy how to respond to such statements in a way that was respectful but true to her own beliefs. In the absence of Remy's guidance, she decided her best bet was to listen and not say too much.

"I didn't want her to come," Queen Clotilde began.

"Her who?" She thought for a moment Queen Clotilde was referring to her, Sam, in the third person, but then she realized the queen must have meant Remy.

The queen's icy glare made her regret voicing her question before figuring out the answer on her own. "They didn't tell me she was coming until she was already on her way, and no one told me she was bringing you." Her pronunciation of English was more deliberate than Remy's, as if she wanted to make certain to say every syllable correctly. Even so, her accent showed in the musicality of her phrasing. She was obviously fluent, but where Remy might have passed sometimes for a native English speaker, Queen Clotilde would not.

She put a long pause after the sentence. Was it the cold forcing her to take time processing her thoughts, or was she waiting for Sam to speak? When she finally looked at Sam expectantly, Sam decided to respond as mildly as possible.

"Thank you for your hospitality. You have a beautiful country."

"If she had told me, I would have said not to. This is not a good time. The people voted for a new prime minister. He is young and charming. They like him. I do not. I can see through him."

There was another awkward pause, but this time Sam wasn't sure how to respond. She didn't think it was her place to talk smack about the democratically elected leader of another country to a woman whose position was only the result of her paternity.

"This is why she must announce her intention this week and show the people the Vallorcin line is strong."

Intention to what? Cease being Princess Remy? Return to graduate school in Boston? Date Sam?

The last one was a long shot, totally out of the realm of possibility, Sam could tell from the moment they arrived at the palace.

The queen was waiting for a response again.

"I'll do my best to offer Their Royal Highness my support in everything they do." It was a vague sentiment, but Sam couldn't be more specific unless Clotilde was more forthcoming. But how was she supposed to ask a queen to explain herself?

Queen Clotilde nodded, satisfied, and Sam felt tremendous relief she'd passed whatever this little test was. The queen took a moment to blow her nose on a tissue she produced from under the blanket, and a maid in a white apron magically appeared with a wastebasket in hand to collect the used tissue. She vanished back out of sight.

"You're quite beautiful," the queen said. "I want you to understand that it's nothing personal."

Sam felt her nerves return as she gave a fake nod of understanding, when in fact she was more confused than ever. What personal gripe could they have between each other when they had never before met, and Remy obviously hadn't spoken to the queen about Sam's existence in the preceding days? Was everyone in this palace always so cryptic?

Madame Pouvoir opened the door to the dim bedroom and beckoned Sam. The meeting was over.

❖

The rest of the breakfast ceremony passed in a blur. After it was over, Remy was ferreted to Clotilde's bedroom for a meeting with Madame Pouvoir. Pierre was there, and he would have been a welcome ally except that his father, Andre, was also present. That meant they were going to perform social niceties instead of having the productive conversations which were so desperately needed but which both Remy and Clotilde so arduously avoided.

For someone who had been reported to be on her deathbed only a day before, Clotilde didn't look that terrible. She was sitting up in bed in silk pajamas. Her hair had been styled, and she was wearing makeup, Remy noticed, but she would have refused any meeting if she couldn't at least tend to her appearance beforehand.

"Mother," they greeted her.

Clotilde didn't move to kiss Remy's cheeks hello, not because she was worried about getting Remy sick, as Remy was now the key to continuing the octocentennial events. More likely, she didn't simply feel affectionate toward them. She was not the type of mother who would have warm feelings over Remy's homecoming after so many months traveling and then settling in the US. Remy knew she was appreciative they'd come to read the proclamation in her absence, but she would also resent them for taking her place.

When she nodded and gave a quick hello, it was fine with Remy. They didn't feel especially warm toward her either.

"The princess has done a remarkable job reading the proclamation," Madame Pouvoir said. Her voice sounded strangely light. Her lips were curving upward and her eyebrows were lifted. Was she actually happy? "After the ceremony, she greeted every attendee, including Prime Minister Âne. She couldn't have carried herself better."

"It's a shame we weren't there to see Her Royal Highness ourselves," Andre said.

Remy didn't understand why the Lefauxes had been absent. They were Montamantien nobility, and they commonly attended royal functions. Remy's friendship with Pierre and Clotilde's with Andre were hardly secret.

"Aren't you even going to say hello?" Pierre chided them. He was wearing a thin black sweater that accentuated his late summer tan. His nose still had its extended regal tip, his cheeks were hollowed in a way that chiseled the contours of his face, and there was a little stubble on his chin. Remy knew many people found him devastatingly handsome, but their affections, while deep, were nothing more beyond familial and friendly.

"Aren't you going to bow to me?" they teased back.

On cue, the Lefauxes gave crisp tucks at the waist. They knew royal protocol, and they knew to respect it, even if Remy had been joking.

"Come here," Remy said, throwing their arms wide. Pierre came forward, and they kissed each other's cheeks four times. "I missed you all summer."

"Me too."

"I'm glad to see you're still so close," Clotilde said, commanding the room's attention once more. Her voice sounded nasal, and she kept opening and closing her jaw as if to pop her ears. "That's what we wanted to talk to you about."

"It's no secret that the princess has been away since certain facts came to light." Madame Pouvoir was obviously reciting a script Clotilde had given her. Her face was pinched tight again, and Remy thought—hoped—she didn't want to be saying whatever awful thing she was about to say. "We've asked Monsieur Lefaux for his discretion on this matter, but we felt it was important that we convene to discuss the princess's reemergence into the public spotlight. Now that she—" Pouvoir seemed to remember that Remy was in the room with them. "You," she corrected herself, "have returned to Montamant and taken up royal duties, it's critical that we ensure seamless operation."

"What? I'm going back to Boston at the end of the week, right after the royal ball. Sam and I have class on Monday."

"Of course you are." Clotilde sounded relieved. "But we must make sure the time you spend here is effective. I'll still be here when you're gone."

"Yes, and…?"

Pouvoir looked down at her shoes in uncharacteristic fear of dealing with whatever issue they were dancing around. Clotilde was staring, as if Remy was supposed to be able to figure out what she had in mind on their own. Opposite her sofa, Andre put a hand on Pierre's shoulder and nodded encouragingly.

"Mother, what is going on?" Remy demanded.

"We've decided you're going to marry Pierre."

"What?" Remy nearly snorted in disbelief. "Why would I marry him?"

"Thanks," Pierre snapped.

"To be frank, Your Royal Highness," Andre said, "the monarchy is in need of stability. Her Majesty agrees that a marriage between you and Pierre will have the effect of ensuring continued support for the crown."

"The Lefaux family is well respected," Pouvoir added, "and can trace its history nearly as far as the Vallorcin line. At a time when traditions are being abandoned, we feel young Monsieur Lefaux will make an excellent match for you."

"Do you have cancer?" Remy asked their mother point-blank.

"No!" she balked. "This isn't about that. It's about you."

"Me?"

"Yes, you. Look at you. You need help."

"And a wedding is going to accomplish that?"

"A marriage between the Vallorcins and the Lefauxes, two of the oldest and most esteemed families in Montamant, is to be expected. It speaks to our tradition."

"An arranged marriage? That's the tradition we want to preserve?" Remy looked from Clotilde to Andre to Pouvoir. "Or is this about the tradition of men being men and women being women, and men and women marrying each other? Is that what this is about? You hate that I'm queer?"

"Control yourself," Clotilde said. Saying the word "queer" in her presence was tantamount to the sound of clipping one's toenails: something unbefitting a queen's ears. "We are ensuring the monarchy's long-lasting stability."

Andre, who was less artful than Clotilde and Pouvoir, put it more directly. "Weddings are very popular with young people. Consider how successful the British monarchy is now that the two princes have married."

And consider how one of them had shucked his title and run for dear life, Remy wanted to add. Not unlike their own choice to find sanctuary in the US for graduate school. The difference was that they always knew they'd be coming back one day. Just not today, and certainly not to marry someone because Clotilde told them they had to.

"You will marry Pierre, and the throne will remain in our family. And you will announce your engagement on Friday at the royal ball."

Remy's face felt hot. They took their glasses off and pressed two fingers to the bridge of their nose, pretending to think while covertly brushing their tears away. They wanted to scream. They wanted to start flipping over furniture and ripping the stupid paintings of their ancestors off the wall and hurling them at their treacherous mother.

Where was Sam? Why were they keeping them apart?

Clotilde blew her nose and tossed the tissue on the floor. Her callous disregard for hygiene was emblematic of her narcissism and its power to hurt those around her. Remy had never felt as much contempt for her as they did at that moment.

When had she crafted this plan? Had this been the real reason Pouvoir had summoned Remy home? Maybe Clotilde's illness had been exaggerated to inspire Remy's sense of duty, and the reading of the proclamation had set the stage for the real trap, which was that they wanted Remy in Montamant to announce this engagement.

"Pierre," they said, "did you know?"

"I didn't." He looked as stunned as Remy felt. He turned to his father. "How could you set this up without even talking to me about it?"

"It's time you settled down," he replied. "You couldn't do much better than king consort."

"I'm not dead yet," Clotilde reminded him.

"Prince consort, then," Andre said.

In Montamant, unlike many other monarchies, the spouse of a reigning monarch always assumed the title king or queen. Remy's father had been named King Georges shortly after Clotilde had inherited the throne. Georges had told Remy he saw it as his duty to ensure his status didn't overshadow Clotilde's, especially since there were so few female monarchs. For Remy, who was struggling to be recognized as someone outside male and female, the situation would be even more difficult. With a marriage to Pierre, Remy would be neatly categorized. Queen Remy and King Pierre. How convenient for Clotilde to finally solve her biggest problem, the one that had been plaguing her for the last twenty-five years.

Pierre was equally angry. "Papa, do you even care whether I want to do this?"

"Mother," Remy protested, "this isn't what I want at all! You can't make us do this!"

Their eyes locked in a battle of wills. Remy wanted to hear her explanation, but Clotilde knew real power lay in making people wait for her to speak. She never rushed into a conversation. She waited. And when she spoke, she usually had the sharpest, most definitive answer.

"My little cabbage." Usually a term of affection, it came out dripping with derision when she said it. "I'm not making you do this. It's already done."

CHAPTER THIRTEEN

There was no point in pleading with the queen any further, but Remy could tell Pierre wasn't going to stop harassing Andre. Remy wasn't certain Pierre had as much effect on his father as Clotilde seemed to have. In the interim, the queen's work was done, and she excused them all from her company and retreated to her bed.

As Pouvoir and Remy found their way out of the suite, Remy tried to reason with her. Sam had been right that she was terrifying, but she was also the only person with enough clout to help.

"Don't you see this is wrong? Forcing someone to marry someone they don't love for the sake of appearances? Hasn't the monarchy moved past that? Clotilde got to choose her husband."

From the stories they'd heard in childhood and from the affection they remembered seeing at a young age, Clotilde and Georges had been in love. Although their father was titled, a count like Pierre's father, no one had forced Clotilde to pick him for her husband, and she hadn't chosen him merely for his rank. The way Remy had heard it, Georges had wooed Clotilde with his wit and his talents on the ski slope. Theirs had been a love match, the kind Remy thought Montamant, as its name testified, believed in.

Remy understood the importance of marrying someone of a certain status. It was unpleasant to think about, and it was unfair, but there was logic to it. If they truly believed nobility and royalty were special, a cut above everyone else, then they oughtn't marry commoners and grant them titles by extension. Remy didn't subscribe to the belief of divine right, but they understood the illogic of inheriting a title based on their birth on the one hand and then advocating the crowning of someone of modest birth on the other. To do so would eradicate the entire principle that some were gifted by God to rule.

And if someone of modest birth was fit to sit by their side, what precluded that person from being able to sit on the throne directly? At what point were the principles of the monarchy abandoned altogether? And if they were, what would that mean for Remy and Clotilde? Where would they live? Would they have to find jobs? And what would it mean for the future of Montamant? The nation had been founded when Remy's ancestor Robert declared independence from the Count of Savoy eight hundred years earlier, and its continuation was the result of one Vallorcin after another maintaining leadership in an unbroken line. Would Montamantiens be able to cast that history aside for an unknown, unproven leader in a new form of government?

But being told to marry Pierre because he was a politically convenient choice wasn't much better. Remy wondered if Clotilde had bothered telling Andre their family's biggest secret: that Remy could not have children, when producing an heir was the primary duty of anyone in line for the throne. If a sham marriage was intended to force Remy into a life of sexual and gender normativity, it wasn't going to accomplish the ultimate product of that normativity, and the Vallorcin line was still going to be in danger. Forcing Remy to marry Pierre wasn't the solution to the monarchy's problems their parents made it out to be.

"Your Highness," Pouvoir sighed. "We have a lot of other business to attend to."

"What could possibly be more important than this?"

"Remy." Her voice was gentle. "You had to know this day was coming. You had the chance to find a suitable spouse on your own. You frittered the time away sailing and skiing and moving to the United States."

"I'm only twenty-five."

"You're also home during the octocentennial and a period of transition with an antagonistic prime minister. Your unexpected appearance has raised questions about you and your suitability as Queen Clotilde's successor. Marriage indicates your maturity and provides reassurance that there will be further generations of Vallorcins to follow in the footsteps of you and the queen. You know this."

"And you know, as does Clotilde, that the problem of further generations isn't solved with a marriage between Pierre and me."

Pouvoir arched an eyebrow. "With a spouse who is close to the family, someone trustworthy, certain arrangements can be made."

As usual, she preferred hints to declarative sentences. Remy guessed she meant that if they needed to fake a pregnancy, they could trust Pierre to go along with it.

"Your father would have been proud of you today, and announcing your engagement to the younger Monsieur Lefaux would have pleased him."

It wasn't fair to remind Remy of what Georges might have wanted. He had been a magnificent king, well-loved by the people for his generosity and warmth. How he and Clotilde had ended up together was beyond Remy. They couldn't imagine the father they remembered ever loving someone as cold, calculating, and vile as Clotilde.

"I hate my mother."

"I know you do."

It wasn't Clotilde Remy hated the most. Because at the end of the day, they could book a flight back to Boston, order a car, grab Sam, and get the hell out of there. No one was going to physically drag Remy down the aisle to Pierre. No, Remy recognized they really hated themselves. Because they would probably go through with this ridiculous engagement scheme out of duty and love for Montamant.

Madame Pouvoir surprised Remy by folding them into a motherly embrace, and though the fabric of her black blazer was starched and scratchy, they buried their forehead into it as the tears began to fall.

"This isn't how I imagined it to be."

They had always known that one day they would return to sit on the throne. But they had never really figured out how that would reconcile with being neither a man nor a woman. They had just imagined being Remy, and they'd avoided ever having to sort out the rest.

Now Clotilde had solved the problem for them. The citizens of Montamant would be reassured of their heir's gender, and marriage to Pierre would assure them that Remy was sincere in their loyalty and respect for tradition. Clotilde had probably already devised a plan for how Remy and Pierre could feign conceiving children together.

That was down the road, a few years into the future. First would be a wedding. Then, once the appeal of that spectacle had worn off and there was another hostile situation with Parliament, she would probably force them to announce they were expecting a baby. Remy could see a whole future ahead, one in which they lost every ounce of personal freedom to Clotilde's master plan.

In the present, Remy and Pierre would announce their engagement and carry on with the week's events. Sam would be sent home, maybe sooner than the royal ball Remy had promised her she'd get to attend. She'd be brokenhearted, and she would probably never speak to Remy again. With time, her wounds would heal, and it would be a fun story she got to tell her friends. The time she nearly dated a princess who wasn't a woman. One day she'd wake up and realize Remy no longer mattered to her at all.

They felt sick to their stomach imagining it.

Pouvoir produced a small package of tissues from her pocket. They took one and wiped their nose. She immediately extended her hand to take it, without thinking, but Remy had already shoved the used tissue into their pocket.

"Sam," they said. "What's going to happen to her?"

"She is a guest of the royal family and will be treated as such."

"She needs some books before school on Monday. Can we make sure she gets them?"

"Of course, Your Highness."

"Do you think she could still stay until the royal ball?"

"She's *your* guest," Pouvoir pointed out. "Her Majesty would not approve of her as your escort for the ball, particularly given your expected engagement announcement, but...If Your Highness ordered me to add a name to the guest list, I would be obliged to do so. Of course, Her Majesty has already approved the final list. At such a late date, if there were any changes, Her Majesty might not have time to review them."

Remy smiled at her for dancing around what she couldn't say. If Remy added Sam to the list of invitees now, Clotilde wouldn't know. But there was a hitch.

"Pouvoir, she's going to need a dress."

❖

It felt good to sleep after the whirlwind trip overseas and her first royal event, and the soft cotton sheets of the bed welcomed Sam after she pulled the heavy drapes shut. Her mind was still replaying the hasty conversation she'd had with Queen Clotilde, but her body had had enough for the day.

She awoke several hours later in darkness and felt around the nightstand for her phone. It was dead. She hadn't charged it during the flight or since arriving, and because there was no clock in the room, she didn't know what time it was. She could try to plug her phone in, but the maid hadn't yet brought the electrical adapter she said Sam would need to use the outlets. Had she slept until evening? Was it the middle of the night? It didn't feel as if she'd slept that long, but she was feeling a little jet-lagged. Her internal clock was probably out of sync.

Although she was worried she was breaking some unknown rule about being lazy in the queen's presence or missing some important function, Sam padded to the adjacent bathroom. It was stocked with quality toiletries, and she took a few enjoyable moments to brush her teeth and wash her face with a rosemary mint scrub. She filled a glass of water, carried it back to the nightstand, and climbed back into the bed.

There wasn't a television in the room, and with her phone dead, she wasn't sure how to entertain herself. She nestled back into the pillows and was dozing again when she heard a faint knock on the door.

"Sam?"

Everyone at the palace had thus far referred to her as "Mademoiselle Ide," so even though their voice was obscured, Sam knew immediately it was Remy. She rushed to the door.

They were still wearing the outfit they'd worn to breakfast, but the shirt sleeves were rolled up to the elbow. This was much more in line with Remy's personality, and the overall effect was a devil-may-care attitude that had both repelled and attracted Sam from their first encounter. She realized how happy she was to see them.

Remy surprised her by pulling her into a hug. Not a courtesy hello hug, but a sincere embrace that lasted a minute and deepened after the first breath.

"I missed you today," they said. "What have you been doing?"

Sam became aware she was in the pink pajamas Remy had given her on the plane. "They took me to meet your mother, and then they brought me back here, and…I guess I fell asleep. Is that okay?"

"It's perfectly okay," Remy said with a smile. "You're adjusting to the different time zone. I saw you at the breakfast ceremony. I'm sorry we didn't get to talk."

Sam smiled at them. "You were awesome, Rem. You did so well. Everyone loved you."

Remy looked sheepish. "Yeah? What did you think of our country?"

"Truthfully?" She waited for Remy's nod. "I thought it was gross there are no women in Parliament, and I don't understand why people who wait their whole lives to visit the palace are crammed in the back and have to eat soggy food that's been picked over. It wasn't the best start to a visit."

Remy bit their lip and was quiet for a moment. "I never thought of the seating arrangement that way, but that's something to think about. Changing it would anger the ministers, but truthfully, Parliament has been a problem since I was a child. I once wrote an essay about why we needed more women in Parliament for my after-school tutoring."

"You did?" Sam tried to picture Remy as a precocious little child, stirring up trouble because they were too enlightened for all the nonsense couched in tradition that surrounded them. "What happened?"

"Clotilde liked it, but my tutor failed me because the essay topic was supposed to be the importance of good communication between the sovereign and the prime minister." Remy sighed. "I was surprised today by some of the concerns the people expressed when I was talking to them. On the subject of the palace, in theory, that is easy to fix. We could open the doors more frequently to guests, but Clotilde would never agree to it. She thinks the mystery is what keeps us in power. The more troubling issue is the economic pressure on the citizens. I'm not sure what to do about that. Inviting someone who can't afford their rent to visit a palace…that might be hurtful."

Sam loved hearing Remy talk like this. They were sincere in their desire to listen to the people, and although they didn't yet have solutions, they were certainly thinking through options in a way befitting a public servant.

"How did your meeting with Clotilde go?" Remy asked. "I'm sorry I wasn't there. They didn't tell me they were taking you to her until it was too late. Was she awful?"

"She told me she was sorry and that it was nothing personal." Sam shrugged. "Whatever that means."

Remy made themselves comfortable on the edge of the bed. Sam took the liberty of sitting beside them.

"They took me to her room, too, and there were several other people there. Including Pierre."

"It's good you got to see your friend."

Remy turned to look, but what they were hoping to see, Sam wasn't sure. "My mother told me I have to announce I'm going to marry Pierre at the royal ball."

Sam leapt off the bed. "What?!"

Remy nodded.

"Are you fucking kidding me?"

"I don't know what to do. The train is moving down the track, and I don't know how to stop it."

"They can't force you to marry someone against your will!" Sam was appalled. "So, wait a second, the queen thinks the people will accept you as...what, a straight couple?" Remy nodded. "I don't get it. Why does Queen Clotilde think you need to get married now? Why not after graduate school?"

"I don't know," Remy said, "but I think she's worried about this new prime minister. She says it's to secure the stability of the crown and the line of succession."

Sam had thus far avoided any prodding questions, but if they were talking about securing the line of succession, there were a few details that needed to be clarified.

"Remy, I don't know how to ask this except just to ask. Are you capable of having children?"

Their downcast eyes were answer enough.

"Then how are you and Pierre expected to produce an heir?"

Remy cleared their throat. "I wouldn't be the first monarch unable to produce an heir, Sam. There are ways."

Sam had never thought about it before, but now that Remy mentioned it, there were probably lots of secret things that happened behind the scenes in a royal palace. When a queen couldn't carry a baby, there was probably someone else who could, and the queen raised the baby as her own. And when a king couldn't father a child, someone else was probably brought in. A brother, preferably, so the baby would have a family resemblance to avoid raising suspicion. Both of those had probably happened in history.

There was some benefit in being transparent with the public, Sam thought. It provided an opportunity to talk about how archaic the inheritance laws were in light of how real people organized their families in the twenty-first century. They could create laws allowing adoptive children to inherit the throne. Or, better yet, they could do away with the whole ritual of familial succession in the first place.

It occurred to her that they were talking about Remy's future with Pierre. Sam still hadn't met the man, but she couldn't help disliking him out of jealousy.

She folded her arms across her chest. "When is all this happening?"

"Clotilde wants to announce the engagement on Friday. We haven't talked about when the wedding will take place."

"I don't want you to get engaged to someone else," Sam admitted. "The thought of it makes me feel jealous and angry."

"It makes me feel so sad for you," Remy said. "I didn't invite you here to abandon you like this."

"Can I kiss you?"

Remy nodded. Sam leaned over and kissed them, and after a second, they kissed back. It was soft and sweet, and it reassured Sam that she was the one Remy wanted to be with. Not Pierre.

After a moment, like on the plane, their kissing grew in intensity. Remy wanted her. And the blood rushing through her veins wanted them badly.

"Do you want to marry him?" Sam asked between kisses.

"No."

"Why not?"

Remy's lips quirked in a telling smile. One of their hands cupped Sam's jawline as they dove in for another kiss.

"Why not?" she asked again.

"Because of you."

The words felt so good to hear.

Remy ran a hand through their hair. "This isn't how I thought this would go at all. I feel so…betrayed and trapped. If I don't do it, what happens to the Vallorcin line and to Montamant? If I do it, what happens…"

What happens to us? It was too soon to make any decisions about the future based on the fact that they were attracted to each other, but it was far too late in the course of events to pretend she didn't want to be the one standing by Remy's side instead of Pierre.

"Monarchies suck." Sam didn't care if she was pouting. "No one is going to dictate to me who I have to marry to preserve society. Or whether I even get married at all. And you know why?"

"Because you're born of common blood and middle-class, so it doesn't matter?"

Sam gaped. She hadn't expected the ugly rich persona to come charging back in, especially after such tenderness, but there it was. A staunch reminder that Remy was not someone well read on feminist and Marxist theory and was, in reality, totally wrong for Sam. Whatever her attraction to them was, moments like this were a reminder that she needed to stick to feminists. Socialists. Radicals. Not pompous relics from another time and place.

"What the hell, Remy?"

"Have I offended you?"

They sounded sincere in their question, but she couldn't believe they were that oblivious.

"Yes, you have. You don't just call me common like that and say my life doesn't matter. Not after you kissed me. Not unless you have some fetish for commoners or something. Is that what this is? Like, it's not me at all, it could be anyone who's not royalty and not rich? It's just the thrill of slumming it with some American?"

"I do not have an attraction to commoners," Remy insisted.

"Well, where I live, in the real world, we don't say rude things about people, and we don't tell people who they have to marry."

"You're naive if you think these problems are unique to monarchies. The one percent, as you call them, they all worry about who their children marry, where they were educated, how much money their families have. It is an illusion to believe those things have changed because so many societies have become democracies. If anything, late capitalism resembles the pre-industrial and pre-democratic era more fully in that regard. As for the middle class, they have less at stake in terms of land and assets. Since marriage has historically been a means for acquiring and protecting property and wealth, who the middle class marries matters less. It always has."

For someone who got confused by the word "spork," Remy was able to express themselves really well on certain topics. Sam couldn't help being impressed by the depth of their understanding of capitalism, even if she hated everything they were saying. And she certainly wasn't going to admit they might be right.

"Look, do you want my common-blood, significantly-less-important-life help or not?"

"I didn't say your life doesn't matter. Of course your life matters. Of course you matter. I meant that it doesn't matter who you marry because economically—"

"The bottom line is you've been indoctrinated into this system where everyone has told you that you're special and better than everyone else, and there's really no escaping that. So maybe you should just marry Pierre, and the two of you can live happily ever after with your lives that matter very much."

She strode to the door and put a hand on the wide knob. "Would you please leave my room now?"

"Are you serious?"

"Yes."

"What are you going to do without me? You don't know where anything is. You don't even know what day it is. Are you going to stay in this room until it's time to go back to Boston?"

It sounded stupid when they put it that way.

"Maybe."

"To be clear, you are removing the heir apparent from a room in the royal palace?"

"Yes," Sam blustered, "since I don't believe in the whole royalty thing, I'd hardly care about something so trivial as offending the heir apparent by throwing them out of a room that belongs to them."

They stared at each other in a battle of wills. Sam's arms were folded angrily, and Remy's hands were on their hips. To an outsider, it probably looked childish. To Sam, it was principle. She wasn't going to back down until Remy recognized they were wrong.

Remy cursed in French. "You win."

"Win what?" They needed to be clear on the terms, after all.

"Your life matters, and I was wrong for how I expressed myself, even though I was speaking about post-industrial economics correctly."

Sam couldn't resist cracking a smile. "That was a roundabout way of saying you still think you're right, and you know it."

Remy gave a cute shrug. "What can you do with me?"

There were lots of things Sam would have liked to do with them, but this was neither the time nor the place.

"Since you're so angry at me," Remy said, "I guess you're not really interested in seeing the archives before dinner."

The royal archives. A treasure trove of historical findings. She could feel her eyes widen at the prospect of seeing them.

Remy smirked. "You're so easy. Put on your clothes, and I'll show you."

"Okay, but for the record, you're still full of yourself." Sam turned to go to the giant wardrobe that lined one of the walls of the bedroom, but Remy caught her hand and pulled her in.

"It's why you were attracted to me in the first place."

CHAPTER FOURTEEN

"Marie-Claire, has the seamstress finished the alterations to Her Majesty's gown for the royal ball?" Pouvoir was standing in the kitchen with the staff as each reported on their progress with various tasks pertaining to the octocentennial.

"Yes, Madame."

"Has Her Majesty had the final dress fittings?"

"Yes, she looks very elegant. We hope she will feel well enough to wear it. We have put hidden pockets in the gown in case Her Majesty needs to hide tissues for her cold."

"Excellent work. Since you have finished that, I would like to put you in charge of another task. Mademoiselle Hyde will be attending the ball, and she needs a suitable gown. Do you think you could find something for her to wear by Friday night?"

Marie-Claire frowned. "That is very little time, Madame, and we will need Mademoiselle to be available for alterations."

"What does she have to do until then?"

Pouvoir resented it when the staff tried to claim they didn't have enough time for a task, especially when they were being excused from all other duties to focus on it. Truthfully, she also resented that her staff had to be responsible for ensuring Samantha Hyde had appropriate attire. It should not have been their responsibility, since Mademoiselle was not part of the royal family. But it was a favor to Princess Remy, in exchange for her favor of coming home on such short notice, and Pouvoir saw the value of getting on the princess's good side after the devastating news of her arranged marriage.

"Marie-Laure will dress Her Majesty for all daytime events for the rest of the week," she continued, double-checking against her notes, "assuming Her Majesty is able to leave her bedroom. We are very lucky that this seems increasingly likely. Marie-Claire, that means you have nothing but time to ensure Mademoiselle Hyde looks her absolute best for the ball."

Pouvoir was finished with the discussion, but Marie-Claire interjected with further questions before they could move to other business items. "What should I put her in? Are there any guidelines?"

Pouvoir resisted the urge to roll her eyes. She was the assistant to Her Majesty Queen Clotilde, chief protocol officer for the Royal Palace of Montamant. She was not a fashion designer.

"Whatever you put her in for breakfast, please continue in the same style."

"It was Valentino, Madame, but we were lucky it fit. I found it in the back of the queen's closet."

"Let's not tell Her Majesty that," Pouvoir suggested. "I trust that you will create something suitable, and of course you will coordinate colors and styles with Her Majesty's gown. There can be no competition between them, no chance that anyone will say Mademoiselle Hyde looks more beautiful, but of course we want Mademoiselle Hyde to look as though she belongs. Not enough to appear as one of the family, but we don't want her to stand out as a foreigner either. Can you create a dress that accomplishes all of that?" Pouvoir didn't wait for the response. "Good. Now, Marie-Jeanne, I'm afraid your task is more challenging."

"The princess?" she guessed.

"That's correct. You will work with Princess Remy and Queen Clotilde to determine the appropriate attire for the royal ball, which will be Her Royal Highness's first as an adult. Her attire must not match Mademoiselle Hyde's, and it must coordinate with what Monsieur Lefaux wears."

Pouvoir didn't explain that this was because the princess needed to look her best for the announcement of her engagement. The staff did not need to know that information yet, lest one of them leak it to the press before it was official. Given the unique nature of Princess Remy's return and the news of the arranged marriage, clothing for the royal ball was a much more important affair than it usually would be. Her Royal Highness would need an outfit that said she had fully matured but was also a young breath of fresh air to the nation. She needed to appear feminine to quell rumors but strong to instill trust in her leadership. Her clothes needed to coordinate with Her Majesty's to show their familial connection and thus the line of uninterrupted leadership of the nation, but they also needed to coordinate with Monsieur Lefaux's to show them ready to enter a new partnership. She was expected to wear a gown, but she was likely to refuse to do so. However the princess ended up dressed, the significance of the evening meant the outfit would end up in public photographs and archives for posterity.

Pouvoir tried to communicate the gravity and the complexity of the matter to Marie-Jeanne. "You understand the importance of what I have asked you?"

"I do, Madame." Marie-Jeanne bowed her head. "I will undertake this task to the best of my abilities."

❖

When Remy kissed her, Sam kissed back. She hated how easy it was for them to ruffle her feathers, but she hated herself for how easily those feelings dissipated when they were together. How fast she forgot she was mad at them and gave in to how much she wanted them.

No one else was in her room, and there was an hour before they were due anywhere. The giant bed behind them looked empty and full of promise. Now would be the right moment. But she didn't want to start something, become emotionally attached, and watch Remy announce their engagement to someone else.

For now, she would take these stolen moments as they came. She pressed her lips softly to Remy's one last time.

"You're still full of yourself." She wiped the traces of her lipstick from Remy's bottom lip with her thumb. "Just so we're clear."

"Just so we're clear, you're a very rude guest." Remy said it with an affectionate smile. "I want to stay here and do this with you all day, but I promised to show you the archives. Come on."

Sam went into the bathroom, where she ran a brush through her hair. She put on the jeans she'd brought and the T-shirt that had been in the gift box. Then she followed Remy down the grand staircase, along a wide corridor, and around a corner that led into the medieval section of the palace. The dark wood floors changed to slick worn stone, and the temperature felt much colder. They passed a few members of the cleaning staff, each of whom stopped their work to bow as Remy walked by. Finally, they descended a tiny spiral staircase that was too small for Sam to stand upright.

They emerged underground in a narrow stone corridor that had never been wired for electricity. A few candles in sconces on the walls provided sparse, flickering illumination, giving Sam the sensation of being in a haunted house, and she was grateful Remy held her hand until they reached a heavy wood door, which they unlocked with a skeleton key.

The door had obviously not been opened for a while. It creaked and stuck until, together, they managed to push it enough to squeeze through the opening. The room inside had cheap fluorescent lights dangling from hooks in the ceiling, and Remy turned them on before checking Sam's reaction.

"I'm a little underwhelmed," she admitted. "It's all just...sitting here. I thought there would be glass cases and plastic sheets around everything."

Remy explained that the Montamantien royal archives existed in two forms. The official archives were housed at the national library, underground in a climate-controlled room with proper air circulation. All the pieces had been digitally scanned and catalogued. Visitors could make appointments to see items, but almost nothing older than a century could be handled. That sounded more in line with what Sam had expected.

This room was the unofficial Vallorcin family archive, the existence of which was unknown to the public. Some of the items stored here were duplicates of what had been given to the library, so the less desirable preservation qualities of the room didn't matter quite as much. Other items were things someone at some point in history had determined inappropriate for public access: an inventory of Queen Flore's underwear dated to the 1650s, love letters written by Prince Alain in Paris to his four mistresses in the midst of the French Revolution, and medical documents pertaining to Remy's birth.

In addition to the papers that were stored in large cartons labeled by sovereign, the room housed copies of leather-bound, gilt-edged books dating back hundreds of years. Some were first edition publications, probably worth a fortune and better off in a library or sold to a collector who would appreciate them.

"My grandfather wouldn't let anyone sell them or donate them to the library," Remy explained. "He said you can judge a man by his taste in literature."

"How did he think you can judge a woman?"

Remy laughed. "Good point."

"Did you know him well?" Sam skimmed the spines of the books, but the titles were in French, and she didn't understand what she was reading.

"He died when I was very little. It is probably one of the few conversations I can remember having with him."

Sam reached for a book. "May I?"

"Of course."

"I don't need gloves or something?"

Remy pulled a clean handkerchief from their pocket and tossed it to her. She used it to remove a thick volume and carry it to the wooden table in the middle of the room. She tucked a finger inside the handkerchief before prying open the cover, so the oils on her hand wouldn't damage the fragile pages.

"It says 'dic-shun-air mont-a-man-tee-un.'"

She knew she was butchering the pronunciation, but Remy nodded and adjusted the frames of their glasses. "It's probably a translation dictionary, Montamantien to French."

Sam hadn't realized Montamantiens spoke a different language than French. Or was it a dialect? She flipped forward to a random page to see if any of the words looked familiar from her high school studies and noted with some relief that English words filled the page. "I think it's Montamantien-English," she reported. "Okay, see, here it says '*ami*,' and the English translation is 'friend.'"

"That's correct."

"'A-m-i' is the spelling, and the word uses a masculine article." She looked up from the page. "I feel like your life would be much easier if your language didn't parse every word into masculine or feminine."

"No kidding," Remy said.

She looked back at the book. The next entry was for "*amiot*," which in English was described as "friend of ambiguous origin." She wondered what that meant. A friend from a faraway land whose home was unknown? A friend who didn't know who their mother or father was? Either option seemed really specific for a single word.

"Is this a word unique to Montamantien?" she asked Remy.

"Let me see." Remy leaned over her shoulder, peering at the book's tiny print and faint ink. "In truth, I am not sure how Montamantien varies from French. I didn't learn much about that in my language and literature lessons. There are some regionalisms, things Montamantiens say differently from the people in the neighboring French and Swiss villages. Our accent is slightly different, too."

That could be the case historically with all mountain settlements, Sam thought, where heavy snowfall had once meant being cut off from the rest of the world for months of the year. Their language and culture were bound to have grown somewhat separate from their neighbors'.

She scanned the rest of the page. It was mostly full of verbs and adjectives that didn't have genders. The adjectives were changed to match the gender of the noun they modified. And all the nouns had a given gender. She looked back at "*amiot*."

"What's so special about that word? Amy-ott? Have you heard it before?"

"Ah-mee-oh," Remy corrected her. "I've never heard it, but that's how you'd pronounce it today." They shrugged the dictionary off. "So do you like it down here?"

"I love it. Can I have more time to dive into everything?"

"Unfortunately, you've been invited to dinner, and as much as I would rather we escaped and found a pizza somewhere, I don't think it would be good if we were missing."

"I guess you do still owe me that fancy dinner."

"Trust me, you will have more fancy dinners than you can tolerate before we leave. You will be begging for a lobster roll. But, in answer to your question, yes, you can spend all the time here that you want." They placed the skeleton key in her hand. "I've instructed the staff that you are allowed to come and go as you please."

Her fingers folded around the key. "Really?"

"Consider this your first research trip."

"This is so cool! Thank you, Remy!" She threw her arms around them. "I'm going to be at that dinner, and I want you to know that I'm on your side. No matter what. We'll figure something out. You're not going to marry anyone you don't want to."

Sam didn't fully understand the sense of duty and commitment that came with growing up royal, but she understood loyalty. She wanted Remy to know she was on their team. Together, they would try to find a way out.

CHAPTER FIFTEEN

The maids gave Sam another beautiful dress to wear to dinner, this one emerald green with a deep v-neckline that showed more cleavage than Sam thought would be respectable. Maybe the Vallorcins liked to tart it up for dinner. The dress had long sleeves and a hem that hit well below her knees, but that didn't make up for the amount of skin showing at her bust or the giant slits across the skirt panels. It was the kind of dress that could pass as decent until someone really started looking at how revealing it was. There were no tags on it, no stains or wrinkles or snags in the delicate fabric. Surely they wouldn't have bought a new dress for Sam to wear to a weeknight dinner? When would they have even had time?

She shivered at the thought that they were raiding the queen's closet to dress her.

One of the maids, Marie-Francine, helped her put loose curls in her hair and loaned her a necklace that, she assured Sam, was not from the royal jewel collection. It was still elegant in its design of a single small diamond resting in a gold heart, and it looked more expensive than any piece of jewelry Sam had ever worn. In halting English, Marie-Francine offered to help with Sam's makeup, but Sam was confident in her skills on that front. Marie-Francine was kind enough to take a photo, so once Sam was back in the US and had cell service, she could send her parents a picture of herself dressed for her first ever dinner at a royal palace.

At 6:30 p.m., Madame Pouvoir arrived with notes to make sure Sam felt adequately prepared. As much as it was probably to protect the Vallorcins from the shame of an uncouth guest, Sam appreciated that Madame Pouvoir also seemed to recognize it would help ease her nerves to have more information. She talked Sam through the guest list and seating chart, as well as the more idiosyncratic customs. Sam nodded as she was told it was a grave offense to slurp soup, but it was entirely expected that she would use a piece of bread to mop up any sauce left on her plate after the main course.

"What do I do with the bread afterward?"

"You eat it."

It was a dumb question in retrospect, but she didn't want to take anything for granted. She was supposed to be on her best behavior, but she didn't know how royal dinners worked. She barely knew anything about dinners that didn't come with free drink refills.

Madame Pouvoir tucked the sheet of paper with the seating chart back into the black leather binder she always carried. "Mademoiselle Hyde, I cannot stress to you the importance of good behavior—good breeding, but then in the absence of it, good behavior."

Good breeding? Were they human beings or show dogs?

"But I also can tell you candidly, from years of experience, that the more you worry, the more nervous you are, the more mistakes you will make and the more uncomfortable you will feel."

Sam tipped her head. "So you're saying I shouldn't freak out?"

Pouvoir couched it in more diplomatic terms. "You should not prevent your anxiety from allowing you to recognize that most of what I've told you is basic manners, and what isn't covered by basic manners can be learned simply by observation."

Instead of being scared of Madame Pouvoir's vague statements, Sam realized she could read between the lines and maybe have a little fun with her. "Basically, I should chill out and just watch what everybody else does?"

"If that is how Mademoiselle interprets our lesson, then so be it."

Sam was chuckling inside, though she kept a straight face. "Remy says nice things about you, you know."

"It is not fitting to gossip about Her Royal Highness."

Her. In French, she had learned today, "highness" was a masculine noun, so "His Highness" and "Her Highness" were expressed the same way. The masculine form doubled as a universal one. But curiously the word for "his" and "her" changed depending on the noun they described. Her table, his pen or his table, her pen—the adjectives remained the same: *sa table, son stylo.* The word for "Highness" was always masculine—likely, Sam thought, because the world expected men to be its leaders.

Remy's title was much more complicated in English, where the adjective had to be changed depending on whether the royal person in question was male or female. His Royal Highness, Her Royal Highness. In English, the terms were landmines to anyone who lived beyond the gender binary. If Montamantiens were accustomed to using the same term for all princes and princesses, then would it really be so hard for them to accept Remy was neither?

Madame Pouvoir was waiting for her to respond.

"I'm not gossiping. I'm paying you a compliment. Remy said you were exceptionally competent, and I can see that's the case. They also said you were the only real source of tenderness they remember from childhood and that you really care about them. And that if I could look past your tough exterior, I'd see that."

"Well?" Pouvoir's eyebrows were nearly raised to her hairline.

"I can." It was only a small white lie. There were glimpses of that humanity, but Madame Pouvoir was still scary and too concerned with protocol for it to be wholly true. But Sam wanted to offer an olive branch.

Pouvoir's eyebrows relaxed, and her lips turned up in the tiniest of smiles. She gave one small nod of her head in gratitude.

Sam figured this was the best moment to go for the kill, while they were…bonding, or whatever they were doing. "Can I ask you something candidly, Madame? How do you really feel about this plan of the queen's to have Remy marry Pierre?"

Pouvoir gave her a rehearsed line about respecting Her Majesty's wishes and wisdom. It was probably the same thing she said when asked about any of Queen Clotilde's crazy ideas.

"I understand that." Sam couldn't at all, but she hadn't spent twenty years serving a queen, and she had never functioned as the glue that held a monarchy together. "I also know you care deeply for Remy, and this plan is making them miserable. Isn't there some way you can use your influence to talk to the queen? If it's not your place to persuade her to change her mind, maybe you could at least convince her to sit down with Remy and listen to them before she makes them go through with it. That's not a lot to ask, is it?"

Madame Pouvoir didn't have time to answer. There was a short knock on the door, followed by Remy poking their head into the room. They were dressed in an eggplant-colored men's blazer with a crisp white shirt underneath. They wore slim gray slacks with their clear glasses, and the overall effect was modern and stylish.

"You look fantastic," they observed, gazing at Sam.

She could feel herself blushing. "Shut up."

"I'm serious. Clotilde is going to be jealous when you steal all the attention."

"Remy, stop!"

"Your Royal Highness," Pouvoir interrupted. "Do you require assistance?"

At face value, it was the question a loyal servant would ask, but it was clear that Pouvoir meant to interrupt their flirting. Of course she did. If Queen Clotilde thought Remy needed to marry Pierre, then Pouvoir wasn't going to stand by and watch genuine affection pass between Remy and Sam. Sam resisted the urge to roll her eyes. The inner workings of the palace were like a bad reality TV show.

"I came to walk Sam to dinner," Remy said.

"You will enter with Her Majesty after the guests," Pouvoir reminded them.

"I can take her to the back entrance to the dining room at least. I'll disappear and wait for Clotilde after that." Remy held out their hand.

Sam glanced at Pouvoir, slightly afraid of her reaction, before taking Remy's hand. It was warm to the touch, and she felt a frisson of excitement pass through her.

As they made their way from the luxurious wing in which Sam's suite was housed to the courtyard, Remy asked if she felt prepared and if she had any questions. They were attentive and thoughtful, and Sam felt protected and taken care of.

"You really do look stunning tonight," they added.

"Really? I love this dress. I don't know where they keep finding me these beautiful clothes." Sam looked at their slick mismatched suit. "How do you feel in the suit? Is that comfortable?"

"Yes," Remy said pleasantly. "It's as if Marie-Jeanne is starting to understand who I am. Clotilde had wanted me to wear a dress. She won't be happy. I would have liked to have worn makeup like you, but with the pants…"

They had reached the entrance to the Tudor wing, and a butler opened the door for them. Sam wondered if he stood waiting in the courtyard all day on the chance that someone might eventually want to use his door. Inside the building, Sam put a hand on Remy's arm to stop them.

"You look amazing, and you're starting to shine here," she said. "And, for the record, I'd love to see you in makeup."

"I'm very lucky to have you here." Remy leaned forward, looked quickly left and right to see who else was in the corridor, and gently kissed Sam. They tasted like minty toothpaste, but their skin smelled of the ocean. A very subtle, very alluring cologne. "Oh, no, I've smeared your lipstick!"

They led Sam by the hand to a mirror on the wall near a full suit of armor. The mirror was probably as old as the armor. Its surface had darkened, and in the dim light of the hall Sam could only take her best guess at fixing her lipstick. She stood up and realized Remy had red on their cheek. She wiped it with her thumb, savoring the last opportunity to touch their skin so intimately before dinner separated them.

When they reached the door to the dining room, Remy reminded her, "I want you to know how much I hate sitting apart from you. I'll be thinking about you all night. Will you remember that?" Their breath was hot on Sam's cheek, which they brushed gently with their lips before releasing her hand and encouraging her to enter the room. They turned and walked away to find Clotilde for their grand entrance.

When Remy entered the dining room with Clotilde on their arm, their guests curtsied and bowed, including Sam. Remy was desperate to catch her attention and give her a wink or a smile, anything to let her know they were thinking about her. It was hard with Sam seated at the opposite end of the long table, and from that distance Remy couldn't gauge whether she was comfortable.

The dinner passed unremarkably. Over the cheese course, Pierre remembered his manners and asked Sam about herself. It was the only time Remy saw Sam speaking during the meal, and she answered each question cordially but succinctly. Whether that was because she didn't want to be there or because she understood that the best way to avoid being the subject of gossip was to give minimal information about herself, Remy couldn't tell. She looked affluent in the clothes the palace staff had procured for her, and her manners were impeccable. If they hadn't known she was a middle-class American, they would have assumed she had spent a lot of time in the company of the European aristocracy.

After dinner, Pierre's father, acting as the man of the house as he had often done since Georges's death, led the older adults to another room for a game of belote, a beloved card game in their region. Clotilde said she was still not feeling well and excused herself to an early bedtime. That left Pierre, Remy, and Sam alone in the dining room.

It was the worst possible scenario for how to finish the night.

"We should leave the table so the staff can clear it," they said. "How about a brandy?"

"Lovely," Pierre said.

Sam looked at them with wide, confused eyes. She'd probably never tasted brandy, Remy guessed, and she didn't know if she should leave them alone or stay with them.

"Sam?" They gestured to the corner of the room. "Come on, let's go over there."

They moved to a cluster of chairs and a peacock blue sofa near a small bay window. Remy made sure to sit in the middle of the sofa, so Sam would feel welcome. Pierre sank heavily beside them and put his feet up on the marble coffee table. Sam watched in surprise.

Remy patted the space to their other side. "Come on, sit by me. Do you know that when I was younger, I often had to ask the kitchen for a second dinner."

"You did?"

Remy nodded. "It's hard to eat when you're worried about spilling or talking with your mouth full."

She looked immensely relieved to hear that. She perched delicately beside them.

Remy let their arm rest on the back of the sofa, not quite touching her but assuring her it was there. "Tell me the truth. Did you eat enough? Did you like the food?"

"The pear and chocolate tart for dessert was really good."

"Do you want another?"

"No, Remy, I'm fine. You're embarrassing me."

"There's no reason to be embarrassed." They waved to one of the dining staff. "Could you have the kitchen send up some brandy, another piece of the pear tart, and…maybe those little fig cookies?"

"You've turned American," Pierre observed. "You're snacking right after a meal."

"We would also like a baguette and some jam," Remy amended to spite him. They hadn't gained an ounce of weight in the US, and they didn't want him making Sam feel badly. Remy knew it could be hard to feel sated when faced with a foreign cuisine. Anyway, whether Sam was hungry or not, Remy was, and they didn't intend to go to bed hungry simply because Pierre thought eating after dinner was gauche.

The dining attendant, whose name Remy didn't know, nodded and retreated from the room. That left the three of them alone. They were seated in a row, Pierre's feet up on the coffee table, Remy's fingers gently brushing the nape of Sam's neck, and Sam sitting up straight as if she was being tested on her posture. No one said anything, and the silence began to feel uncomfortable.

The attendant returned ten minutes later with a silver rolling cart. He placed the three brandy glasses on the table, one in front of each of them, neatly avoiding Pierre's feet. Then he uncovered the rest of the dishes.

"The pear tart, cookies, baguette with jam and butter, and Chef also made for you three savory crepes—two with ham, one with gruyère. *Bon appétit*."

"Thank you," Remy and Pierre called reflexively.

Once he was gone, Remy put the food on the coffee table, kicking Pierre's feet off when he wouldn't move them himself. Remy explained to Sam in English what the food was. She said she'd never eaten a crepe before, but from the expression on her face, she didn't much like it. She gobbled down the pear tart, though, and they all passed the baguette back and forth, tearing off pieces and not caring if the crumbs got all over their clothing.

After his brandy glass was empty, Pierre decided to speak. "Shall we address the secret of Polichinelle?"

"The what?" Sam asked.

Pierre, who was less confident in his English than his German and Italian, repeated the phrase in French. This only confused Sam more, and she turned to Remy with a comical expression on her face.

They thought for a moment for an explanation in English. "The thing we all know and do not discuss with each other."

"Oh," she said, "the elephant in the room."

"Which is what?" Remy asked Pierre.

"You and I will be married if our parents are successful, but where does that leave you and Sam?"

Sam leaned around Remy to speak to Pierre directly. "It leaves me out of the picture. I don't want to intrude, and it obviously seems you and Remy have some things to discuss." She rose to her feet. "I'll find my way back to my room."

"Sit down," Pierre ordered her.

"Excuse me?"

"You're being boring. Sit down. We can talk about this like adults."

Remy had known Sam long enough to know that she didn't react well when others were brusque. Despite the lavish setting and her earlier timidity, this was no exception.

"I'm being boring? I'm trying to be polite! And I don't have to take orders from you. I may be new to your country, but I'm pretty sure you're not royalty. Yet," she added, her voice dropping.

Pierre nudged his elbow into Remy's side and mouthed in French, "Why is she so upset?"

"Why did you start this conversation right now?" they snapped back in English.

"I wanted to tell you two that I know there is some relationship between you, and I don't intend to interfere. If you would listen to me. Instead, you indulge in self-pity."

"Remy is not self-pitying," Sam shot back. "Do you have any idea what their life has been like?"

"Yes, of course," Pierre retorted. "I grew up with her. You have known her for a few weeks?"

"Them." Sam's tone was final.

"One minute, please." Remy didn't like the idea of them fighting. They had foolishly hoped tonight's brandy and snacks session might bring them together. "Please sit down, Sam. There is no reason for shouting."

"He keeps misgendering you."

"I know."

"You don't correct him. No one corrects anyone around here. Do you want to be called 'she'?"

"No." But neither did Remy want the responsibility of policing the language of people they had known their whole life. No one was trying to be hurtful. It was a big adjustment. "Thank you for trying to protect me, but it's my decision."

Slightly mollified, Sam sat back down on the sofa.

Remy turned their attention to Pierre. "You said something about not interfering? What did you mean?"

"Look, I love you." He looked at Sam. "But not in the way of lovers. It is nothing for you to be jealous of. I don't have those feelings for Remy." He turned to Remy again. "Queen Clotilde wants us to marry, Papa wants us to marry, and I can think of worse things than becoming part of the royal family."

Next to them, Remy could feel Sam tensing again. They didn't blame her. They didn't want to be someone's lesser fate, a convenient entry into a more privileged lifestyle. Pierre had plenty of money and privilege on his own. He didn't need to wear a crown to think of himself as royalty.

"I don't love you either," Remy told him. Their stomach was in knots over having this conversation in front of Sam. Pierre had put them all in an awkward position. There was no way for Remy to win. "You're my best friend, and I don't want to hurt you, but…I don't want to marry you."

"I was not finished," Pierre told them pointedly. "You see, if anyone had asked my opinion on this plan, I could have said that it will not work for one simple reason. I'm gay."

❖

"Since when are you gay?" Remy was leaning forward on the couch aggressively, their body turned toward Pierre so Sam could barely see. She leaned against the back cushions to peek at Pierre's face.

Sam's first impression was that Pierre was an arrogant snob, the kind who'd been brought up rich and, although he knew which fork to use with which course at dinner, had very few practical manners. She suspected he'd had a long life of doing and saying whatever he wanted and getting away with it.

And, to be honest, it was hard to like someone who was intended for marriage to the person that she—well, Sam wasn't ready to say she was in love with Remy. But she hated the idea of someone else swooping in and claiming them before she had a chance to see how deep her feelings ran.

"You have been gone for weeks," Pierre explained. "Don't presume you know everything about my life. You are usually only concerned with yourself."

That, Sam had observed, was kind of true.

"You're saying that while I was in New York, you suddenly became gay? That's not how it works!"

Sam felt an internal sigh. Because she didn't like Pierre. She saw him as a rival. And, Remy aside, she also saw him as selfish, overprivileged, and obnoxious. But, on this particular issue, that didn't matter. Sam was going to have to defend him.

She laid a gentle hand on one of the arms Remy was flailing. In a soft voice, she reminded them, "Sometimes that *is* how it works. He's the only one who can decide what his identity is. Same as you."

"Thank you, dear," Pierre called from the other end of the sofa. "I need a drink."

"You've had plenty," Remy said grumpily. But they took his glass and theirs and walked over to the cart to refill them.

Sam looked down at her own empty glass, wondering if the peasant folk had had enough of the fine royal liquor or if Remy had forgotten she was even there.

"I don't understand why you are upset," Pierre continued. "Shouldn't this news make you happy? Now they cannot force us to get married, since you are close to being a woman."

Sam gasped. She waited to see Remy's reaction, but they just said, "This is the worst thing that you could have done to me."

After that, Pierre began speaking in French, nearly spitting in Remy's direction. Sam was dying to know what he said.

"Don't talk to me that way!" Remy yelled back in English. They handed him a glass of brandy, actions and words showing opposite feelings toward him. More French back and forth between them. Sam couldn't tell which parts were swearing. There were a lot of explosive consonants and spitting.

They were rehearsing a play, she realized. Reciting lines they didn't really mean, wrapped up in their own drama with no room for Sam in the script. She was merely the audience.

Frankly, the show had long since ceased to be interesting. She rose again and cleared her throat quietly. "I think I'll—"

"Where are you going?" Pierre asked crisply.

"I am going back to my room."

"You're being a rude host," he told Remy. "She is about to flee."

"That's because you like to make yourself the subject of the conversation. It makes people uncomfortable."

Their quick banter, their easy rapport, the way neither flinched at the other's insults. Even if they weren't in love, they obviously had deep affection for each other, not to mention their shared childhoods and prestigious bloodlines. It probably was a good idea for them to marry each other. It made sense politically, and who else would want to put up with either of them? Neither seemed capable of making space in their life for anyone else anyway.

Remy probably wasn't angry at Pierre, just in shock. A coming out was always a surprise to those around the person, even when the signs had always been there. Usually because people overlooked those signs in order to craft their own vision of who their loved one was. If they'd paid a little more attention, they—and the person who came out— probably would have recognized it had been there all along. That's how it had been for Sam anyway.

She thought there might be additional reasons Remy was so uncharitable about this revelation of Pierre's. Maybe Remy had counted on being the lone queer person in Pierre's otherwise boring heteronormative life. Or maybe part of Remy wanted Pierre to find them attractive, and this ruined it. Whatever it was, their feelings for each other were too complicated for Sam's taste.

Summoning her remaining dignity, she announced, "It was very nice to meet you, Pierre. I want you to know that I always support personal journeys. Congratulations on yours." She turned to Remy. "Good night."

That was it. Just "good night." She didn't know what the schedule for the following day was and when she would see them. She wasn't sure she wanted to. If she had had a choice at that moment, she'd have asked for a ride back to the airport. But she had promised to help Remy, and she would keep her word. As an ally, nothing more.

She pretended not to hear them calling her name as she strode out of the dining room.

❖

"Are you happy?" Remy unleashed all their anger on Pierre the Homosexual.

"What did I do?"

"What you always do when I'm interested in someone! You chased her away!"

"How did I do that exactly?" he snapped. "The trees are hiding the forest from you. If I'm gay, then we are hardly a match for marriage. Everyone thinks you're a woman."

Remy ran a hand through their hair. "You're the one who can't see the forest. When people find out you're gay, it will make them start thinking about queerness in general, and they'll remember the story about how I wasn't really born a girl. Instead of stopping the rumors, it will encourage more. And then Clotilde will want us to prove our relationship. We'll be expected to have sex and have children."

"I don't want to have sex with you!" Pierre said in horror. "What do you even have down there? Is it even normal looking?"

"Do you hear yourself? How rude you are? I can't imagine anyone wanting to be married to you unless they were forced to do it."

"The same for you! Do you think anyone but me could even tolerate being with you? My God, Remy, why can't you pick one? Why can't you just be a boy or a girl?"

The words stung like a slap to Remy's face. They set their brandy on the table and moved away from him. They weren't entirely sure they could resist lashing out, physically or verbally. They counted *un-deux-trois*, and by the time they got to twenty, the rage had simmered enough for them to speak. It wasn't worth wasting energy explaining everything Pierre did and said wrong to him. He was too obtuse, and Remy suspected he might be incapable of changing.

"You don't understand anything," Remy told him.

At least Pierre looked remorseful. "I'm sorry. I didn't mean it."

"Yes, you did. Because you don't understand. Not really."

"I suppose *she* does?"

"Yes, she does."

"She's perfect for you, then."

"Are you jealous of her? Is that what this gay nonsense is about?"

"It's not nonsense," Pierre said crisply. "If you want me to respect you, you should respect me in return."

That was exactly what Sam would have told them if she was still there. Remy took a breath. "It's hard to respect you when you say such hurtful things to me."

Sam would have been proud of them for standing up for themselves so calmly and directly.

Pierre looked contrite. "I only meant that choosing whether you're a boy or girl would make things easier for you."

"That's what people say to bisexual people," Remy pointed out. "If you would choose whether you want to fall in love with a man or a woman, things would be easier. They say it to gay people, too. If you would choose to be straight, your life would be easier. It's not how it works for them, and it's not how it works for me. A choice was made for me when I was born, and now that I can undo it, I feel whole. That is my choice."

Pierre gestured for Remy to join him on the sofa. "I'm sorry," he said again. "I didn't think about the implications of what I was saying."

If Remy had learned anything from Sam in the past three days, it was how to accept an apology graciously. They nodded, sat beside him, and tried to change the subject to something less tense.

"Tell me how you found out you're gay. I want to hear all about it."

Pierre threw his head against the sofa cushions and spread his arms wide, a blissful smile spreading across his face. "I've fallen in love!"

"With whom? When?"

"Remember when I went to that yacht party in Barcelona with Manon?"

"Your girlfriend whom you dated for an entire year, yes." He had talked about nothing but Manon all of the previous summer. She came from family wealth but had also accumulated her own through investment banking, and they'd met at a dinner party hosted by mutual friends. When Pierre had first shown Remy pictures of them together, Remy thought Manon looked bland and boring, but Pierre had declared himself in love after only one week. Remy had never understood why.

"One of the other guests at the yacht party was a model named Giovanni. He's from Milan, and I'm still not sure who invited him. I think he knows Pedro—he's the one who owns the yacht. At some point, Manon abandoned me to discuss business with this Saudi guy in the oil industry, and Giovanni and I were alone, and we had a few drinks, and…"

"You just described what most people experience at university. You're having a delayed adolescence."

"I am not."

"One sexual encounter with a handsome Italian model hardly makes you gay."

"You're an asshole, Remy." His voice, which had been dreamy, was cold. "I'm trying to tell you about the biggest thing that's ever happened to me, and you're making jokes. Do you think it's the first time I've ever kissed a man? Do you think I'm that unsophisticated?"

"You've kissed other men before?"

"This was different! Yes, we had sex, but then we started talking to each other. At first it was in secret, but then I started feeling more connected to him. I didn't want to live a double life, so I broke it off with Manon. Giovanni and I spent a week in Milan together while you were in New York. We talked about everything, and do you know what he told me? That he didn't want to be my first boyfriend. He said he wanted me to make sure I understood what I was doing."

"What did you do?"

"I came home. I saw my therapist. I attended a support group for LGBTQ people in Chamonix."

"You went to a support group?" These were hardly the actions of the person they'd grown up with and left behind. Could it be that he was sincere in his coming out?

"We decided to pause our relationship while I figured things out," Pierre continued. "I dated other men. Giovanni knew. He encouraged it. He thought it would help me sort out my feelings."

"And did it?"

"Yes."

"What are your feelings?"

Pierre smiled, and it wasn't the usual artificial smile he used to get what he wanted. Nor was it a mere turning up of the lips in what was really a sneer. This smile was sweet.

"I'm in love with him. I don't know why it happened now and not when I was younger, and I don't know why I dated so many women before. I only know I'm in love with him, and everything feels like it makes sense now."

Remy took his hand in their own. "I'm happy for you. Really."

"I'm sorry I didn't tell you. I didn't know how, and you were—"

"I was only concerned with my life in New York and then settling in Boston. I've been a lousy friend. I haven't even asked you about your life."

"I haven't volunteered." He squeezed their hand once and took his back. "You're forgiven as long as you respect my feelings."

Remy nodded. Even if Pierre decided next week he had been wrong and went back to women, they owed it to him to respect how he felt now. But something told them he wouldn't be changing his mind.

"Pierre, what you said about everything feeling right? I wish you could understand. That's how I feel when I don't have to be a man or a woman."

He shook his head. "I don't understand."

Remy struggled to put it to words. Sometimes the world made them feel like they were aberrant, a freak of nature who needed to be changed. That was usually an outside feeling, the pressure of the world influencing them. Alone, away from the palace and its expectations of them, Remy felt right. They felt like they finally understood who they were. And that person was not Her Royal Highness Remy. It wasn't "he" or "she." It was somewhere in between. It was neither and both.

They told him what they'd learned about intersex from the doctor in New York and how this new knowledge had helped them make sense of their life and who they were. Pierre listened, which Remy appreciated, even if he didn't or couldn't fully understand. At least he was trying to be a good friend.

"I'm happy you feel like you've found yourself," Pierre said.

"Same to you." They kissed each other's cheeks affectionately.

"As for this American," he asked, "are you in love with her?"

Remy hesitated, and Pierre rushed to the assumption that their hesitation meant they weren't sure how they felt about Sam.

"I'm glad your feelings aren't clear. That means there's time to forget about her."

"My feelings are clear," Remy said. "She means everything to me."

"Already?"

Remy nodded. "I have never felt this way about anyone."

Pierre shook his head. "You can't get involved with an American. It's not proper. You're the next monarch!"

"I know, and that's why I am trying not to let myself fall in love and start something and hurt her feelings. Or, worse, have her hurt mine."

"Why would she hurt your feelings?"

"She hates all this royal nonsense." Remy spread their arms wide to encompass the palace, the mountain, the whole country. "She's focused on getting her PhD and doesn't want any distractions."

"You didn't say anything about the most important part."

"Which is what?"

"You didn't say, 'She's not in love with me.' Everything else is an obstacle, not a barrier to the relationship."

He was turning his usual advice about women in committed relationships on its head. Now it was meant to encourage Remy to look beyond surface details that seemed to stand in the way of what could otherwise be a great relationship. With Sam, they shared political and social values, they laughed together, and they challenged each other in ways that were necessary for each of them to grow. If the make-out sessions they'd been sneaking in were any indicator, they clearly had great sexual chemistry.

"I do have strong feelings for Sam," Remy said, "and I think she feels the same way about me. I don't know for certain, and I don't know how to ask her in the middle of announcing my engagement to you. I don't want to hurt her like that."

"In that case," Pierre said, "let's figure out how to get ourselves out of our engagement."

They stayed on the couch for a few more hours, talking. Although they had been friends for years, Remy thought it was the first time they had shared their feelings so candidly with each other. They were reconnecting on a new level. The conversation affirmed for Remy how much they loved Pierre at the same time that it solidified how ridiculous Clotilde and Andre's plan really was. Neither of them wanted to marry the other, and together they tried to determine how to end Clotilde's plot.

When the clock on the mantlepiece chimed one, Andre and the remaining guests returned to the dining room from the small drawing room where they had been playing cards. They said their good-byes, and Pierre got up to leave with his father. Although the hour was late, Remy felt invigorated because they finally had a plan.

CHAPTER SIXTEEN

In the morning, Sam ate a few bites of croissant and took a few sips of the creamy espresso Marie-Francine had brought before heading down to the archives. She had hoped Remy would come to her room after they'd finished talking to Pierre, but by midnight she had realized they weren't coming and had gone to bed—a little mad, mostly sad. It was her own fault for leaving them the way she had.

She would still be in Montamant for a few days, and whatever happened with her shaky new romance, she was going to use that time effectively to enjoy access to resources she'd never have again. Dr. Grant might have thought her research was inviable because Sam didn't know historiographic methods, but how could she possibly argue against the value of sifting through a royal archive firsthand?

She got lost a few times on her way to the archive, and she kept expecting a staff member to yell at her for being in places she wasn't allowed to be. But most of the rooms she stumbled into were empty. She saw more exquisitely old furniture, oil paintings, and plush carpets and drapes, but not much else. If the palace was hiding secrets, she hadn't found any on her way to the archive.

Finally, she reached the solid old door and let herself in. The fluorescent lights hummed overhead as she took a box off the shelf and settled at the table to dig through it. She wasn't really sure what her process ought to be, other than opening every single box, and she didn't have her phone to take photos or any paper for making notes. Maybe these were the sorts of things Dr. Grant had meant about research method. What she lacked in organization, though, she made up for in enthusiasm. In the quiet of the room, she easily passed several hours looking at old family photographs, bank statements, and menus from state dinners from bygone centuries.

Sam confirmed what Remy had told her: they were the last surviving Vallorcin. No generation of the family had ever had more than one or two children, a first child who was the heir and a second child who served as the "spare" in case something happened to the elder sibling. As the line of succession passed down, many of these spares became further removed from the throne, which could have been beneficial at a moment like this when they needed to find more blood relatives. But many of their progeny had died in the two World Wars, others from old age or disease, and thus the possible alternative branches to the family tree had been snipped. Like Remy, Clotilde had been born an only child, meaning the Vallorcin name would end with Remy if they didn't have children of their own.

In another carton, Sam learned that state dinners had once been entirely vegan, despite the region's heavy reliance on cheesemaking for cultural and economic gain. The vegan phase had been instituted after Queen Flore had read a pamphlet describing how meat and dairy caused mental weakness. The menus of that time looked kind of dreadful: vegetable broth with bread, plain noodles with olive oil, and fresh fruit for dessert. Nothing like the rich, flavorful cuisine Sam had been served the night before, and nothing like the vegan food she'd eaten at trendy bistros inspired by the flavors of the Mediterranean and India.

As she returned the carton with Queen Flore's papers to the shelf, she noticed that the cobweb-covered bricks behind it were loose, and she couldn't resist pushing on them. One wiggled in place, and she was able to wedge her fingertips in. She pulled the brick out.

In the space behind it, in a hidden nook in the wall, was a small metal box. Sam lifted it out and brought it to the table. Its surface was intricately carved silver. It had a hinged lid, which she opened.

Inside was a tiny painting of a person with cherubic cheeks, piercing blue eyes, and wispy blond medium-length hair. Along with the painting were a few folded papers, which Sam opened carefully so as not to tear them. They were written in calligraphy.

She remembered the English-Montamantien dictionary she'd found the day before and hurried to retrieve it. Some of the words on the paper she could guess, and others she had to look up. After a steady hour of piecemeal translation, she understood she had found something extraordinary.

❖

One of Pierre's ideas had been to boost the public's attitude toward Remy by having them make appearances while they were in town, instead of remaining secluded. Truthfully, Remy had wanted to stay in the confines and safety of the palace. Clotilde might have been their enemy, but they at least knew her and what to expect. Out in public, among people they didn't know, people who hadn't seen them in years, Remy wasn't sure how to behave or what to say.

"Don't be absurd," Gilles said when Remy confided this in the car. "I heard you were excellent at the reading of the proclamation yesterday."

"That doesn't make me less frightened, but thank you."

As he had done the night before, Pierre assured Remy that granting the public closer access to them was a better way to combat rumors than remaining hidden in secrecy. Remy agreed in principle, but now that they were driving down the mountain for their first public outing, they feared it had been a terrible idea.

The nation-state of Montamant was organized around a central square with a giant fountain. On one side was the cathedral, where regular Sunday masses, in addition to the more ceremonial events like the royal family's weddings and funerals, were held. On the other side of the square was the library, and a few meters down the block was the building that housed Parliament. Montamant was a small enough country that the important government buildings were right next door to the places people frequented in the course of their daily lives. In a small building next to Parliament was the civic center, a space Remy had heard about but had never actually been to.

Today, that was about to change.

"Are you nervous?" Pierre asked from the back seat.

"Terrified."

"Remember to keep your chin up and remain calm. No one is going to say anything rude directly to you. People are too polite for that. As long as you listen to them, they'll appreciate that you're giving them your time, and they won't have a chance to think about whether they approve of your appearance." He laughed. "They all think you're some important person who's so busy that a half hour of your time is some great gift. God knows why they think that way."

"Did Madame Pouvoir tell the press we are doing this?"

Pierre shook his head. "When I suggested it, she said that if we alerted the press, we would run the risk of Queen Clotilde finding out what we're doing. Madame Pouvoir thought Her Majesty was likely to put a stop to the whole outing. I think it'll be better if we have viral publicity because it will register as more authentic."

Meaning they were going to leave it to the good people of Montamant to whip out their phones and document their future monarch's appearance. As much as Remy didn't want to do this, they wanted it to work. They felt torn between hoping no one would take a picture, so they could remain in the safety of relative obscurity, and hoping the visit would "go viral," so Clotilde would be forced to see that Remy was liked on their own terms, regardless of gender or marital status.

"But, Remy," Pierre reminded them as Gilles pulled in front of the civic center, defying the "parking forbidden" sign, "this is only going to work if you let them call you 'princess.' Now is not the time to correct them."

"Great final words of advice." They got out of the car without waiting for Gilles, who instead rushed to the front door of the building and held it open.

Remy and Pierre stepped inside the civic center. A modest front desk and a few chairs occupied the lobby, along with a woman who was staring down at her phone.

"*Bonjour*," Remy said.

"*Bonjour*," she replied without looking up.

Remy looked at Pierre and shrugged. Pierre took a step toward the front desk. "Mademoiselle, I hope it's not inconvenient for you to have an unannounced visit from Princess Remy today."

The woman looked up at them. Her eyes narrowed, and Remy suspected she was trying to remember what they'd looked like as a child and whether this could really be them now. Hadn't she seen the news from the proclamation reading yesterday? They offered a slight smile and waved their hands beside their face, and she dropped her phone and leapt to her feet.

"Your Highness!" She attempted a clumsy impersonation of a curtsy. "Your Highness *here*! To what do we owe this pleasure?"

Remy took a breath to muster the public persona they'd only crafted a day before. Then they offered a hand for the receptionist to shake, to show they were down to earth. The receptionist, when she stopped flailing in surprise, introduced herself as Matilde.

"We heard you have an octocentennial exhibit," Remy said, "and we'd like to see it and meet some of the staff involved in putting it together."

"And the seniors," Pierre said softly.

"I'm also told that Wednesday is senior day?" Remy continued as if they hadn't been prompted. "We were hoping to meet some of them. I am hoping they have some good stories to share about Montamant's history."

"Of course!" Matilde led them to a small office immediately off the lobby, where they met Dominique, a woman about Clotilde's age who ran the center. The four of them then toured the exhibit that had been installed in the main room for the week of the octocentennial celebrations.

Remy knew they only had to pretend to be interested in the displays, but once they started glancing at the version of history written alongside the maps and artifacts, they were sincerely intrigued. The exhibit told a different history of Montamant than the one they'd learned in school and private tutoring sessions, the version that was told at the palace. They hadn't known there had been an anti-royal uprising after the French Revolution or that it had been thwarted not through absolutism but through reforms that included a citizen advisory committee.

Did such a committee exist today, or had it been replaced by Parliament? Admittedly, Remy didn't know as much about the day-to-day functions of Parliament as they should have, but in broad terms, they knew the ministers hardly represented the people of Montamant. The youngest was forty-four, they were all men, and the least wealthy was a millionaire two times over. By contrast, the average age of the population was slightly younger than Remy, and that was because Clotilde's pregnancy announcement had triggered a birth wave. The country presently had more women than men, and the average household income was only around forty thousand euros.

They got lost in the exhibit for a moment, thinking about what Montamant had been and what it could be in the future, until they heard Pierre whisper, "It's working!"

Remy looked over their shoulder to see a few people standing nearby with their phones pointed at them. In the past, they would have ducked and run away from cameras, but that was the goal of today's visit: to let them gawk.

Or maybe that didn't have to be the only goal.

Publicity for publicity's sake wasn't going to change the hearts and minds of people. Remy couldn't expect to be loved simply because they'd made time to appear in public. No, people were smart enough to see through things like that. What Remy needed was sincerity.

They turned toward the crowd. "Put your cameras down," they said, hoping their voice sounded gentle and friendly, "and come over here. There is no need to be shy. I'm here to meet you."

"Oh my God, what are you doing?" Pierre asked, but it was too late.

For the next two hours, Remy shook hands, exchanged jokes, and even played a hand of belote with women old enough to be their grandmother. The cell phone cameras kept reappearing, which they supposed was understandable, but they encouraged people to speak to them, rather than making videos from a distance. They put their arm around people as Pierre, who had figured out the value in what they were doing, agreeably served as photographer.

One older child, with shortly cropped hair, a square jaw, and pink eyeshadow, covered their mouth in surprise when they walked into the center and saw Remy. Spotting their intense reaction, Remy waved them over and greeted them. The child started to curtsy, then stopped, looked over their shoulder as if someone might catch their mistake, and started to bow from the waist. Remy could feel their hesitation and knew from experience it wasn't because they were worried about how to behave in front of royalty. They knew they were supposed to show deference. No, their confusion had been about whether to bow like a boy or curtsy like a girl, and that kind of confusion, that panic about making the wrong choice, was something Remy had felt too many times to count when they were younger. Remy's heart ached for the life this child must have been living, and they spared them the discomfort by giving them a kiss on each cheek in the manner of friends greeting each other. Out of the corner of their eye, they could see the phones being raised to video the moment royalty greeted a local kid with so much familiarity.

Remy put their arm around the child. "You seemed very excited to meet me."

The child choked and wiped at their eyes as they admitted, "I never thought the day would come when I would get to meet you, Your Highness."

Remy felt the weight of their role in addition to their immediate affinity for the child. "How old are you?"

"Eleven."

At that age, they'd probably never seen "Princess Remy" in public, since for most of their life Remy had been in boarding school or college abroad. They wondered how the child even knew they existed as someone to feel so emotional over one day meeting. If their excitement was for the reason Remy suspected—that they saw Remy as a role model—then all the years away from Montamant hadn't done any good, and neither had the palace's publicity machine. Clearly, some of the citizens knew Remy was nonbinary anyway.

"Why were you so excited to meet me? How did you learn about me?"

"Grandmother always says I remind her of you. Then when she saw the newspaper this morning with the picture of you in it, she said I look a little bit like you with my hair and eyes."

On a superficial level, Remy supposed they did bear some resemblance to each other. They both had dark hair and round, revealing eyes. But the sculpt of their noses, jaws, and brows were totally different. To see Remy in this child was not a simple matter of their appearances.

"Do you get along well with your grandmother?" The child nodded. "You're very lucky. Mine has been dead for a long time, and I miss spending time with her."

"I don't spend that much time with her," they said, "since I'm at school all day."

"And how is school?"

They glanced over their shoulder again. "I get good marks."

Remy smiled and leaned down to meet their height. "But how are things really? Do you have good friends?"

They shook their head. "They don't like me."

"Why do you think that is?" Remy had their suspicions, but they wanted to know if the child understood yet.

"I don't look like a girl, but I am one. The boys' voices are changing, and all the girls are interested in boys, and I don't belong with either group."

"I can understand how hard that must be," Remy said. "When I was your age, I felt the same."

"You're not really like a princess."

"How is a princess supposed to be?"

"They wear beautiful dresses, and they have long hair. You don't wear any makeup."

"Sometimes I wear makeup," Remy added to push her preconceptions a little.

"I like makeup, but Maman doesn't like me to wear it."

"She's trying to protect you, do you know that? She wants to protect you from people who might judge you or hurt your feelings. Not everyone understands people like us. Did she bring you here today?"

"Grandmother. She doesn't mind if I wear makeup. Sometimes she helps me put it on."

"She sounds nice." Remy wished they'd had a family member who was that supportive when they were younger. Even now, there was no one, save maybe Sam, who would help Remy with things like that. "What's your name?"

She hesitated.

"Not the name your parents call you. What name do you want to be called?"

"Sandrine."

"Sandrine, it's nice to meet you. When you feel that no one likes you, I want you to remember that I like you very much." Remy meant it. It was hard not to empathize. Although the particulars were different, Remy remembered experiencing the same sense of confusion, fear, and sadness that Sandrine was going through. "I want you to promise me you will stay strong and write to me when you have trouble." They stood up, before the emotion of the encounter became too overwhelming. "Pierre, can we get a pen and paper?"

He relayed the request to Matilde, who returned a moment later with the items. Remy scribbled one of their email addresses down and gave it to the kid.

"Write to me when things get hard. I'm here for you." They pressed the paper into Sandrine's hands and started to move away before they teared up in public.

"Your Highness!" the grandmother called. "Your Highness, thank you! Thank you a thousand times!"

Remy waved as they muttered to Pierre, "I have to go. I'm about to start crying over that."

Pierre nodded, then turned to the crowd that had gathered. "We have really enjoyed our visit, but unfortunately Her Royal Highness has to return to the palace to prepare for the evening's octocentennial event. Thank you all so much for your time!"

Remy put their brave face back on and turned around. They waved and smiled. "I had a wonderful day!" They were surprised to realize they meant it.

CHAPTER SEVENTEEN

Her Majesty twisted and turned in the bed sheets but couldn't find a comfortable position. "I felt so much better yesterday," she croaked. One hand rubbed her sore throat while the other protectively covered her infected ear.

"Dr. Lemal told you not to drink any alcohol at dinner," Madame Pouvoir scolded her. "You didn't listen." She strode to the breakfast table, poured a glass of water, and set it on the bedside table. "You need to rehydrate. He warned you that dehydration would only complicate your loss of equilibrium. I will have to call him to give you the IV he wanted to use yesterday."

Queen Clotilde looked at her. "Honestly, Pouvoir, I can see your lips move and guess what you're saying, but I can't hear a word." She put a finger in her right ear and swished it around. She puffed her cheeks out comically and then opened her jaw as wide as it would go. "What if my hearing never comes back?"

"The doctor said it would come back as soon as the fluid in your inner ear has gone down, which will happen when the ear infection has passed, which is why you need to take your morning antibiotics."

"You have the patience of a saint, Pouvoir." The queen's voice was scratchy, as if she'd spent the night before screaming at the top of her lungs, and it was evident how much it hurt to talk. She reached for the glass and dutifully swallowed the blue oval pill that was sitting next to it. Then she blew her nose and coughed for a few moments, finally producing a ball of phlegm into a tissue. "I don't know how you can put up with me like this. I can't even stand myself."

"It is a pleasure to serve Her Majesty."

Queen Clotilde tucked her legs under the blankets and pulled the comforter all the way up to her chin. A few moments ago, she had complained it was too hot in the room. "Where's my child? She needs to attend every remaining meeting for me today."

"On that matter, I have news." Pouvoir took the iPad from the bedside table and pulled up a page on the internet. "Princess Remy made a visit to the octocentennial exhibit at the civic center. Here are some photos taken by the people Her Royal Highness and the younger Monsieur Lefaux met."

The queen took the iPad and scrolled through the page. "She took Pierre? Not the American?"

"No, Your Majesty."

"Did you know she was going to do this?"

Pouvoir hesitated. She had lied to the queen a few times in their decades of working together—a very select few times, which she could justify for important reasons. This time, she hadn't told the queen what the princess was planning because she didn't want the queen to stop it. Pouvoir had sensed that the princess and Monsieur Lefaux would make the day into a success, and she had wanted them to have the opportunity to do so.

Before she could decide whether to admit she had known about the trip, the queen sensed her hesitation. "And you didn't tell me because you thought it was a good idea? It looks as though you were right. Can you make sure Andre knows about this? Tell him I want him to see me as soon as possible. I don't care if I'm still in bed. And, Pouvoir, see what you can find out about Mademoiselle Hyde."

It was the third time Queen Clotilde had made the request, but each time she made it before falling asleep or after taking medicine and forgot. A basic criminal background check had been done before Mademoiselle Hyde had been permitted on the airplane with Princess Remy, and since their arrival at the palace, Pouvoir had authorized a more thorough check into her credit, employment history, and social media usage. She was awaiting the results.

"Of course, Your Majesty, we will conduct a thorough check on her."

"What prompted Remy to visit the civic center?"

"If I may speak candidly, Your Majesty, I think it was partly to spite you."

Pouvoir awaited Her Majesty's reaction. She had learned in her time serving the royal family to gauge when the queen would value candor and when she might find the truth difficult to swallow. Today,

Pouvoir sensed that the queen needed to hear that the princess was developing nicely in her role as heir. It was also helpful to know that if Queen Clotilde didn't like hearing that Remy had taken liberties with a public appearance, she'd likely forget after her next nap and round of cold medicine anyway.

"She's decided to win the love of an adoring public to show me she doesn't need the security of marriage to be a good heir." Queen Clotilde scrolled through the photos for a moment until a smile spread slowly across her face. "Sometimes I wonder if I really did give birth to Remy, but moments like this remind me how alike we are." She handed the iPad back to Pouvoir. "Do you think you'll manage today without me? You can coach her through the rest of today's events?"

"Of course, Your Majesty."

"Good! It sounds as if you have everything under control." The queen snuggled more deeply into the covers and closed her eyes. "You will tell Andre I want to see him, correct? I'm going to close my eyes for a little bit before he comes."

❖

Around one o'clock, Sam made her way back to her suite, and one of the kitchen maids brought a lunch tray to her. She was trying to swallow a bite of baguette sandwich without shredding the inside of her mouth on the crusty bread when a man walked into the room. He introduced himself as Monsieur Lapin, Pouvoir's right-hand man. He had arrived with a stack of books, which he announced were a present from Remy. As he set them on the desk, she saw that they were the schoolbooks she had left with the cashier on their last day in Boston. Monsieur Lapin handed her a crisp white linen envelope, inside of which was a textured white card that said simply, *This way you won't fall behind while you're here helping me—R.* It was a romantic gesture, one Sam wasn't sure how Remy had even managed to pull off.

Before he departed, Monsieur Lapin told Sam he was at her disposal for "anything at all," which Sam suspected wasn't really true. But she did have one request: she needed to call her mom.

Lapin set her up in a small office with a mahogany desk and executive chair. The room was the size of a large closet, but it was well-appointed and made Sam feel very official. Lapin dialed the numbers for her, and Sam hoped they didn't mind paying for her long distance. Was it even legal for them to use the phone for personal use if the taxpayers funded the monarchy? Then again, it wasn't like they were elected officials at their office. The palace was their home. Should she offer to pay them for the expense? At the very least, she decided she should keep the call short.

As the phone rang, Lapin left the room and shut the door behind him. A moment later, Sam's mother answered. Sam missed seeing her face and wished they were on a video chat, but it was good to hear her voice. Soon she found herself telling her mother how unexpectedly difficult and complicated life in a palace was.

"I don't know how these people can stand living like this," she said. "There are rules for everything. It's not glamorous at all."

"Maybe it's good you're seeing that," Mom said, "so you'll stop fantasizing about it."

"I never fantasized about being royalty." The very thought made her bristle. "This lifestyle is completely undemocratic. Everything is organized by gender and social class. Frankly, I think all the rules are intended to distract us from the reality that there's no real difference between them and us, other than who their parents were. It makes you wonder why they think they're so special."

"You don't like royal life, hmm?"

"No, Mom, I absolutely do not."

"Then why are you so intent to research it?"

Sam huffed. "First of all, I'm not researching royalty. I'm researching the *aristocracy*."

"Honey, what's the difference?"

Sam paused. Bloodlines, maybe, because both had money and power. As Remy had pointed out, though, the wealthiest people in a society were inevitably as invested in pedigree as royals were. Was Sam merely interested in a rose by another name?

She avoided the question and returned instead to Mom's initial one. "It's not about the fantasy. It's fascinating, but at a critical distance."

"Oh, I see," Mom said, her voice ringing false. "My mistake."

She'd made a surprising point—one Sam would need more time to reflect on. Not the point about wealthy commoners being pretty much the same thing as royalty. No, she had been earnestly asking that as a question, and Sam could see that extreme wealth, whether through bloodline or business, was pretty much all the same. The part about Sam's line of research stemming from her own interest, and maybe envy, was something Sam needed to spend some time considering. She knew she felt uncomfortable in the Montamantien palace. Out of place and poised at any time to get in trouble for doing something wrong, even though the staff had always been pleasant to her. It was less their demeanor and more the opulence of the place, the hushed tones with which everyone spoke, and the blind adherence to centuries-old traditions that made Sam feel lost in the rule book.

At the same time, she had to admit she enjoyed how easy life was. Clothing appeared by magic. She didn't have to cook or clean up after herself. Her room was incredibly comfortable, and Remy had given her license to use the archives whenever she wanted. She enjoyed the creature comforts and the proximity to history. And she liked being able to see Remy in their native, if disowned, habitat.

She wondered how Remy would feel visiting her family in Indiana.

"Whether you like it or not, I want you to remember two things," Mom said. "First, you are having a once in a lifetime experience, something most people would never even dream of being able to have. Take advantage and appreciate that. But, second, don't forget you are a guest. Remember when you went to your friends' houses for slumber parties? What did I always tell you?"

"Be gracious, don't complain, and pick up after myself," Sam answered by rote.

"That's right. Even though it's a palace, you're still a guest. This is their way of life. You might not understand it or approve of it, but you owe them the courtesy of respecting it."

She was right. In a parallel way, it was the same thing Sam said about gender and sexuality. During her own coming out process, she'd asked her parents to consider that even if they couldn't imagine having feelings toward a person of the same sex, they should respect that she did. The Vallorcins had welcomed Sam into their home. Their wealth and generosity had enabled her to make this phone call. Even if she didn't like that kind of wealth, she owed it to them to respect that it was their lifestyle.

Sam's problem was that Remy seemed so trapped by their birth, so harassed by Queen Clotilde and haunted by the prospect of becoming the sovereign in the future. The privileges and wealth seemed like meager compensation for the ways Remy had been obligated by their status as heir apparent.

"What else?" Mom asked. "I can tell there's something else on your mind."

"Queen Clotilde wants Remy to announce their engagement to a local nobleman on Friday. He and Remy don't want to get married at all. It's none of my business, but I just…" She choked back tears. Maybe she was suffering from exhaustion due to jet lag, or maybe it was the stress of trying to follow protocol all the time, but a dam inside broke. The tears came flooding out. "I don't want them to get married!"

"Oh, Samantha, honey," her mother said gently, "you're in love."

"I don't know." She sniffed. "It's way too soon for that."

"Maybe, but it sounds like it's way too late for you to put your feelings back in the bottle."

The inevitability caused another wave of tears. Was she really in so deep that there was no turning back? What would that mean if they weren't able to figure out how to stop the engagement? Sam didn't want to be the other woman any more than she wanted to be someone who cried over the one that got away.

"It doesn't matter anyway," she managed to explain in chokes and fits, "I'm American. I'm not important enough to marry."

Mom let out a breath. "You know, this is all way over my head. I don't know anything about royal families and castles. I never imagined you'd call me from one."

"It's a palace, Mom, not a castle."

"My point is, I don't have any experience or wisdom I can guide you from on this one. You're going to have to feel it out for yourself. But if I can tell you one thing I've learned in my time on this Earth, it's that the best option is never sitting back and not saying something when you have strong feelings."

By the time their phone call ended, Sam had managed to calm down and could see a few things more clearly. Her mother was right about her feelings for Remy. Being "in love" was an ideal Sam wasn't sure described their situation after so little time together, but her feelings were present and strong. It was too late to deny them. She was hooked, and that wasn't going to change, no matter what happened with Remy and Pierre. More than that, she recognized she didn't want her feelings to change. She liked the way she and Remy kept teasing each other and stealing moments together. She liked the little gestures Remy made, like having her books shipped to the palace or ordering an extra piece of dessert from the kitchen to make sure she didn't go hungry, and she liked being the person Remy leaned on.

She also understood that if she really loved Remy—or liked them or was on the path to loving them, whatever they might call it—then she couldn't be a silent witness as the week unfolded. If Remy wasn't able to change their mother's mind, if they had to announce their engagement at the royal ball, Sam would regret it. She owed it to herself, to Remy, and to this thing developing between them to try to find a way to get them out of it. One that still honored Montamantien tradition.

When she met up with Remy and Pierre that afternoon, the two of them were beaming with delight about their expedition, which they recounted in a combination of English and French, with Remy interrupting to translate and Pierre speaking right over them. Watching them, Sam realized her jealousy the night before had been unfounded. There were two peas in a pod, but their rapport wasn't that of lovers. They acted like siblings.

When Pierre excused himself to the restroom, Remy leaned close to Sam and took her hand. They had a way of looking deeply into Sam's eyes that made her feel as if they were the only two people in the world.

"You're not mad, are you?" they asked quietly. "That I went with Pierre?"

"Mad? No! It was a fantastic idea. I'm glad you did it. I think you're right to try to make yourself more approachable to the public, even if it's the opposite of what you want to do and what feels safe."

"Do you wish you had gone with me instead of him?" Remy murmured, stroking her hand lazily with their thumb.

Sam leaned into the touch, their faces close. "Mm-hmm."

"You like watching me?"

"You know I do." She dared to lean forward and plant a lingering kiss.

"I see you two have apologized," Pierre said with his usual lack of tact as he came sauntering into the room.

"We didn't have to apologize for anything," Sam said. "We weren't fighting in the first place."

"Yes, you were."

Sam resented that Pierre didn't think it was rude to say whatever he thought. In the world Sam knew, people had enough decency not to speak the truth when it was going to make someone feel badly. Pierre subscribed to the belief that all thoughts should be uttered aloud, and if they hurt people, too bad. He had probably never had to deal with the consequences of hurting someone. There was probably someone who followed after him, offering money and cleaning up whatever messes he made.

"Mind your own business," Remy said to Pierre.

"I'm sorry. I thought it concerned me, since I am going to propose to you tomorrow."

"What?" Sam and Remy shouted it at the same moment.

"Tomorrow?" Remy repeated. "My mother said Friday!"

Pierre plopped onto Remy's bed and toed off his shoes. Sam wondered if his feet would smell bad. Rich people could probably take their shoes off all the time without foot odor. It was probably some cosmetic procedure they could all afford that no one in the real world knew about.

"I thought you were gay," Sam said.

"I am. Why? Are you interested in me?"

"No."

It came out harsher and faster than Sam had intended, but there was no question. She recognized that Pierre was picture-perfect: lean and tall with thick and well-styled brown hair, clear skin with a light tan, a face that looked sculpted with just enough stubble, and elegant yet simple fashion. If Sam were interested in cis men, she still wouldn't be attracted to Pierre. The model look didn't do it for her. Her attraction to someone was shaped by their personality and their chemistry with her. It's what made Remy, who on paper was wrong for her, so desirable.

Pierre merely shrugged. "Too bad. I have never done a threesome before."

"Please stop!" Remy demanded. "No one wants to hear that."

"Why did you say you are going to propose tomorrow?" Sam asked.

"Our parents have planned it that way."

"Since when?"

"Since I saw my father outside the queen's suite. They said we gained the support of the people during the visit to the civic center, so now would be a good time to ensure the proposal was well received."

"Our plan backfired," Remy said. "Clotilde must have realized what our goal was, and now she's turned it against us."

"How exactly did you respond to your father?" Sam asked.

Pierre shrugged again. "It is not as if I want to be married. You can ask Remy. I told her last night after your explo-see-un that I am in love with my boyfriend. I do not want him to see me ask Remy to marry me. Can you imagine what that might do to our relationship? We just started seeing each other."

Yes, I can imagine how your engagement to someone else would ruin a blossoming relationship. Look what it's doing to mine. But Sam was already conjuring up ways to foil the proposal.

"Them," she corrected Pierre automatically. "Where is your boyfriend?"

"He is not in Montamant. I told him I had to come home for this week and asked him to join me, but he could not. He is in Milan."

Sam chewed her bottom lip in thought. What if they put Pierre on a plane to Milan immediately? If they sent him away for a few days to visit his boyfriend, he would conveniently be gone when Clotilde imagined the public announcement happening, and it would have to be postponed. If the queen were really intent on the marriage, she'd simply wait for Pierre to come back, but they would have at least bought themselves some time. This plan had the added benefit of giving Sam and Remy time to themselves. But Pierre would have to agree to it. As much lip service as he gave to not wanting to marry Remy, he seemed nonchalant about the proposal.

"I'm not going to accept a proposal from you," Remy said.

"Oh, why not? I think it will be fun."

"Fun?" Sam scoffed.

"It won't be serious," Pierre assured her.

"Then why do it?" Sam thought she knew the answer. Pierre liked being in the limelight. He'd go through with a sham proposal to see his picture in the paper and his name splashed across the internet. He would probably get on one knee and expect Remy to wear a big, fat diamond ring, something Sam had never imagined for herself.

"If our parents insist on the announcement, we should make it as pleasant as possible," Pierre explained. "We tell everyone we are engaged, collect the presents, and in a week or two, we can tell the press we are canceling the wedding. At this point, it will be easier to do what our parents want, and we might get some good gifts from the experience."

"I thought you were worried about what your boyfriend would think," Remy reminded him. "What's the real reason he's not here with you?"

Pierre looked away slightly. "We are on a petite pause."

Sam could see through the depths of Pierre's guile. "You want to announce your engagement to someone else to force him back into your life. You hope he'll be jealous and come running back to you. That's a terrible thing to do to Remy and your boyfriend."

"Schemes like that are never successful, Pierre," Remy said with none of the venom that was in Sam's voice. If anything, they sounded tired.

Sam found it frustrating that Remy was so placid when the stakes were so high. How could they muster outrage about a moving cart but not about marriage?

"Do you want to do this?" she asked them suddenly. "Do you actually want to be with him? Or are you so go-with-the-flow that you won't say no?"

"Stop it," Remy said quietly. "It's not that simple."

"It should be."

"You don't understand what it means to carry this burden of being next in line. *Last* in line. I don't have the freedom to do things simply because I want to."

Sam could never fully understand, but she was beginning to see how little freedom royalty had after being in the palace for three days. "I'm starting to get it. But when it's just you and me—and him—you could make it a little clearer what you actually want. Otherwise, what am I doing here?"

Remy sighed, their eyes warm with compassion. "You're here because I need you."

"You *need* me. To help you. But you don't *want* me."

"She's very dramatic," Pierre said to Remy.

To Sam, Remy said, "Of course I want you. Why would you think I don't?"

Because you didn't follow me last night. You didn't come to my room.

She didn't say it because she didn't want to look pathetic in front of Pierre, and she wasn't sure she wanted to hear Remy's explanation for why they hadn't. In the pit of her stomach, something lurched, and she dreaded the idea that Remy hadn't come to her room because they had taken Pierre to theirs. It was a dumb thought, she knew, but she couldn't help feeling jealous and worried.

Remy watched her carefully and seemed to understand that Sam didn't feel free to speak. To Pierre, they asked, "Can you please excuse us?"

To his credit, he nodded without fuss. "I will see you both at dinner." He jumped down from the bed, put his shoes on, and left them alone.

Remy closed the distance to Sam. "I want you more than anything. I'm the one who's not sure how you feel."

"What do you mean?" Sam asked. "How could you doubt my feelings for you?"

"You've never…made a sexual move toward me."

"What do you call all the making out and groping?"

"Kissing, but not more than that."

"You're royalty."

"But you're American."

She wasn't sure what that meant. Did Remy think all Americans were sexual aggressors? "I'm still capable of being intimidated."

"You don't act intimidated. Madame Pouvoir told me you called me by my given name the entire time you talked to her. She was scandalized."

"Madame Pouvoir can shove it." Sam mustered the courage to say some of the things she'd been thinking through since her conversation with her mother. "I thought you should take the lead because I'm not sure if there are rules about it and because I don't know how comfortable you are with your own body or with someone else touching your body. What if I did something, and it was the wrong thing to do, and instead of bringing us closer, it backfired? Plus, you said you have all this sexual experience, but you never made a move other than kissing, so it seemed like…I don't know. It seemed like maybe you were hot and cold toward me because you weren't sure."

"It's not always easy for me sexually," they admitted. "You're right about that. Letting people become close to me is hard. When people know I'm royalty, sex with me is a great story they can tell other people, and when they realize I'm different, it becomes an accomplishment. A different story to tell their friends: the night they slept with the freak."

"You're intersex," Sam said, "not 'different,' not a 'freak.' It's who you are, the same way I'm built the way I am. I wish you valued yourself for how special you are. I wish you saw what I see when I look at you."

Remy licked their lips. "I am starting to see myself differently, and I believe you feel it very strongly, but not a lot of people regard me that way. Relationships are hard for that reason."

"Have you had many? Any?"

Remy shrugged. "I've dated people and thought the relationship was serious, but it seemed as if the other person never felt the same. You?"

Was this the time to confess the number of sexual partners they'd had and all the scars they carried from past relationships? If they weren't going to develop a relationship of their own, it wasn't any of Remy's business. But they had just confided something important to her, and she wanted to return the favor.

"I had two girlfriends in college. One of them broke my heart, and I broke the other's."

"What about the sex with them?"

Sam could feel herself blushing. "I don't want to talk about that."

"We must."

"Why?"

"Because I want to know if you would ever have sex with someone like me."

Sam looked at them. Now she was just angry. What were all the long looks and excuses to touch each other, not to mention their make-out sessions, about if not a lead-up to sex?

"I know your body may be different from other bodies I've had sex with," Sam said. "I also know there are plenty of things we can explore together. We can find out what each other likes and how our bodies respond to different things." Did Remy really think she hadn't considered what it meant that Remy was intersex? Or, worse, that she had considered it, knew about the range of bodies that were classified as intersex, and had been restraining herself from sex in case she didn't like what she found once they took off their clothes? "Do you think I'm so shallow that I would be bothered by your body?"

Remy looked contrite. "No, I don't. It is always my worry, but I don't think you are that type of person."

Maybe it was the opposite, then. Maybe Remy was afraid that when they finally had sex, Sam, too, would only be interested in uncovering the mysteries of their body.

"Are you worried that I would fetishize you? Is that what this is about? Is that how you've been treated in the past?"

They shrugged. "I suppose sometimes."

Sam was sad to think about the bad experiences Remy had had and all the joy they hadn't experienced that came from sharing sex with someone who treasured their body as more than an object of fascination. Although she had long moved past her first girlfriend, she looked back fondly on the way Sarah had taken time to cherish Sam's body as a thing of beauty. Sam had learned that it didn't matter if she had stretch marks on her hips or if she'd forgotten to shave. She was still beautiful to someone—and to herself. Celebrating the unique parts of her partner's body, rather than turning away from anything that didn't match some beauty magazine standard, was a lesson she'd taken into future experiences. She wanted to make her partners feel whole and sacred, and that made her feel loved back.

"I think bodies are all weird and different in their own ways, and if you care about someone, you appreciate their body, no matter what size or shape or color it is. Please don't use that as an excuse not to get close to me. It's an insult to me."

"Be kind. This isn't easy for me to talk about."

She was turning a conversation about Remy's discomfort into a conversation about herself. "I know it's not easy to talk about, but I'm glad we are. I appreciate that you're willing to share your feelings with me."

"Sex must be so easy for you."

"Why do you think that?"

"You seem to know so much more than I do about these things," Remy admitted. "When I listen to you talk about gender or sexuality, I see how little I know. I thought I was so…How do you say it? Cultured?"

"Remy, you know I feel completely ignorant around you, don't you? It's funny to hear you say you feel less cultured than me. Knowing you has helped me grow as a person, and for that I thank you."

"You're perfect."

Sam grinned. "That's what I've been trying to tell you about yourself."

They came together, reaching for each other's waists, their mouths finding each other. As they kissed, Sam felt the blood rush from her head as her legs turned to wet noodles. One look, one word, one kiss from Remy, and she was a melted puddle of goo. How could Remy ever think that she wasn't into them?

"You're the most complicated person I've ever met," Sam said, "but I'm so attracted to you. I just want to be with you. I was hoping you would sneak into my room last night after you were done talking to Pierre."

"You did?"

"Yes! I can't very well go to yours, can I? Until this afternoon, I didn't even know where it was! You were supposed to come after me, and we were supposed to have makeup sex."

"Fuuuucck." It was the first time Sam had heard Remy swear in English, and it was the most erotic word she'd ever heard. "I can't believe I missed my chance."

"Doesn't have to be your only chance."

They kissed again and let it go on for a while, tongues dancing together. They found their way to the bed, and Remy reclined against the pillows, pulling Sam on top of them. Sam felt the heat rising in her body as her limbs fit in between Remy's, and she wondered—hoped—that this would finally be the time they went beyond kissing.

But Remy stopped kissing and held her at arm's length. "I don't want to start something with you if our hearts are going to be broken over this engagement."

Sam gave herself a moment to let her breath slow. Every time they started to get close, something happened. It was helpful to hear that Remy was apprehensive about showing Sam their naked body and that it wasn't a matter of her not being good enough. Remy wanted her. They just didn't want to break her heart by announcing their engagement to someone else while sleeping with her.

Sam thought about the two extremes she had seen in the past week: the person who had tried to hide their royal identity in Boston and the person who had rushed onto a plane to save the fate of the nation. Royalty was Remy's biggest curse—maybe even more than the way others felt about their gender—but it was also their defining characteristic. Montamant would always be their first love, the thing they were committed to, around which all other relationships and commitments had to be organized.

Sam shifted her weight to her knees so she was straddling them and took a moment to enjoy being in a position of power. "You're worried about hurting me because something else might come before me. And it's not Pierre, not really. Whether you announce an engagement to him or not, your first love, your truest love, is Montamant."

From below her Remy looked sheepish. "I didn't know how deep that love was until we got here. I hope you understand."

She did, and the amount of respect she had for Remy grew with this new understanding. But that didn't mean she liked the idea of waiting alone in the palace for her royal lover to make time for her.

"Montamant will always be here," she said, dragging a finger down Remy's chest. "I understand that it needs you and that I might have to share you with it. But you know how easily you landed your role as heir apparent? Just remember, it's not that easy to land the role of my partner. If you play your cards right, maybe you can have me. When I decide you've earned it."

CHAPTER EIGHTEEN

When Sam told them she wasn't going to let them take things too far sexually yet, Remy had been incredibly turned on. It was the first time they'd seen her act so dominant, and they were both aroused by the reversal of power in their relationship. They were in a good place. They had been honest about their feelings, and their choice to go slowly gave them time to get to know each other better as they sorted out the mess Clotilde had made.

After Sam disappeared to go hunting in the archives again before dinner, though, Remy felt regret kicking in. They knew Sam meant it when she said bodies were all different and okay in their own way. That made Remy feel safe with her in a way they never really had before. Why hadn't they made love? The afternoon was free. Pierre had left them alone. Remy wanted it. Sam wanted it. It would have been the perfect moment. But Sam was going to make them work for it, and Remy spent a solid hour lying on their bed fantasizing about her in frustration.

Before dinner, Madame Pouvoir came to their room to tell them Clotilde had fallen over while bathing from the loss of equilibrium due to her inner ear infection, and while Remy was angrier at their mother than they'd ever been before, they also didn't want her to drown in her own shower. Dr. Lemal had ordered Clotilde to bed, tended to her wounds, and given her an IV of vitamins and electrolytes.

That meant Remy would have to preside over dinner, at which the usual inner circle, including Pierre and Andre, were invited that night along with members of Parliament. Pouvoir felt Remy needed briefing on the newest members and their political affiliations, as well as a few words of caution about the prime minister.

"He'll be glad to hear you're thinking about marrying nobility," she said. "He's expressed concern about your absence from the country."

She said something else after that, but Remy didn't hear. "Is that the biggest concern? Marrying noble blood? Does it even have to be a Montamantien?"

"Young Monsieur Lefaux will be a pleasing choice," Pouvoir said, "as a noble and a citizen, but Prime Minister Âne is a pragmatic man. He knows there aren't many nobles left in Montamant, and a marriage to a noble who is a suitable fit would be preferable to a marriage to any commoner. I think he would accept a foreigner if they were of noble birth."

One of the problems facing an eight-hundred-year-old nation that spent months of the year cut off from the surrounding French and Swiss villages was that there was a limited pool of people with whom anyone, nobility or not, could marry and procreate. The civic center kept careful records of all marriages and births, and the ordinary person had to have theirs triple-checked before being allowed to marry. It would not have done the nation well to have people marry within their family tree. Despite its small size and limited resources, Montamant had always had a very welcoming attitude toward foreigners for that reason. They presented the opportunity to infuse the nation's genetic pool with new material. The Vallorcins proudly traced their roots to the nation's founding, but historically, it hadn't been uncommon for them to marry among the French nobility.

Sam wasn't of noble birth, though. There was no getting around it. Even if a foreigner was welcome at the palace, there was still the problem that she was a commoner.

"Is there someone in particular Your Royal Highness is thinking about?"

"No. Maybe. It doesn't matter."

"Because Americans don't have nobility?" Pouvoir asked sagely.

"Yes. Not that we're considering marriage. We haven't even…" Remy didn't want to discuss their sex life with Pouvoir. "We haven't been on a proper date yet."

Marie-Jeanne held up another brightly colored belt to accompany the pair of Georges's pants Remy had chosen. They didn't fit very well, but she had hidden pins in seams to give them the illusion of being tailored to Remy's body.

"You look nice this evening," Pouvoir said. "The clothing you have chosen is working quite nicely on you."

Remy turned to her, feeling proud of their combination of casual suits with lively colors and surprised she wasn't angry they'd forgone dresses and skirts. "Thank you, Pouvoir. That's one of the nicest things you've said to me."

She cut down any positivity by adding, "It's a good thing your mother is in bed and won't see you dressed that way."

Internally, Remy groaned. One gain at the palace was always swiftly followed by a loss. They didn't think Clotilde and Pouvoir would ever understand who they were. To them, Remy would always be their strange little girl.

Their briefing over, Pouvoir folded her black binder and tucked it against her chest. "Your Royal Highness—Remy—I hope you know that I have always supported you. I know you haven't had it easy, but, for what it's worth, I am proud of you."

She exited swiftly, leaving Remy to share a surprised look with Marie-Jeanne.

❖

As she strode to the kitchen to check on the chef's progress, Pouvoir replayed her last words to Remy in her mind. She was proud of the princess, even when she had done foolish things, because she had always owned up to her foolishness and tried to make things right. When they needed Remy to come home, she had come immediately. The stunt at the civic center to appeal to the public had been a stroke of genius that showed the lengths Remy was willing to go and how well she understood her duty.

Duty, Pouvoir regretted, that meant Remy would likely have to marry someone she didn't love. Pouvoir hadn't known Queen Clotilde before she'd met King Georges, but it had been clear in the early years of their marriage that they were in love. Her Majesty had been lucky on that front. She'd found a man of noble birth, a Montamantien, who had fallen in love with her and had been a wonderful king consort. It was a shame Remy wouldn't get the same, especially if she preferred to date women over men, but if she had to marry nobility, a childhood friend like the younger Monsieur Lefaux was better than a stranger.

Pouvoir sighed. It was evident the princess's feelings for Mademoiselle Hyde were growing more serious. And Mademoiselle Hyde, who lacked in decorum, had made her feelings for the princess transparent with every word she spoke and step she took. If only

Mademoiselle Hyde... It was not her place to speculate. To do so would be to disregard the code of discretion her job required. If she were the type of person to engage in such contemplation, however, she would wonder whether Princess Remy and Mademoiselle Hyde had yet professed their feelings for each other. She hoped that Samantha Hyde was the kind of person who could see that beneath the princess's hard exterior was someone physically and emotionally vulnerable and would treat her accordingly.

Although Remy was not her child, Pouvoir had raised her, and having no children of her own, she felt protective of Remy and her nephew, Gilles, in the way she imagined mothers to feel. She wanted what was best for them. Perhaps it was time to acknowledge that what the palace thought was best for Remy was at odds with what Remy believed was best for herself. Unfortunately, the palace always won, by necessity. It was perhaps time to find justification for terminating the princess's love affair.

On the way to the kitchen, she used her phone to summon Monsieur Lapin and took a detour to the security office. She entered the access code to the door on the panel next to it, and the door unlocked, admitting her into a dark room with the footage from a dozen security cameras on a block of monitors behind a desk.

"Madame!" The guard, Jean-Michel, leapt to his feet. As the chief of staff, she was technically everyone's boss, though it was equally his duty to investigate her if she were ever suspected of a security violation.

"You can relax, Jean-Michel. I have not come here to check in on you, and I know there is very little time until the members of Parliament begin arriving."

Once that happened, he would have to coordinate with the front gate staff and any personal security the ministers had brought to ensure seamless and safe entry into the palace. And to ensure the exclusion of anyone or anything unwanted.

"How may I assist you, Madame?"

"Let's wait until Lapin arrives," she said, and it was only a brief moment before the door opened and her deputy entered. They greeted one another. "Mademoiselle Hyde. Have we received the rest of the results from her background check yet?"

Lapin had personally requested it through the security office as part of his regular duties. Lapin reported that they had pulled her credit report, which was terrible; her criminal background report, which was thankfully nonexistent; and a profile of her parents and sister, which had yielded plenty of biographical details but little by way of scandal or threat.

Jean-Michel reached for a file that was still sitting on his desk. "The original criminal check is right here. Her social media usage seems on par with young women of her age. She is outspoken about her modern—and, may I say, bizarre—attitudes about gender, but otherwise nothing inflammatory or damaging to the royal family."

"Any other observations about her in her time here?"

"She made a telephone call to her mother in the United States," Lapin reported. "I gave her privacy for the call."

"Jean-Michel?"

"We are not in the business of listening to personal phone calls," he said, "but, on your request, we have been keeping close watch on her. Her phone call contained nothing worrisome, except…"

"Except what?" she asked with some alarm.

Jean-Michel looked between her and Lapin. He seemed embarrassed. She pressed him to respond, and he finally said, "Except she said she was falling in love with Princess Remy."

In keeping with their training, neither Pouvoir nor Lapin showed any external response to this news. Internally, however, Pouvoir heaved a great sigh. It was settled, then. They were in love. Remy might follow through on her duty to marry Monsieur Lefaux and engage in an extramarital affair with Samantha Hyde. If discovered by the press or public, it would be as damaging to the palace as simply allowing Remy not to announce an engagement at all. Or Remy and Samantha might walk away from each other, heartbroken, and they'd be left with a princess in emotional turmoil. Neither possibility was ideal.

If they could find something that would tarnish Mademoiselle Hyde's reputation, they could alert the princess. They could help her fall out of love.

"I appreciate the work you have both done," Pouvoir said, and she meant it. With such little time, her team had done a superb job ensuring a guest was suitably vetted without causing any delay to her entrance within palace grounds. "Now I am hoping you can dig more deeply."

"How deep?" Lapin asked.

"Absolutely anything we can find. Read her graduate school thesis. Find her social media from ten years ago. Expand your search to her family as well. Let's find everything about the Hyde family of Indiana that we can."

Lapin made a face. This was beyond his regular job description,

Pouvoir knew, but he also had access to information that would make the task much easier than it would be for someone else at the palace. But it was an unusual request.

"Is there something in particular you're looking for?" he asked.

"Yes, but I can't tell you unless you find it."

Dinner that evening was far more elaborate than the preceding night. Instead of one long banquet table, the dining room had been fitted with ten round tables with place cards instructing guests where to sit. On the center of each table was an arrangement of small yellow and purple flowers, which Sam would later learn were the yellow pasque and pansy flowers that blossomed in the mountains this time of year. The room felt soft and warm, where the night before it had felt blue and gray and cold. It was the candles, she noted. In addition to dimming the lights, the staff had placed white pillar candles across the fireplace mantle, and votives decorated every table. Facing the windows was one rectangular table, where the queen and the prime minister were supposed to sit in a show of united governance. In addition to the floral centerpiece, the head table had a candelabra with long tapers.

As a non-citizen, Sam was relegated to a table at the back of the room with a few of the least important political figures. That was fine with her. She didn't want to be in the spotlight, and although their table wasn't close to the head table, they had a good view of it. She could watch Remy without attracting attention.

The hitch was that everyone at her table expected her to speak French. She knew *bonjour*, of course, and *merci*, and she remembered a few words she'd picked up from the dictionary in the archives. But how to put words together to make a sentence was beyond her, and she wasn't sure which had the potential to be more insulting to Montamantiens: not speaking French at all or butchering their language.

A pleasantly plump woman who looked fiftyish sat beside Sam. She introduced herself as Madame Bone-cur, a name Sam repeated several times with correction before the woman said, "You may please call me Delphine." She told Sam she was delighted to have her at their table because she was a translator and always needed to practice her English with native speakers, who were not frequent visitors to Montamant. Sam wasn't sure if Delphine's kindness was authentic to her personality or stemmed from pity for Sam, but she readily accepted it.

Delphine introduced Sam to her husband, Paul, who was seated on her left. His English was much less proficient, so Delphine translated that he was pleased to meet Sam and was the official minister of health, which meant his job was to see to the overall health of the populace and supervise the small medical clinic in town. Montamant, Sam learned, didn't have a hospital with surgery or an emergency room, so part of Paul's job was to teach the clinic staff urgent care procedures and triage, as well as ensure preventive health for everyone. In the event that a trauma happened, the patient had to be rushed to a hospital outside Chamonix. Sam wasn't sure how far that was, since Delphine gave the distance in kilometers, but she imagined that the winter snow made the travel long and grueling. She hoped Paul and the urgent care staff were very good at their jobs, for the sake of Montamant.

Over a heavy dish of potatoes and cheese her new friends said was called *la tartiflette*, they talked a little about a new health initiative Paul had launched to combat the growing obesity epidemic, which had hit perfect little Montamant the same way it had the United States and the rest of the world. There was irony in discussing fitness and health while chowing down on potatoes and cheese, but Delphine explained that the food was a regional specialty and a point of pride with the many local cheesemakers. It was interesting to learn about life for the ordinary citizen outside the palace, and Sam was pleased to hear that Queen Clotilde had given her blessing for Paul to create a series of fun exercise classes for children and adults at the civic center with financial support from the royal coffers. Maybe, she thought as the never-ending supply of wine began to have an effect, Remy's next public appearance could be a community yoga class.

"Fitness must be fun," Paul explained in halting English. "The body is…natural. We thought in the past that…" He turned to his wife and said a string of sentences in French.

"He says in the past doctors thought thin was good and fat was bad." Delphine pinched her own middle. "I would be bad!" She gave a delighted chuckle, which Paul shared. "Now, he says, we must accept the body is natural as it comes. Some are fat, some are thin, but we must all eat healthy food and exercise, then it is okay."

Sam smiled. They clearly adored each other as they were, and Sam was heartened to hear Paul's thoughts on body positivity. Sam had never been overweight and couldn't fully fathom what life would be like if clothing lines didn't make her size and she felt constantly pressured to lose weight. Pretty awful, she expected. As someone who had been born with a thin body, genetically gifted to her from her equally thin parents, she had still experienced the pain of not having a body that conformed to social expectations. She had had doctors assume she was anorexic and insist she gain weight without bothering to ask what her diet and exercise regimens were. She'd been taunted in middle school when the other girls began wearing bras and her breasts hadn't yet developed. How refreshing it would have been to have a doctor tell her she was just as she was supposed to be.

If only Remy could experience the same.

The conversation turned to Sam, and without being intrusive, they asked her what she was doing in Montamant. When she said she was a friend of Remy's from school, and remembered to call them "Princess Remy," Delphine was visibly awed. When they asked her what she studied, Sam hesitated. Should she say she studied gender and sexuality, or would that simply call attention to Remy's transformation? They seemed like open-minded people, but she didn't want to sour her first positive encounter with Montamantiens by hearing that they were homophobic or transphobic. She opted to tell a partial version of the truth.

"I'm doing historical research," she explained. "The royal family has given me access to their family papers."

Delphine made a squeal of delight. "Of course, you know about Queen Flore?"

Sam nodded with a smile. "She sounds amazing."

"In my family it is tradition to make a book—how do you say it?—with pictures and newspaper articles about each king or queen."

"A scrapbook?"

"Yes."

"Do you have one for Queen Clotilde?"

"Of course! My mother had one for her father, and I have one for her."

She didn't mention any children, and Sam wondered if there was a Petite Delphine to carry on the tradition by making a scrapbook about Remy. The hobby sounded sweet, though Sam wasn't sure what to do with the information.

For now, she turned her attention to the head table, where Remy was sipping a glass of white wine with a pout on their face while the prime minister was looking in every direction except Remy's.

"Do you know the prime minister well?" Sam asked her new friends.

"Monsieur Âne?" Delphine looked over her shoulder toward the head table. "Paul and Jacques were at school together."

"Can I ask you about him? Do you know how he feels about the royal family?"

Delphine's face clouded. "Officially, his job is to do the laws of the queen."

"But unofficially?" Sam wasn't sure if Delphine would reveal anything useful, especially not if the prime minister was a family friend.

She leaned closer and dropped her voice. "There are rumors he prefers democracy." Delphine made the sign of the cross. "Can you imagine?"

She gasped as if they were talking about inviting Satan to dinner. For someone whose family legacy was making royal scrapbooks, it was probably the equivalent. They struggled through the conversation due to language barriers, but by the time Sam spooned up the last puddle of sauce that was drizzled over the blueberry tart they had for dessert, she had a much better understanding of Montamantien politics. Despite its abiding Catholicism, Montamant as a whole was fairly progressive in its social values. The prime minister, however, had been elected by a conservative segment of the population which had previously tried to block a marriage equality law. Âne hadn't made any public speeches against the monarchy, Delphine said, and Sam remembered that Remy had said such speech was illegal anyway. But there were rumors he believed the monarchy had outlived its usefulness in the twenty-first century.

"What about you?" Sam tried to sound curious but not probing, as if it were an idle thought and not a calculated search for an ally. "How do you and Paul feel about Remy's reemergence? What do you think of their appearance?"

After a moment of careful thought, Delphine gave Sam the good news. "We feel that Princess Remy is the heir to the throne, so we must support her in all cases."

"Delphine," Sam said, leaning back in her chair with her glass of wine, "I could kiss you."

CHAPTER NINETEEN

The next morning, Remy and Clotilde were invited to Parliament. When Pouvoir burst into Remy's bedroom before they had awakened to tell them the news, Remy understood that "invited" was a polite way of saying "summoned." Of course, the prime minister had no actual authority to summon the royal family anywhere, but the urgency of the request indicated that Remy would be wise not to ignore it. They raced through a shower and had a few bites of the croissant that had been brought to their suite while they were getting dressed.

Clotilde had slept through Madame Pouvoir's three attempts to wake her. When Pouvoir reported this to Remy as they laced up their shoes, Remy resigned themselves to the fact that Clotilde would not be joining them for this morning's mission. They told Pouvoir to let the queen sleep. In the right state of mind, Clotilde would have been an asset at any meeting with the prime minister. She didn't have a lot of respect for Jacques Âne, but she was adept at charming people to get what she wanted. In her present state, coughing phlegm into mountains of tissues and asking for everything to be repeated because she still couldn't hear out of one ear, she could do more harm than good.

Besides, Remy had Pouvoir, who knew everything Clotilde did about current politics. For good measure, they asked Sam and Pierre along as well, the former for her outside perspective and emotional support, the latter for providing some of the cunning that Clotilde wasn't present to offer.

Looking barely awake, Gilles drove them down the mountain to the town square and parked in front of the modest building that served as Parliament. On the outside, it was hardly noticeable. Inside was a different story. Remy remembered entering the building a few times as a child, but they had forgotten how stunning it was. The marble floors and dark wood beams lining the ceiling gave it elegance. One of the guards led them to a back corridor, away from the members' individual offices and the main entrance to the floor.

"You don't mind that Pierre is here, do you?" Remy murmured to Sam as the entourage followed the guard. They held Sam's hand while they were out of the public eye.

"Not at all," Sam said. "He knows a lot more about this stuff than I do, and he did an awesome job at the civic center yesterday."

"I don't understand why we were invited here, since they came to us yesterday. And so early in the morning, too. They don't usually convene until after breakfast."

"Did the prime minister say anything about it at dinner last night?"

Dinner had been painful and long. The prime minister's behavior was cold and rude. He hadn't even attempted to make any of the usual, empty conversations about the weather or sports people usually had at these state dinners. Instead, Âne had acted insulted by the substitution of Remy for Clotilde and had refused to acknowledge Remy's presence.

"He barely said two words to me."

Madame Pouvoir, who had been keeping a respectful distance, interjected. "This cannot be good, Your Royal Highness. You need to be prepared. There aren't any octocentennial events scheduled today at Parliament, so Monsieur Âne must be up to something."

"Stay calm, no matter what," Pierre said. "You will sit facing everyone, so it is imperative that your face remain neutral."

"He's right," Sam agreed. "The more easygoing you seem, the better. If the prime minister wants you to be rankled, but you stay totally calm, you'll make him look like an ass."

They reached the double doors that led to the chamber floor, each flanked by a guard in a suit of Montamantien blue. For ceremonial purposes, they each held a Lucerne hammer that stood from the stone floor to just above their heads. They were intimidating to look at, but in Remy's lifetime there had never been any violence at Parliament. There had never even been a situation in which two people spoke at the same time.

This would be the first time they sat at Parliament, and the prospect, especially when it was unscheduled, was nerve-wracking. They took a deep breath in as Sam squeezed their hand and Pierre fussed with their clothing. Then they nodded to the guards, who opened the doors and announced their presence.

The chamber floor featured seats in rows with narrow tables in front of them, much like the lecture halls at older universities. The seats faced the front of the room, where a podium stood next to the prime minister's chair. To the left of that was a dais, upon which sat the throne. It was a giant chair in white velvet with gold leaf covering the wooden legs and arms, and it was usually only occupied once a year for the prime minister's briefing to the queen on the state of the nation. Today, with Clotilde absent, a smaller but still ornately decorated chair had been placed beside it. Traditionally, it served as the seat for the consort, the husband or wife of the reigning monarch, but it was in this chair that Remy would sit as the heir apparent filling in for their mother.

The entire room stood when Remy was announced, and in unison, they bowed their heads until Remy had climbed the dais, gracefully they hoped, and taken a seat. Once they were settled, the prime minister approached the podium. He summoned the chamber to order, banging a wooden gavel on the edge of the podium twice. He announced the first item of business would come directly from him.

"For eight hundred years, the House of Vallorcin has overseen the daily lives of the people of Montamant," he began. "For eight hundred years, we have looked toward their family to maintain our traditions and way of life. But times change, and people change. We can no longer deny that the royal family remains out of touch with the realities of life for the average citizen. Last night's dinner was a reminder of how distant the family has become, philosophically and geographically."

Remy clenched their fists on the arms of their throne. The dinner menu the preceding night had been carefully arranged to represent the best of Montamantien cuisine and had been prepared using only locally sourced ingredients. The dishes had been exquisite, but that was because the royal chef was a master at his trade, not because the palace had tried to show off and make everyone else feel lowly.

As for Remy's geographic distancing, that had been beyond their control. Clotilde had sent them away, but that wasn't because she thought Montamant wasn't good enough for them. On the contrary, she loved Montamant so much that she didn't want her aberration of a child to taint her relationship with it.

When they were younger, Remy had hated being so far from

home. They understood that Clotilde was embarrassed by them, and they felt ashamed of themselves as a result, but they still missed her company and the familiarity of life at the palace. By the time they finished university, they had come to understand that Clotilde was the one who should be ashamed for treating her own child so badly. It had become easier to stay away than to return and face her and the judgment of people who had known them as a child.

But Remy's long-term absence wasn't a sign the Vallorcins were uninterested in Montamant. It was a sign of how much they cared about it. If Clotilde and Georges had had a different child, that child would have grown up in the public eye.

Remy wondered what Âne's goal was. Was he about to rebuke the royal family? Would he really do that in the middle of the nation's biggest celebration ever, a celebration that united the history of the monarchy with the history of the nation itself? Surely, he would have given Remy and Clotilde the courtesy of warning them in advance, wouldn't he?

"The Vallorcin family is essential to Montamant," Âne continued to Remy's relief. "Montamant is Vallorcin, and the Vallorcins are Montamant. We need to ensure the stability of that relationship for posterity. We need to ensure that the reigning sovereign and heir are truly Vallorcin and, by extension, truly Montamantien."

Remy glanced up to the gallery to see if Pierre and Pouvoir could make sense of the circular language. Pierre shrugged. Pouvoir was frowning. Remy next caught Sam's eye, and she gave them a wink and smile of encouragement. They could feel their own cheeks about to burst into smile in return but willed themselves to look serious.

"Therefore, I am introducing today the Legitimate Inheritance Bill, which will ensure a proper and smooth line of succession for the throne."

"We already have one," Remy muttered.

But Âne wasn't finished. "By requiring all in the line of succession to certify medically their legitimacy as either male heir or female heir."

On the surface, the words sounded meaningless, but the emphasis Âne put on the words "either" and "or" unmasked his true meaning. Remy understood why the prime minister had looked so uncomfortable the night before. It wasn't because they didn't know each other well or because Âne was resentful the palace had substituted Remy for Clotilde at such an important dinner. The prime minister didn't know what to do with someone who looked like Remy, and now, to settle his confusion, he was proposing legislation that a doctor would have to determine if Remy was a boy or a girl.

If Remy was found to be intersex, they would be exposed to the entire nation. The shock and disgust of the people would play directly into Clotilde's belief that Remy should have stayed out of sight, and Remy would have to go through another round of humiliation and rejection, this time publicly. The idea of it made Remy's palms begin to sweat and their stomach churn.

Additionally, if they were intersex, they could no longer be Clotilde's heir. As the last Vallorcin, if Remy were delegitimated, they'd be back to where they were when Clotilde couldn't read the proclamation of sovereignty. They'd be in danger of letting the prime minister declare the end of the House of Vallorcin, the end of the monarchy. For all his lip service to tradition and the Vallorcin family, Âne was proposing the end of the Montamantien way of life.

The chamber erupted. Men who never fidgeted during a Parliament meeting broke out into conversation with the people sitting next to them. Some rose to their feet and cheered. Others rose to their feet and banged fists on the table, shouting their protests. In the galley, Sam grabbed Pierre's arm in confusion. She couldn't understand what had been said and why everyone was reacting so strongly. Pierre looked shocked. On the floor, Monsieur Âne turned around to face Remy, smiled with cruel satisfaction, and returned to his seat.

In that moment, Remy understood what dire circumstances they were now in. There was no physical exam Remy could pass, and somehow Âne knew it. If his bill was approved by Parliament, and it seemed like it might as the cheering and shouting grew, then Remy would lose their claim to the throne. And face the terror of having the truth about their body become public.

❖

Remy spat a curse in French as they paced the floor in front of the queen's bed, wearing tracks in the carpet.

In English, Pierre reminded them, "Sam cannot understand you, and your anger does not help the situation."

"I agree with my daughter," the queen said.

"Child." Sam didn't think the queen was listening, but her label for Remy bore correction all the same. "What did you say?" she asked Remy.

"I called him the son of a cheesemaker!"

"That may be," Madame Pouvoir said, "but he may have enough support to get the bill passed. And quickly."

"Then we have to act quickly in return," Queen Clotilde said.

Remy flopped backward on their mother's bed and covered their eyes with their forearm. "It's easy for you to say 'we,' but this is really about me."

"If the Vallorcin line ends with Remy, surely there's a distant cousin or someone who would assume the throne?" Sam asked. "Would it be Monsieur Âne's family? Is that what this is about?"

"No, he really is the son of a cheesemaker," Pierre explained. "He is a commoner. I don't think he wants to move the line of succession, but you are beginning to think like a royalist now."

Sure, Sam thought with a frown, she was beginning to understand royal machinations, now that they were all hurtful to Remy.

"Perhaps he thinks you will surrender your title to avoid the medical examination," Pierre suggested.

"I'm not going to surrender my title! I'm the heir apparent!"

Sam could understand their anger and concern at the idea of stepping down from a role they'd spent their life preparing for, especially without anyone to take their place, but the alternative wasn't much better. "Then you'll submit to a medical exam? You're okay with that?"

"I cannot," Remy said with the same level of anger. "I won't do it. It's a disgraceful idea, and it wouldn't serve a purpose because I would not pass the examination."

"Then there is nothing we can do," Pierre said. "He wins either way."

"He must think he has enough support for this dreadful bill to pass," Queen Clotilde decided, "or he would never have proposed such a preposterous idea." She looked at Remy for a moment. "I'm sure he doesn't like you, especially when you look like that, but I'm not convinced this is about you."

"What do you think it's about?" Remy asked, one eyebrow raised in hope.

"Me," Clotilde said. "We haven't gotten along since he took office, and he must think he has enough support to take control of the government for himself. It's why he was angry Remy was here for the reading of the proclamation, and it's why he wants to delegitimate the Vallorcin line. With us out of the picture, he gets to form a provisional government, and he must know he has enough support to establish himself as the provisional head."

"This isn't an inheritance bill," Sam said. "It's a coup."

Pouvoir nodded in agreement. "That's why he said Montamant and Vallorcin were synonymous. He wanted everyone to think there can't possibly be another royal family, so if Remy is delegitimated, then the clear solution is no more monarchy."

The door to the queen's bedroom opened, and Pierre's dad stormed in. He screamed at the queen, shocking Sam, but the queen was unruffled. She waved a hand dismissively at him and said something back in French.

"What are they saying?" Sam asked Remy.

"Andre says Pierre and I cannot get married now. He says this is the final straw and the plan is over now."

"Yes," Andre agreed in English. "It is out of the question."

"Papa—"

"What do you mean 'out of the question'?" Queen Clotilde interrupted. "Your son would be lucky to marry into this family!"

"Mother," Remy began, but despite lying in bed with a stuffy nose, the queen wielded her royal power to silence them with one raised finger.

"Everyone out!" As the group turned to leave her bedroom, she added, "Except you, Andre."

Pierre's dad was stoic as they left him behind. Once they were in the corridor, Madame Pouvoir closed the double doors to the bedroom for privacy.

"I hope she doesn't kill him," Remy grumbled.

"She will try to convince him that marrying nobility is your best option if you are no longer royalty," Pierre said. "Maybe the new government will agree to recognize the Vallorcin family as nobility. If they do not, you can marry me, since Lefaux is still a noble family name."

"Haven't you watched a single documentary about the end of monarchies?" Sam said. "They don't end with people getting big houses and fancy titles. They end with people's heads getting cut off!"

"This is Montamant, not eighteenth-century France."

"Wait a minute," Remy said. "I remember something from the civic center's history display."

Before Remy could explain, however, Pierre continued his relentless and stupidly optimistic prattle. "My father will not allow anything bad to happen to Queen Clotilde. They will probably decide how to turn the engagement announcement into something positive, so our family does not get hurt from our association with you."

"As long as *you're* protected," Sam scoffed, disgusted by Pierre's self-interest at such a horrible time. "Look, your parents cooked up the engagement together. Maybe they can plan how to cost the prime minister the votes he needs, so the bill doesn't pass."

Madame Pouvoir opened her black binder. "I remind you we have more pressing work than standing in the corridor, speculating. Mademoiselle Hyde, you are due to complete the reading for your first graduate school seminar today."

"How did you know—"

Pouvoir ignored her and continued, "Monsieur Lefaux, I'm told you have received several phone calls from Milan, despite the palace having a private number and you possessing your own cell phone."

"Giovanni!" Pierre clapped his hands and beamed. He either didn't notice Madame Pouvoir's reproach, or he didn't care. He hurried off down the corridor, presumably to find a private spot to call his boyfriend.

"Your Royal Highness," Pouvoir continued, "we have much to discuss about the rest of the octocentennial events. Regardless of what happens with the prime minister, we must carry on with the celebration as scheduled unless we are otherwise notified by Her Majesty."

Sam put her hands on her hips. Sure, she had reading to do for school, but that wasn't due until Monday. Right now, Remy was facing some serious shit, and it didn't seem right that they would simply wait for the queen to figure out what to do. Why was it up to Queen Clotilde, anyway?

The door to her suite opened, and Andre tentatively poked his head out. His jacket was off and his shirt buttons were undone. "Eh, Pouvoir?"

Madame Pouvoir strode into the suite behind him and firmly shut the door behind her.

Remy and Sam looked at each other for a moment. Remy sighed and rubbed their fingers on the bridge of their nose, and Sam put a supportive hand on their shoulder. Remy leaned in for a full embrace, exhaling as if they'd been holding their breath for her touch.

"You don't have to wait here with me," they said quietly. "You have your reading to get done."

"I can read later. This is more important."

"Do you really mean that?"

"Of course." Sam was surprised they would even ask. School was important, yes, but Remy's life was on the line. "How are you feeling?"

"Angry. Scared. Tired," they said. "Very tired."

"Tired of fighting battles you shouldn't have to?"

Remy nodded. They leaned in for another long hug, and Sam could feel how much they needed it. But after a bit, the embrace wasn't about empathy but something more. They shifted their feet, finding ways to get closer and to feel each other's bodies more clearly. Sam put a hand on Remy's cheek and brought their lips together. It was Remy who deepened the kiss.

"Sam," Remy whispered, "why do you stay around?"

"I need this." Her answer surprised her. She hadn't realized that was the reason yet. She heard Remy's little moan of pleasure. Their fingers interlaced at their hips. Sam didn't think they could stand any closer to each other, but they pressed together, kissing, and Remy stumbled backward into the gold-trimmed wall.

Remy's hands framed Sam's face. Their eyes were serious and intent. "Sam, I think I'm falling—"

"Your Royal Highness, Her Majesty requests you!" Pouvoir called from down the hall.

Sam's heart stopped.

Remy's eyes squeezed shut, and she felt their body go limp beneath hers. They were clearly disappointed at the interruption, as she was.

She dared to think about what they had been about to say. *I think I'm falling*…in love? Were those the final words?

"Will you come with me, please?"

Sam took a second to share a warm smile with them. They wanted her at their side while they faced the queen. "Of course," she said, holding out her hand for them to take.

❖

They held hands all the way to the queen's suite. Clotilde was seated on her silk couch with Andre beside her. Dr. Lemal had arrived, but when? He must have come through the door in Clotilde's chambers that led to a back corridor, intended for use by inconspicuous servants and secret lovers. His presence could not mean anything good. He was seated on the sofa opposite the queen's, and Madame Pouvoir was standing behind them. All four were watching Remy expectantly.

Clotilde began, but Remy interrupted her.

"English, please, Mother."

"We have made a decision on how to proceed," she repeated for Sam's benefit.

Remy awaited further explanation, but after a silent moment, Madame Pouvoir said cryptically, "Our goal now is to ensure a smooth transition for you, Your Royal Highness."

Transition to what? Remy wanted to ask. But Pouvoir wouldn't say any more.

They suddenly understood what she was hinting at. It sent a shock wave through their body, and they resented that neither she nor the others had the courage to say something so awful aloud. They were going to turn Remy into a man. Or a woman. Something easily defined to pass the prime minister's disgusting medical certification.

Remy had the urge to flee the room, but they kept their feet glued to the floor. The only thing worse than being present for this conversation would be being absent and suffering the consequences of whatever the others decided without them.

"What are you talking about?" Sam demanded.

"We can't risk obliteration," Clotilde croaked. "Dr. Lemal is going to help make you into a woman."

They were talking about altering Remy's body. What the doctor in New York had said was usually done to people like Remy when they were children. Surgery. Mutilation.

"What the fuck?" Sam screamed.

Everyone else in the room was stunned to hear her language and rage. Remy expected it, but they did not expect her to lunge toward the sofas.

"Are you fucking kidding me?! This is your plan?! You're talking about your own child!"

In a flash, Andre and Dr. Lemal jumped between Sam and Clotilde. No one threatened the queen.

"Stand back, Mademoiselle!" Andre shouted.

"Call security!" Lemal commanded to Pouvoir.

"Don't touch me!" Sam jerked her body away from them.

She let Remy take her elbow, and they gently pulled her a few steps back. Her body was tense. She wanted to fight.

They were grateful for her anger, which they shared, along with a mix of dread and mortification. To be having this conversation in front of so many people—to be having it at all—was worse than embarrassing. It was unconscionable, yet twenty-five years of being Clotilde's child had taught them that nothing was beyond her consideration, no matter how morally reprehensible it might be.

At last, they were able to ask, "How?"

"There are some promising new procedures and a very skilled surgeon in Lausanne," Lemal explained. "I will accompany you there, and we will return in approximately seven weeks, depending on your progress. At that time, we expect you will be able to be examined by another physician and be understood as visibly female."

Remy had learned from the doctor in New York that it was theoretically possible to remove or add breasts, remove or recreate a penis, help undescended testicles descend, create a small vagina. Doctors could also remove a uterus, ovaries, or testes. The possibilities for surgery were many, but, as the specialist had explained, the risks were great, and many of the procedures were irreversible. It was unusual for one surgery to solve everything. Thanks to their experiences in New York, Remy knew now that Dr. Lemal was an idiot who didn't know what he was talking about. It was highly unlikely that one surgery and a few weeks of recovery time would be enough for Remy to pass the prime minister's physical examination.

"What procedures will you or the other surgeon be doing?" Sam demanded.

"We have determined that the simplest course of action is to focus solely on external indicators," Lemal said. "Enlargement of the breasts and reshaping of the genitals."

"No! Absolutely not!" Remy said. "You are not doing that to my body!"

Once the New York specialist had taken the time to explain how the different procedures worked, what their benefits might be, and what the possible consequences were, Remy knew surgery was not for them. The thought of undergoing surgery to change their body gave them cold sweats. They still didn't love the way they looked, but they had spent the last six months learning to become okay with it. In New York and Boston, they had been on a path toward self-love they had craved their entire life. This, now, would erase all of that.

"Your body is the body of the nation." Madame Pouvoir was quoting a line in the original charter to Montamant, a document that was historical but no longer legally binding in the wake of the formation of Parliament and the creation of a constitution. The abstract idea that the sovereign's body was symbolic of the nation as a whole remained, but certainly no one had ever used it as justification for coerced medical procedures.

"Then her body is also the body of the nation," Remy said, pointing to Clotilde. "I don't recall asking the public to vote on whether she should get a new nose!"

Pouvoir gasped at Remy's willingness to mention aloud something that was supposed to be a family secret. Dr. Lemal looked embarrassed. How pitiful, Remy thought, that they were scandalized by mention of Clotilde's cosmetic procedures to feel more beautiful but not by the idea of Remy's body being altered against their will.

Clotilde wasn't impressed with their attempt at shock. "I underwent the surgery without complaint to improve my appearance, and you will do the same."

"Mother, it might surprise you to learn that I have actually spoken to a doctor about my condition." Remy pointed to Lemal. "He doesn't know what he's talking about. He's not an expert in this area of medicine. In New York I visited a doctor who was, and I gathered enough information to determine I do not want surgery. It will be a long process. You cannot expect to send me to Switzerland for a few weeks and return magically changed."

"Okay," Clotilde said. "Then we'll send you there for as long as is necessary."

They looked to Sam for help making their point.

"It sounds dangerous and stupid and totally unnecessary to me," she said with her usual disregard for tact. "Unless it's something you want."

"I can't be gone for seven weeks," Remy said. "I'm in school. That's half the semester."

It was hardly the most important detail, but it bothered them that once more, Clotilde had found a way to intervene and ruin something important to Remy.

"Boylston University's policy is to refund ninety percent of your tuition if you withdraw for medical reasons in the first week of classes," Pouvoir recited. "We will ensure that proper documentation of your surgeries is provided to the university to secure a timely withdrawal. Of course, your housing fees will not be refunded."

She had already researched Boylston's refund policy. Dr. Lemal, who had not given Remy an examination in seven years, had already determined which procedures would be best to perform, despite the fact that the prime minister had only announced the bill a few hours earlier.

Remy began to wonder if the queen had been planning this for a long time. Maybe this, not the engagement to Pierre, was her real endgame, and being ill was the excuse she needed to get Remy home, where she could ensure their abduction and transfer to Lausanne.

It was a matter of protecting her reputation. She was no doubt deeply concerned at the thought of their family losing their hold on the monarchy, as was Remy. If Montamant entered an unknown form of government for the first time in eight hundred years, it would invoke panic and uncertainty among everyone, palace and public. But it was Clotilde's legacy at stake. She didn't want to be forever remembered as the queen who let Montamant slip from her grasp, the queen who first disappointed the country by only producing one child and no spare and next disappointed everyone when they found out that child was not a suitable heir.

This was infinitely worse than their plan to force Remy to marry Pierre. Which they would probably still expect once Remy returned from Switzerland as a certifiable woman with breasts.

In their mind, they saw a flash of a white hallway and white starchy sheets on a metal bedframe. They broke out into a cold sweat imagining the operating room and the *beep-beep-beep* of the heart rate monitor. They clenched their hand into a fist, and they wondered where they could channel the rage building up inside at the injustice of it all. They wanted to scream, to hit, to break things, to cry—all of it at once.

Somewhere, behind a thick veil of gauze, they heard Sam calling their name, but they couldn't answer. In their head, they counted *un-deux-trois*, but it didn't calm them.

Remy took one deep breath in, looking slowly around the room at their traitorous family and friends, and without a word to them, walked out.

CHAPTER TWENTY

T he way Remy had stormed out of the queen's chambers, Sam
thought they might want to be alone. Every impulse was telling her
to follow them, so she could make sure they were okay and talk through
the impossible situation they were facing with them. She lingered in
case it was rude to leave the queen's company without being dismissed,
and for a moment everyone was silent, stunned by Remy's departure.

Then Pierre's dad said something, and he and Madame Pouvoir
began arguing with each other in French. Pierre jumped in, and the queen
was listening intently to all of them. They made no effort to translate
for Sam's sake. Without Remy present, she was inconsequential.

"I'm going to check on Remy," she said for the sake of politeness.

She remembered learning in a guest lecture by an intersex professor
that intersex babies often underwent surgery, which some doctors
and parents considered to be corrective but which many advocates
considered unnecessary and cruel. She remembered hearing that later
in life some of those children regretted the choices that had been made
for their bodies without their consent. But she didn't know as much as
she wished she did. In her studies, she had spent a lot of time reading
about the history of gay and lesbian rights, and she'd taken courses on
queer feminist theory. All she had learned about intersex had been from
that one guest lecture, and she felt disappointed in herself for feeling so
smart when there was still so much she had to learn.

The door to Remy's suite was open, but she knocked on the frame
anyway. Remy was sitting on their bed, their head resting on their bent
knees.

"Do you want to be alone?" she asked. "Is it okay that I'm here?"

"You can come in. Only you."

Sam joined them on the bed, but they didn't look at each other or touch. When Remy didn't say anything, Sam didn't press. She was content to sit beside them and just let them process what had happened.

"I don't want to do it," Remy said at last.

"I know you don't."

"I don't see how I can say no."

Sam looked at them. Remy's jaw was clenched, but there were tears in their eyes.

"If I say yes, what happens to the person I am starting to become—the person who, for the first time in my life, I like? This is the first time I have ever felt like *me*." Remy huffed out a breath. "And if I say no, and the bill passes, then everyone learns I'm intersex, and I lose my place following Clotilde on the throne. Then what? Everything is lost. My privacy, the monarchy, everything."

"Not everything." Sam put an arm around Remy's shoulder. "Whatever happens, I'll still be here. We'll figure this out together."

Remy leaned against her. "How? You heard Pierre. We have two options, and whichever we choose, Âne wins."

Sam sat up as a thought occurred to her. "But that's it, Rem. That's what we have to do: find a third option."

"A third option?"

"Yes!" Sam felt a niggling of excitement. Maybe things weren't as hopeless as they'd seemed. "Your mother is reacting to the prime minister's bill, right? But the bill hasn't passed yet. If we can stop the bill, we can stop the surgery."

"How are we going to stop the bill?"

Sam couldn't argue with bloodlines and eight hundred years of tradition, but if the bill had been written specifically because Remy was nonbinary, maybe they could find a way to persuade the other members of Parliament that binary gender identity was not a prerequisite to good leadership. Then there was the prime minister himself. Clotilde believed the bill was just a power play on his part, so he could take control of the government without her.

"I think there are two fronts we have to wage our campaign on," Sam explained. "First, we have to convince the other members of Parliament to vote no."

"Monsieur Âne said this is a matter of tradition. Montamantiens value tradition more than you Americans. Think about what this week is celebrating…"

Remy kept talking, but Sam didn't hear what they were saying.

They had said the one word that was probably the most important of all: tradition. The prime minister had framed the bill around tradition and the long history of Vallorcin rule.

Sam remembered the hidden box she'd found and the confusing entries in the dictionary. She didn't think it was worth explaining until she was certain what it all meant, and she was eager to go to the archives. She jumped off the bed.

"Remy, I think I have an idea, but I need time to do more research."

Pierre came bursting into the room. "I heard the news!"

"Wait a minute," Remy said to Sam. "What is the second front?"

She looked at Remy and thought about the duty and obligation that drove so much of their life and Queen Clotilde's. But in the last few days, Remy had also demonstrated they were capable of leading, and leadership was about acting, not just reacting.

"Your mother," she said as she lingered in the doorway. "Everything she's done so far has been in reaction to someone else, and everything you've done has been in reaction to her. Don't let Âne and Queen Clotilde call the shots. Change the strategy."

"What strategy?" Pierre asked.

Sam didn't have an answer. Her mind was already in the basement with the hidden box. But she was certain Remy would figure it out. They looked less despondent now, and they nodded at her in understanding.

"Sam, you go to the archives. Pierre, you stay here and help me. We're going to think of a way to outsmart two very smart people."

It was good to see some of the fight coming back in them.

"Hey, Rem? What you were about to say earlier? Same."

Sam waited a moment for it to dawn on Remy what she meant, and they shared a secret smile.

"What are you talking about?" Pierre asked, and that only made Sam's smile grow.

She blew a kiss to them both and headed back to her own room, where she'd left the key to the archives.

Once in her room, she thought about the dictionary and the old documents. She needed a translator, and without a computer or working phone, she couldn't rely on the internet. Anyway, she needed someone who knew the language well enough to understand historic text. She rummaged around her suite until she found the scrap of paper on which Delphine had written her name and number after their pleasant dinner. Then she scouted the corridors until she found Marie-Francine.

"Do you have a phone?"

Marie-Francine didn't answer. She must have thought it was a trick question. She probably wasn't supposed to have a phone on her during the workday or inside the palace for security reasons.

"My phone can't dial Montamantien telephone numbers," Sam explained. "Could you help me make a call to someone in the country?"

"*Oui, Mademoiselle.*" Marie-Francine produced a sleek new iPhone from her pocket. Sam entered the ten digits Delphine had scribbled onto the scrap of paper. A moment later, the call connected. She introduced herself and asked Delphine if she could come to the palace once again.

"Will that be a problem with security?" Sam asked Marie-Francine.

"It is unusual for a guest to invite another guest here."

Sam nodded in understanding. "How do you feel about Their Royal Highness?"

"Princess Remy? It is an honor to serve."

"Yes, yes, of course." They didn't have time for all that. She needed to know how willing Marie-Francine was to stick her neck out to save Remy. "Do you want to see the end of the Vallorcin line? The end of the monarchy? Or are you willing to let Remy be…unconventional if it means carrying on an eight-hundred-year tradition? I need your help."

Marie-Francine bowed her head. "Anything for the family. I know Jean-Michel, in the security room. We can talk to him."

Sam nodded, and they finished setting up the urgent meeting with Delphine. Then Marie-Francine raced with Sam to the security office, where they explained the sudden visit. Because Delphine had already been vetted as a guest the night before, Jean-Michel told them it was only a matter of alerting the guards at the front gate to her arrival, and having someone at the palace door to escort her inside to find Sam.

"I'll be in the archives," she told him.

When she got to the room, she realized she didn't have the key on her, and she had to run across the courtyard and up the stairs to her bedroom to find it. On her way back down, she took the wide stairs two at a time, not caring the cleaning staff who were staring at her thought she lacked class. She dashed across the courtyard and back into the medieval wing of the palace, pushing on the heavy door as she twisted the skeleton key in the lock.

Inside the archives, she went immediately to the spot on the shelf that covered the hiding place. She shoved everything aside, jiggled the loose brick, and produced the box hidden in the wall.

She set the box on the table and searched for the Montamantien-English dictionary. She was just sitting down to look at her findings when Marie-Francine and Delphine arrived.

She jumped up to greet her new friend, who offered a kiss on each cheek as a hello. She introduced Delphine and Marie-Francine in case they hadn't already exchanged names.

"Thank you so much for coming so quickly!"

"You said it was urgent. Is the princess okay?"

Sam didn't know how they could defeat Prime Minister Âne and his insidious bill without others knowing Remy's truth. But Remy's body shouldn't have been the subject of public discussion, and it wasn't up to Sam to decide whom to tell what.

For the moment, she opted for history instead. She opened the box and pulled out what she thought was a birth certificate. "Can you translate this?" She pointed to a particular line after the numerals that must have indicated weight and length. "You see this word? I have been searching for it in the dictionary, and I can't find it."

Delphine carefully took the paper from her and studied it. "Ah, you wouldn't," she explained. "In English you would say 'male' or 'female,' and in French you would say '*masculin*' or '*féminin*.' Do you see the 'ot' on the end here? That comes from Montamantien, a dialect that has been dying for many years but was once the official language."

"What does it mean?" Sam asked.

"It is most unusual," Delphine said. "I am not sure I understand. You see, every noun and adjective in French has a gender, unlike in English. We add 'e' to the end of words to make them feminine, though sometimes you must add other letters. The male 'Bernard' becomes 'Bernadette,' and an adjective like '*vert*' meaning 'green' becomes '*verte*' if the noun it modifies is feminine. You must know the gender of every noun in order to use an adjective correctly. As for articles, masculine nouns use '*le*,' and feminine nouns use '*la*.'"

Some of this was basic grammar Sam could hazily remember from French class and had inferred from the past few days, but it was helpful to hear Delphine spell it all out so concretely.

"In Montamantien, however, in the past, we had a variance for words that had no gender or for which we did not know the gender. In that case, we added 'ot' to the end."

"Which adjective form do you use with words ending in 'ot'?" Sam asked. "How do you know if you should use '*le*' or '*la*'?"

"In contemporary practice, we use the masculine," Delphine explained. "It is one of the ways Montamantien is disappearing. Words of unknown gender have become masculine by default."

"What about in the past?" Sam asked.

"'*Li*.' It was borrowed from Italian, which had an influence on Montamantien, but our use of Italian grammar was…how do you say? Bastardized for our own purposes. The article G-L-I in Italian has a different use. In Montamantien, L-I was simply the word 'the' before a noun of unknown gender ending in 'ot.'" Delphine pointed to the birth certificate. "This person would have been known by their given name, their first name, but if you were to speak of them in the third person, you would say, '*li filiot*.'"

"So '*li filiot*' would mean 'the child' without any attached gender? Not boy or girl?"

"Yes." Delphine studied the paper with admiration. "I must tell you, this is remarkable. I have only ever heard of this structure to refer to a person when the speaker did not know the gender, not when the person did not have a gender." She pointed to the first line of the birth certificate, which asked for the first name. "There is no name? Only this written? I do not understand why this would be on a birth certificate."

Sam smiled at her. "I think, Delphine, that Montamant once had a royal family member who was neither male nor female, and I think someone tried to cover up their existence. But this birth certificate proves it."

Marie-Francine came forward. "But no!" She pulled the paper from Sam's hand, and Sam cringed at her careless handling of the paper. "The date of birth is 1763. That would be…" Marie-Francine thought for a moment. "A child of King Robert and Queen Louise de Chamonix."

"What do you know about them?" Sam asked. She turned to the shelf to pull the appropriate box from that period. "Who was their heir?"

"We called him Prince Emmanuel." Marie-Francine's voice betrayed her doubt that what she knew about the prince was correct. "He died before his father, so he never assumed the throne, and the line passed to his younger brother."

Like Hrodohaid. Sam wondered, with sinister dread, if Emmanuel had died from natural causes.

They looked into the box together, sifting for answers. Sam had seen the name Emmanuelle in the feminine on the family tree at some point, but she hadn't thought much about it because it was before she had found the birth certificate.

"Emmanuel married," Delphine said. "The wife, Germaine, was from Alsace, and she died…Marie-Francine, do you remember how she died? I cannot remember now. I haven't studied the lineage." She gave a bashful smile. "The family scrapbooks do not extend so far in history!"

"That's okay," Sam said.

They found several letters belonging to Emmanuel's parents, King Robert and Queen Louise, but none about or by Emmanuel. Sam let the others continue searching while she turned her attention back to the box and the tiny portrait. Whoever had painted Emmanuel had done an honest impression that didn't give away any clues to their real sex or gender, and the tiny size of the painting probably meant it had never been for public consumption anyway. She asked Marie-Francine to borrow her phone again and took a picture, which she then zoomed in. In the corner of the painting, too small to be seen by the naked eye, was a delicate signature. *Germain.*

"Was this the name of Emmanuel's wife?" she asked Delphine.

Delphine peered at the image on the phone screen. "That is Germain, without the 'e' to indicate feminine."

Still, Sam thought, given what they'd seen on the birth certificate and the occurrence of Emmanuel's name as Emmanuelle, it was too great a coincidence.

"Did Emmanuel live at the palace? Or abroad?"

"I don't know," Marie-Francine said. "I will look." She went to the shelf of books and skimmed the spines. Then she pulled one down. It was a history book with engravings and photographs of all the homes in which the extended members of the royal family had lived. After flipping for a moment, she showed Sam a photograph taken in the early twentieth century of a beautiful, but fairly small, old house. It was in Alsace, a province between France and Germany, far from the prying eyes of the Vallorcins. In small letters, the caption gave the title to the home.

Chez Hrodohaid.

Sam gasped. "We have it!"

"Have what?" Marie-Francine asked.

They had the research that Sam could take back to Boylston to show Dr. Grant that her dissertation was viable. It just needed patience and special access. They had information that would stop the axe over Remy's head from falling. But, most importantly, they had historical precedent to prove Monsieur Âne wrong.

"We have to get to Parliament," Sam told them. "Right now."

Chapter Twenty-One

R emy, look," Pierre said. "I know I'm sometimes…I'm not always the best at…I can act…But this is different. I wanted you to know that."

Nothing he had said was clear, yet somehow Remy understood. Pierre wanted them to know that, for once, he recognized how serious the situation was, and he felt badly about the things he had said about Remy's gender in the light of the situation Remy was now facing. Pierre wasn't good at apologizing. In fact, it was one of few times Remy could remember him even attempting to do it. While he was unable to say the words he meant, Remy knew from their lifelong friendship that Pierre didn't wish them any harm and would stand by them through this latest mess.

"Thank you, friend. In that case, help me to determine my next action."

"We need to talk to our parents again," Pierre said. "They made this decision in a split second and weren't thinking."

Remy climbed out of bed and put on their shoes. "Unfortunately, I don't think that's true. You didn't hear them. They had too many details already planned. I think Clotilde has been planning this for a long time. She was waiting for the best moment to tell me."

"She can't force you. What is she going to do? Have the bodyguards drag you? Will they drug you to put you on the train to Lausanne? I can't believe my father would play a role in anything like that."

"He was there." Remy wasn't sure what part Andre had played in crafting this heinous plan, other than pressuring Clotilde to do something before the Lefaux family lost its chance at upward mobility via royal marriage. "I don't know what good talking to them will do. They have already told us what will happen, voilà."

"Since when did either of us quit anything without a fight?"

He was right. They might have appeared to be lazy, spoiled brats, but they were both very good at achieving what they wanted. Remy wanted graduate school and New York, and they got it. They were not the type of person to give up without trying.

Remy thought about what Sam had said. They needed to show Clotilde that it was not up to her to make choices about their life anymore. They weren't going to be a passive child awaiting her instructions. They were in charge now.

They nodded at Pierre, and together they marched down the hall to Clotilde's suite. They didn't know what they would say, other than heated insistence that their parents were wrong and impassioned pleas to change their minds. At the very least, Remy would feel they had tried to do something.

They pounded on Clotilde's door with their fists and rattled the doorknob. It was locked. They looked at Pierre, puzzled. Ordinarily, their rooms were never locked, not even when they wanted privacy, because it would interfere with the servants' ability to do their jobs. A locked door, preventing them from returning for further discussion with Clotilde, was the final straw.

They resumed banging, and Pierre joined in. This time, they also resorted to kicking the door and shouting, which was something neither had ever been permitted to do in their delicate upbringing.

"Your Majesty, we must speak with you!"

"Mother, I know you're in there! You can't hide from me!"

After a moment, Marie-Claire, Clotilde's chambermaid, appeared in the hallway through one of the hidden doors. She offered Remy a curtsy. "Your Highness, Mademoiselle, please forgive me, but Her Majesty has asked for no interruptions at this time." She looked uncomfortable telling them, and since she was staff and Remy her superior, they could have just barreled past and entered the suite through the maid's door.

"Did she say when she would be available for an audience?"

Marie-Claire's eyes were trained firmly on the floor. "Only… when Monsieur Lefaux had left," she murmured.

Remy could see she was desperate to flee an awkward situation, and they didn't blame her. It was wrong of Clotilde to ask the staff to intercede with her own family. That was something they'd never done when Remy was little and Georges was still alive. If they had needed to talk to each other, they had found each other and spoke, and if they needed space from each other, they had said so. There had to be a good reason that Clotilde didn't want to be disturbed, beyond her general desire to avoid Remy.

They dismissed Marie-Claire out of pity and turned to Pierre. "Now what?"

"I have no idea. Yesterday, we were supposed to be getting married, and now you're getting your pieces cut off."

Remy cringed. "Don't say it that way."

"How should I say it?"

"I'm not the only one who is ruining their plans," Remy said. "Have you told your father about Giovanni?"

"Yes."

Possibly out of spite for the crude manner in which he spoke of the surgeries Remy was facing, they suggested, "Maybe Clotilde is giving Andre advice about what to do with you. Perhaps Andre wants to know how to convert you back to heterosexuality."

It was Pierre's turn to glare. "That's not funny, Remy."

"No," they acknowledged. "Nothing about this situation is funny." They adjusted their glasses and took a few seconds to contemplate. "We're not thinking enough like Clotilde. She doesn't beg people to change their minds. She calculates her risks and maneuvers in advance. She is always two steps ahead of everyone else. What would she do in my position?"

Pierre thought for a moment. "The prime minister wants a medical certification, yes? Presumably from the royal surgeon?"

"Dr. Lemal is loyal to Clotilde and will do whatever she tells him to."

"Will he lie about your body for her?"

"I don't think so. He seemed eager to take me to Lausanne, as if he wants to do it to please her."

"Why?"

Remy didn't know the answer. They had suspected Clotilde had once had an affair with the doctor, but they had no evidence. At any rate, she didn't express any sentiment toward him other than appreciation for his professional services. If there had been something between them, it was now one-sided.

Lemal wouldn't lie about Remy's body, that had been clear during their conversation in Clotilde's suite. Even if he were willing to, Jacques Âne would never accept his word because of his loyalty to the queen.

"What we need," they said, "is a different doctor. Someone respectable enough that Âne can't argue with their ruling, but someone who will be favorable toward me."

Montamant had two medical doctors in positions of power. There was Lemal, whose official duty was defined as "ensuring the health and longevity of the monarch," though taking care of the other members of the family also fell under his purview. But there was also the minister of health, whose job was to oversee the entire nation. The position required the credentials of a fully trained medical doctor or surgeon, though the role was largely administrative—supervising other medical practitioners, implementing nationwide programs for fitness and health, and tending to research studies on the population. Remy had only met the minister of health once, at the full cabinet dinner the night before, and they didn't remember his name. He wouldn't be difficult to track down, though there was no guarantee he'd agree to what Remy was asking.

"Pierre, what do you know about the minister of health?"

His eyes lit up. "Yes, excellent plan. His name is…" He rubbed a hand on his brow, and in that moment, Remy no longer saw the friend who gallivanted around the Mediterranean in an endless cycle of yacht parties. He had transformed into someone politically minded, bright, and capable. "Boncoeur. Dr. Boncoeur." He reached into his pocket and pulled out his phone. "Shall we find his number?"

"One minute. How do we know he will be sympathetic to me?"

They looked at each other. "Lapin," they said simultaneously, and they hustled off to find Madame Pouvoir's deputy.

He was the logical choice for an aide and confidant, since Pouvoir herself had been involved in the decision to pursue surgery. Lapin knew everyone of importance in the kingdom, in keeping with the requirements of his job, and had as many connections as Pouvoir did, but since he wasn't the one who handled business directly, he had a much gentler reputation. He also didn't have such a long history with Remy, since he'd only taken his post a few years earlier. Ordinarily, when it came to their secrets, Remy thought trust was earned over time. In this case, it was better to trust someone newer who didn't have the tangled past with Clotilde that Pouvoir did.

Lapin was in his office, working on his palace-issued laptop. He rose to his feet when Remy and Pierre walked in and offered a crisp bow. Feeling that time was of the essence, Remy opted not to sit or make pleasantries and asked directly for the minister of health's contact information. They explained that they wanted Dr. Boncoeur to perform a physical examination as soon as possible.

"That is out of the bounds of protocol, Your Highness." Lapin's face was quizzical. "Is there some larger medical concern that needs tending? Dr. Lemal can be at the palace in only five minutes."

"He's probably still in the palace," Remy said. "I assume your response means Pouvoir hasn't notified you of the queen's recent decision regarding me?"

Now Lapin appeared concerned that he had missed an important aspect of his duty. "Should I confer with her?"

"Absolutely not. I'm happy to hear she hasn't spoken to you." Remy sat in the wooden chair in front of Lapin's desk. They felt the tension momentarily ease from their body. Pouvoir wouldn't notify everyone, of course, since the surgery was supposed to be a secret, but if she hadn't taken Lapin into her confidence yet, then there was a chance the plans for travel to Lausanne had not yet been arranged.

Pierre pushed in front of Remy and laid his palms flat on Lapin's desktop. "We need to know Dr. Boncoeur's political leanings, specifically with regard to gender and sexuality issues. We don't have time for careful language."

Lapin studied Remy's face for a moment, gauging his response in light of Pierre's demands. Remy met his gaze and held steady, showing that they would not back down. Lapin cleared his throat and opened his bottom desk drawer. He produced a slim file folder and handed it to Remy.

"This is everything we know about the doctor."

Remy took the file and got to their feet.

"It's not my place to ask, Your Highness, but is this concerning the prime minister's proposed new law?"

They paused in the doorway, turning over their shoulder to look back at Monsieur Lapin. He couldn't have been more than forty years old, relatively new, compared to others whose families had worked in the palace for generations. Remy wondered what the depth of Lapin's knowledge about contemporary Montamantien politics was. Did he realize the things that were said and done, the things regular people knew, were the mere surface?

If he did know there was more to Montamant, which side was he on?

"Do you happen to know anything about the prime minister that we might not?"

Lapin cleared his throat again. He bent down to the bottom desk drawer and returned with another file folder. He placed it squarely on the desk, resting his hands protectively over it.

"Madame Pouvoir doesn't know about this."

Pierre eagerly sat in the chair Remy had occupied, leaning forward to hear better. "And?"

Lapin looked at Remy, who nodded encouragingly. "We're all friends here," they said. "Pierre and I will appreciate anything you tell us, and rest assured we will work to protect your name from it."

Tentatively, Lapin opened the cover to the file folder. Remy came forward to take the chair beside Pierre's as Lapin perused the first paper.

"Last May, the park beside my home was demolished," he said, "and now there is a new building with retail on the ground floor and housing on the top three. At the time, I didn't think much of it. Although we aren't prone to construction booms here, housing is in short supply, and I assumed the building was permitted by Parliament as a way of responding to the shortage."

Remy could see the paper showed an aerial view of a construction site, but they couldn't read the fine text around the image. "Go on."

Lapin turned the sheet of paper face down on the folder cover and tapped his index finger on the next page. "Last week I noticed the old church—Saint Michel, near the river?"

Remy and Pierre nodded that they knew the church in question. Its stained glass windows had been boarded up for a dozen years after plumbing and electrical problems had forced its closure. As the oldest remaining church in Montamant, the nation had been hesitant to demolish it, but the prohibitive costs of restoration had meant shuttering it and sending the churchgoers to the larger, newer cathedral in the national square.

"I saw two cars in front," Lapin said, "one with French license plates. I happened to be walking along the river that day. I noticed that the man who emerged from one of the vehicles was Jacques Âne."

A private meeting at an abandoned churchyard. What was Âne up to? Bribery, Remy supposed, or drug trafficking? A legitimate business meeting, and the church was conveniently located halfway between his and the other person's offices?

"I don't think they saw me, and please understand, Your Highness, I did not intend to overhear them."

"Of course not."

"I heard them say something about a sale, and two days ago, I observed several cars with French license plates in the parking lot. People were inside the church. It aroused my suspicion, so I did a little research." He turned to another page in the file, which Remy could see was a printout from a news website. "I found an article in the *Le Dauphiné Libéré* announcing a new building project from Agences Loriaz, the same company responsible for the commercial building that is now located where the park used to be. Agences Loriaz is headquartered in France." Lapin let out a sigh. "To be honest, it's a relief to share this information. I'm uncertain what it means, but I have my suspicions. Nothing supported with enough evidence to mention to anyone else, but it has been weighing on my conscience."

Remy opened the file and looked at the pages. They'd need to research Agences Loriaz to find out who the stakeholders were and whether there were any public records of a building contract in Montamant. Given its size, Montamant did not have any cities, so the parks were all nationally owned and operated. If the land had been developed, there would have to be records of a sale, permits for construction, financial commitments from the development company. As for the church, the nation owned the grounds and leased them to the Catholic diocese of Montamant, which consisted solely of the bishop as administrator. Parliament technically had the authority to sell the land, but they wouldn't without the bishop's blessing. Even so, the prime minister had no authority to enter the church for business purposes or to grant a foreign company permission to do work there. Everything within the walls was the bishop's responsibility, and frankly, it would be sacrilegious.

Remy tried to digest Lapin's findings and suspicions. Their initial judgment was that the prime minister had gravely overstepped his bounds, but they needed to review the file carefully and do a little more investigating on their own. The situation with the church was more mysterious than the park. Because of the nation's small size, national law prohibited land ownership by foreign entities. The law had been designed to prevent wealthy foreign tourists from buying up holiday property and displacing residents from their permanent homes. If the prime minister had sold the park land to a French company, was there a vote in Parliament supporting the sale? Had

Parliament passed an amendment to the local ownership law without Remy knowing it?

And the biggest question, of course, was where the money for the sales had gone.

Remy thanked Lapin for sharing the information, and they left with Pierre.

"We should bring this to light. If Monsieur Âne wants to make my life difficult, I'll do the same with this."

"You can't go public with that yet," Pierre said firmly. "You have to find out if he was authorized to make those sales. Otherwise, it looks as if you're trying to shift focus away from yourself and the inheritance bill."

"Did you hear anything about an amendment to the local ownership law?"

Pierre shook his head. "The legislation could exist, but you and I have been out of the country. The money, however—"

"Precisely what I was thinking. We need to find out how much was paid and to whom, and what it has been used for since then." Remy handed him the file folder on the minister of health. "Will you do a little bit of background research on Dr. Boncoeur? Find out what his attitudes toward people like me might be."

"People like us," Pierre said. "Queer people."

Remy appreciated his solidarity, but fortunately for Pierre, the days of trying to medically intervene in homosexuality were long past. Montamant had legalized same-sex marriage in 2013 after France had, despite the opposition to it in the bordering Swiss canton. If Pierre wanted to get married to Giovanni or even adopt children, public opinion and the law would support him. Remy's rights, however, were more in question.

"I'm going to look into Âne and these real estate deals," they told him.

"Remy? This is getting much bigger and more serious than I expected."

"Are you scared?"

"I'm scared for you and for Montamant, but I believe in you. Thank you for trusting me to help you."

CHAPTER TWENTY-TWO

After quickly reading the clippings Monsieur Lapin had assembled, Remy was convinced that the prime minister had done something dubious, if not outright illegal. But Pierre was right. They needed more proof. Real estate transactions were recorded by the cadastral registry, which had kept track of property boundaries and ownership for the entirety of Montamant's eight-hundred-year history. Unfortunately, Remy, like an ordinary citizen, only had access to the registry via written notice and a three-day waiting period.

They certainly couldn't submit a written request for information. That would tip off Prime Minister Âne. A waiting period was also out of the question, since they had no idea how long Âne would entertain debate on the Legitimate Inheritance Bill before calling for a vote. There was also the concern that additional lands could be sold in the interim.

Remy needed to access the cadastral registry immediately, and the only way they knew to do that was to go directly to an employee. Officially, three people worked in the registry office. Unofficially, one person oversaw them.

They needed the help of Madame Pouvoir.

Remy didn't want to find her and ask for her help. They were stung by her betrayal over the surgical plan, and Lapin had chosen not to confide their findings to her. Apart from her, however, Remy's only chance was to storm the registry office to demand the staff help them. Given the confidentiality of this investigation, that didn't seem like a good idea.

They set off for Pouvoir's office, which was down the hall from

Lapin's. Hers was more spacious with a small conference room adjacent for staff interviews and meetings, and it was here that Remy found her. She was sitting at the oval table with reading glasses on, sorting through her own pile of file folders next to her laptop. She looked up when she heard them in the doorway and removed her glasses.

"I was expecting you," she said, rising to her feet.

"You don't have to do that." Remy entered the room and sat across the table from her. They gestured at the pile. "What is all this?"

Pouvoir set her glasses on the table. "Employee files. I am trying to determine who will be able to retain their employment after you return from Lausanne and who may not be able to keep the matter confidential."

"If you don't deem them able to keep a secret, then what?"

She didn't look away or back down. "They will receive a severance package."

Remy shook their head in disbelief. "Do you see how out of control this is getting? We're going to fire people who have done nothing but serve us because you're worried they might tell someone Clotilde sent me away for surgery?" Their voice nearly cracked. "Pouvoir, this is too much."

"I expected you to come to me and beg me for understanding." She gave a wistful smile. "That's what you always did when Their Majesties told you something you didn't want to hear."

"This is more than something I don't want to hear. This is my life. My body. This is wrong, and you know that."

"And you know that Her Majesty is desperate to hold on to the throne. You know that monarchies are a dying breed, and Queen Clotilde feels that the only way to protect your family legacy is to ensure that you are so beloved by the people that they will defend your right to rule. I think you are intelligent enough to know that it's not about whether Clotilde cares about your body and your identity. It's about whether the people do."

"We haven't even given them a chance," Remy said. "She has hidden me away and masked who I am. When I went out yesterday, people liked me. They wanted to engage with me. Do you know what I learned? There was an anti-royalist uprising before. I never knew that. Do you know how it was stopped?"

Pouvoir pursed her lips and gave a tight nod. "I do, but I'd like to hear what you learned."

"I learned that opening up the monarchy to greater involvement from people was the solution. Citizen advisors. Transparency. Not secret medical procedures and hiding away in this palace."

"This is a somewhat different conversation than I expected to have," she admitted. "Maybe the time in the United States has been good for you. You've grown into an adult."

It was the first kind thing she'd said about Remy's choice to move to the US. They couldn't help smiling, the way any child might when praised by a parent. "Then help me do something more adult than I expected to do."

"Stage a conspiracy against your mother?"

"No." Remy slid the file folder across the table to her. She put her glasses back on and opened it. "Help me access the cadastral registry, so I can figure out why public lands have been turned into private businesses and why Jacques Âne has been having secret meetings about these sales."

"He's what?"

"When I met people at the proclamation breakfast, they told me they were concerned about rising housing prices. Now I see that part of the cause is a decrease in available stock because land is being sold and redeveloped into expensive new apartments that our people can't afford," Remy said. "Âne has been involved in real estate transactions with a French company called Agences Loriaz. I need to see the deed transfers, and I need to know who profits from business done by the company. I need you to help me."

Pouvoir's face was its usual blank mask, and for a moment Remy feared she would say their suspicions were outrageous and refuse to help.

"One minute," was all she offered. She turned to her computer and began typing.

Remy didn't like sitting and waiting for her to do the research, but they felt something vaguely monarchical about giving commands to loyal and competent staff. They leaned back in their chair and drummed their fingers on the glossy tabletop.

"Agences Loriaz is a subsidiary of a larger French real estate company," she said.

"Go deeper."

"That will take time. Shall I access the cadastral records? For which properties?"

Remy named the park and the church, prompting a small look of surprise on her face as she typed and clicked. While she worked,

Remy looked through the employee files she had been reviewing. There was one for Gilles, who of course already knew Remy's secret and needn't lose his job, and all the maids whose name began with Marie. In Remy's experience, maids were trustworthy. They saw the royal family in various stages of undress, tended to Clotilde when she wasn't in the makeup that served as her suit of armor, and knew who came into bedrooms late at night and crept out early in the morning. Remy saw no reason any of them should lose their job. If anything, the family owed it to them to be open about what was happening.

"Your Highness?" Pouvoir's voice sounded shakier than usual.

"You found something?"

"One million euros were paid for the sale of the land underneath Saint Michel, and the money was transferred directly to Agences Loriaz. A foreign sale."

"Which is against the law in Montamant."

Pouvoir looked up from the computer. If Remy had to describe the face she was making, they might have said it was fear.

"What is it?" they asked.

"Jacques Âne was able to circumvent the anti-foreign sale law because he's one of the owners of Agences Loriaz. He's been selling public land in Montamant to himself."

Remy leapt to their feet, their fists pounding into the table. "That's what this is about. Don't you and Clotilde see? He doesn't care if I'm nonbinary or intersex. He wants to delegitimate me and send the country spiraling. And when the dust settles, there he is, in power, with all the land and wealth to support him."

Remy was furious at Âne, but they were equally enraged at Clotilde and Pouvoir for being so paranoid about Remy's body that they hadn't seen what was right under their noses.

"Print that out! I'm going to confront him!"

"Your Highness, you cannot hurl accusations at the prime minister when—"

"Watch me!" Remy roared.

❖

"Gilles, Mademoiselle Ide!" Marie-Francine cried as they rushed into the courtyard with their findings packed in one of the large cartons. She stopped in front of the perfectly clean black SUV that Sam and Remy had arrived in. "The fastest way is to have Gilles drive!"

"Where is he?" Sam yelled.

"I'm here!" Gilles called, popping out of the medieval door. "What is going on?"

"We have to get to Parliament to save the crown," Sam told him. "Now!"

Gilles didn't ask any questions. He took the box from her and put it safely in the back of the vehicle while she, Marie-Francine, and Delphine climbed into the SUV. While their arrival at the palace had been meanderingly slow to avoid bumps, this time Gilles peeled out of the courtyard in a squeal of rubber, and they bounced down the steep incline to the front gates so hard that Sam and Delphine kept falling into each other despite wearing their seat belts.

"How are we going to save the crown?" Gilles asked once they had cleared palace grounds.

"You heard the prime minister's announcement this morning?" Sam asked.

"I didn't vote for him, Mademoiselle."

"Good," Delphine interrupted angrily. "We are about to stop his reach for power."

"What's in it for you?" Sam asked her quietly.

Delphine's eyes grew steely. "He has always been rude to my husband, Paul."

"I am taking you to Parliament, yes?" Gilles asked. "To stop a vote on the Legitimate Inheritance Bill?"

"Yes, so please drive faster!" Sam said.

In a few minutes, they arrived at the square. Sam unbuckled her seat belt before the car had completely stopped. She leapt out and went to the rear hatch. "Pop the trunk, Gilles!"

A moment later, she and the carton were headed into the building without any plan for how she would get admitted.

She stopped in front of the guards. Unlike the last time, she wasn't with Remy. She had no visitor's pass and no formal invitation to be there. She was trying to run onto the chamber floor like a lunatic. There was no way they were going to let her in. Why hadn't she thought this through?

Delphine walked up beside her, talking in French on the phone. Then she stabbed at the screen. "They are still in session, thanks to God. Paul is coming out. He will take us in as his guests."

They waited a moment for Paul to arrive. He spoke to the guards, and then Sam and Delphine were scanned and the carton sent through an x-ray machine. Sam was given a bright red badge to wear on a lanyard around her neck.

"You have good timing," Paul said as they hurried along the dimly lit corridor. He continued in French, with Delphine translating for Sam's benefit.

"They are currently debating the bill, and Paul may be called to speak from his professional expertise."

"What will you say?" Sam dared to ask.

Paul cast an odd look in her direction. "Her Royal Highness did not speak to you?"

"Remy? Speak to me about what?"

"Pierre Lefaux phoned me five minutes ago," Paul explained. "He asked if I could replace the royal surgeon in performing the examination."

Smart idea, Remy. Sam breathed a sigh of relief. Remy hadn't given up fighting Clotilde's plan.

"Of course I said I am happy to do this," Paul said. He looked to Delphine and spoke again in French.

She smiled fondly at him before explaining to Sam, "He says this bill does not reflect the current attitudes in the medical or psychological communities."

He pushed open an almost unnoticeable wooden door with a simple brass handle, and suddenly Sam found herself in a crowded and quiet room. Fifty men in suits turned to look at her entrance.

Shit had gotten real. Sam had been operating on adrenaline, rushing around the palace and now rushing into town. She hadn't taken a moment to reflect on the fact that she, Samantha Hyde from Lafayette, Indiana, was standing on the floor of the parliament of a tiny country in Europe, where she was madly in love with the heir apparent. And trying to do her part to save their life.

From his seat at the front of the room, Prime Minister Âne leapt to his feet and began shouting. Two security guards moved from their positions in the corner of the room and headed toward Sam. The members of Parliament began talking in rapid-fire French, and Paul was shouting back at the prime minister, who banged his gavel uselessly on the podium for quiet.

She braced herself for a guard to grab her arm and force her from the room. Instead, one of them said to her, "If you please?" and gestured toward the podium.

Sam cradled the carton tighter, lest their precious evidence be lost. Delphine murmured gently, "It is your time to speak."

"On the dais? I'm allowed?"

"My husband has yielded his time for an expert opinion," Delphine said. "You are the expert."

Sam blew out a shaky breath, which she was certain the now silent room could hear. She slowly made her way to the lectern at the front of the room. She heard every crunch of the mauve carpet under her feet and every creak of wood in the chairs as the members of Parliament turned to follow her progress. The journey to the podium felt like it took an hour. She wasn't sure she would make it without dropping the box.

Finally, she was there. She pulled the microphone down to her own height, and it gave an electronic whine of protest that left the members of Parliament cringing. "Hello?"

Delphine was right by her side, offering support. "*Bonjour.*"

"*Bonjour,*" Sam replied. Then, foolishly, she understood Delphine's intention to translate for her, and she felt herself blushing. "Uh, I'll just speak in English."

Delphine nodded encouragingly. At the back of the room, Gilles and Marie-Francine had arrived. Gilles gave her a thumbs-up.

"This morning, the prime minister announced a new bill to determine the legitimacy of the heir to the throne. He said it was to ensure Montamant's long tradition of rule by the House of Vallorcin remained uninterrupted. What the prime minister didn't say, but what I'm sure you all understood, like I did, was that the bill is really intended to reiterate a distorted understanding of legitimacy through binary gender." She hoped Delphine was able to translate effectively. She had no idea if the concepts even made sense in the French language or in Montamantien culture.

She decided to be more direct. "The prime minister doesn't like Remy Vallorcin. That's what this is really about. None of you has seen Their Royal Highness in years, and when they arrived to read the proclamation of sovereignty, some of you were shocked at their appearance. The new bill requires that heirs be determined purely male or purely female, and Monsieur Âne says this will preserve tradition. But I've been researching in the royal family's archives, and I have found evidence that contradicts the prime minister's claims."

This was the moment of truth. Someone in the palace had obviously wanted Emmanuel's life to remain a secret, and now that history would be revealed. She could only hope that Emmanuel or Emmanuelle, whichever they had preferred to be called, would understand why she was dredging up their history and how much it would benefit Remy in the present.

Sam couldn't figure out where to set the box, and in a rush of thoughtlessness, she placed it on the throne behind her. There were mumbles of protest from the crowd, and she quickly realized her mistake, but moving the box would have been more awkward. She took another shaky breath and reached for a few of the items inside. Then she returned to the microphone.

"In 1763, Queen Louise gave birth to a child called Emmanuel. On the birth certificate, Emmanuel's sex is listed as neither male nor female."

Someone burst into the room and yelled in French.

The room gasped at the intrusion, and Sam, along with everyone else, turned to look at the private sovereign's door behind her, through which Remy had just emerged.

They looked at each other in disbelief.

"Remy—what...?"

"What are you doing at the podium?"

She blinked. "I was in the middle of a speech."

Remy looked around the room and must have recognized the signs that Sam was indeed the official speaker at the moment. They nodded and sat in the second throne, gesturing for her to continue.

She was even more nervous with them there and hoped they wouldn't be hurt or insulted by the things she was about to discuss. She hoped they understood the goal of what she was trying to do.

"On Emmanuel's birth certificate, the sex is listed as neither male nor female," she repeated. "Emmanuel was officially pronounced as having an unknown sex. In 1783, Emmanuel left Montamant for Alsace, where they lived in a house with a person they married, whom documents alternately name as Germain in the masculine and Germaine in the feminine. In some documents I found, Emmanuel is also called Emmanuelle—" She turned to Delphine. "Can you translate that? Feminine with an 'e' at the end?" Delphine nodded, and Sam continued. "Here is a portrait of Emmanuel painted by Germaine." Sam held up the tiny painting. It was too small for the members of Parliament to see from their seats, and she wondered if she should pass it around. "In this picture, Emmanuel's face is deliberately painted so as not to appear obviously male or female. The house Emmanuel and Germaine built was named Hrodohaid, after a Danish royal who was assigned male at birth but wore women's clothing. Hrodohaid was heir to the throne but abdicated because they didn't want to live as a male king. I think naming their house after Hrodohaid was probably Emmanuel and Germaine's secret joke—a name testifying to the fact that they identified as trans or nonbinary." She stopped again. "Does 'nonbinary' translate?"

Delphine shrugged and whispered back, "I'm trying my best."

Sam continued. "I believe Emmanuel, or Emmanuelle, sets a historical precedent within the House of Vallorcin. As the heir to the throne, Emmanuel's life shows that Montamant has already had a legitimate heir who was neither male nor female. Their Royal Highness Remy is not breaking tradition or threatening it. They are actually upholding tradition."

A man with a gray handlebar mustache leapt to his feet and argued in English, "Prince Emmanuel never assumed the throne!"

"This is true," Sam answered calmly. She had anticipated this challenge. "Emmanuel died before their father and so never assumed the throne, and their brother became king. But he died without children. Emmanuel and Germaine had a son, whom you know as King Henri. Because the line of succession returned to Emmanuel's children, it proves that Emmanuel's claim to the throne was never invalidated."

From what she had learned in her research, Henri's father was listed as Emmanuel and his mother Germaine. If the ministers wanted to dispute paternity, that was a matter that might open a floodgate. As Remy had reminded her, there were ways for infertile monarchs to secure their line of succession, and that was something done more commonly than most people realized, and not just for intersex or trans royals. Sam hoped the ministers wouldn't probe that deeply yet.

For now, she explained, "King Henri's reign shows how the Vallorcin line descends directly from Emmanuel and extends to Remy. Princess Remy." She hated calling them that, but that's how the ministers would understand. "It's time for you to celebrate this history." She turned to look at the prime minister, and feeling emboldened, said directly to him, "And to celebrate your current heir."

She nodded to Delphine that she was finished and gave the documents to one of the security guards. No doubt the ministers would want to vet their authenticity and look at them on their own, rather than trusting Sam's simple word they existed. But maybe that would mean stalling the vote and buying them more time.

Then, to Sam's surprise, the man with the handlebar mustache rose from his seat again and said something that caused a ruckus. Delphine translated. "In light of these discoveries, he moves the Legitimate Inheritance Bill be voted on immediately."

Sam gaped. That was the opposite of what she had been hoping to accomplish.

Someone seconded the motion, and suddenly, Sam could see Remy's future swirling down the drain. What had she done? How could they continue with the transphobic bill in light of the evidence she had presented?

Prime Minister Âne looked as stunned as Sam. Maybe he thought he would have more time to marshal votes. With the motion seconded, he had no choice but to call for a vote, and Sam and Delphine were asked to leave the chamber. No guests were allowed during the voting procedures. Gilles and Marie-Francine followed them into the vestibule.

"Is there a television or something we can watch?" Sam asked.

"The gallery," Delphine said. "Everyone is allowed in the gallery as Parliament is supposed to be transparent in its business."

They hurried up the flight of stairs that led to the gallery, where Sam had been sitting that morning with Madame Pouvoir and Pierre. Rushing wasn't necessary, though. The voting was done by secret written ballots cast into a large wooden box. It lasted an eternity as each member of Parliament rose from his seat, came forward to deposit his vote, and returned to his seat before the next person repeated the ritual. Once the last vote was cast, Âne opened the box and read each vote aloud.

"*Oui*," he declared, setting one slip of paper to his left. He unfolded the next. "*Non*." This paper went to his right.

He continued through all fifty ballots, his voice growing despondent as the number of "no" votes rose. By the time he was finished, the "no" pile was sprawling while only a few scraps sat to his left in the "yes" pile. It was hardly worth counting.

Protocol must have dictated the votes were formally counted anyway. Three men came forward and sifted through the ballots, each of them counting twice. They compared results. Then one man spoke to the full chamber, which erupted into applause.

"He said the vote is 'no,'" Delphine said as the prime minister returned to his seat with his head hanging. "There will be no law requiring either male or female heirs."

Remy rose from the throne and stepped toward the microphone. Delphine translated quietly to Sam as Remy explained that they knew it was not customary for members of the royal family to interfere with the business of Parliament, but they had special information that must be immediately shared. Then, to Sam's astonishment, Remy said the prime minister had been illegally selling public land for his own personal gain in an effort to destroy the Vallorcin reign and the nation itself.

The chamber erupted into chaos once more. Âne's face grew red as he protested the accusations, but like Sam, Remy had come armed. They waved a series of papers in the air. In desperation, Âne jumped to reach them, and an unstately game of keep-away ensued until Delphine's husband, Paul, was able to snatch the papers and read from them aloud in the microphone.

Next to Sam, Delphine beamed in pride.

The man with the handlebar mustache called for another vote, and this time the chamber unanimously declared, "*Oui!*" Their cries echoed throughout the chamber. Two guards came and flanked Âne, and Remy took the gavel from Âne's hand and banged it twice before thrusting it in the air in celebration.

Sam was on the edge of her seat. "What happened? What did they say?"

"Jacques Âne has been removed from office! He's no longer the prime minister of Montamant!"

❖

As the guards escorted Jacques Âne from the floor of Parliament, Remy felt mixed emotions: a sense of amazement that this had actually happened and they'd played a part in it, surprise and delight at learning there had been another Vallorcin like them, concern for the nation that something so terrible had happened under their family's watch, and tremendous appreciation for Sam. They could see her in the gallery, her mouth as wide as theirs must have been, and they felt the urge to run to her. They waved her down to the floor instead.

She came rushing in her casual style, not caring about the rules of decorum that traditionally governed Parliament. Those had been destroyed in the last few hours anyway. Remy ran across the floor to meet her halfway, and she threw her arms around them in a tight embrace.

"How did you even get here?" she asked. "I took the car with Gilles."

"I drove myself in another vehicle and left it outside. It's probably received a parking violation. I can't believe what you found out. That was in the archive?"

She nodded. "Hidden somewhere. I hope your family doesn't mind that I brought it into the open."

"How could I mind? You saved me."

"You saved yourself! I can't believe what you found out about Âne. I'm so proud of you! And so happy! I can't believe we did it!"

We did it. They had operated from two different lines of investigation, but they had come together to stop the madness. Remy looked at her and didn't see a friend or potential sexual conquest or even a confidant. They saw all those things, but for the first time, they also saw a partner.

They leaned forward to kiss her in front of fifty fussy old members of Parliament, a chauffeur, a maid, and a translator whom they could hear cheering for them.

"Sam," Remy said, touching their foreheads together, "I love you."

CHAPTER TWENTY-THREE

Madame Pouvoir?" Jean-Michel's voice nearly cracked as he approached. For a security guard, he was too easily intimidated. Pouvoir would have to take that under consideration when his annual performance review came up.

"Yes?"

"I have the background material on our guest."

"Excellent." Pouvoir followed him into the security office. One of the monitors showed the chamber of Parliament instead of the usual views of the palace and grounds. "Why are you watching Parliament?" She doubted the ministers knew the palace had access to their security cameras.

"It's protocol to follow the crown princess when she goes somewhere we have surveillance." That answer would have been sufficient, since Pouvoir had expected Princess Remy at the Parliament building, though not directly on the floor. But Jean-Michel, again perhaps showing a lapse in discretion, volunteered further information without being asked. "We had switched the monitor when Mademoiselle Hyde left, since protocol dictates we follow guests of the royal family as well."

Pouvoir was familiar with the dictate. It was less about concern for the guests themselves than that one of the royal cars could be bugged or planted with a bomb or the guest held for ransom to extort the royal family. Unlikely though any such scenario might be in their usually tranquil nation, she appreciated that young Jean-Michel was being attentive to security procedures. She was not, however, familiar with any plan for Samantha Hyde to leave the palace grounds.

"Mademoiselle Hyde went to Parliament? To the chamber floor?" She leaned forward to look at the monitor. Through the grainy view, she could only see the usual group of aging men standing around talking. "Where is she now?"

"After she spoke to Parliament and the bill was defeated, she and Princess Remy returned to their car. Gilles is on his way back with the other vehicle. Unfortunately, we don't have direct surveillance on the cars, though we can track them via GPS."

Pouvoir put a hand over her mouth to think for a moment. In thirty years of service to the royal family, she had never seen a guest take the royal family's car and chauffeur, storm Parliament, and certainly not speak on the chamber floor. In fact, in her entire lifetime, she had never seen a non-citizen even visit Parliament. Who did this Samantha Hyde think she was?

"Did you say a bill was defeated?" she asked.

"After Mademoiselle Hyde spoke, they called for an immediate vote on the Legitimate Inheritance Bill, and it was defeated."

"What did she say to them?"

Jean-Michel shrugged. "I don't have audio access." He glanced sideways at her. "I assume you heard the other part, Madame?"

"Other part?"

"About the prime minister being removed from office?"

Pouvoir was stunned. And annoyed to hear the news secondhand. She checked her phone and saw that it had been switched to silent mode, and indeed it was full of messages regarding Jacques Âne and the new interim prime minister, who would need to meet with Queen Clotilde immediately to be granted authority to govern.

"Here is the additional information you requested on Mademoiselle Hyde, Madame." Jean-Michel handed her a thick manila folder. Pouvoir took it absently, her attention still on her phone, as he briefed her. "No criminal record in the last two generations of her immediate family, and we traced the Hyde family to the originating ancestor who arrived in the United States."

She had hoped Jean-Michel would find something that would make it necessary to terminate Samantha Hyde's relationship with the princess. Now, though, she had mixed feelings about what might be in the file. She flipped through the pages in the folder to search for the information Jean-Michel conveyed.

"When?"

"Arrived from Paris as a small child in 1753, though he was

British. His name was Samuel Hyde. It's uncertain why he left Paris, though his father died there the same year."

This foray into Mademoiselle Hyde's ancestry would have to wait, since the news of the prime minister's ousting was far more important. Pouvoir closed the file folder and tucked it under her arm. "Thank you for your hard work, Jean-Michel. Will you notify me when the car returns?"

She left the security office and first checked on Queen Clotilde, briefing her on the events that had transpired that afternoon. When the queen expressed her own disbelief and asked more questions, Pouvoir shrugged for the first time in all her years of service.

"I don't know anything anymore," she said, showing herself out of the queen's room before she had been officially dismissed.

She went to the kitchen and fixed herself an espresso. Then she sat down to read the findings on Samantha Hyde. The security team had found the educational records for her father, as well as items of interest about her maternal grandmother in the local newspaper. She had apparently been an award-winning pie baker. While these were interesting tidbits, they were hardly significant. In fact, the more Pouvoir read about how utterly banal the Hydes were, the more she bristled at Samantha's upstart attitude toward Montamantien law.

She hadn't been able to get far before one of the butlers came to tell her the princess and Samantha had returned. She strode toward the courtyard at a fast clip and arrived as the two lovebirds climbed out of the car and immediately reached for each other's hands.

"Welcome back."

Pouvoir hadn't always been so imposing, but through years of royal service, including raising an obstreperous heir apparent, she had learned how to channel her voice and posture. She had learned that a terse phrase or simple nod could be far more effective than shouting.

Unfortunately, it didn't work. They didn't quake in their boots. Instead, Samantha leapt at Pouvoir, hugging her fiercely.

"We did it!" she shouted, her voice echoing around the courtyard. "We did it!"

Pouvoir kept her arms tight against her sides, lest Samantha think she was returning the embrace. "When you have composed yourself, Her Majesty is waiting to see you."

Remy nodded solemnly. "Of course. I will see her right away."

"Not you." Pouvoir pointed to Mademoiselle Hyde. "You."

Pouvoir led her to the queen's suite and opened the door, gesturing for Samantha to enter unaccompanied. She had a few suspicions as to what Queen Clotilde wanted and how she would react to Sam's brazen actions, and some of those reactions Pouvoir shared. These things simply weren't done.

On the other hand, her quick thinking and careful research had unearthed something that saved their beloved Remy from the embarrassment of a public physical exam and the agony of a legitimacy claim. Or worse. Although she wouldn't say it in the presence of the queen—her training and commitment to her job prevented her from doing so—Pouvoir was relieved. The queen's plan was not good for anyone, and she had seen the genuine terror on Remy's face when it was announced. For the part she played in sparing Remy that trauma, Samantha Hyde would have Pouvoir's gratitude.

As she pulled the door to the queen's suite closed behind her, she couldn't help murmuring, "Well done, Mademoiselle, and thank you."

The door shut and Sam left to fend for herself, Pouvoir went to her office and took a seat on the green velvet couch that stretched between two tall bookshelves. She switched on the floor lamp, took off her black loafers, and stretched her legs on the sofa cushions. Then she reopened the file and began to read again.

It took her thirty minutes to read everything from cover to cover, and by the time she was done, she saw something of utmost value. The ancestor who had first arrived in the United States from Paris was the son of Henry Hyde, an earl who had died in Paris in 1753. When Henry died, his title had been made extinct, as the child Samuel's existence had been unknown in Britain and all other sons had predeceased Henry.

Pouvoir double-checked the marriage records, but Jean-Michel had included suitable proof that Henry Hyde had secretly married a French noblewoman before Samuel's birth. That meant Samuel, who had arrived in the United States at the age of three, should have become the heir to the now defunct earldom of Clarendon.

Given that Henry Hyde had had a previous marriage and other children, Pouvoir traced the family tree carefully. When she didn't trust her own interpretation of the background findings, she went to her desk, took out a piece of paper, and mapped out the lineage in ink. From the Earl of Clarendon to Samuel, who had a son named Edward, and forward a few generations to when the oldest son in the family had died in World War I, moving the line of inheritance to his brother, who had three children. She continued through the twentieth century, flipping the paper over to keep the family tree going, and when she arrived at

1995 with the birth of Samantha, it was clear. She was a child of the oldest son of an oldest son.

Samantha Hyde was nobility and didn't even know it.

❖

After Sam was sent to the queen's chambers, Remy felt some of the elation of the day beginning to fade. They suspected Clotilde would yell at Sam for exposing family secrets and ruining her plans to mutilate her only child, and it was unclear if Remy was still going to be forced to announce an engagement to Pierre.

They headed to their own suite, where Marie-Jeanne had requested a final fitting on the outfit they were supposed to wear for the royal ball. They were standing with one arm outstretched while she pinned the sleeve cuffs when Pierre came flying into the room, unannounced and largely unwelcome. He thrust his phone at them, and he was talking so fast that Remy couldn't really tell what was going on. They took the phone and looked, but the screen was locked.

"Slow down and take a breath!"

On the ground, Marie-Jeanne glanced up from the hem she was pinning. "Shall I...?"

"No, stay. Pierre, what is it?"

"Your girlfriend," he managed to say. "I can't believe she stopped the bill!"

"I got the prime minister removed from office!"

"I know, I saw!" Ignoring Marie-Jeanne's hard work, Pierre threw his arms around Remy. "You're still the heir!"

"I know, I was there. Where were you?"

His smile flipped into a deep frown. "I was looking up the doctor's records, as you told me to do. You should have told me you were planning to topple the government. I would have wanted to be there."

"We didn't topple the government. We removed a corrupt prime minister from power. Clotilde will meet with the interim prime minister until a new one can be elected."

"No, Remy, you don't get it!" Pierre waved his phone again. "The internet is exploding. Everyone is saying we should get rid of Parliament, that the ministers can't be trusted. They're saying the Vallorcins are the only ones who should govern!"

"Are you kidding?" Remy didn't want to be a news story, and they certainly didn't want the public to have lost faith in a democratically elected government. A return to absolute monarchy was the last thing Remy wanted, especially as the future monarch. They asked Marie-Jeanne to give them privacy, and she took her leave.

"Where are the news alerts?" Remy asked Pierre.

"Well, Montamantien Twitter is exploding, anyway," Pierre said. "That is all that matters right now. Think about it, Remy. Sam's speech made it clear you are neither male nor female, and the people don't care. They want you and Queen Clotilde in power."

Remy would need to speak with Clotilde, who would probably want to confirm their next line of action with their lawyer. She had friends among the old guard, and it was unlikely the issue of who or what Remy was would come up again, especially if the favorability of the family was running so high.

And, if that were true, Remy could stop masquerading. No more pretending to be a princess. They were going to be true to themselves and let the public see that they were no different than they had been. In fact, if the week had taught Remy anything, it was that they were far more responsible and dedicated to duty than anyone realized. The people of Montamant had seen them firsthand, and what they valued wasn't femininity. It was someone who listened to their concerns.

If Remy did that, if they pledged to be a loyal servant to the people, they wouldn't have to go through with a sham marriage. In fact, now that they were publicly labeled as nonbinary, marriage to Pierre might even seem strange to some of the public. Remy was probably going to have to marry one day, and the House of Vallorcin still needed another generation of heirs. That was a matter Remy was going to have to figure out down the road. But there was time. And they'd figure it out with someone they actually wanted to have children with.

"Pierre, can we have a serious conversation for a second?"

"Of course."

They settled on Remy's bed, and Remy held one of Pierre's hands in theirs. "You know I love you."

"Of course, my friend, and I love you."

"But I'm not in love with you."

"I know. Neither am I."

"I don't want to marry someone I'm not in love with. Maybe that's naive of me, but I don't see the need to rush to an engagement anyway, especially now. I don't care about the attention or the presents. There are other things I'd like to do before settling down here in Montamant. I want to finish my graduate degree."

"You're not really going through with that, are you? I thought you had only started that to get away from Queen Clotilde. Now that you're back and everyone has seen how you look and act, why bother with school?"

Maybe graduate school had begun as a way of escaping Clotilde and Montamant, but it meant more to Remy now. It meant opening their mind and preparing them to be a better leader, not someone so shielded they didn't understand how to protect the country in the twenty-first century. They needed to understand the world around them. They needed to gain other perspectives.

Pierre didn't understand. That was one of the many reasons why he was not someone Remy could fall in love with, why he was wrong for them.

What Pierre did understand was Montamant. He had been the one with the stellar idea to put Remy into the public eye to boost their approval, and he had played a role in helping Remy uncover the prime minister's plan. Pierre had a clear sense of who the major players in Montamantien politics were and how to charm them, and the stunt at the civic center showed he also understood the importance of connecting with the people.

He wasn't a prospective spouse. He was a prospective Madame Pouvoir.

Yes, Remy realized, the idea made perfect sense.

"I have an important question to ask. You don't have to answer right now, and it won't actually happen until I finish graduate school, or at least until I return for the summer break. You see, when I think of coming back here and taking leadership, I see you by my side."

He looked confused, and rightly so. It sounded as if Remy was still considering marriage.

"Will you be my chief secretary?" they asked.

"What?"

"You'll be to me what Pouvoir is to Clotilde. You can live here in the palace, or we'll get you a house nearby, whatever you want. You'll be involved in the day-to-day governance, attend all the social functions, you'll have the royal life. And you'll make sure I don't screw up. But you'll get to do it all with someone you actually love by your side."

And someone I love by mine.

They thought about Sam and how she might complete the picture. She had worked so well with them, and she had shown her commitment to Montamant's history and Remy's place in the nation. Without the announcement of an engagement to Pierre, they had time to explore their relationship with Sam now, and maybe Pierre could help them figure out how to defeat the rule about royals marrying someone pedigreed.

In the meantime, the prospect of putting together their team was exciting. Although Clotilde hopefully had a long life ahead of her, there was no reason they couldn't get started on some pet projects. If the public continued to view Remy favorably, Clotilde would be thrilled to see them taking a more active role in daily Montamantien life.

"What do you say, Pierre? Are you desperate enough to work for a paycheck?"

"When you put it like that, how could I possibly say no?"

❖

If Queen Clotilde's goal was to intimidate Sam or make Sam regret her actions, she was going to be disappointed. Showing off her findings at Parliament and squelching the prime minister's vote had emboldened Sam. She wasn't scared of these royals and their highfalutin attitudes any longer. It didn't matter that she was a nobody from Indiana. She had proof she could hold her own.

She still gave a curtsy to show she understood and respected the queen's station and Montamantien tradition, which she knew was important to Remy. "You asked to see me, Your Majesty?"

"Yes, Mademoiselle."

Queen Clotilde was reclining on the sofa with one elbow holding her head up. She wore a gray hoodie three sizes too big for her, and a puddle of used tissues decorated her lap. She gestured for Sam to sit on the matching sofa facing her, which Sam did, careful to keep her knees tight together and her hands politely folded on her lap.

"That was quite a display this afternoon." The queen leaned forward for a glass of fizzy water that was sitting on the glass coffee table between them. She took a long drink and rubbed her temples.

"Your Majesty is still feeling ill?"

"I've gone from sneezing nonstop to feeling as if my head is made of bricks. I'm dizzy, and I still can't hear out of my right ear, but of course we can't let anyone know that. Who knows what they might say behind my back if they did?"

"Of course." Sam didn't really understand where the conversation was going.

"I have to appear at the ball tomorrow night. To be out of the spotlight for a few events was disturbing enough, but to miss the royal ball would be unthinkable. Maybe unforgivable. With all the scandals about Remy this week, I'll be needed to smooth things over." The queen paused in rubbing her head to look pointedly at Sam. "Of course, some items have already been smoothed over."

Sam wasn't sure that was an invitation to begin presenting her case, but she spoke nonetheless. "Remy gave me access to the archives in the old part of the palace. They told me I was allowed to look around. When I found those documents related to the royal person known as Emmanuel, it seemed like I needed to share them, to stop the vote on the inheritance bill."

"Where did you find them? Never in my life have I heard anything about a secret house or a wife who was really a husband in my own family."

Sam explained about the hidden box inside the wall. "Someone must not have wanted anyone to know about Emmanuel and Germaine."

"And you, an American who arrived a few days ago, thought better?"

Sam sighed internally. She didn't want to be chastised by Queen Clotilde. Frankly, it only made her think she was a lousy mother. She ought to have been praising Sam for helping her child.

"Respectfully, Your Majesty—"

"No sentence that is truly respectful ever begins with the word 'respectfully.'"

"With respect, I care a lot about Remy—"

"Are you in love with my daughter?"

"Remy isn't your daughter."

The queen glared at her. "Answer the question."

"I can't answer your question because you asked me about someone who doesn't exist."

Clotilde's eyebrows nearly met her hairline. She set her glass of water on the table with a clink and sat up. "You are a guest in this palace. An outsider. What gives you the right to talk to the queen of Montamant this way?"

"I care a lot about Remy," Sam said, rising to her feet, "and I know they haven't been happy. I saw an opportunity to help, and I took it." The queen said nothing, and Sam began to feel nervous in the hot seat of her stare. She fumbled to continue. "Frankly, your plan to send them for surgery was cruel and horrifying. You've treated them like something is wrong with them instead of treating them with love. I don't regret what I did. I would do it again."

"Good."

Sam looked at the queen in surprise, and the queen nodded, confirming that Sam had heard correctly. The queen smiled, not with the vain coldness of before but with genuine warmth. Her real smile, Sam saw, made her eyes crinkle and her cheeks glow. She looked radiant and not unlike Remy when they were laughing.

"Some people think the ideal partner for a monarch is someone who will smile and keep their mouth closed," Clotilde said. "If she's a woman, she should know how to throw fabulous parties and never get involved in politics. If he's a man, like Georges, he should know how to support the queen without appearing to be running things in the shadows. This is nonsense."

"Your Majesty?"

"When I took the throne from my father, the palace advisors told me to watch out for Georges. They said that in order to preserve my power, I should find a weak husband who wouldn't try to interfere in policy. They even advised me to give him the title prince consort, despite centuries of tradition." She sighed. "Samantha, sit down. You are hovering."

Sam sat as instructed. "Was King Georges that way? Did he try to govern from the shadows?"

"Luckily, no." Queen Clotilde's smile turned wistful. "He freely shared his advice and questioned some of my choices. He was deeply involved, but he always understood when it was time to let me make the decisions as sovereign. I miss him very much. Remy has probably told you we drifted apart after Georges's death?"

Sam wasn't sure if she should admit to knowing that or not.

"You're loyal to Remy, I understand." She paused to blow her nose. "Whatever she's told you—"

"They," Sam couldn't help correcting her.

Queen Clotilde held up a palm in apology. "Whatever they have told you, I'm sure it's true. I haven't been a very good mother. Georges's death made me realize how fragile life is, and it scared me. I realized Remy would one day take my place, maybe sooner than either of us thought, and I saw a child who didn't know who she was. I wanted to protect her from the watchful eyes of this place."

"They."

"Samantha, when I die, Remy will be facing the greatest challenge of their life. This week they have only had a small taste of what being the monarch means. They need friends and allies who will challenge them to be their best self, people smart enough to understand the politics inside and outside Montamant, who won't be cowed by Remy's authority. The way Georges always challenged me."

Sam held her breath, expecting this to be the moment the queen told her to get out of the country and leave Remy alone.

Instead, Queen Clotilde said, "Based on what I have seen from you today, standing up to Parliament and to me, I think you may be that kind of person. If Remy chooses to continue their friendship with you, I would be happy about it."

"Thank you, Your Majesty."

Inside Sam was quaking. She had not expected the queen to be so forthcoming, and it was a victory that she believed Sam was good for Remy. But friends and allies? Was Clotilde saying that she was comfortable with Remy's continued association with Sam, as long as it was never romantic? Or was "friendship" royal-speak for "relationship"?

In terms of speaking truth to power, that was something the queen needn't have worried about. Partly because Sam cared about Remy, but partly because it was her nature. And she saw one more necessary occasion.

"If I may speak freely, Your Majesty, I think you owe Remy an apology. Forcing them to marry Pierre and making them pretend to be a girl—they've been tortured by this when all they wanted was love and understanding. Remy doesn't even know you love them."

"Watch it, little girl." The queen stretched out on her sofa and pulled a blanket over her legs. "Part of the job is knowing when not to speak."

"You're right. I just know that we both care about Remy, maybe more than we care about anyone else in the world."

"We do. I think Remy is lucky to have you. It's a shame you're American."

The way she phrased it was cutting: Sam, the lowly American. But it was supposed to be a compliment, Sam understood. The queen was telling her she would have supported a match between her and Remy if she were Montamantien or otherwise noble. Sam decided to accept the queen's words as she had intended them.

"Thank you, Your Majesty. That's incredibly kind of you. Should I leave you to rest?"

"Yes." Clotilde closed her eyes, and Sam got to her feet again.

But there was one more honest thing she wanted to say. "Queen Clotilde?"

"Hmm?"

"Maybe it's not Remy's love life you should be so concerned about. Maybe it's okay if you concentrated a little more on your own."

"Mademoiselle Hyde, please mind your own business."

"But I think if you told Remy and Pierre about you and Andre, they'd—"

"Good evening, Mademoiselle."

Sam gave one more curtsy in case Queen Clotilde's eyes weren't fully shut and then crept out of the room.

❖

When they heard a knock on their door, Remy assumed it was Marie-Jeanne coming to finish alterations to their attire for the royal ball. Or maybe it was Sam returning from her meeting with the queen, who they hoped hadn't attacked her for her brazen actions or for ruining the insidious surgery plan. But after Remy called, "Come in!" in English, they were surprised to see Clotilde standing in their doorway.

She was wearing fluffy slippers and one of Remy's old sweatshirts. She looked haggard, and Remy wondered why she had made the trek to their suite, especially when she was ill. She always summoned people to her. Had she ever come to their room? Remy hadn't thought she even knew where in the residential wing of the palace it was located.

"Mother, if you've come here to say anything other than 'congratulations,' you're not welcome here."

Clotilde made her way to Remy's desk and collapsed into the chair. "I deserve that."

Remy glared. "And more."

"I came to tell you I was impressed with what you and Samantha did today. And to apologize."

"Apologize for what?"

She wiped her nose. "All I have wanted since you were born was to protect you and this family. These past few days, since you've been home, I can see that I was wrong about how I did that. I thought that if I changed you, I could give you a happier life and protect the monarchy at the same time. But I had it backwards. I see now that what makes you the happiest is letting you be the person you are, and you showed me today that is also how we can protect the House of Vallorcin."

Remy was stunned into silence. They sat on the edge of their bed, facing her, not sure how to respond. From the time they were a small child, they had sensed they weren't good enough for her. Georges and Pouvoir had been the ones to say they were proud of Remy when they did well at school or accomplished some clever feat. They had supplied hugs and kisses. It wasn't as if Remy's life had been devoid of any affection, but they had still felt inadequate and imperfect and longed for Clotilde, just once, to tell them they were okay. As they had gotten older, her rejection had begun to hurt less, and the emptiness inside where her love was missing became filled with resentment. If they were honest with themselves, part of what they had wanted to do this week was to show her she was wrong about them. That they were just as good at her job as she was.

"You want me to be happy?"

"Oh, Remy." She shook her head a few times and sniffed. Her voice cracked as she said, "I've mistreated you. I'm so sorry. Can you ever forgive me?"

Hearing her voice crack broke something inside Remy, and they rushed across the room to her. They hugged, with Remy's head buried in her shoulder, and they stayed that way until she had a coughing fit that forced them apart. They found a box of tissues on the nightstand and brought one to her. She accepted it and caressed their face.

"I love you, my little cabbage. You're so special."

"Apparently not, if Sam's research is correct."

"Yes, it was impressive of her to find another Vallorcin like you. Does it change how you feel about yourself?"

Remy reflected on their newfound knowledge of Emmanuel and Germaine. It was sad to learn they'd had to run away, as Remy had done, but it was inspiring to know they had found a way to be happy. If there were more nonbinary, trans, or intersex Vallorcins, it meant Remy wasn't special in that they weren't alone, but that didn't make them sad.

"It's reassuring to know I'm not the only one. I'm eager for Sam to show me everything she found and learn more about this person." They glanced at their mother. "Is that what you came to talk about?"

"No," Clotilde said. "I would like for you to share what you discover, but I came to ask what I can do to make the situation between us better. It's time to repair our relationship, if you want to."

Remy wanted to. They wanted to call her and tell her about their day the way Sam did, but it would take time to see her as that kind of mother. And they weren't willing to do everything on her terms anymore.

"Under certain conditions," they said.

"What are those conditions?"

"I'm not going to announce an engagement to Pierre. There is no rush for me to marry, I don't date men, and Pierre is gay. An engagement between us is not tolerable."

"Pierre is gay?" Clotilde coughed into the tissue. "Has he told Andre?"

"I don't know. Do you think Andre would accept him if he did?"

"I'll make sure he does. I can tell him about the dangers of becoming estranged from your child." She patted Remy's hand. "No engagement to Pierre. But it can't be the American. It has to be someone with an appropriate background."

Remy rose to their feet. "I don't even know if I want to marry Sam yet. At least give me time to find out, and if I decide I do, give me some time to figure out a way. You got to marry someone you loved. I ask that you give me the opportunity to try to do the same."

"Discreetly. We don't want to have any situation like the Grimaldi disasters. What else?"

"Marie-Jeanne has worked very hard on my outfit for the royal ball, but—"

"But it's all wrong for you?" Clotilde guessed. "Oh, this one is difficult for me. Our appearances are important."

"Yes, which is why I need to look and feel true to myself."

Clotilde let out a small groan. "Wear what you wish, but promise to keep within the bounds of decency."

Remy tried not to take offense at what was a major concession for someone who had forced them into girlish clothing for most of their childhood and who prided herself on being named to "best dressed" lists. "Of course," Remy said. "You're giving in very easily to my demands."

"I'm trying to show you how serious I am about fixing our relationship." She coughed and spit into her tissue, and Remy tried not to gag. "It occurs to me we're going to need to find you a new title."

A concession here and an apology there were surprising but perhaps overdue. This, however, far exceeded Remy's wildest dreams, and in the back of their mind they wondered if this was more of Clotilde's diabolical cunning. Maybe she intended to ingratiate herself to them before moving in for the kill. Remy didn't want that to be the case, and they wanted to believe she was trying to turn over a new leaf, but there was a lot of history between them that couldn't be so easily forgotten.

"Are you sincere about all this?" they asked. "How do I know I can trust you now?"

She hoisted herself to her feet. "I don't expect you to forgive me or trust me for a long time, but I would like us to try."

They hugged again, and this time Remy was sure they felt her crying against their shoulder.

"I would like to try, too, Maman. I love you, too."

CHAPTER TWENTY-FOUR

The palace of Montamant was glowing, literally and figuratively. Small lights had been strung around the central courtyard and woven through the bushes to give the night a warm glow. Inside the ballroom, blue and silver lights echoed the national color scheme, and candles covered every table. Guests arrived in the central courtyard and exited their cars next to a red carpet, which led them through the Renaissance wing of the palace. After their jackets and personal items were stored away, the guests were escorted down a long corridor. At the end of it, they gave the small name card they had received with their invitation to one of the butlers, who formally announced them as they stepped into the glittering ballroom.

In spaces the guests were allowed, the palace staff were quiet and calm, their uniforms clean and pressed. Behind the scenes, things were bustling. A crew of valets ensured each car was quickly parked out of the way to make room for the next guest. Extra security stations had been set up in empty closets, and waiters scrambled back and forth between the kitchen and the ballroom with silver trays of hors d'oeuvres.

Upstairs, Sam was shampooed and blow-dried by a stylist, her nails buffed by a manicurist, and false eyelashes applied by a makeup artist. Two maids helped her into her gown, taking care that no makeup rubbed off on the material and no folds of the dress ruffled her hair out of place. They even put her feet into her shoes and fastened the straps for her.

Sam had never felt so pampered. She couldn't believe what efforts had been made for her, the lowly American guest. A custom-made dress of lavender and sky blue chiffon with a sweetheart neckline and a billowy tulle skirt had been created, and because it was custom made, it fit Sam's body like nothing she had ever worn before. Marie-Francine helped her slide a pair of elbow-length sky blue gloves on her hands to complete the effect. She felt like a princess.

More accurately, like Cinderella. Because there was an expiration date on it all.

While she experienced this extraordinary night of glamor and luxury, Marie-Francine would be packing her things. At six in the morning, Gilles was going to drive her back to the airport in Geneva, where she had been booked on a commercial flight to Boston in time for classes Monday. Sam would be back to her jeans and empty bank account, and Montamant would become a distant memory. She didn't even know if Remy was going to return for the semester or stay after the announcement of their engagement to Pierre.

For the rest of the night, she didn't want to think about the future. She wanted to enjoy one last taste of the good life, a celebration of what she had managed to accomplish in her short time in Montamant. A few last final moments before the engagement ruined everything.

"Have you seen Remy?" she asked Marie-Francine.

"No, Mademoiselle. Marie-Jeanne won't let anyone know how the outfit looks, and she told me Their Royal Highness dismissed everyone from their suite to dress in private."

Sam didn't know what Remy was planning to wear to the ball. Her own dress had been a secret even from her until yesterday when she had fittings. It didn't matter. If she had been involved in the design, she would have chosen the same thing. Somehow it was perfect.

"Don't worry about fitting everything into the bag you brought, Mademoiselle," Marie-Francine reassured her. "I have a suitcase for your dresses."

"My dresses?"

"Yes, the ones you have worn this week."

Sam looked at her in surprise. "They're not mine."

"But, yes, Mademoiselle, Madame Pouvoir told me to pack them for you. She has given me an extra suitcase for this purpose."

There was a knock at the door, and Madame Pouvoir came in. She was slightly more dressed up than usual in a black bolero with sequins and a floor-length black satin skirt. Her dark hair was tucked up for the first time, showing off her elegant, long neck.

Pouvoir put a hand on her heart. "Mademoiselle Hyde, you look stunning!"

Sam hadn't heard that kind of emotion come out of Madame

Pouvoir the entire week, and she definitely hadn't expected it to be directed at her. "Really? Do you think I'll fit in?"

"More than you realize," Pouvoir said cryptically. "If you're ready, it's time to announce you."

"But, wait, Marie-Francine said she's packing the dresses I wore, but I didn't—those aren't mine—I didn't know they had been bought for me. I thought I was borrowing them."

"Mademoiselle, you were our guest, and you needed suitable clothing. The dresses are a gift to you."

"I don't want the people of Montamant to fund my wardrobe. Some of them can't pay rent."

Pouvoir smiled. Sam could see she had said something that pleased her. "The dresses came from the queen's personal funds and not any money belonging to the people. If you feel uncomfortable with the gift, why not resell them and donate the money to charity?"

"That's an excellent idea. I'm surprised to hear you suggest that."

Pouvoir gave a slight raise of her shoulders. "These are strange times. Now, please, we must go downstairs, so you can be introduced with the rest of the guests."

Sam followed her down the main stairs to the central corridor with the rest of the guests. She had explained to Sam that she would be introduced early in the evening before the royal family. Sam didn't mind. It meant she'd get longer to enjoy the ball and get a chance to see Queen Clotilde's entrance. She could imagine the queen would have a spectacular dress and tiara. She couldn't wait to see Remy either. What Remy was planning to wear was the talk of the palace, and Sam wanted a front row seat to watch their entrance.

In the ballroom a band was set up on a small raised stage, and Sam recognized the strains of "The Way You Look Tonight." No one was dancing yet—they were expected to wait for the queen's arrival—but the bar was open, and Sam took the opportunity to get a glass of champagne.

She found Delphine and Paul and was chatting with them when the room fell quiet. It was time for Remy and Queen Clotilde to enter.

As the heir, Remy was supposed to be announced first, with the queen as the grand finale. But the butler yelled something in French, and the women in the room dropped to deep curtsies, and the men bowed. Sam joined in and remained in her curtsy as Queen Clotilde's heels clacked down the parquet flooring to the bandstand.

The queen turned to the room and gestured with her hands, and the crowd rose.

As Sam expected, Queen Clotilde looked beautiful. She wore a full ball gown in a shade of ivory with a wide blue satin belt. The skirt billowed out and made her hips look slim. Like Sam, she wore long gloves that extended to her elbows like a movie star from a bygone era. Her brown hair was curled in loose waves that framed her face, which made her look much less imposing and more romantic than she had seemed during their tense conversations throughout the week. She wore a diamond tiara, elegant and understated, and she looked perfect. If Sam hadn't known the queen had had a cold, she wouldn't have suspected anything.

Queen Clotilde began to speak, and Sam nudged Delphine, who offered a translation.

"Some of you may be wondering why I have arrived first when there are two members to the royal family. This week, as we have celebrated eight hundred years of our country, eight hundred years of fair and just leadership by the Vallorcin family, I have come to appreciate how important it is to be a part of that family. There have been some questions about the person you know as the princess and her future in the monarchy, and I am sorry to tell you that the princess will not be following in my footsteps."

The queen paused for dramatic effect. Sam looked at Delphine, who seemed greatly concerned. There were murmurs of surprise around the room. Was Remy about to abdicate their claim to the throne? Surely they would have told Sam if they were?

"The princess," Queen Clotilde continued, waiting a moment for the gossip to hush, "will not be following in my footsteps because there is no princess. Tonight, I am happy and proud to reintroduce my child, the heir to the throne, whom we shall now call…Princiot Remy!"

She gestured with one gloved sweep toward the main double doors, and the band began to play. Instead of the Montamantien national anthem, they offered a jazzy rendition of Lady Gaga's "Born This Way." The crowd turned away from the queen to look in anticipation at the double doors.

The butlers opened them, and Remy came striding in, looking more confident and prouder than Sam had ever seen them. Their hair was styled in a puff swept up and curled over, the shaved undersides on full display. They weren't wearing any glasses, and even from a distance Sam could see magenta eyeshadow and thick black eyeliner. But the real attention grabber was their outfit.

Remy was wearing a white tuxedo blazer with a blue cornflower pinned to the label and a baby blue bow tie. Instead of matching pants, they had on a knee-length skirt in a shade of baby blue with lavender accents in the pleats that gave it body and made it swish as Remy made their way across the crowded and silent room.

Sam glanced down at her own gown and realized their outfits were made from the same fabric.

But that wasn't the only surprise. Remy's skirt was short enough for everyone to see that they were wearing a pair of silver glittery high-heeled ankle boots.

Remy looked masculine and feminine at once. Ethereal, a queer movie star on the red carpet, but also more like the real person Sam had gotten to know than they had looked in any of their previous outfits. Her heart felt full looking at them and thinking about how hard they had fought to get to this point and how exciting it was for them to appear in public like this, and with Queen Clotilde's blessing no less. Sam was sure the smile on her face matched the wide one on Remy's.

Remy stopped next to the queen, who immediately kissed their cheeks. The two clasped hands and raised them high. Sam looked around the room, some of whom looked scandalized, others confused, and some were smiling. She clapped her hands loudly and nodded at Delphine and Paul, who joined in. Madame Pouvoir clapped as well, as loudly as she could, nodding to the rest of the room to join them. The applause grew solidly in volume and increased in pace until the ballroom erupted in cheers for the new heir.

Princiot Remy, a refashioning of the title that gave a nod to the future and, hopefully, the end of binary gender politics while reaching toward Montamant's beloved past. It was perfect.

When the applause died down, Remy and Queen Clotilde were swept into conversations with the local elite, and Sam started to feel as if she'd stayed too long. She was contemplating how to make her exit, whether she should just leave or tell Remy and the queen good-bye, when Madame Pouvoir summoned her to join the royal family in the center of the room, where they were holding court.

"Sam!" Remy pulled their phone from their jacket pocket and held it up. "Take a selfie with me?"

Sam remembered how stern Remy had been when she had offered to take a first day of school picture. "Are you sure?"

But Remy was smiling. "Do you see how good we look? Come on!" They angled the phone so they were both in the frame. "I'll text it to you, so you can send it to your mom." They tucked their phone back in their jacket pocket. "I wish Hrodohaid and Emmanuel could have had this experience."

"Maybe they're here in spirit. And think about all the future kids who are going to be able to be themselves because of you. How does that feel?"

"Terrifying." Remy laughed. "It's a lot of responsibility to be a role model. But fantastic."

"Mademoiselle Hyde," Queen Clotilde interrupted, "what do you think of my princiot?"

"I think they look perfect. I'm really glad you two were able to work things out."

"We owe it to you," the queen said.

"I was actually about to leave."

Remy's beatific smile dropped, and a crease formed between their eyebrows. "What? Why?"

Sam didn't want to spoil the night, but she wanted to remember it this way, with them sauntering so proudly into the ballroom and being honored with cheers for living their truth. She didn't want to stay and listen to the person she loved—the person who had declared their love for her on the floor of Parliament—tell the world of their intention to marry someone else. If she went now, she would leave with precious memories of her time in Montamant and her time with Remy.

"I don't want to be here when you make the announcement about your engagement to Pierre. Would you mind if I went back upstairs?"

"If there is to be an engagement, it's probably one you should be present for," Madame Pouvoir said.

Remy looked at her with curiosity. "What?"

"Samantha Hyde," Pouvoir explained, "you are the daughter of the man who should be the thirteenth Earl of Clarendon, Baron Hyde, of Stittenham."

Sam frowned. "I'm the daughter of Richard Hyde from Lafayette, Indiana."

"The fourth Earl of Clarendon, Henry Hyde, was believed to have died without male issue. In fact, he married Henriette de Beauharnais, a French noblewoman, and they had a son, who fled to the United States and is your ancestor. Your father is the direct descendant and the oldest male heir, meaning he should be an earl in the United Kingdom."

"My father what?"

"You are French and British nobility," the queen told her.

Remy and Sam looked at each other. This changed everything. The one thing standing between them wasn't anymore.

"Remy! Your Majesty!" Pierre approached, dragging another man by the hand. "This is Giovanni, everyone. I wanted him to meet the queen."

Giovanni offered an elegant bow to the queen. "Your Majesty."

"And this," Pierre said, "is the person who lost me to you. Meet the…?"

"Princiot," the others supplied.

Giovanni turned to Remy, and in clear but musical English said, "You look stunning, Your Highness."

"He's a model," Pierre reminded them. "He knows good fashion."

"Lost you to him?" Sam asked in confusion.

Pierre looked sheepish. "Giovanni flew here to surprise me. We made up, and we are now engaged to be married."

So Remy and Pierre weren't going to announce their engagement anymore? And Pierre was planning to marry someone else? And Sam had British nobility in her family tree? She felt the need to sit down. It was all too much at once.

The band was playing a slower song, and Madame Pouvoir clapped her hands authoritatively. "Your Majesty, it is time for you to begin the dancing."

"I don't have a partner," the queen said, smiling at Remy. Sam loved watching her express love for her nonbinary child.

"I was hoping I might help with that." Pierre's father, Andre, was standing outside their circle in a dashing black tuxedo with a white bow tie and cummerbund. "Madame Pouvoir, if you will permit a break from tradition and allow a simple man like me to start the dancing?" He looked as if he was going to say more, but instead he gave a great sneeze and reached into a pocket for a handkerchief. "Please excuse me."

Sam bit back a smile. She knew exactly where Andre had gotten that cold, but she didn't think Remy and Pierre had caught on yet. The queen narrowed her eyes. Sam shrugged benevolently. She wouldn't tell. She'd let the queen and Andre confess their romance when they were ready.

"Papa," Pierre said, "Giovanni and I are engaged to be married!"

"Well," Andre said easily, "the idea of you marrying Remy was never a very good one. Congratulations, my son." He kissed each of Pierre's cheeks, then each of Giovanni's. To Remy he said, "I am sorry for everything that has happened this week. If you see fit to forgive me, my son and I would like to continue our places in your court."

"You'll do better than that," Remy said. "Pierre's agreed to be my chief secretary, beginning this summer when I set up my offices."

The queen was surprised at this news. "You're coming home this summer? To begin working?"

"I want to finish my degree, but I also think there's a lot that could be done here. I want to make Parliament more gender-balanced and establish services for children like me. I think we can preserve the monarchy through progress. We can show everyone that Montamant is welcoming and forward-thinking."

"That's fantastic," Sam said. "I think you'll be great at it."

"Our new prime minister agrees with you on that front," Queen Clotilde said. "He's very eager to appoint a female deputy, and I have personally pledged funds to buy back the land Jacques Âne sold from underneath us."

"It sounds as if Montamant is entering the twenty-first century." Perhaps Sam had been wrong about monarchies. This one seemed to view its role as serving the people, not being served by them. She was proud of what Remy had accomplished and eager to see what the future held for the tiny kingdom.

"There's room for an archivist," Madame Pouvoir said. "The royal archive needs a researcher to catalogue and organize—"

"Digitize," Remy added.

"And the princiot needs a partner," Queen Clotilde finished.

Remy reached for Sam's hand, and they interlaced their fingers together. "We can talk more on the way back to Boston," they said. "I'm flying with you to start school on Monday. But what do you think about the summer? Will you come back with me?"

"Yes," Sam gasped. "Yes, I will."

Right in front of the queen and a room full of curious onlookers, the newly minted princiot kissed their American girlfriend, and the history of Montamant—and two lonely people—was forever changed.

About the Author

Jane Kolven is an author of contemporary, fun LGBTQ romances. She is proud to create stories that show a variety of LGBTQ people finding happiness—because everyone deserves love. Jane currently lives in Michigan with her wife and their pets.

Books Available From Bold Strokes Books

A Fae Tale by Genevieve McCluer. Dovana comes to terms with her changing feelings for her lifelong best friend and fae, Roze. (978-1-63555-918-7)

Accidental Desperados by Lee Lynch. Life is clobbering Berry, Jaudon, and their long romance. The arrival of directionless baby dyke MJ doesn't help. Can they find their passion again—and keep it? (978-1-63555-482-3)

Always Believe by Aimée. Greyson Waldsen is pursuing ordination as an Anglican priest. Angela Arlingham doesn't believe in God. Do they follow their vocation or their hearts? (978-1-63555-912-5)

Courage by Jesse J. Thoma. No matter how often Natasha Parsons and Tommy Finch clash on the job, an undeniable attraction simmers just beneath the surface. Can they find the courage to change so love has room to grow? (978-1-63555-802-9)

I Am Chris by R Kent. There's one saving grace to losing everything and moving away. Nobody knows her as Chrissy Taylor. Now Chris can live who he truly is. (978-1-63555-904-0)

The Princess and the Odium by Sam Ledel. Jastyn and Princess Aurelia return to Venostes and join their families in a battle against the dark force to take back their homeland for a chance at a better tomorrow. (978-1-63555-894-4)

The Queen Has a Cold by Jane Kolven. What happens when the heir to the throne isn't a prince or a princess? (978-1-63555-878-4)

The Secret Poet by Georgia Beers. Agreeing to help her brother woo Zoe Blake seemed like a good idea to Morgan Thompson at first…until she realizes she's actually wooing Zoe for herself… (978-1-63555-858-6)

You Again by Aurora Rey. For high school sweethearts Kate Cormier and Sutton Guidry, the second chance might be the only one that matters. (978-1-63555-791-6)

Fleur d'Lies by MJ Williamz. For rookie cop DJ Sander, being true to what you believe is the only way to live…and one way to die. (978-1-63555-854-8)

Love's Falling Star by B.D. Grayson. For country music megastar Lochlan Paige, can love conquer her fear of losing the one thing she's worked so hard to protect? (978-1-63555-873-9)

Love's Truth by C.A. Popovich. Can Lynette and Barb make love work when unhealed wounds of betrayed trust and a secret could change everything? (978-1-63555-755-8)

Next Exit Home by Dena Blake. Home may be where the heart is, but for Harper Sims and Addison Foster, is the journey back worth the pain? (978-1-63555-727-5)

Not Broken by Lyn Hemphill. Falling in love is hard enough—even more so for Rose, who's carrying her ex's baby. (978-1-63555-869-2)

The Noble and the Nightingale by Barbara Ann Wright. Two women on opposite sides of empires at war risk all for a chance at love. (978-1-63555-812-8)

What a Tangled Web by Melissa Brayden. Clementine Monroe has the chance to buy the café she's managed for years, but Madison LeGrange swoops in and buys it first. Now Clementine is forced to work for the enemy and ignore her former crush. (978-1-63555-749-7)

A Far Better Thing by JD Wilburn. When needs of her family and wants of her heart clash, Cass Halliburton is faced with the ultimate sacrifice. (978-1-63555-834-0)

Body Language by Renee Roman. When Mika offers to provide Jen erotic tutoring, will sex drive them into a deeper relationship or tear them apart? (978-1-63555-800-5)

Carrie and Hope by Joy Argento. For Carrie and Hope, loss brings them together but secrets and fear may tear them apart. (978-1-63555-827-2)

Detour to Love by Amanda Radley. Celia Scott and Lily Andersen are seatmates on a flight to Tokyo and by turns annoy and fascinate each other. But they're about to realize there's more than one path to love. (978-1-63555-958-3)

Ice Queen by Gun Brooke. School counselor Aislin Kennedy wants to help standoffish CEO Susanna Durr and her troubled teenage daughter become closer—even if it means risking her own heart in the process. (978-1-63555-721-3)

Masquerade by Anne Shade. In 1925 Harlem, New York, a notorious gangster sets her sights on seducing Celine, and new lovers Dinah and Celine are forced to risk their hearts, and lives, for love. (978-1-63555-831-9)

Royal Family by Jenny Frame. Loss has defined both Clay's and Katya's lives, but guarding their hearts may prove to be the biggest heartbreak of all. (978-1-63555-745-9)

Share the Moon by Toni Logan. Three best friends, an inherited vineyard, and a resident ghost come together for fun, romance, and a touch of magic. (978-1-63555-844-9)

Spirit of the Law by Carsen Taite. Attorney Owen Lassiter will do almost anything to put a murderer behind bars, but can she get past her reluctance to rely on unconventional help from the alluring Summer Byrne and keep from falling in love in the process? (978-1-63555-766-4)

The Devil Incarnate by Ali Vali. Cain Casey has so much to live for, but enemies who lurk in the shadows threaten to unravel it all. (978-1-63555-534-9)